Jaralii Chronicles

Gilraën and the Prophecy

I Conquered

by J. R. Reid

ISBN: 978-1-7344680-5-2

Cover by 100 Covers

Dedicated to Denise Trask

It was your idea and your character.
I built the story,
But it was your inspiration.
I miss you

I Came, I Saw, I Conquered

Julius Caesar, 47 BCE

Report to the Roman Senate

victory over Pharnaces II of Pontus at the Battle of Zela

A High One among High Ones shall come from Beyond.

She shall wear an old face of the Verdant Hills

She shall befriend the Mighty and the Weak.

She shall unite the High, the Deep, the Many, the Few.

The Usurper shall fall before her; all will rejoice.

Unite and be Free."

Thane Cadrazhulea, Seer of Clan Camazhule

Table of Contents

The Usurper shall fall before her; all will rejoice.

Unite and be Free.

Chapter 1 – Separations and Departures

I awoke with a start. I feared I was late for something terribly important. Mummia was peeking over the horizon, but I wasn't ready to climb out of my comfortable bed. Then I remembered! Today is the day!

I leapt out of bed and raced to the loo. By the time I had washed my face and returned to the bedroom, Rosie was there, hot thrak in hand. I thoroughly inspected my quiver to ensure that I had packed everything I needed and forgotten nothing. When I was thoroughly satisfied I had everything I needed, I dressed for travel with minimal armor or other encumbrances. Then, I remembered what I'd forgotten – Justice.

I sat quietly and concentrated on him. I met a solid rock. Evidently, Justice had protected his mind most ably. However, I battered his defenses until I detected a tiny bit of interest. *'Justice!'* I demanded of him.

I detected a shred of responsiveness. *'Reuben! It's Tony! Listen to me.'*

'Tony?'

'Justice, it's Gilraën. Meet me on the road to Willicamp this morning.'

'Gilraën?'

'Yes, you massive hunk of Krell. Meet me half way to Willicamp later this morning.'

'Gilraën? Willicamp? OK.'

I raced down to breakfast, only they call it first meal. My Tribe and my Ghillies were already there, as was the Palace Guard. Prince William arrived just moments later. None of us had much to say. All of us were far too apprehensive for banter, even Harold.

I asked William, "So, what's the order of march?"

"Brown Hills will lead. They're fastest, so there's no sense in getting in their way. They'll probably get to Barstough before mid-day. Your Charioteers will go next, followed by Viscount Geoffrey with King Richard behind him. So, it will be a huge spectacle with lots of cheering and excitement. Finally, you and I will leave. I'm guessing we get started about mid-morning. We should make it to Willicamp before nightfall. We'll get an early start the next day. We'll push hard to get to Easbister by nightfall. It'll be a tough march for all of us, but we've been practicing our long-stride with full packs. We're in good shape, so should be able to do it.

"Of course, you will leave Willicamp about the same time as we do. You'll be through Higgleston and to Tamvill after mid-day."

"Ah, I forgot to tell you something," I said. "My friend Justice, the Krell, will be joining us. We'll be meeting him on the road to Willicamp. Hopefully, he will bring a few of his friends. It'd be nice to have some Krelli on our side."

"Krells?" William asked, a strong note of concern in his voice. "Are you sure?"

"Why not? I know Justice. He's an old friend of mine. He's huge and strong and will be a powerful ally."

"Yes, but a Krell? You're going to scare the life out of my men."

"That's why I'm warning you."

Harold stood, as did all the Charioteers. "We're going now, Gilraën. We'd love to be going with you and our friends." He indicated my Tribe. "But, you'll outpace us."

"How many zhaks are going?"

"The zhaks decided on two males and six females. So, there'll be more than a hundred of us. We'll go first, with our herds behind us, leading Geoffrey's Battalion. So, we'll be Richard's vanguard."

"How long before you arrive in Barstough?"

"We're figuring three days. That's why we have so many zhaks. And, of course, it's another three to four days to Shalal'm Caer, so it's a long trek."

"So, I guess we'll see you when we arrive in Barstough."

"Yes," he replied gloomily. Suddenly, he grabbed me in a big hug. "Take good care of yourself, Gilraën. We will miss you." Following his lead, each of the twelve hugged me.

I couldn't help it. I wept openly.

I joined William, along with my Elves and his Guards, and we walked the winding road to the wall gate. Only a few people cheered us until we arrived at the gate. It seemed the entire population of Shesol Vys had gathered outside the gates to send the army on its way accompanied by their highest hopes and best wishes.

A horn sounded from my right. A shimmer of color became an Elvin army as they slowed to pass in review. King Glorfindel was resplendent in auburn armor and high crown. Queen Eilol was dressed in fire red, her crown reflecting the morning light. As they reached the gate, they stopped and beckoned to me. When I joined them, they hugged me and kissed me on the cheeks.

Eilol said, "Daughter, our ways part, but only for the moment. We will meet before the gates of Shalal'm Caer." Again, they kissed me. They turned to their Tribes and raised their arms. A horn sounded, and the entire Tribe raced southward in a splash of brown, orange and red.

Shortly afterward, I heard a clatter of hooves. My twelve Charioteers led the armies of Umbeqjaralii. They were closely followed by a mighty herd of one hundred zhaks, their hooves prancing lightly and their heads held high. I couldn't help but whoop and yell along with the multitudes gathered to cheer them on to victory.

Sir Geoffrey's Battalion followed. The bedraggled rats that had hauled themselves back to the castle covered in mud and mire had changed dramatically. Their armor was properly blacked, their halberds glinted, and their shields were held proudly before their chests.

King Richard followed at the head of the four Battalions of Umbeqjaralii high-stepping in review. The King's subjects roared and cheered and leaped into the air to show their love and appreciation. The men of the Battalions laughed and waved as they passed, acting far more assured than they felt in their hearts.

When the last of the King's army passed, it was my turn. I stepped out followed by my Tribe. Quite unexpectedly, Dorothea, Rosie, Beryl and Daisy raced out to hug and kiss me. At this show of affection, the entire crowd cheered lustily. I waved to them, as did my Tribe. Then, at my signal, we raced off at a modest two-fold walk. Just moments later, we slowed to await Prince William's Company. We heard a huge cheer – far larger than even that for the King. Then, William and his Guard appeared, racing towards us.

We joined them, trundling along at a modest two-fold walk. Regardless of this 'modest' pace, we were eating up the distance at a rate far greater than could be accomplished by any Human army. I guessed that we were loping along at something around fifteen miles per hour. At this rate, we'd be in Willicamp in three hours or so.

We'd been running for about an hour when a huge voice yelled, "Gilraën!" Suddenly a huge man-shape some eighteen feet tall loped out of the wood and fell in beside me. "Hey, girl, good to see you. Another quest?"

I laughed, "Yes, another quest." I nodded towards the Prince. "Prince William, meet my old friend, Justice. Justice, meet my friend, Prince William. That's his castle back there."

William was a bit overawed. I must admit that Justice was awe-inspiring. Justice said, "Hey, great to meet you, William. Gilraën has spoken highly of you. But, the rest of your army marched south. Why are you heading to Willicamp?"

William finally found his voice. "My Battalions are in the east. I have one down in Barstough, a few Companies in Easbister, and two Companies passing through Tamvill on their way to Phaedham. I'm going to Easbister to take command of my wing of the army. I understand that Beckworth has seized the bridge at Phaedham and is holding it in force. I plan to trap them between my forces."

"I'm not sure. I've been watching the south road. I've got a few friends out east. I've sent word to them. We'll see how many show up."

"How many of your friends will be joining us?" I asked.

"Maybe four: Integrity, Retribution, Vengeance and Retaliation. But, Beckworth has twice as many, and they're some of the worst."

I said, "It's important to know what's happening around Phaedham. If Beckworth's got a big force down there, it could mess things up."

"How so?"

"Well, he could defeat us in detail. He could attack our Companies, and the Dwarves coming south from Tazhela. If so, he could then attack the Elves of the Green Mountains coming up from Phaedport. Then, he could head south and attack Duke Armjurst marching up from Eastport."

"Napoleon in North Sicily?"

William interrupted. "Napolion? Zizzily?"

I explained, "Yeah, back on Earth there was this military genius who conquered a huge continent. One of his most famous campaigns was in the country of Northern Sicily, where he out marched his enemies, defeating them in detail before they could come together to defeat him."

Turning back to Justice, I continued, "I have no idea if he has the troops or the speed to pull it off, but with Adjudicars on his side, who knows?"

"Yeah, and with eight or ten Krelli, Caierne just might pull it off."

"My thoughts exactly. Can any of your friends help us out?"

"I've asked them to scout about in the east and report back to me when they can. We'll see." He glanced over to William. "Hey, Prince, how come you're running so fast? Humans aren't supposed to be this fast."

"Indeed, most aren't. We're part Elf."

"Aha! That'd explain it. Does that mean you fight more like Elves, too?"

"We're better than most Humans, but Elves are still faster and stronger."

"OK, sounds right. Well, look, I'm going off ahead. I'll look around Willicamp and let you know. Just remember to save me a place at the dinner table!" He laughed uproariously and disappeared up the road.

William shook his head and looked searchingly at me. "Your friend?"

"Yes," I answered. "Scary isn't he?"

"He almost stopped my heart. He's huge!"

"Yes, he's large, strong, fast, and eats Porg by biting their heads off and then swallowing the rest of the body in a single gulp. He's not for the faint of heart!"

Little happened for the next hour. The heavier forest had given way to more open fields and meadows. Herds of different herbivores grazed in open fields, and porg grunted in large enclosures. I even saw flocks of bird-like creatures pecking in the dirt.

"What are those?" I asked. I was sure they were birds, similar to the ones I'd seen while scouting near Shalal'm Caer.

"The smaller grazers are charder. The big spotted ones are bov. The birds are puldry. We believe the bovs and the puldry were imported from Earth, but I can't be sure. I've heard that Adjudicars transported them and some other Earth animals to feed our armies back in the early days when they were still trying to act as though they were neutral. We've been experimenting with them to find out how to raise them. We even sent large numbers of them to the Orcs to rear."

I informed him, "If they are what I think they are, we call them chickens. The females are hens, the males are roosters, and the babies are chicks. The hens lay eggs, roughly once a day and will produce about 200 oyes. They only live a year or so. If roosters are around, they will fertilize them. The hens will sit on the eggs, producing chicks. The roosters live for four or five years. If you have enough of them, the eggs are good eating. They can be boiled or fried or mixed with meat or veggies to create a really nice meal. The adults are meaty and tasty. They can be baked, boiled or fried. Whoever brought them here may have done you all a great service.

"The bovines are also excellent food sources. They produce two young every year, assuming there are bulls as well as cows. The cows produce large quantities of milk, which makes excellent fron, chedz and guk. However, they do consume a lot of vegetation. Learn from the Orcs the best way to preserve their feeding grounds.

"So, when we get to Willicamp, where will you and your Company stay? Have you made provisions for provisions?" I joked.

He laughed, saying, "Oh yes. Talbot contacted the Guilds, and we have reservations. There's a nice field just north of the town, and the mayor has made arrangements with the townsfolk. As far as you are concerned, the Guild of Thieves has a room for you and the barn is available for your Tribe. They will be expecting you for dinner and breakfast."

"Thank you, My Prince. I appreciate your many kindnesses and forethought."

It was mid-afternoon when we arrived at the edge of the town and slowed to a trot. We entered the town square, where the mayor greeted us. I excused myself, letting the Prince handle all the protocol. I headed to the Guild of Thieves, where I was greeted warmly. I was ushered to the same room I'd occupied before, while my tribe was directed to a large auxiliary building directly behind the inn. The Warden led us to the tavern. As expected the meal was excellent, and the cook, barkeep and serving staff received well-earned coins.

We walked to William's camp. They had finished their dinner meal and were preparing to bed down. Tomorrow, they'd take the southern road to Easbister. We mingled, wishing each other good fortune. William held me closely, saying, "I am loathe to release you, My Queen, but I must. Journey well, and, though we are separated by all of Beckworth's armies, I shall hold you in my arms when this war is over." He kissed me passionately, and released me.

I couldn't focus properly through the tears in my eyes.

* * *

Early the following morning, we were ready. "Let's go." We were off and running, quite literally. Unlike the previous day, we were racing through open countryside. It was mostly meadows, farmed lands and pastures, but every once in a while we race through a hamlet of just a few houses. We crossed the Stone Bridge over the Phaed River about an hour later. It was nearing mid-morning when we came to the side road that led to Tamvill. Although traveling through Higgleston was fifty miles further, I wanted to travel through the village we'd saved just a few weeks ago.

We were about half-way to Higgleston, when Justice suddenly appeared at my side. "Gilraën, you'd better hold up for a moment."

We stopped, and Justice explained, "I was just talking with Vengeance. He's been hanging around these parts. Evidently it's pretty good pickings. Anyway, he says a big army is marching north. It'll be here in two days or so."

"How big? How many? Where?"

"Too many questions and too few answers, Gilraën. Vengeance says it was big, and they had other Krelli, so he avoided them."

"Damn!" I cursed.

"Gather 'round!" When my Tribe assembled, I told them what Justice had told me. "We need to find our troops and theirs. We need to establish a defense or line of retreat.

"Galdor, you're going to find the enemy. Take the trail to Tamvill and then south.

"Nienna, Caranthir, Justice, you're with me. We're going through Higgleston and then south. We need to find Tazhela. If they've passed through Higgleston, so much the better. If not, we'll find them and send them to Tamvill. Go!"

We all raced ahead at our best speed. Even Justice was hard pressed to keep up with us. We arrived in Higgleston within the hour. I found John the Barber and Maude the Wise Woman.

"Have any troops passed through Tamvill?" I asked.

"Yes, just yesterday. Two Companies under Baron Richmond passed through yesterday morning. Then late yesterday, a whole army of Dwarves arrived. We fed them as best we could, but there were hundreds of them. This morning they left, heading south."

"OK, everybody, we're heading to Tamvill at top speed."

We ran as fast as we could. We raced through Tamvill, leaving only a gale in our wake. Moments later, we overtook the Dwarves. Justice and I stopped, but I sent Caranthir's Cohort on ahead to find Richmond. "Jharl Tazmatahela, there may be a large enemy force to our front. My Elves are exploring the area to find them. I'm hoping Baron Richmond is nearby. If we can, we will pull him back to you.

"Return toward Tamvill. We need a defensive position, or we'll be forced to retreat."

Jharl Tazmatahela looked askance at Justice, and then at me. "Queen Gilraën?"

"Yes, My Jharl," I replied, pointing to the lip of the coronet peaking from under my helmet. "This is Justice the Krell. The Elves are my Tribe. Now can we think about not getting killed?"

That seemed to focus his thoughts. He spoke earnestly with his Thanes. I understood most of what he said, but his accent was different from the Dwarfish I had learned from Ez-Tansk and Ghamarazh. However, I did understand enough to learn he was asking if they remembered a nearby defensible position. None had.

"Let me ask my Elves." I concentrated on the minds of my Elves, asking what they'd seen.

None reported anything. The land was mostly flat. There were rolling hills, covered with grass and copses of deciduous trees. Small farms were scattered about. Occasional hamlets were sparsely spread throughout the area, connected by small trails. It was a terrible place to defend. In my computer games, we'd have described this as 'tank country.'

I asked Caranthir if he'd found Baron Richmond, yet. He had. Richmond was only a few miles ahead. I ordered them to retreat with all possible haste. Then, I realized that would be an extremely difficult maneuver. Richmond's supply train was between him and us. Turning a multitude of carts, wagons and wains would be slow at best. If the enemy fell upon them, they'd be wiped out.

"Jharl Tazmatahela, Baron Richmond and two Companies of Humans are a few miles ahead of you. He has a supply train behind him, meaning it's between your army and his. It will be difficult for him to turn his Companies and to then head back toward Tamvill. I ask if you will advance to bring your army to him. Then, as a combined force, we can retreat ahead of the enemy. I believe that our combined force can retreat to Tamvill. I doubt the enemy can advance any faster than we can retreat.

"I can easily communicate with Tamvill, and order them to prepare a defense. If so, we will have a prepared defensive position awaiting us.

"I will also inform King Amder of our position. I believe he is near Phaedport. If so, he can reinforce us within two days. If so, I doubt that Beckworth can send an army large enough to defeat our combined forces.

"What are your thoughts?"

The Jharl translated my words to his three Thanes. Once again, I tried to follow their conversation, but their accents were difficult for me to understand. I did get the gist, but lost the details.

Finally, the Jharl turned back to me. "Advance we will not. Instead, prepare a temporary defense we will. Let them return to us, pass through our lines. Then, as a united army, we retreat."

"Done!" I replied.

I concentrated on Caranthir's mind, telling him to stop Richmond and have him retreat to the Dwarf's position. He replied that Richmond was anxious to avoid a battle with a vastly superior force.

Richmond would turn his supply train around, but maintain his position as a rear guard between them and the advancing enemy. I told Caranthir to monitor the enemy's advance and advise me of their position and rate of advance.

Reaching into one of the hidden pockets in my quiver, I found my mirror. Turning it toward the north, I commanded, "Margaret the Witch of Tamvill!"

A face appeared. "Who calls for Margaret?"

"High Queen Gulámae."

"High One, how may I serve you?"

"A large force of the enemy is little more than a day south of Tamvill. I am retreating with the Dwarves of Tazhela and Baron Richmond to Tamvill. Alert the town and prepare a defensive position. I will send help to assist you in fortifying Tamvill and prepare your village for battle. Do you understand me, Margaret?"

"Yes, High One, I understand. I fear that everyone will evacuate when they hear the news. What do you suggest?"

Quite frankly, I had no idea. Turning to Tazmatahela, I said. "My Jharl, I leave you in command. I will return to Tamvill and gather the villagers before they disappear into the countryside. I will bring Justice and a Cohort of Elves with me. We will prepare a defensive position for your Clan and Baron Richmond's Companies. I will leave two cohorts of Elves with you to scout your front and defend your flanks. Is this arrangement all right with you?"

"Agreed, My Queen. We will return to Tamvill this night."

After I had contacted both Galdor and Nienna, informing them of my arrangement with Jharl Tazmatahela and my orders for them, I led Justice and Caranthir's Cohort back to Tamvill. I headed to the Guild of Witches, where I met Margaret and several of our sisters. After I explained the problem, we walked to the center of the village.

Tamvill was tiny – less than half the size of Higgleston. There were half a dozen buildings. One was the Guildhall of Witches, Truth-Seekers and Wise Women, which was also the village inn and tavern. The largest building was a general store, meeting hall and barber's shop. There was also a small blacksmith's forge, a bakery, a tanner, a miller, and a weaver. The total population was around one hundred, with three to four times that number in scattered farms surrounding the town.

Needless to say, the last few days were the most excitement this town had ever seen. Two Companies of the King's troops had encamped overnight. Then more than five hundred Dwarves had come through. Then, my tribe and a Krell raced through, only to return.

I raised my voice, "People of Tamvill! The King commands! Attend to me! Attend to me!"

Although they were reluctant, they slowly assembled. The first two or three saw an eighteen-foot monster and turned to run. "Stop!" I yelled. "He is with me. I am Queen Gilraën! I come from Prince William and King Richard to save this village from the enemy. Attend to me!"

More and more arrived. Caranthir lit a small fire in the middle of the intersection. I walked around it yelling, "Attend to me!" while my Elves and Justice sat before the Guildhall. After a while, some fifty or sixty people had arrived. I guessed that was about all that were coming.

"People of Tamvill! Subjects of the King! I am High Queen Gilraën, here to save your lives, your property and your town. The army of the Dwarves of Tazhela is returning to your town. The Tribe of the Elves of the Green Mountains-Maidstone Forest is returning to your village. The Tribe of the Elves of Green Mountains is racing at this very moment to rescue you and save this village. Perhaps the fate of Umbeqjaralii will be decided right here, tomorrow, and you will determine whether good King Richard rules or the evil Lord Beckworth and his Adjudicars reign over you and your children forever and ever.

"Will you help me defeat them? Will you help me save your town? Will you help me save your property, your family, and your very lives? Will you help me?"

Margaret leapt to her feet, shouting "Yes, My Queen! Lead and I will follow!"

Her enthusiasm was contagious, evidently. The others jumped up, yelling, "Lead us!" or "We will fight!" or other such encouragements.

"Here is what we need," I confided with them. "We need a barrier behind which the Dwarves and the King's men can stand and fight. We need eyes and ears that can tell us that the enemy is approaching or attempting to surround us. We need everyone to dig a ditch and build a redoubt.

"Let me introduce my Elves and my friend, Justice, the Krell." I could see their apprehension. "Yes, he is a Krell. Now, here is one Cohort of my Elves." I introduced all nine of them. "We will lead you, and we will help you. Now, who is the head man or woman of this village?"

A tall, overweight and balding man stepped forward. "I am Mansfield, the Headman. I am the proprietor of the store, which serves everyone for ten miles around."

"Mansfield, we face an emergency. We need builders, woodsmen and masons. We need to build a fortification to the south. We need to barricade the road and prevent Beckworth's forces from invading the Kingdom and sacking this village. You know the people in this region. Who do we need?"

Mansfield thought for a few seconds, and then began spouting names.

"Whoa! These names are meaningless to me. Are they here? If not, can you send someone to bring them here? Who is reliable? Ask them to bring these people here."

He looked around and issued orders. Several men raced off in different directions.

"Now, you know the lands. Where can we build a wall to defend the village?"

"There is no special place, My Queen. The lands hereabout are flat. The soil is rich, and the farms prosperous. We send much food and produce to the cities ... as far as Phaedham and even Shesol Vys."

"Could we build a wall of rocks to the south of the village?"

"Rocks we have in aplenty!" he laughed. The villagers joined him in laughter. "We build rock walls to separate one field from another. Our fields are littered with a new crop every spring. We say the first crop of each season is rocks. After that, we can sow, and tend, and reap."

"Ok, so we have the raw materials. We will need tools, and we will need to transport all those rocks."

Mansfield nodded.

"We will want to dig a ditch in front of the wall, and line it with sharpened sticks and thorns. We will have to make it long – long enough so that the enemy can't get around us. We will also need for you to help protect your village. Who among you has military experience or is familiar with arms?"

Three men stood forward.

"Do you still have arms or armor?"

All three said they had swords, shields and long knives.

"And are you familiar with fortifications?"

All had served under Captain Gracie, who was from Tamvill. All were familiar with building field works and had both attacked and defended mock attacks of those works.

"Excellent, you three will coordinate your actions through me as needed. Where would you build a fortification to defend against an attack from the south?"

After a brief discussion, they began telling me. I interrupted them. "No, show me. Let's lay this out so that you can show everyone else where to go and what to do."

The three agreed to a line perhaps five hundred feet south of the village. There was a small declivity that wandered west to east, under the road, and into the distance.

One man, named Tinslow, said, "This is the place. It's a small creek in the Spring, when it's wet and rainy. We should be able to dig a ditch here and pile the dirt behind it. We can build the rock wall on top of the dirt. There aren't many trees in this area, but there are more than enough thorns."

The other men nodded in agreement.

By that time, men and women bearing shovels, picks, hammers and other tools began arriving. The three men directed their friends and neighbors to the task. They pitched in, not just helping, but leading the project. Justice grabbed two picks, one in each hand, and began slamming their points into the ground. Clouds of dust and dirt flew up into the air. Great clods of dirt and mud flew left and right.

Townsfolk dug into the loosened dirt, heaving it up the ever-deepening trench to the northern side. The only place we didn't dig was the road itself. These roads were old, tough and well tended. Besides, the road was needed in good repair to supply our armies. However, that didn't mean that we couldn't build a wall.

People began arriving with cartloads of rocks. My Elves began sorting, positioning and piling rocks, building a strong barrier. The biggest problem was that we had no cement to bind them together. The only things holding our wall together were the weight of the rocks and the friction between them.

However, we were Elves, after all. As each section was laid, an Elf concentrated on the rocks themselves. We 'welded' them together, creating a single solid boulder. By nightfall, we had a ditch and wall extending more than five hundred feet to the west and bending back around another hundred. A second ditch and wall extended to the east almost four hundred feet, before bending northward at a 45-degree angle for another one hundred feet. Two huge piles of rocks were deposited on opposite sides of the road where it cut through the wall. When all our troops were north of it, Justice and my Elves could shift them into the gap on the road, sealing it against the assault.

Night fell, but there was still no sign of Richmond or the Dwarves. I concentrated on Galdor and Nienna. '*Where are you? What's happening?*'

'*We are only a few miles south of Tamvill. The Krells, Vengeance and Integrity, have joined us. We had some difficulties with the*

*animals, but we persuaded them to hurry, with the promise of a good
meal. Be prepared for a hundred tired and hungry animals.'*

I informed Mansfield, who hurried off to make appropriate
arrangements. We lit torches to guide the men, Dwarves and animals
through the opening. After that there was nothing to do but wait.

Just as I was about to leap out of my skin, we heard the sounds of
marching feet. Shortly, a long double line of Dwarves appeared,
Jharl Tazmatahela at their head. I rushed forward to greet him.

"My Jharl, we have prepared a defense. Although it is not to
Dwarf standards, it should be effective. I shall ask the town's folk to
provide provender for us. However, this army outnumbers the entire
village six-fold, so they will be hard pressed to provide. And, as you
have observed, Baron Richmond is ill-prepared to feed our army. Do
you have any suggestions?"

"We are provisioned for five days, My Queen. We need not
burden your supplies until we reach Phaedham."

I laughed, "Unless Lord Beckworth has other plans, My Jharl."
We shared wry smiles. "I suggest you deploy your Dwarves along
the ramparts. Since Baron Richmond's forces will be the last through
the gap, I suggest he defend the gap and you defend the flanks. My
Elves and our Krell allies will be the reserve force to reinforce our
lines as needed. Is that acceptable, My Jharl?"

"Eminently, My Queen. I would have suggested such a
distribution, had you not done so. However, if we are attacked we
may become besieged. We may have to consider a longer term plan
for supplying our forces."

"Yes, we may. I will alert Higgleston and Tazhton of our need so
that they can begin to gather supplies for us. Regardless of whether
we are besieged or not, we will need the extra provisions since we
will be delayed in arriving at Phaedham.

"I will also communicate with King Amder. When I last talked
with him he was at Phaedport, heading west on the Great Southern
Road. There is a trail about half-way between Phaedham and
Phaedport that arrives in Tamvill, avoiding Phaedham entirely, and
cutting off forty miles of distance. He could be here by morning.

When he arrives, the battle is won. So, our objective is to delay the enemy until the Elves arrive. Then, we annihilate them."

Jharl Tazmatahela thought for a moment and then nodded sagely. "Yes, I would like to defeat them myself. However, if their forces are that strong, then the best I can expect is a stout defense worthy of remembrance. Will you die with me, Thanelish Gulámae?"

"I would be honored to do so, Jharl Tazmatahela, but I'd prefer to defeat our enemies and sing a song while dancing on their graves."

We shared a nervous, perhaps cynical, laugh, before we went our separate ways.

Justice clapped a hand on my shoulder, almost crushing me. "Hey, Gilraën, I want to you meet my friends. This here is Vengeance, and this ugly brute is Integrity. Guys, this is Queen Gilraën Gulámae. She's the one I told you about." He turned to me, "Hey, introduce my friends to your family, why don't you?"

"Sure! Good to meet you, Vengeance, Integrity. Here's my Tribe." I introduced one and all. Then we sat together while I explained our dispositions and plans for the upcoming battle.

Vengeance licked his lips. "Humans and Orcs, both? Good eating, either way. Whacha think, guys?"

Both Justice and Integrity laughed.

"Yup, good eating," Integrity replied.

"Warm and juicy, I expect," Justice laughed. "They've been feeding at Beckworth's tables, so they'll be round and fat and juicy." He glanced at me. "We'll need wine with our meal, Gilraën!" he laughed exuberantly.

As night fell, a long line of wagons, wains and carts rumbled through the gap in our wall. Richmond's Companies followed them. The Baron was the last through.

"Welcome, Frederick," I greeted him.

With Richmond's Companies behind the wall, Krelli and Elves heaved and pushed a fused rock barricade across the road, filling the gap in our defensive wall. Richmond's Companies took up their positions behind this new section to defend the center of our line.

With our defenses completed and our troops in position, I called a meeting of the leaders. After a brief discussion, I concluded, "I have three cohorts of nine Elves – eight warrior-mages and a healer-mage. I will defend each wing with one of these cohorts while I remain here in the middle with the third. I suggest one of you Krelli accompany each of my cohorts. They will protect you, while you protect them.

"These cohorts of Elves and Krelli will stand in reserve, while Jharl Tazmatahela and Baron Richmond defend the wall. We will maintain mental contact with each other so that we know what is happening on each flank. We will be the last line of our defense.

"Let me also warn you. My Elves and I are very fast and extremely well armed. We're the best archers on this world, so don't jump in front of us. Our arrows will kill you; our spears will penetrate your armor; and our swords will stab straight through you. We are unlike any others you have met on this world, including Caierne. So, work with us."

Vengeance turned to Justice, asking, "Is she always like this?"

He shrugged. (See? Even Krells shrug) "Yah, she is … serious and all that. Regardless, she's really good, and she can party when she wants to do so."

"OK, you guys," I joined in, "Time to get to work: Galdor to the West; Nienna to the East; Caranthir, you're with me in the middle. Keep your minds open to each other, but remain a blank to the world. Feel, without being felt. Act only when you are sure, but never alone or without informing the Tribe. Go! Take up your positions."

Caranthir's Cohort, Justice and I joined Baron Richmond just off the road overlooking the battlefield spread out before us. None of us spoke. Instead, we stared out into the night awaiting the enemy. I knew we Elves had excellent night vision. I assumed Justice was a predator, and, therefore, had good night vision. And, I assumed that Dwarves had excellent night vision, based on their subterranean existences.

Regardless, none of us was aware of them until they were almost upon us. With a mighty yell, hundreds of Humans attacked from the east, and Orcs from the west attacked the walls. Dwarf's axes smote mightily, building a wall of bodies before their ramparts of stone, and still they came on. But, these were Dwarves standing on stone, defending that stone as though they were made of animated rock. The battle raged for minute after minute, as waves of enemies rose as a tide against the land.

"Breakthrough!" Galdor announced.

"Breakthrough!" Nienna announced just moments later.

Almost simultaneously, I watched a gigantic form leap over the wall. Kicking and flailing, he destroyed a four-foot section of the wall. As the wall crumbled, a river of men flowed through. Richmond's Companies engaged them. I raced forward, leading Caranthir's Cohort to attack the Krell who was thrashing about, killing with every swipe of his mace.

I raised Bohesta. Regardless of how quickly he moved, my arrow was faster. I loosed my arrow at his heart. My Elves volleyed, killing Humans with a fusillade of arrows. The Krell fell, crashing into the ground, much to the consternation of the Humans who had been counting on the supremacy of the giant to carry the battle to the enemy and achieve the victory promised to them.

Baron Richmond's Companies surged toward the center. Friend and foe became intermixed.

"Spears!" I yelled, yanking Death Leaf from my quiver. I strode forward. Caranthir and his Elves were blurs as they stabbed and slashed. Our spears darted, our shields were battered, but our force of arms was superior, and we drove through them.

A hulk reared up before me. An enormous sword swept down towards my head. I ducked and rolled to the side. The sword slashed once again, only to be countered by a similar gigantic blade. Justice stepped over me to engage the Krell. I slid aside, and leapt to my feet just in time to deflect a sword with the shaft of my spear.

A powerful blow landed on my vambrace. I fumbled Death Leaf just as a sword stabbed me in the chest. Although my chest plate deflected it, I fell on my back, weaponless. As the sword withdrew to stab again, I shouted, "Blade!" Dashemba appeared in my hand. "Kill!" The Soul Blade found its mark long before my enemy could strike.

Rolling to my feet, I reached over my shoulder and grabbed the hilt of Vaerorderol. I sliced at an arm. Severed, it fell to the ground, accompanied by a scream of pain and anguish. I deflected a sword stroke with Paeraelaes and stabbed upward. Spinning on my heel, I delivered a killing thrust through a man's chain mail. Turning a sword thrust with my blade, I returned the complement with another killing thrust. Sensing a threat, I ducked and spun to my shield side. As the blade passed behind me, I thrust upward skewering the man, and then slashed left and then right. I lifted Paeraelaes over my head, just as a mace fell, and then hacked at the legs, severing them at the ankles.

I leapt into an open space, my head on a swivel. I stood at the circumference of a circle of nine Elves. Each of us was covered in blood and gore, but unharmed. Bodies or parts of bodies lay scattered around us.

Justice rushed to me. "Well done! Great fight! Thanks for inviting us." The gap in the rock wall was behind us. Somehow we'd fought beyond it. Justice laughed, "But, I think we should be on that side of the wall, not this." We returned to our side, where Justice and I shoved large rocks back into place, temporality restoring the integrity of our redoubt.

Richmond slapped me on the back. "Thank you! I thought we were dead." He turned away, shouting orders. His men were still engaged in the battle for their lives.

I signaled to my Cohort. Each of us loosed four volleys of arrows. By the time the fourth was gone, our first arrows had returned. Just minutes later, the road was cleared of enemy. Only corpses remained, piled before our walls.

Still, the battle raged. Yet, it had morphed into something far more deadly. I felt magic in the air. Sorcerers had entered the fray, determined to achieve the victory we had so far frustrated. Although Dwarves are resistant to most forms of magic, the spells directed at us were solely for the purpose of death. Even the strongest Dwarf was vulnerable to aneurisms in the heart or brain. While Richmond's lower-ranked Sorcerers protected his Humans from the magical attacks, my cohorts organized the defense of their flank. Both Nienna's and Galdor's cohorts engaged the enemy's magical attack with only one Elf. We were determined to hide our strength and numbers until it was necessary for us to reveal ourselves.

Slowly, inexorably our defenses failed. In spite of their numbers, their skills and their strength, Dwarves fell – some dead, others wounded. Humans fell, some never to rise again. Gaps appeared, but Dwarves and Humans redeployed to close them. Yet, by doing so, the defensive line was shorter, and our flanks more exposed. My Elves moved to the flanks, volleying flights of arrows, slowing, but not halting the tide of men.

For some reason, our Elvin arrows turned aside, missing their targets.

Magic!

My cohorts countered, extending control of their missiles to their targets. But, this took time and concentration, slowing their rate of fire.

Our arrows seemed to lose their speed. Again, magic was being employed against us. We countered, using magical energy to overcome the resistance encountered. But, as we did so, others of the enemy turned our flanks, and a Krell raced toward us, a sword slashing a swathe of destruction.

Slowly, we retreated, blunting every attack, maintaining our rate of fire. A Krell dropped, felled by Elvin arrows. But a new ward materialized; more powerful than any that had been erected previously. Dwarves fell under the onslaught of invulnerable Orcs and Humans protected by this new and powerful magic.

I concentrated on the Sorcerer that had created this shield. At first, he was just a shadow. I pushed into the shadow, and, in spite of the resistance I encountered, penetrated to its core. A being of immense power was before me. He saw me as I saw him, and engaged me with an all-embracing blanket of magical energy, trying to pin me in place and reduce me to impotency.

I would have none of it. I stabbed through it with a blade of adamantine. I sliced it open and stabbed at his chest.

He reacted instantly, forming a shield, which deflected my blade to the side. As he did so, he grasped at my mind.

I hardened my mental defenses, polishing them to reflect every quantum of energy back at him. But he was powerful.

"Caranthir!" I gasped.

I felt his Elvin mind merge with mine. Together, we fought the enemy. Others joined – first one and then a second.

Our defenses began to crumble. "Cohort! Help us!" I screamed.

Instantly, seven minds joined ours. Together, we stymied the attack upon us and turned it back upon them. We felt three minds, two Sorcerers and a dark, mighty one beyond us, forming a powerful, encompassing darkness reaching out toward us.

Slowly, I built my magical helmet into a sun, beating back the darkness. Still menacing, the darkness slowed and then stopped, thwarted by our resistance. Taking advantage of the respite, I empowered my magical helmet until my brightness was a nova. Reaching into the darkness, I seized a mind in my hand. Caierne! I had felt his presence before, deep in the mountains when he and his henchmen had captured me. Now, it was my turn. I enclosed him in my hand. He squirmed in pain. I felt his desperation, and …

He was gone!

The fervor and pace of the attack suddenly abated with his departure. Men and Orcs fled in terror. We would have pursued, but our numbers were too few, our casualties too great. Even we Elves of the Green Mountains-Maidstone Forest were exhausted from our labors. Pursuit was not one of our options.

A cloud of dust arose in the southeast. It raced towards us at breakneck speed, and then went beyond us. It seemed to halt in the west and turn southward. The cloud raced eastward and then westward. It seemed to stop and then settled south of us. Five hundred lithe figures emerged from the cloud of dust and dirt. A tall thin figure led the way. His robes were sky blue, and he wore a tall, blue-white crown with six points.

I stepped forward. "King Amder Melwasúl, I am Queen Gilraën Gulámae. Welcome. However, before we greet each other more formally, I request your assistance in healing the many wounded Dwarves and Humans on this battlefield. Come, let me show you."

He waved his arm, signaling his Tribe forward. Many moved to either side, discovering my Healers hard at work. They rushed forward, quickly performing a triage to provide immediate care to those most seriously wounded. The King joined Jharl Tazmatahela and me.

The Jharl greeted him, palms pressed together before his face. "I am honored to greet you, King Amder, my friend and neighbor of old."

The King pressed his palms together, facing the Jharl. "Greetings Jharl Tazmatahela, my friend and neighbor of old. I apologize to you for my tardiness. Had we arrived but an hour earlier, much of this death and destruction might have been avoided. My healers have joined yours and those of Queen Gilraën to heal the injured."

I asked, "King Melwasúl, have you destroyed them?"

"Most of them. The rest are scattered, no longer a military force. I fear Lord Beckworth has lost a substantial portion of his armies. It will make the assault upon his fortress easier."

"Let us hope so, My King."

The King, the Jharl and I walked the length of the wall to view the field of victory. Bodies of hundreds goblins and men lay scattered in awkward poses that no live person could assume. Body parts – arms, feet, and heads – lay scattered. The very ground beneath our feet was muddy reddish brown. And, it stank! Dying men and goblins had defecated and urinated in death. Torsos, violently rent apart, had spilled intestines, which had split open, leaking their filth. The reek filled my nostrils.

This was no game. No game I'd ever played had presented the true horrors of war and battle. Yes, they'd tried to present them, but even when they did, it was still imaginary – a game. And, no game could present the smells! It was beyond the capacity of even the finest VR to present such revulsion. I was nauseous almost beyond my capacity to control.

Even King Melwasúl seemed to be affected. He looked askance at the scene around us. He seemed distracted, glancing around, and grimacing as we walked.

Dwarves and men had separated the dead from the living. Healers were hovering over the injured and maimed, working mightily to save their lives and restore their bodies as much as possible. The Jharl and I stopped often to talk with one or more of the survivors. Slowly, the full extent of our losses became apparent. More than fifty Dwarves had been killed, and three times as many wounded. Of these, more than one hundred could be restored to full health. The others would bear the damage of battle and war for their lives.

Of Baron Richmond's Companies, fully half had been wounded. Fortunately, only nine had been killed. The healers worked diligently, but two more died in the next hours. At the same time, they restored seventy-eight to health. The rest were so badly injured or maimed their time as warriors of the King had come to an end.

Fortunately, none of my Elves had been killed. Seven had been injured, but only Lenwë Tasardur badly. A spear thrust had penetrated under his breastplate puncturing a lung. Fortunately, Lessien Melwasúl was at hand, and she had saved his life. Given a few hours of care, he would recuperate fully. And of the Krelli, only Integrity has been injured, and it was just a minor wound, easily healed.

We inspected the lands beyond the walls. Bodies were stacked like cordwood in the ditch and along the wall. A huge body lay blocking the road. Justice kicked the corpse over so we could see its face. "Chaos," he said, "one of Caierne's favorites. A real kiss-ass." A broken arrow had penetrated his forehead. "Nice shot, Gilraën."

We went beyond the road, where a second huge body lay. Justice said, "Thunder! He's a real bastard, but he wasn't that good. At least that's two of them gone."

We walked around, searching for survivors. The Elves had been most efficient. We found a third Krell, who Justice identified as

Ruin. Human and Orc alike were dead. I had tried to count them, but failed. I knew there were more than one thousand, but the exact count was beyond me. Indeed, this was a victory of magnificent proportions. It was, however, a telling blow to Lord Beckworth's power. No matter how large an army he had, losing more than a thousand plus three Krelli in a single battle would be devastating,

When we returned beyond the wall, I called my Elves to accompany me. King Amder asked several of his lords and Tazmatahela asked three of his Thanes to join us. Justice, Integrity and Vengeance also sat with us. I began, "When we have recovered, we will march to Phaedham. I expect a small holding force at the bridge, but nothing large. Once we have crossed the river, we will march to Easbister.

"I will leave a small force behind to await Duke Armjurst and King Aeradir Séregon. When they arrive in Easbister, they will turn south to approach Shalal'm Caer from the east. King Amder and Jharl Tazmatahela, you will advance upon Barstough to join with Prince William's Battalions. You will move southward to attack Shalal'm Caer from the east. King Richard will lead his army, Grampus' Battalion and King Glorfindel's army from the north. Princess Cassandra will lead her Battalion, King Fingolfin's army and that of Yurchist Linda from the west. I will ensure that the Dwarves of the Mountains along with the Orcs of the Meadows are prepared to attack from the south."

Everyone nodded in understanding. Then, after a long silence, Jharl Tazmatahela asked, "But once we are there and in position, what is our plan of attack?"

"That's a good question, My Jharl. The answer is, I don't know. I have spoken with William about the fortress, but never asked for a full description. Further, I'm sure Beckworth has been busy as a beaver changing, modifying and rebuilding the old place to serve his new needs."

"A beezer?" Séregon asked.

"Ah," I replied. "A semi-aquatic animal on Earth that builds dams to block rivers and domed houses in the pond it created to protect itself and its family from terrestrial carnivores. They are always most industrious."

When both Séregon and Tazmatahela nodded their understanding, I continued, "I know, for instance, that Beckworth has imported birds and animals from Earth. He's built farms, new facilities and distributions. He's built a support and infrastructure for a large army. And, if he can afford to send a thousand troops off on such an expedition as this, he's got a lot more in reserve and ready to defend that fortress.

"What we really need is inside information about the castle, the troops, the supplies and all sorts of things that we don't know right now. Then, once we know, we can make definite plans. Worse, we have to know all that stuff really quickly. We're not prepared to lay siege to Shalal'm Caer. We just don't have the ability to supply an army of ten thousand for weeks on end.

"So, I'm going to lead my Tribe to Barstough. On the way, I'm going to talk with Prince William, and, when I get there, King Richard. I also want to talk with King Glorfindel and Queen Eilol. But first, have either of you ever been in the old fortress of Shalal'm Caer? Can you tell me about it?"

King Amder shook his head, but Jharl Tazmatahela replied, "Not me, but you might talk with Jharl Azkhalish, Jharl Morthanzhemian, or the elders of Clan Ghamarazh. Their clans helped to build it."

"How about you Krelli?" I asked.

Justice replied, "Sure, we've all been there a lot, but I doubt that any of us knows all its secrets. Still, we can give you a good start."

The fortress they described as impressive. With their permission, I extracted their memories of it from their minds. I got the impression of a three-tiered defense. The outer wall was massive, turreted and heavily defended with ballistae and catapults. The main gate was heavily turreted and well defended. The inner wall was higher and also turreted. At the heart of the fortress was a tall, rectangular keep. Each of the Krelli envisioned deep cellars and catacombs, but none with any details. Each remembered massive barracks and storerooms, but, again, little detail. They had just enough information to arouse my curiosity, but not enough to satisfy it.

I thanked them for their help, and I thanked the King and the Jharl for their suggestions. I was not ignorant as I had been, but I didn't know enough to form a definitive attack plan. However, it was an appropriate time to inform all my commanders and allies of our victory. I could use that time to ask for further information about Wayland's Keep.

The surest way to inform them all was by using the *Waking Sleep*, but that was out of the question. This was war, and everyone's minds were doubly and triply protected. I could batter my way into their minds, but that would only cause problems. Instead, I sat with my mirror and called Richard, William, Cassandra, Albert, Abuahad and all the Kings, Queens, Jharls and Thanes involved. Then, I contacted the Seeress.

When everyone was 'on line', I announced, "Early this morning, Jharl Tazmatahela, Baron Richmond and I defeated an army of Humans and Orcs immediately south of Tamvill. King Melwasúl arrived in time to destroy the army before they could escape. I am pleased to report that, although we did suffer significant casualties, we lost few Dwarves, Humans or Elves. We estimate that we killed more than one thousand of the enemy, which has to be a significant loss.

"We are now preparing to march upon Phaedham, and then to Easbister to take up the siege of Shalal'm Caer. However, we must now consider our attack in greater detail. Although I have a general description of Beckworth's fortress, I do not know the details. I have no idea of the number and kind of its defenders. I have no idea of the true strength of the walls, or the state of the defenses. I have no knowledge of their weapons or their preparations. I have no knowledge of the layout, passages, tunnels or any other architectural features.

"Therefore, I ask all of you for your intimate knowledge of Beckworth's fortress, his dispositions, his defenders or defenses. What do we know of the place?"

The silence was deafening. "Nobody? None of you know what's inside that edifice?"

Jharl Azkhalish replied, "My Thanelish, centuries ago we did aid the newly arrived Humans to build a defense against those who might do them harm. At first, it was no more than a high, stone cylinder. Later, they built a wall around it. Then, during the reign of Ulrich, they discovered iron ore near the Jaralii Hills, and removed themselves to the new capital of Jhal'm Thaer. In those halcyon days, Humans seemed to eat the lands. They built roads and harbors. They established towns and farms. They undertook great works, of which the great castles Jhal'm Thaer and Shesol Vys are but two.

"During those times, the old fortress was abandoned and fell into disrepair. When Ulrich built the Great Southern Highway, he bypassed Wayland's Keep and went through the village of Barstough instead.

"It was during the reign of Ambrosius that the family of Beckworth came to Shalal'm Caer. They came to control the region over time, and, as they did so, they rebuilt the fortress. Although they did employ the artisans of Clan Zhaenstain to rebuild the fortress, they also employed their own masons to perform much of the work. Our knowledge of the interior of their castle is limited, and you would have to speak with Jharl Galmerstain for further information. However, I can say they were secretive of their restoration.

"It was when King Patrick took a second wife that the fortress of Wayland became the estates of Beckworth, extending from Soubister to Easbister. George Beckworth, the only issue of that mating, became Lord Beckworth. Since that time, the exterior of the fortress has changed little. Yet, construction is almost continuous within. We know, for instance, that he has extended subterranean passages to meet our circumferential tunnels joining Ex-Tansk to Ghamarazh to Ozhemia and Zhaenstain. Unless Zhaenstain can add additional information, we have no knowledge of what goes on beyond the main gate."

For the next half hour, we discussed our dispositions and plans. Duke Armjurst had landed at Eastport, and King Aeradir had arrived at Bursk. They would both advance on Goerskim to eliminate any hostile presence, and then to Easbister. They figured four days to make the journey.

We would arrive in Phaedham today and Easbister a day later. Richard would arrive in Barstough in two days, but his train would take another week to arrive.

Fingolfin would arrive in Soubister tomorrow, with Yurchist Linda and Sir Domnall arriving six days later. Princess Cassandra would not arrive for another week. Depending on our plan of attack, she might or might not make it. It was possible that the Elves of the Blue Lake would be the only force in the west when we first engaged.

Of course, the Dwarves were already in position to attack. They'd been fighting wave after wave of attacks, directed primarily at Clan Ghamarazh. Clan Worfellsten had reinforced them, preventing a breakthrough, but it had been close. All four Clans were angry, and Thane Defghamask expressed their frustrations.

"Jharl Regent Gulámae, you promised aid in our fight with Beckworth, but we expected such reinforcements would prevent an invasion of our dwarrows. Instead, we are fighting for our lives. Had Jharl Worzhemacht not reinforced us, we would have been utterly overrun and defeated. Who knows what would have become of us?"

"Yes, Thane Defghamask, I apologize for the delay. But, I am here now at the head of a mighty army of Dwarves, Elves, Orcs, Humans and Krelli. As you have heard, we have just delivered him a stunning defeat, from which even he may not be able to recover. We are closing a trap around Beckworth.

"I had hoped that the other Clans would have been more supportive. For that, I will not apologize. Instead, I ask why Jharlmor Azzele hasn't come to your aid. Instead, it seems to me, he has done everything in his power to deliver you into Beckworth's hands.

"I do not have a similar indictment of Elvin tribes. Five tribes are represented here in this army. Three others are providing material aid. Similarly, I have no indictment of the Orcs. Yurchist Linda has led her army under Princess Cassandra's banner. The Orcs of the Great Eastern and Great Western Meadows are now actively defending the passes into the Dwarf Mountains, over which Lord

Beckworth could be marching to invade and overcome the Dwarves of the Dwarf Mountains.

"Thus, I suggest you direct your anger against your own kinfolk, who have not come to your aid, while directing your gratitude towards the Humans, Elves, Orcs, and Krelli of these lands who are your allies."

Thane Defghamask hung his head for a moment. "I apologize to you, My Jharl. I have held the fate of my Clan in my hands for many days. My only concern day and night is the defense of our Dwarrow. Too few have come to our aid, and I blamed you and everyone else for our plight. I now see that you have accomplished a great deal in assembling this army and coming to our aid. I have served my Clan to the best of my abilities, My Jharl."

"Yes, you have, My Thane. You have served our Clan with honor and distinction. And, because of you, we now have the opportunity to defeat Beckworth and his Adjudicars. Fear not, My Thane, your opportunity to avenge your losses is near at hand. Just hold out for a few more days."

I wrapped up our impromptu meeting, saying, "OK, everyone?" By this time, everyone understood my aphorism and just nodded. "OK, get to your jump-off points. King Fingolfin, be sure to link up with King Richard's forces on your left and Jharl Azkhalish on your right. I don't want Beckworth to be able to isolate and attack you. Jharl Azkhalish, extend your front toward Barstough and seek King Fingolfin's right. King Richard, extend your right to meet the Elves. If he'll expend two Battalions in the east, he surely can expend one or two in the west.

"Anything else?"

The Seeress interjected, 'When you are done, Queen Gilraën, I would like a few words with you."

"As you wish, Seeress. Anyone else? Terminate."

The Seeress reappeared in my mirror. "Gilraën, you have accomplished much in the past few weeks. I am so proud of you."

Once again, I demonstrated my mental acuity and quick wit. I blushed and stammered meaningless syllables.

"Now, you need to learn more about Beckworth's fortress."

I nodded, thinking, '*Duh!*'

"And, you've asked everyone, including your friendly Krelli. Further, it is doubtful that anyone other than Beckworth himself is aware of what is going on in his castle. You need to enter his domain without being seen … without being detected … beyond *Divergio lepto*. You must *Transfer*, but without a destination. You must *vanish into the Void*, which is *Sia sai Balor ailai si Byr*. To do so requires the greatest of precautions. You will need your entire Tribe, so that none of you are lost forever. Concentrate and be careful, Gilraën. You will never do anything more dangerous in your life."

She terminated before I could ask what she meant.

* * * * *

Chapter 2 – The Void

Regardless, we had to get there before I could take her advice, whatever that was. "My King, My Jharl, Justice, let us consider when we can resume our march upon Phaedham. I'm sure a small force remains there, and, no doubt, they expect their armies to return victorious. So, we can expect some defense of the bridge. Yet, we must also be prepared for their contingency of destroying the bridge before we can liberate it. Suggestions?"

Justice spoke first. "We know, Gilraën, that the only way to take a bridge is from both sides."

"And," King Melwasúl added, "we must act quickly, so they do not have time to carry out their plan."

I answered, "I believe my Tribe and I can handle that. We can *transfer* to both sides of the river and grab it before they even know we're there. But, we'll need reinforcements just in case. King Amder, how long would it take you to arrive at Pheadham?"

"We could also *transfer*," he replied, "or *Fugitos* for a turn."

"And you, Jharl Tazmatahela?"

"We could arrive late on the second day," he answered.

"And you, Baron?"

He considered, before answering, "Two days, but we wouldn't be ready to attack before the third day."

"Excellent. Then here's my plan. We will *transfer* to Phaedham and seize the bridge. King Amder, Justice and the rest of the Krelli can reinforce us immediately. Jharl Tazmatahela can reinforce us in less than two days, and Baron Richmond within three days. So, by three days from now, we can have seized Phaedham and be in a position to advance on Easbister. That's another five to six days. We should be in position to attack Shalal'm Caer in a week or so."

* * *

By morning, those who had been healed had recovered. The people of Tamvill were generous in every way. They had little, but shared a morning meal with us. Headman Mansfield was most magnanimous in his thanks and his praise. The people of Tamvill cheered us as we stepped off on our southward journey. My Elves and I set out at a ten-fold pace, accompanied by the Elves of the Green Hills and the Krelli. When we were just a few miles north of the Phaedham, I called a halt.

"We'll *transfer* to the south of Phaedham. Give us a short time to orient ourselves. I will contact you, My King, to let you know when to advance."

I gathered with my Elves. "We have practiced this before. Let us concentrate our far sight on the southern extreme of Phaedham. Do you all have it in mind? Concentrate on our objective. Now, *Divergio Lepto! Sia sai Salaes!*"

This time, instead of simply *transferring* from point to point, I tried to peep at my surroundings as we passed through non-space. However, my instantaneous glimpse was of a great, black nothing. I wondered, *'If it's so flat and featureless, how can we enter it at one defined point and exit at a second pre-defined point? There has to be some kind of coordinate system linking the two points in space-time.'*

My conjecturing ended abruptly as I stepped onto the ground. I looked around to count the rest of my tribe. All twenty-seven had made it. "Everyone OK?" I asked. When they all answered, I contacted King Amder, "We are here. Let's attack." When I felt his affirmative, I said, "Let's go!"

We raced through the streets, dodging people, carts, and the occasional animal. Suddenly, the bridge was before us, along with a dozen or so soldiers. The emblem of a red tower on white displayed on their helms and their chests identified them as Beckworth's. Most of them were at their leisure, sitting to the side and talking with each other. Only two or three were standing guard, alert for trouble.

We raced ahead, covering the last few yards in the blink of an eye. Vaerorderol passed through the neck of the first guard. The other two died nearly simultaneously.

"Stay here and guard the bridge," I told Galdor.

I led the other two cohorts to the other side of the bridge, just as King Amder arrived. We quickly disarmed the few soldiers on the north side. Our speedy arrival had surprised them completely, and they were unprepared to defend the bridge. Quickly, we passed back to the south side, where Galdor and his Cohort had overpowered and disarmed Beckworth's troops. Altogether, there were only thirty of them.

We marched them to the center of Phaedham, just south of the bridge. King Amder's Elves spread out through the village seeking others of Beckworth's forces. The citizens quickly discovered our presence, and soon a large throng had gathered. I stopped a passing cart and stepped upon it so everyone could see me.

"Citizens of Phaedham and subjects of King Richard, greetings. I am Queen Gilraën Gulámae of the Elves of the Green Mountains-Maidstone Forest." I waved to King Amder to stand beside me. "I introduce the King's ally, King Amder Melwasúl of the Elves of the Green Mountains. In three days, Frederick Baron Richmond will arrive with the Companies of Tamvill and Higgleston. Another ally, Jharl Tazmatahela of the Dwarves of Tazhela, will accompany him.

"We have met the armies of Lord Beckworth in battle near Tamvill. I am pleased to tell you, we defeated them utterly. They will not return to disturb the peace and tranquility of Phaedham ever again!"

A great cheer interrupted me. People laughed, cheered, danced and cavorted about elated that Lord Beckworth's armies were defeated and wouldn't return.

When the uproar subsided, I continued. "As we pass through your pleasant village, we will need your support. You will host more than twelve hundred Humans, Elves and Dwarves, along with three Krelli."

At that point, Justice, Retribution and Retaliation walked across the bridge to join us. "Hey, Gilraën!" Justice yelled. "Any problems?"

"No, Justice, everything's OK. You three come over here."

The crowd parted in fear. Several cried out. A few ran in terror.

"Hold, good people!" I shouted. "I introduce my friend, Justice, and his friends and our allies, Retribution and Retaliation. And, yes, they are all Krelli, and no, they will not try to enter your homes. I doubt any of them could fit through your doorways." We laughed, easing the tension somewhat.

"Again, I say to you that a mighty army will pass through your village. Go forth and get the food and other supplies that they will need. I understand that Beckworth's armies may have devoured everything they could grab. We will not. I will work with your head man to ensure that you receive proper payment, and, if possible, some reparations for the depredations heaped upon you."

This brought a mighty cheer.

"So, go forth and inform everyone that the King has returned and needs their help to drive out the Usurper and his minions."

King Amder and I stepped down to rejoin our troops. A man approached. "Elf Queen, Elf King, I am Gifford Gibbsson, village smith. You speak of proper payment and reparations. Do you speak for King Richard?"

"Master Smith Gibbsson, I speak for myself, Prince William, and Baron Richmond. I believe I also speak for the King in this matter. Regardless, if you will assist me, I will begin both repairing the damages to the King's subjects and considering the payments for the goods and services my armies so desperately need. Is that satisfactory, my good smith?"

"Well spoken, Queen Elf. I am here. Shall we converse now?"

"Master Gibbsson, I would ask you to take the time to speak with the people of Phaedham. I need to know the extent of the damage inflicted upon the King's subjects and in some detail. I ask that you meet with me for supper, at which time you will report to me your findings, if you can withstand the company of Elves and Krelli, that is."

He smiled, and answered, "Where will you be, Queen Gulámae?"

"Our Tribes will be just south of the village between the Great Southern Highway and the Great Eastern Road. We will obtain our own food from the countryside and woodlands. Understand that Elves eat mostly vegetables and little meat, but, for you, I will also provide some meat."

He nodded, turned and left.

I turned to my Elves and King Melwasúl, asking, "Can you forage for us? I'm guessing southeast? Remember to ask; don't take. Tell the farmers to come here with their produce and for payments." Almost immediately, fifty Elves disappeared towards Phaedport and Eastport.

King Amder and I worked with the rest of the Elves to set up our camp. It was a nice area, mostly flat with scattered trees not far from Phaedham. The setup took but minutes. Afterward, we sat and talked. Although we were Elves among Elves, we felt like children among grandparents. They spoke of things long since, of which we knew nothing. When we asked for explanations, the stories often began in the distant past before they had come to this planet. We sat listening, amazed and astounded as we learned of people, events and times we could never know, yet now would remain in our memories and lore.

Slowly, Elves returned, bearing armloads of produce. My Elves also brought carcasses of puldry, bhar and porg. By nightfall, we had prepared a wide variety of baked veggies and meats.

When Master Gibbsson returned, he was dumbfounded. "Where did you get all this? We in Phaedham are hungry for the lack of food."

I had been unaware of the scope of the problem. I looked to King Amder, and he nodded his approval. "Master Gibbsson, return to Phaedham and tell the people that we have prepared food for them. However, they must bring their own plates, bowls and utensils, for we do not have them. Further, let them know that farmers from Phaedport to Eastport will be arriving to sell their produce. I will ask you to administer disbursements and payments, if that is satisfactory. However, you must maintain a complete record for the King's inspection. Have you learned your letters and numbers?"

"I thank you for your confidence, Elf Queen. Certainly, I have both my letters and my numbers, as is required in my trade. However, were I to accept, then I could not fulfill the jobs that await me. My journeymen and apprentices are among the best, but I am the Master, and am needed at the forge, anvil and bellows."

I turned to King Amder, asking, "Is there some way we can compensate Master Gibbsson?"

The King nodded and said, "Master Gibbsson, you are a smith, working in iron and steel?"

"Yes, My King, but I also work in copper, silver and gold when I have the metal and the commission."

"Then, I will ask my artisans in black and precious metal smithing to teach you some of our arts. With this knowledge, you will become the finest smith in all these lands, if that is sufficient to compensate you."

"I am overcome with your offer, My King. I will gladly accept such knowledge and skills as recompense."

"Then, go to your village and lead your people here, where they will be fed."

We set to work cooking most of the food we had gathered. Using our skills and knowledge, we enhance the meal, preparing enough for a multitude. It was but a short time before the first trickles of that host arrived. For over an hour, we fed man and woman, elderly and infant. Never had we seen such gratitude. Old women dropped to the ground to kiss our feet. Young parents wept openly. Children, wide eyed at the sight of Elves, sat on our laps wolfing down bread and vegetables. We were so busy helping others that we forgot that we, too, needed nourishment. It was only when they were all sated that we alleviated our own hunger.

* * *

Using our magical skills, we had increased the amount of food we had gathered, leaving plenty for our morning meal. It was well that we had. Many of the good folk of Phaedham, who had eaten with us the previous evening, returned seeking a meal. We barely had enough for ourselves. We did not have enough for them as well. Instead, we fed the people and tightened our own belts.

Fortunately for us and them, farmers began arriving at Phaedham's marketplace. As the market reopened to perform its function, Master Gibbsson presided over the distribution and the payments as needed. During the day, more farmers arrived, slowly returning the important village of Phaedham to a state resembling normality.

The King and I sent patrols out to reconnoiter the area. We knew that Duke Armjurst was marching northward on the South Highway and King Séregon was marching northward on the Great Eastern Highway. However, until they arrived and joined forces with us, we felt vulnerable.

Within an hour, Nienna reported, "Duke Armjurst is just outside of Goerskim. He'll encamp there overnight. And, King Aeradir Séregon sends his regards."

"Where is Aeradir?"

"He took the cut-off trail between Bursk and Easbister. He should arrive in Easbister tomorrow. Looks like everyone's in place."

I recalled my cohorts and sat back to contemplate what we should do now. My armies would be in position in just a few days. But, as I'd been asked, what then? I didn't know. So much for my leadership. And what was this stuff the Seeress had said to me? "… beyond *Divergio lepto* … *Transfer*, but without a destination." What did she mean?

How could I transfer without a destination? *Sia sai Balor ailai si Byr?* I'd been able to *Divergio lepto* and then synchronizing with the warp and woof of the universe. I didn't know what it was called, but I knew it was different from just disappearing. Still, *transfer* was different. *Transfer* involved using the Void to pass from one place to another. To do it required the Sorcerer to know where they were, and then to specify the exact place to go. The Sorcerer had to use prescience to envision where to terminate the *transfer*. But what would happen if there was no 'to'?

The question bothered me all night. I just couldn't figure it out. Yet, the Seeress had insisted that I had to do it. By morning, I was exhausted. I had slept poorly. Baron Richmond started out first thing, trailed by his long supply train. Jharl Tazmatahela followed an hour or so later. Before he could leave, I consulted King Amder, asking him what the Seeress had asked of me.

"The Void?" he answered in alarm. "Avoid it at all costs! High Elves access it to secure an Elf Realm. In the past, we used it to emigrate from world to world. However, even I do not willingly go there. It is utterly featureless, with no dimensions, directions or guides. Once you are lost, you will never find your way.

"You are young and inexperienced, Gulámae, so let me advise you. Nèssa Narmőlanya is unique to this continent, although there are several others like her on Trahe. She has unusual abilities. Your very presence attests to that. However, she seems to believe you have such extraordinary powers that you can accomplish the most remarkable tasks without preparation, training or assistance of any kind. I don't agree with her. To suggest such a thing is unconscionable."

"You say that, but she seems to think it's important. Tell me, how should I approach learning how to do this?"

"You are determined in this, I see. Unfortunately, I can be of little assistance. I created an Elf Realm by using my powers, but I can't say that I knowingly controlled the Void. Although I have traveled its null-space, I have never enjoyed it. I admit, I followed Mother Nessa, our Seeress, but I never learned the secrets of the Void."

Disappointed, I returned to my camp, still unsure of what or how to do anything regarding the Void. I called my tribe together and related the Seeress' comments. Then I told them of Melwasúl's warning. Finally, I said, "I am determined to understand this, and how to use it to our advantage. But I need to take it one step at a time or suffer the fate of King Amder's warning.

"So, I ask you to join me. My idea is to create an Elfin chain between the here and now and the Void. We will start with the basics of *transfer*. Nèssa Narmőlanya said something about *transfer* without destination. I wonder if that's the same as making the start and the end the same.

"So, here's what we're going to do. I'm going to try to enter the Void. Some of you will come with me. Some of you will use our *Vanish* to get as close to the Void as you can. Some of you will stay here maintaining mental contact with the rest of us. Your job is the most critical. If we get in trouble, you will be our anchor… our destination… our salvation. Those who are close to the Void will maintain intimate contact between us and them. We who attempt the Void will maintain close contact with you, making the chain that we will use to find our way back.

"So, which of you goes, which stays, and who's in the middle?"

As expected, they all volunteered to do the most dangerous part and come with me into the Void. I had to decide. "OK, Galdor, you are our rock. If we get in trouble, your Cohort must rescue us. Caranthir, you are the chain between us. Nienna, you come with me."

They all nodded.

"Let's find a quiet place.

We sat in a spiral, with me in the middle. I held Nienna's hand, and she held Lenwë's. Lúthien held Caranthir's hand and so forth to Idril. Idril held Galdor's hand and ended with Celebriän.

I explained, "I'm going to try entering the Void. I think I've done it before, whenever I've *faded* completely from sight. As you know, when you *fade* like that, there's an energy barrier that you can touch but not penetrate. However, when we *transfer*, we seem to bounce and rebound from a kind of energy barrier. I will try entering the Void by using *transfer*, but not going anywhere. That's why I need to hold hands and keep track of each other in every way. If I get in trouble, you pull me back. Got it? OK, I'm going to concentrate on this."

I considered *fading*, but decided against it. Instead, I considered the sense of the universe I'd felt before. I quickly entered that in-between world where I could perceive the entire structure of space-time laid out all around me. From that vantage point, I considered the properties I used to *transfer*. I grasped at the essence of the magic, seizing the spell, and seeking a transitionless *transfer*.

As I applied the energy to *Vanish into the Void*, I felt the energy barrier, and I pushed against it. It yielded like a huge pillow, but I couldn't get through it. I reinforced my finger to create a hard, pointy tool, attempting to penetrate the barrier. When my finger poked through the barrier, I jammed my hand into it to make the hole big enough to poke my head through the barrier to see… absolutely nothing… an utter, profound blackness.

A clamor of voices penetrated my mind, "Gilraën, stop! Pull out! Come back! Gilraën, hear us!"

I withdrew and terminated my spells. It took a few seconds to re-acclimate and see my surroundings. Twenty-seven Elves were strung out in a long line. We were not where I had started. Somehow we'd moved. "Where are we?"

Nienna answered, "You disappeared, but I held onto you. Then, you started drifting to the west. We did everything we could to keep you in place, but you pulled us about half a mile."

I explained what I had done. They explained what had happened. After a while, we correlated my actions with the results they had observed. Essentially, we concluded that our space-time was moving relative to the Void.

"OK, let's try this again. I'll try to maintain my position. And, I think I can get into the Void more quickly, too."

We formed up. I kept my attention on the place I was standing, while stretching through non-space to the Void. I punched through it and squeezed into the Void. Concentrating on my initial position, I discovering I had drifted some small distance.

'*Hmmm*,' I thought, '*I can "see" what's "down there."*' I moved back to the starting point and left the Void to return to the tribe.

"How was that?" I asked.

Sure enough, I started to drift, just as I had the previous time. But then, I had 'corrected' and returned to the original position. Further, this time, they all experienced everything that I had done.

When I returned, we discussed my movement. Our consensus was that the planet was spinning beneath me. However, I had noticed it and had compensated for it. So, if I was aware of it, then I could maintain my relative position. If so, it might be possible to navigate in the Void using real-world spatial orientation.

"OK, let's try it again." I was tired, but I had to learn how to do this. I stretched my mind, quickly finding and penetrate the energy barrier. It was getting much easier, now that I knew it could be done. I stood in the Void, Nienna standing beside me holding my hand.

Lenwë was only partway into the Void, uncomfortable and struggling with the constriction the energy barrier was imposing on him. "Hey! Let go or pull me through. This is awful." We pulled him through, but let him lie there, his arm through the barrier holding Elrond's hand.

I had carefully monitored my position relative to my starting point. Oddly, it wasn't a matter of my moving or walking. It was more a matter of awareness and anchoring myself to the space-time world.

"Let go, Nienna, I want to move around a little bit."

Tentatively, I released her hand and took a 'step.' Oddly enough, I traversed space. I turned – another surprise – to look at Nienna. I looked 'down' and stepped in that direction, to find myself about even with her chest. I stepped 'up' again.

I tried to consider Cartesian coordinates in a non-Cartesian space. Then I stopped because my brain hurt. How could such things as up, down, angles and such exist? I thought 'up' and moved 'up.'

I looked at Nienna, and asked, "How do we move around here? There has to be a way."

Nienna performed a basic reality check, saying, "No! That's why they call it the Void. There is no orientation. It's like space, without all the atoms and stuff. Without the planet, and gravity and stuff like that, we wouldn't have words like 'up', 'down' and directions like that. Without gravity, we couldn't walk or run or jump. This is a new reality."

"Let's get back and try to figure this out."

We returned to the real world, back where we started. Each of us had experienced what Nienna and I had lived. We all contemplated what we had lived. We shared our minds, exploring what we had done, what we had felt and how we could cope with it. No matter how we considered it, we just couldn't put unlimited non-existence into our limited, Cartesian, space-time brains.

"But wait," Daeron interjected, "how can we *transfer* if the Void is directionless? We start at a known position in space-time, and we end at a different position in space-time. I can get how we start, but how do we get where we want to go. I mean, how does the Void know where to kick us off the bus?"

That was a poser. How did we know where to get off if we didn't know how or when to get off? There had to be something or someplace or… something. But what?

"You know," Alassë commented, "coordinate systems are arbitrary. North, south; up, down; right, left – it's all arbitrary. So, why don't we just impose our own coordinate system?"

I answered, "Well, it's easy if you've got a starring point and nothing changes. But, the Void is infinite, with no coordinates and no fixed positions. How do you impose a coordinate system on something that essentially doesn't exist?"

"It's sorta like when I was in the Navy," Eo said. "I was a submariner, and we had similar navigational problems. In the old days, we had to come up to shoot the stars to know where we were. But, that exposed us to hostiles. So, they developed this inertial navigation system. We'd start by establishing where we were in the computer. Then, no matter where or how fast we went, the computer kept track of it. The computer always knew where we were. So, why don't we just create a mental inertial guidance system?"

"And," Camthalion added, "We could use a distant point in space-time to fix our position. I'm an amateur astronomer, and one of the problems I had was the rotation of Earth. We used to use a clockwork mechanism to counteract the rotation. However, I now use a sighting scope to fix on a star. The computer observes the apparent motion and drives the motors to adjust the position to maintain a fixed image. Is there some way we can fix on a distant object or position to maintain the orientation?"

We were discussing the different solutions to our navigational problem until they reminded me we had to depart toward Easbister. We decided to take advantage of the long trip from Phaedham by *transferring* several times. We hoped to study the magic itself and the Void. Our first stage took us only twenty miles or so to the bend in the Great Southern Road northwest of Phaedham.

We were exhausted. *Transfer* was an energy sapping process; *Balor* was worse. Add to that puttering around in the Void, we had spent a great amount of energy and needed to replenish it. But there was no town nearby. In fact, we'd just transferred from the largest town in the whole region. We reasoned that we weren't the only travelers on the main artery from the east coast to the west coast. Again, we reasoned that there had to be inns or the equivalent at semi-regular intervals corresponding to a day's travel, or about 20 miles. Regardless of which way we went, there just had to be something in the next twenty miles or so. Even at a gentle five-fold walk, that was less than half an hour.

One hour later, we were concerned… and hungry. There was nothing even slightly representing an inn. "OK, let's find something to eat," I told them, "Hunt, scrounge, buy – something." We split going twenty-eight different directions. I trotted through a wooded area near the Phaed River. There, in a muddy section, I found the tracks of a charder. I faded and trotted stealthily following the spoor. When I found the animal grazing in a meadow, I dropped it with a single shot. After I'd dressed it, buried the guts, and hoisted it on my shoulder, I trotted back to the meeting place.

Some of the others had already returned. Some had found wild vegetables such as tavor. One had stumbled on a farm and purchased several tans. I set about building a fire and preparing to slow roast the charder. I set the liver, heart and kidneys aside to cook on hot rocks. We cooked the veggies in a skin bag filled with water. We dropped hot rocks into the water to heat it to a boil and then dumped the prepared vegetables in to cook. In the end, we had a wonderful meal of charder, tans, tavor and maidzh, along with plenty of excellent river water to wash it down. And we had plenty left over, which we wrapped in oilskins and packed in our quivers. We figured we had enough for a second meal.

It was mid-afternoon. We had time for at least one more try at transferring before we arrived in Easbister. This time, we tried Eo's suggestion. I stood looking to the north, orienting myself with the planet's coordinates. Then, being careful to maintain my personal orientation, we formed our chain, and I entered the Void. Low and behold, it worked. I could perceive a coordinate system, which I imposed on the Void. Suddenly, I had a Cartesian system that I could use, at least temporarily. Considering Camthalion's suggestion, I searched for a fixed point I could use to adjust my orientation, but found nothing. The Void was universally flat, black and featureless.

"Let me go," I asked Nienna. Then, I took a step towards my imposed westerly direction. I sensed the distance and the speed at which I had moved, feeling my new position relative to where I had been. I deliberately wandered about, trying to sense where I was. When I felt the world moving under me, I adjusted my internal guidance system accordingly. I moved off further and further, reorienting myself as I went, then turned and walked directly back to my initial entry point.

I was elated. Grabbing Nienna's hand, we returned to our own space-time. We sat together, and I explained, "It worked, Eo, but I couldn't find anything else to fix upon. It's just featureless and utterly empty." I explained what I had done and that after walking around I could walk directly back to Nienna. That could only mean I had mapped the terrain mentally. My inertial guidance system had worked. It was only a single test, and the distance was short, but it had worked.

We transferred to a meadow a few miles southeast of Easbister. A small wood separated us from the town. We set up our camp and took a quick nap. It had been a long, tiring but successful day.

* * *

When I awoke, it was full night. My tribe was already awake, waiting for me. They had lit no fire and had erected a simple barrier around us to hide us from prying eyes.

I yawned hugely.

"About time!" Galdor quipped.

"OK, I got it. How long you been waiting?"

Nienna laughed, "Not that long, actually."

"So," I asked, "Shall we see who's here?"

We *faded* and strolled through the wood, making no noise. We extended our prescience to detect anything, but withheld any probes, lest they be detected.

The first group we found was a patrol of humans in a roughly east-west line, looking southward. Obviously, they were the sentries. Since there was no sense in disturbing them, we continued southward to the town. Easbister was another small village typical of the entire east of Umbeqjaralii. Its reason for existence seemed to be the junction between the South Highway and the trail northward to Willicamp. Why it wasn't on the Great Southern Road is a good question. In fact, there was only a small inn at that intersection.

We reappeared and walked through the town. Suddenly, this quiet, little village had become a massive supply depot and military base for ten times the number of villagers. Hundreds of Humans and Elves ambled through the town. Wagons and carts blocked narrow roads, where Humans and Orcs had established depots. We found the inn at the center of town on the northwest of the intersection. Men were rushing in and out. Obviously, this was an important place, so we approached cautiously.

Several men, dressed in Prince William's livery, stood guard. When we approached, they lowered their halberds to point them at us.

"Halt! This inn is restricted unless you have business with the Eastern Army."

"I am Queen Gilraën Gulámae. I am here to speak with Prince William or General Abuahad."

Although the man who had challenged us showed no recognition of us, the others did. One of them stepped forward to whisper into the first man's ear. He blanched and raised his halberd. He stammered, "I apologize, Queen Gulámae. The Prince and the General are inspecting their troops. One of my men can escort you to them."

"No, sentinel, just point us in the right direction."

"They are south and west of the town. Go back to the Road, go west about a mile."

"Where are King Melwasúl and King Séregon?"

He pointed to the north. "The Green Mountain Elves are north of the town to the east of the trail. The White Cliffs are also north of the town on the western side of the trail."

"Ah, good," I said, "King Aeradir arrived. When?"

"A few hours ago."

"I'll bet you feel a lot better now that you have a thousand Elves reinforcing you."

He smirked, "You're right, Elf Queen. With just three Companies, we felt a bit exposed. We're only fifty miles or so from Beckworth, so if he'd come after us, our only choice would have been to flee. At least now, if he comes out, we can stage a fighting retreat."

"Be comforted then. Jharl Tazhela has passed through Phaedham and is marching to your relief. Baron Richmond is behind him, so your Battalion will be united once again. You will march to Barstough, where you will join with King Richard's army and the Elves of the Brown Hills. You will have a mighty army of some four thousand, and when you do, Beckworth will be the one fearing your attack. So, be of good cheer. Sharpen your halberds and be prepared to march."

I made a quick decision and headed north. If I found William, I just might not get back to my own camp. So, it'd be better if we visited with our allies first. King Amder's camp was just a mile or so due north. They greeted us warmly. They had arrived this morning and had found an excellent site along a small stream flowing toward the Phaed River. They had found their own food by searching in the nearby woods and waters. They had found edible roots and berries, along with ample fish from the stream.

After we found they were comfortable, we turned westward to find the Elves of the White Cliffs. At first, they were reluctant to let us pass, but when I introduced myself, they eagerly escorted us to their king. I hadn't met King Aeradir, except at the congress in which we brought my tribe to Trahe. As I had remembered, he was dressed all in white with black trim. Oddly, his crown was a white square with black trim. What I had not remembered was how tall and thin he was. He was at least seven feet tall, but couldn't have weighed more than 175 pounds. He appeared emaciated, and I would have been concerned were he not an ancient High Elf.

King Aeradir stood when I appeared and greeted me, saying, "Welcome, Queen Gilraën. I see you have brought your entire tribe. Have you eaten? Are you encamped already?" He waved us to his pavilion. We sat with him on pillows, which were simultaneously high and soft. As we sat, other Elves entered to serve us wine and small cakes.

"Yes, we are, King Aeradir. We are all here, eager to meet our Elvin friends and allies. I cannot express my deep gratitude for your military alliance in this crusade. What was it that changed your mind?"

"Ah, right to the business at hand, My Queen? Yes, the young are always eager to get on with it, aren't you? But first, you must answer my questions, don't you think?" he gently admonished me.

I laughed and replied, "You are correct, and I accept your gentle reproach. Thank you for your kind welcome." I sipped the wine. It was superlative, but then again, it was Elvin. The cakes were light and sweet, tasting of crumbly honey. "And your refreshment is most excellent. We encamped earlier this afternoon. We had hunted and gathered earlier in the day and had found more than plenty. We are camped to the south of Easbister. We came to the town a short while ago, seeking Prince William and General Abuahad. We were informed they were with their troops and were also directed to King Amder's camp and to yours. We visited with King Amder and found they were comfortable and had eaten. So, we came in search of you to find how you were situated.

"So, I must ask how was your trek from your homes to this distant locale? Is your encampment suitable? Have you sufficient food? I know the Human supplies are limited, and may not be as appetizing to you as they are to them, but are they suitable?"

"Ah, thank your for inquiring about our comfort. We are a people of the sea coasts. We embed our domiciles within the high cliffs overlooking the sea. We miss the salt air, the wind, and the waves that are our homes. Our food is that of the sea and the mountains. We enjoy the fish, the shellfish and the mollusks. Equally, we enjoy the berries, the fruits and the bulbs of the land, and the several mountain beasts that inhabit our lands. So it is that the foods available in these realms are foreign to us. Both King Amder and Prince William have introduced us to these new foods. We find that some are to our liking, and some are so new or different that they are not to our tastes. With the help of King Amder, we have found various roots and fruits that are more to our liking. Yet, it is always interesting to sample foreign foods and preparations. Even after all these millennia, it is refreshing to find something new and different to savor or experience."

"I agree whole heartedly, My King. None of us are native to this world. We come from a different planet, which is splintered into thousands of realms, both large and small. The large realms are themselves split into much smaller locales, each of which is unique in some way. These locales differ in foods, or manner of dress, or language, or physical attributes or social mores. It is either educational or daunting to travel through these many domains, and to experience the differences between them."

"Ah, so your world is larger than ours?"

"I'm not sure about the physical size of our planets or the size of the continents or the number of inhabitants of this world. If they are about the same size, then I would say that our continents are larger, even though the seas cover over two parts in three of our world. However, our world is fecund. We have millions of species of plants and animals. We have one hundred thousand species of mammals, including both prey and hunter species. We have over seven billion Humans, many of whom are violently disposed to others. Although we have no magic such as we have here, we have science and technology, which is so awesome that we could destroy all life on our planet in a single day or we could send our people into the space between the stars to seek out other lives.

"The twenty-eight of us were utterly different before we arrived here. Some of us could have been enemies. And so, our tastes in food, clothing, social mores and all other things were different. We each had to become accustomed to our new forms, our new abilities, and our new societies. We, however, are now a single tribe, encompassing our differences, delighted in the strengths they have brought to us."

King Aeradir nodded in understanding. "I was aware you were from a different world. However, I am surprised at the vast numbers of different types of creatures that inhabit it. Even more so, however, I am astounded at the vast numbers you describe and the immense power your science has granted to you."

"Quite true, My King, we are an interesting study in differences and how societies manage disputes both within a society and between them. King Melwasúl was kind enough to explain some of the political and social problems of this world. His analysis reflected the problem the Adjudicars have imposed on all the societies of this land. That was one reason I expressed my surprise and gratitude towards your military alliance with King Richard's forces. Perhaps you could explain to me how you came to this decision?"

"Aha!" he exclaimed, "Do you see now that by taking the few moments to build the social bridge between us that an appropriate time came for your inquiry?" He chortled and patted me on the shoulder. "Diplomacy is important when dealing with beings that have seen worlds born, grow old and die in the violent explosion of their stars. And now that this subject has arisen so naturally, I am pleased to discuss the politics between the Realms.

"The extension of the Dwarf Mountains to the Eastern Sea divides North from South. In the North lies the great Human realm of Umbeqjaralii. To the south lies the realm of Narwortland. We, the

Elves of the White Cliffs and our neighbors, the Dwarves of Stone, inhabit those lands. By long agreement, the Grau River serves as the boundary between our realms. However, there is much commerce between us.

"The lands to our north are wild and untamed until they arrive at the hamlet of Wendleford on the Wendle River. Yet, this Human enclave is utterly isolated from the rest of the Humans of the North. So the people of Wendleford have learned both our language and that of the Dwarves. They have developed commerce between us, and, using their port on the Wendle River, they have developed commerce with Eastport, Phaedport and Talishport. And so, they have become a part of the peoples of the Eastern Mountains.

"To our south are the Dwarves of Worphelia, noted for their flocks and herds. They are a pastoral people. Although we are friendly with them, they have little to do either with Clan Zhaenstain or us beyond their beasts.

"Beyond them is King Arafinwë in the Green Glens and Duke Armjurst on the coast immediately south of us. We are friendly with the Green Elves, although they are a strange people of wood and bough. Yet, they are the greatest artisans of arms and armor of all our tribes. They have a great rivalry with Clan Worfellsten, each trying to produce the better weapons or armor or works of metal.

"But, it is with Duke Armjurst we have the greatest commerce. My daughter, known to you as Roselyn Graymass, is the love mate of Duke Albert. Their children are my grandchildren, for whom I bear a great affection.

"The Duchy of Armjurstton lies to our south on the Great Eastern Road which leads to Duke Armjurst's great port. His ships rival those of the Tribes of the Sea and of Gray Havens. His fertile uplands provide a great part of our foodstuffs, and his armies defend our southern borders.

"Thus, two tribes, two clans and two Human habitations form the intersection between Umbeqjaralii and Narwortland. For many years, this was a most satisfactory arrangement. Each of us prospered because of the other. None of us suffered, because we each provided what the others needed.

"However, then the Adjudicars arrived, and Lord Beckworth came to power. We believe he has two of these evil mages at his beck and call. We believe a third resides in Narwortland, as does another in Farrowspike. Just as Beckworth and his Adjudicars threaten the North with war, the one in Narwortland is the threat in the South. We, in the middle, are threatened by both.

"When your call to arms was raised, we were still in the middle. Lord Armjurst pledged his aid almost immediately. We understood this, since he is obligated through his family ties to King Richard. However, that left us undefended from the South.

"Duke Armjurst's people, lands, and port were open to attack if he departed with his army. Knowing this, he negotiated with me, Green Glens, Worphelia, and Zhaenstain to defend his realm from the depredations of Narwortland's forces. Then, Zhaenstain armed to defend against the event of an invasion from the North. Jharl Galmerstain moved the bulk of his forces into Ozhemia while Jharl Morthanzhemian moved his into Ghamarazh. Yet, it was that movement that protected us from Beckworth.

"I appealed to Jharl Bethmathalia and King Lossëhelin to extend their forces into Armjurstton and the coast. I explained that if they did so, I could advance my armies to aid Duke Armjurst and defeat Lord Beckworth. Once that had been accomplished, then we could turn our attention to the one vexing us. Again, Worphelia demurred, but I insisted, getting much support from Jharl Galmerstain. Eventually, Jharl Worzhemacht recognized the threat to his flocks and herds, and mobilized his forces to defend the city and port while Green Glens defended the lands between. Thus, with my lands and people defended, I could assemble my forces and march northward.

"We did encounter some minor resistance at Bursk. A small force with a Human Sorcerer attempted to delay my forces. However, they were too few and their sorcery insufficient to delay us. By agreement with Duke Armjurst, we advanced along the Bursk trail, while he advanced upon Goerskim. Evidently, that village was defended. However, they were not expecting such a massive army to attack them. Armjurst quickly surrounded them and attacked from all sides. His force of arms and superior sorcery soon reduced the defense to impotence. Since then, he has been upon the South Highway. If I understand these things, he should arrive in the next day or two. Thus it is that we are here, and I am prepared follow you to the attack on the fortress of Shalal'm Caer."

"My King!" I exclaimed, "I had heard that Elves were terse in their speech, seldom amplifying on events and disparaging their own accomplishments. Instead, I have heard a saga, involving history, geography, social interactions and politics. Thank you for such a stirring and elucidating narrative."

"You are young, My Queen, and have much to learn. As any elder would, I explained to teach a youth, such as yourself, what we have learned through our countless years. Thus it will be that, in the future, such things will be obvious, and we will have no need of such explanations."

"Ah, you have reminded me of my duties, My King," I said, rising. "I must seek Prince William and General Abuahad. It will be necessary for him to march to Barstough before we turn upon Shalal'm Caer. We are so pleased to have met you and to have shared a repast with you."

We left, slowly wending our way through the throng of Elves, curious about us as we were of them. When we finally exited their camp, we turned south, crossed the Highway and quickly discovered a tent city filled with men. The smells of familiar foods filled the air. A sentry shouted, "Halt! Who goes there?"

When I replied, I heard a whoop of joy, and a sentry broke and raced to the rear. By the time we arrived in the camp, a crowd had gathered. As we approached, they broke into cheering and yelling. We greeted many faces we hadn't seen since we left the castle. Then, out of nowhere, a pair of arms engulfed me. I was lifted off my feet and spun about. Then, a kiss was firmly planted on my lips.

The arms were familiar. The lips were familiar. The smell was familiar. The face was the one of the man I loved! (*'What? The man I loved? Tony, what's happened to you? Oh, shit! What has happened to me?'*)

I kissed him back. So much for my conundrum.

"Gilraën! So good to see you."

"William, is this how you wish us to be viewed by your entire army?"

"They can be as jealous as they want to be. I have you in my arms after all this time, and I may not let you go again."

I kissed him and wiggled free. I glanced at my tribe, who were all grinning, but looking in other directions as though they had seen nothing. However, the Prince's army was standing around, staring at us with broad grins on their faces.

"Come, all of you, to my pavilion. General Abuahad is anxiously awaiting you. He has been beside himself since he learned of the battle of Tamvill. I have summoned Sir Xander's Battalion, but Richard prevailed, demanding I march to Barstough instead. We will march tomorrow and arrive in three days. When Richmond and Tazhela arrive, my armies will be complete, and we will be prepared to march on Shalal'm Caer."

I signaled to my tribe, leaving them to converse with the Palace Guards and the three Companies of Richmond's Battalion. I returned with William to his pavilion, where the General awaited us.

Abuahad leapt to his feet when we entered. A huge smile split his usually placid and taciturn face. He nodded, and said, "Queen Gulámae, I am beyond delighted that you have arrived. Where is Baron Richmond?"

I just had to laugh. The juxtaposition of the two sentences was just too funny! Evidently, Abuahad didn't see the funny part, just my laughing at him, and he was upset. It took me several minutes to convince him I wasn't laughing at him, but with him.

Anyhoo, I hugged him, and told him I was happy to have finally arrived. Then, I told him of the battle of Tamvill, our capture of Phaedham, and my efforts to feed not only ourselves but also the populace. I explained that I had spent a large sum to get the economy kick-started.

Prince William nodded sagely, replying, "Well done, My Queen. My lieges need to know their King and their Prince have their welfare in mind. Commerce is the very heart of wealth, and wealth is necessary for happiness, and without happy subjects, we have revolution and chaos. So, once again, you have renewed our kingdom, and at a minimal cost."

"Thank you, My Prince. And, General, have I answered your questions satisfactorily?"

"How many did we lose?"

"Eleven dead and fifteen maimed. Jharl Tazhela lost fifty dead and more than thirty maimed. As for us, none, although Lenwë Tasardur was severely injured, and we feared for his survival."

Abuahad sighed deeply. "I am relieved that our casualties were not worse. It was good that you built the field works, else they would have overwhelmed you. And, you were fortunate that Dwarves were there to defend the wall. Always place Dwarves upon rock, for it is there they are invincible."

William nodded in agreement, before he asked, "Now that we have gathered our forces, what is your plan of attack?"

I sighed before answering, "I'm not sure."

William gasped.

"Well, it's that I don't know what the castle looks like, do I?"

William looked blankly at me. "You know, neither do I. I grew up in Jhal'm Thaer, as did Richard and Cassie. However, Georgie spent some considerable time in Shalal'm Caer. It was his family's castle, you see. It was only when he murdered father that he escaped to the old castle and rebuilt it. I'm not sure if anyone I know has been there since he renovated it."

"Well, we've got to find out... somehow. I wonder if Richard knows anyone?"

William asked, "How about the Dwarves? Do any of them know?"

"No," I answered, "I've asked them. They helped Wayland build his original fortress and with some early modifications, but nothing thereafter."

"So, they're no help."

"No, not at all. However, I think I know how to investigate the place. We've been working on it, and we've made great progress. I think I may just be able to do it."

"And, what is that plan," he asked.

I contemplated the answer. No matter what I said, I wouldn't be able to explain it. Further did I want to? Perhaps this was one of those things that I shouldn't divulge, except to my Tribe. Knowledge of the Void was not a something that should be broadcast. "No, I think I'll not say anything more until I have figured it out."

"Sure, but when you do, will you tell me about it?"

"We'll see, but until then, we have lots to consider. Most importantly, at least for now, how are you feeding all these people?"

He sat back, nodding sagely. "It is the greatest problem we have ever faced. Had King Ulrich not built the roads, and King Ambrosius not begun the domestication of the different animals, we could not have done any of this. Had King Adelbert and Canisius not befriended the Orcs, we could not have done this. Had our father not trained us all, we would never have had the skills, the knowledge and the strength. And, had he not divided his kingdom among us, even George, we would never have had the numbers or the allies or the friends we needed to challenge the Adjudicars. This has been a long time in coming, and if we had missed a single step along the way, we would not be here now.

"There are hundreds of carts, wagons and wains on every road between Shesol Vys and the Great Southern Road. Our greatest problem was not getting them here, but returning them so they could receive a new load and return. We widened the South Road deliberately. That way they can pass each other northbound and southbound.

"We had to solve the problem of distance. The animals can trot rapidly for many miles, but then they require a prolonged rest with plenty of food and time for them to digest it. That gives them a range of about thirty miles. So, we planned waystations roughly every twenty-five miles. Each has its own herds and herders. The animals race from post to post, where we swap them for fresh animals. That way, the animals race to and fro from one home to their other home. Yet, the wagons travel onward at the highest speed possible.

"Of course, this has been the work of generations of herders. These animals are difficult to raise and even more difficult to train as beasts of burden. However, we did it, and now, with the help of the Orcs and the farmers and herders and those who till and work the fields and all the others who toil endlessly just to survive, we stand here today. And, because of them… and on their behalf, we shall be victorious."

"My Prince, you are an orator and poet! Your eloquence fills my heart with wonder and joy. We must be victorious for them."

"So, My Queen, our troops are assembled. When we march upon Shalal'm Caer, we will rely on your battle plan for victory. I hope you figure it out quickly, else all this is for naught."

* * *

I couldn't sleep. William's words had stirred my passions, while scaring me half to death. He was right. Everyone was counting on me, and I did not know what to do. I really had no choice, did I? OK, call me reckless. Maybe I was, but I had to know more about what Beckworth was doing.

I led my tribe some sixty miles to the west. Sighting the fortress, we *faded*. As usual, Galdor Míriel's Cohort was our anchor. However, this time, I entered the Void with both Nienna's Cohort and Caranthir's Cohort. I left Caranthir's Cohort where we had entered the Void to maintain contact with Galdor. While Nienna's Cohort maintained contact with Caranthir's and me, I extended my presence from the Void into the fortification.

The fortress was some forty miles south of Barstough on the South Highway. It extended from the northwest to southeast roughly a mile. I guessed that it was not quite as deep. It was roughly a rectangle but wasn't: the long walls bulged slightly outward. Where the segments met, there was a huge, round turret extending from the wall to give plenty of room for archers to sweep the length between turrets. The wall itself was thirty feet tall and built with outward extending tiers so it was wider at the top than at the base. That is not to say that the wall was thin at the base, because it wasn't.

I studied the base of the wall. One sure way to overcome such a defense was to mine beneath the wall and set a fire. Such a tactic undermined the wall, weakened the dirt and stone base beneath it, and caused it to collapse. However, Wayland had been clever. He had built his original fortress on a granite outcropping of the Dwarf Mountains. Perhaps it was a volcanic flow or maybe even the core of a long dead and eroded volcanic core. Regardless, it appeared all too solid to me. I'm not a geological engineer or a Dwarf, but I knew granite is tough stuff.

The main gate was slightly offset to the western side of the northern wall. It was massive. A broad road, wide enough to be a four-lane highway back home, led to the gate. Two large, wooden drawbridges spanned a wide ditch. A portcullis peeked from the lintels. The port disappeared into the darkness, but did not penetrate directly into the courtyard beyond. Instead, a tunnel led between the turreted portals of the outer wall of the gatehouse to another turreted portal at the opposite side. Direct entry into the outer courtyard was limited, under guard, and easily defended.

Inside the outer fortification was a gap of one hundred feet or more ending at a second fortified wall. This interior wall was much taller, perhaps fifty feet in height. I could see similar turrets distributed along its length.

Deep within the complex was the tallest wall. It had to be over seventy feet tall, again with turrets at the corners and distributed along the length of the long walls. This innermost keep was perhaps five hundred feet each side. This was easily the largest castle I'd ever seen, although I'm sure ancient Earthmen had built larger ones.

I began to consider how we might attack this monster. I envisioned a three-level attack. At first, Dwarves would mine beneath the walls. The Elves would go over the top. The Humans would attack the gates. We'd have to build a battering ram… and siege towers… and catapults… and all sorts of stuff.

Once inside the outer courtyard, Dwarves could dig under the inner wall, while Humans and Elves attacked the gate.

Then we'd have the keep isolated. It'd be over. Maybe.

But what of Beckworth's troops, reserves, other defenses. What about a sally or a counterattack? What could he do?

I descended through the earth to explore beneath the castle. Immediately, I encountered barracks with great caches of arms. Humans filled chamber after chamber. Orcs filled as many others. I kept careful count as I went. There were more than fifteen hundred Humans and two thousand Orcs – an immense army in a strong castle.

There was a second level below the barracks. These were storerooms for food and equipment. There were kitchens, forges, and all the other necessities of warfare.

I was about to leave when I noticed a dark tunnel heading southward. Curious, I explored it. It was twenty feet wide and almost six feet in height. I explored its length for a short time until I was convinced it ran straight and true directly into the Dwarf Mountains. I guessed that it went directly to the junction between Ghamarazh and Ozhemia where it intersected the Dwarf's perimeter tunnels.

Someone 'tickled' my mind. It was the slightest touch, but someone was searching for me and may have discovered me. I closed my mind and with it my perceptions of Beckworth's fortress. I signaled to Nienna's Cohort. Alerted, we remained utterly still, hidden within the Void. Another probe penetrated the Void, passing beyond us. We remained serene and still. I focused my mind in the general direction of the probe. I dared not even think, fearing that even the act of thinking might reveal my presence.

A second probe! Two were searching for us. First, who knew of the Void? Second, how many could gain access to it? Third, who knew how to traverse it?

I knew of a few. I could, as could my tribe. We'd been here several times. I'd brought my tribe here. Caierne had demonstrated that he could transfer. He might know of the Void and he might be able to use it effectively. If the other Adjudicar also knew, it could be them. If it was them, they had more experience in the Void than I had. However, I believed that, regardless of their experience, I was better at this than they were.

But then, I reminded myself of the research exploring why the unskilled were unaware of their ineptitude. Did I really want to fall prey to my ego? Nah!

Slowly, we withdrew toward Caranthir's Cohort. As we approached, I directed a thought to them, 'Serenity!" We stood quietly, holding hands, maintaining our calm and tranquil state.

I extended my perception to watch the Adjudicars as intently as I could without revealing myself. I could learn from them... at least that's what I thought.

After a while, I figured out they were doing an interlocking box search. How mundane! I let them exhaust themselves, bumble around and wear themselves out.

Eventually, one of them stopped. He circled a position, appearing to have discovered something. He mentally contacted someone else, signaling he'd found something. The other person replied, but continued to search.

I was curious. After all, I was here to reconnoiter. Slowly, and as stealthily as I knew how, I circled around to find what they were viewing. As I approached, I felt a male mind searching beyond the Void into the material, baryonic world. I tried to eavesdrop on the mind, to see what he was seeing, touching his mind as gently as I knew how. Evidently, he was concentrating on whatever it was and was unaware of me.

I saw five objects. They were moving... walking. Mountains were in the distance. The five were... no, not walking... running toward it. Could they be Krelli?

The other man sent a mental message that almost felt like 'Aha!' I turned slowly and stealthily approached the other person navigating the Void. I didn't want to repeat my mental contact, so I just observed the baryonic world, letting whoever it was guide my mental visualization. Nine blobs appeared. Again, it took time for me to judge their speed. When I did, I knew it was Galdor's Cohort.

'*So, they know who we are, and where we are.*' I thought to myself.

They seemed satisfied with their discoveries. They moved away from me, and I followed. I used the skills they had just shown me to 'see' the baryonic world as I watched them. They moved directly over the keep and suddenly disappeared from the Void. Then I saw them standing in a large room in the keep.

I looked around to see Nienna's Cohort in a long line disappearing into the distance. We retreated until we joined with Caranthir's Cohort. Together, we returned to our baryonic world of space-time and Galdor's Cohort.

We sat around, exhausted. Our exploration had been demanding and exciting at the same time. We all sat looking at each other giggling nervously. We'd done it. We'd explored his castle; we knew his secrets. Now we could make plans.

* * *

My first obligation was to my Clan. I thought, '*Damn, what I'd give for Skype®!*' Instead, I dug out my mirror, directing it towards the dwarrow of Clan Ghamarazh. "Thane Defghamask!"

It took a few moments for Tildorhamask's face to appear. "Who calls for Thane Defghamask?"

"Jharl Gulámae!"

"Oh! My Jharl! Apologize, I do. Thane Defghamask is at the border, leading our defenses against the Usurper."

"I have an important message for him, Jharl Azkhalish, and Jharl Morthanzhemian. It is critical that they receive this warning immediately. Do you understand, Steward Tildorhamask?"

"I understand completely. What message I should deliver to them?"

"I have located a tunnel from Shalal'm Caer into the mountains between Ghamarazh and Ozhemia. I believe it is Beckworth's plan to use this tunnel to attack our dwarrows. See my mind, Tildorhamask, and transmit my memories to the Jharls and Thanes of the Dwarves."

I concentrated my mind on the memories of Beckworth's castle, the catacombs, and the tunnel heading southward. "Did you understand my thoughts?"

"Yes, my Jharl. Most disturbing this is. Immediately inform I shall to Thane Defghamask."

"Remember this, Steward, I am available to consult with them. I have my mirror ready for them. I will consult with my other commanders regarding our battle plans. If they have any questions, they must contact me immediately."

"Of course, My Jharl."

I terminated and then contacted Prince William, King Amder, King Glorfindel and Queen Eilol. "We must meet immediately. Let us gather at Prince William's pavilion. Bring your lords as well."

When they agreed, I gathered my Tribe and left for Prince William's camp. When I arrived, William was yawning broadly. Abuahad looked as though he had been on parade.

'Does he never sleep?' I wondered.

"Gilraën, do you know what time it is? The night is but half completed. What is so urgent?"

Queen Eilol had entered without me noticing. She scared the life out of me when she said, "Don't forget me!"

I spun around to see her, the King, and King Amder. "Hello, everyone, I have made a great discovery. Come, let us sit."

We gathered and sat by the dying embers of Prince William's campfire. "So?" he yawned.

"Earlier today…."

"Yesterday!" William interrupted.

"As I was saying before I was so rudely interrupted, yesterday, we explored Shalal'm Caer. We entered the Void…"

The three Elves gasped in unison. Queen Eilol exclaimed, "The Void? Are you insane, Gilraën? What are you doing in the Void?"

"Yes, mother, the Void!" I felt like I was in a sit-com or something. "We now have knowledge of the fortification as rebuilt by Beckworth, its garrison, and its defenses. I have already communicated some of our discoveries to the Dwarves, since they may come under attack."

I turned to my tribe, "Please help me to recall all that we saw."

I turned back to the group. "Here are our memories." I concentrated on revisiting our adventure inside of Lord Beckworth's fortress. When I finally completed relaying my explorations to them, including our encounter with Beckworth's Adjudicars, I looked around to see their reactions.

Prince William was looking at me with an expression of awe on his face. Abuahad's face was a mask. King Amder stared at the fire, while King Glorfindel sat with his eyes closed. Queen Eilol stared at me, a look of wonder on her face.

"My daughter! Such powers! I am amazed. We knew from the Seeress that you were extraordinarily powerful, but until this moment, I had no conception of how strong you are. And, your whole Tribe involved? What powers do you all have? I believe that even should all the Adjudicars attack, you could defeat them. But, the awesome responsibility you have shouldered. NO! That was burdened upon you. Oh, my daughter, I am sorry to have done this to you." A tear rolled down her cheek as she grabbed me in a huge hug.

"Eilol," King Glorfindel whispered, as he gently tugged her from me and held her in his arms. "I'm sure she is aware of the dangers she has faced. But now, we need to consider how .glanced toward me. "Is that not so?"

"Yes," I replied, "this is our opportunity to consider Beckworth's dispositions and how we can overcome him. You are the second persons to whom I have divulged this information. Obviously, I need to communicate this knowledge to King Richard, Princess Cassandra, Duke Armjurst and every King, Queen, Jharl, Thane, Yurchist or leader within our coalition. However, I wanted your thoughts and suggestions before I communicated with all of them. I felt that a few might develop a strategy more easily than the many. If so, we can present the first vestiges of a plan to them, and let them fill in the details."

Abuahad, the third professional soldier among us, spoke first. "I see several problems. We must consider each as we develop our battle plan. Both the eastern and western sides of the fortress are sheer slopes of hard rock. The rear rises above the terrain closer to the Mountains, making it difficult to access except from the castle or the mountains. The broad meadow to its north provides the only clear path of attack.

"That broad expanse is littered with rocks of all sizes. These would prevent us from driving siege towers and such against his walls. The uphill slope will be difficult to manage. The moat prevents us from abutting siege towers against the walls.

"The gatehouses are formidable. The towers are large, armed with catapults and ballistae, with arrow slits and sluices. The drawbridges make passage and access to the gates impossible. When they are drawn up, the moat protects them from direct attack. Further, they protect the gates by their presence, as does the iron portcullis.

"The passageway within the gatehouse is a killing zone. There is a second portcullis and gate at the opposite end. While attacking it, any forces within the gatehouse will be exposed to arrows, spears, fire and burning liquids poured on their heads.

"The outer walls are tall and broad, with an excellent concourse at their summit, permitting large forces to stand atop it, defending with arrow, spears, hot and burning liquids. The walls themselves are rounded, not flat. Ladders will not hold, but will slip aside, easily.

"With the large numbers of defenders and the size and depth of this fortification, this will be a most difficult position to assault successfully."

I snorted, "You're a font of good news."

He gaped at me. "My Queen, I provided you an analysis of the situation, as you asked."

"Yes, you did, General, and it was a professional analysis in every aspect. However, it is disheartening."

"Indeed, it is, My Queen. Shalal'm Caer is a mighty fortress. It is supposed to be intimidating, and Lord Beckworth has succeeded in making it so."

William chuckled, as he said, "Abuahad has no sense of humor when it comes to warfare. Once he has adopted his military persona, he is utterly professional. It is maddening, not comforting."

He turned to Abuahad. "How would you go about attacking it?"

"I cannot be sure. If it were only Humans, we would have to consider three approaches to be accomplished simultaneously. First, we would lay siege to the place. They have vastly too many troops to withstand a prolonged siege. With three to four thousand, they cannot be taken by force, but they do have to eat. Yet, a siege would be most difficult to maintain.

"Second, we would mine the eastern and western approaches to gain entrance and to undermine the walls. Again, the hard rock would be a problem. However, since we were besieging them, we would have plenty of time.

"Third, we would need siege engines, including trebuchets and catapults. We would batter the walls continuously until we had reduced them sufficiently to breech them.

"Finally, as the siege engines were being produced, we would need to clear the rocks from the fields, smooth the approaches, and fill in the moat so we could move the siege towers into position to scale the walls.

"We bombard the walls and turrets, launch fire bombs, and kill as many as we can, trying to create breaches, destroy the catapults and ballistae. We roll the siege towers into place to seize the walls and attack the turrets from both sides. We break through the mines to the surface within the outer courtyard. We seize the gate houses, lower the drawbridges, raise the portcullis and gates to open the way for the mass of our armies."

"Sounds like a plan, General. Comments?"

King Glorfindel added, "Remember your power singing, my daughter. We have long used the power of song to unite our strength."

"I had forgotten. Thank you for reminding me."

"And," King Amder added, "we know nothing of the powers of the Orcs. We understand they are ferocious warriors, but what does that mean? At what are they best or worst?"

I added, "And then, there's the Krelli, the Trolls, and the Octopods. If they are not involved, they might feel slighted."

I waited for someone else to add something, but, after an extended silence, I said, "Well, I guess it's time to call King Richard."

"No!" William shouted, "No, Gilraën, it's the middle of the night. King Richard would not appreciate being awakened in the middle of the night. Wait 'til morning, Gilraën! And, maybe, you should get some sleep, while you're at it."

"Perhaps you're right. I wonder if we should run to Barstough to talk directly with King Richard."

"Gilraën!" William shouted, "No! You can't. Just relax, and we'll talk to everyone in the morning. Now, get some sleep and stop bothering people."

I started to argue, but Galdor grabbed my arm. "Great idea, Prince William. We'll help our Queen to her quarters, and, if we must, we'll tie her to a tent pole until dawn. Come on, My Queen, beddy bye time." Suddenly, I was out of the Prince's pavilion and hustling towards our encampment. Every time I tried to say something or to pull away, all of them said, "No. Wait 'til dawn." After a while I got the idea.

So, I lay there in my blankets, wrapped up against the coolness of the night. My mind was awhirl with ideas and plans and hopes. I thought of the steep slopes to the east and west of Beckworth's fort. Dwarves… Dwarves were the key. Clan Tazhela was with me in the east and could easily cross from Easbister to those slopes. With a little help from Ozhemia, they just might burrow through the hard rock and into the castle.

Duke Armjurst's massive army would protect them from attack, while providing the large numbers needed to invest the western flank of the castle. And the Elves of the White Cliffs would provide the song needed to crush the eastern defenses.

The west was a problem. Perhaps Ez-Tansk could swing out from their dwarrows and those of their allies in Ghamarazh to attack the fortress from the west. If so, their allies would be the Orcs of the Chrystal Crags, the Companies of Dungrampus, and the Elves of the Blue Lake. Cassandra wouldn't get there. However, by liberating Coephalli, she permitted Yurchist Linda to advance eastward with Dungrampus and Blue Lake.

The north was our strength. King Richard's army, reinforced with Viscount Geoffrey's Battalion and Prince William's two Battalions, was the largest single force against Beckworth. Best of all, they were a single, unified command, utterly loyal to their King. Then, there were the armies of Brown Elves and the Green Mountain Elves, which was another army. Thinking of them helped me clarify my plan. Perhaps King Richard's humans could attack one part of the northern face, while the Elves would attack the other part.

In fact, the northeastern corner attracted me. I began thinking of the Elves at that corner, between King Richard's army and Duke Armjurst's. They would both be very large. Armjurst's would have some twenty-five hundred, while Richard would have some four thousand. If I could squeeze the one thousand Elves between them right on that corner, our effort would go unnoticed.

But that's where my thinking ended. I need other people's ideas to develop the final plan.

* * *

Mummia's bright smile peeked over the eastern curvature of Trahe. Elated, I sprang to my feet. "It's time!" I yelled.

My tribe was not happy. Enelya threw a tunic at me, yelling, "Go back to sleep!"

Findecáno yelled, "Enough! We need sleep. If you want to disturb the rest of the universe, do so quietly."

Thoroughly abashed, I dressed quietly and left them resting. Instead of just hanging around, driving myself and my entire tribe crazy, I dug out my mirror and contemplated who to call. Obviously, I had talked with everyone locally, so I didn't need to talk with them. Other folk were still asleep.

"Bah!" I said and ventured into Easbister. I wandered around, looking for a sigil of any kind. I found the Guild of Coopers and Barrel Makers, but I wanted something else. I continued wandering and looking. I found the Fletchers in a side street, and then the Pawnbrokers. Then, I found one that I liked – the Guild of Assassins! I knocked and gave the proper password. I didn't want a room, but I did want breakfast. The bar wasn't open, but the inn was serving breakfast. It was wonderful! They had large slabs of brot with a guk-like spread that tasted a lot like butter. Then they served a plate heaped with fried oyes with baked tans and boiled maidzh. Best of all, they served a mug of hot thrak! Fantastic!

By the time I got back to my tribe, they were awake and had eaten. I didn't discuss my breakfast with them. "Are we ready, now?" I asked.

They weren't, but that really didn't matter. I was.

"Has Tazhela arrived?" I asked everyone and no one in particular.

Nobody knew. "Bah!" I exclaimed. I grabbed my mirror. "Jharl Tazmatahela!"

The mirror remained a cloudy mist. "Jharl Tazmatahela!" I insisted.

A face appeared. "Who calls Jharl Tazmatahela?"

"Queen Gilraën Gulámae."

"Oh, you it is, Gulámae Queen Elf. Arisen my Jharl has not."

"Mummia has peered over the lip of the world. Why is Clan Tazhela not marching to Easbister?"

"Last night arrived we did. Now, we rest from our exertions."

"You're here? Where?"

"South of road near town."

"Inform the Jharl that I will be with him in a few minutes. Terminate!"

"Come on," I shouted. I was off and running. I didn't know where they were, but I was sure I could detect the presence of four hundred Dwarves. Sure enough, just moments later, I sensed a huge Dwarf presence off to my right. Within seconds, four Dwarves blocked our path.

"I am Queen Gilraën. I must speak with Jharl Tazmatahela."

The four glanced at each other as though unsure of what to do. I couldn't just wait there. So, I leapt over them and raced toward the center of the camp. Jharl Tazmatahela's pavilion was obvious. It was the huge purple one with the gold trimming. "Jharl Tazmatahela!" I yelled. "You up yet?"

Three dwarves rushed out, brandishing axes. I held up my hand and yelled, "Stop!" They bounced backward as though they'd run into a glass door.

"Who calls?" a voice came from within the pavilion. Jharl Tazmatahela poked his head around a tapestry. "Oh, it's you! What are you doing here? It is barely day, and first meal hasn't been served." He shook his head. "Oh, well, you are here. Enter and enjoy first meal with me."

I didn't have the heart to tell him I'd already eaten. "Your sentinels are detaining my tribe. Would you send word to permit them to join us?"

He waved his hand at one of the guards. Then, he turned to a Dwarf standing in the corner. "Tell them to prepare a meal for thirty. Summon my Thanes for first meal." Looking back to me, he muttered, "Assume this important is?"

"Yes, My Jharl, it is."

"Bah!" he growled. "Too early it is for important discussions. Perhaps my Thanes will be more awake than am I."

I was beginning to feel that I should have waited, but it was a bit late for that. Too late – my tribe was arriving, accompanied by the four Dwarves who had attempted to stop me. Then, three very important looking Dwarves arrived. I recognized them by their coronets. "My Thanes, I am Queen Gilraën Gulámae, and the reason why you were summoned at this early hour. I apologize to you, but I'm sure that you will find my information most illuminating."

"Bah!"

I turned to see Jharl Tazmatahela standing behind me. "Come. I do not have room for all of you at my table. Let us sit here and be as comfortable as we can be."

As he spoke, several Dwarves arranged tables, moved chairs and benches, and in general prepared places for all thirty-two of us. I sat with the Jharl and his three Thanes. Each of my cohorts sat at tables clustered around us. It was quite cozy. The meal was almost a duplicate of what I had eaten at the guildhall. I just didn't eat much of it. Everyone else tucked in as though they were starving.

The conversation was about the battle of Tamvill and their subsequent march on Phaedham. They were still in mourning for their lost Clansmen. Yet, they were proud of having defeated a force more than twice their size. They paid little heed to the contributions of my Tribe, Baron Richmond's Companies, or that of the Krelli, but I let it pass. This was not the time to reopen old Dwarf-Elf rivalries.

Finally, the Jharl asked me, "Why, Queen Gulámae, have you demanded this meeting?"

"My Jharl and Thanes of Clan Tazhela, I have come for your advice, assistance and expertise. Yesterday, my Elves and I entered the fortress of Shalal'm Caer."

As I had expected, they were amazed. "How?" Tazmatahela asked. His Thanes each expressed their amazement.

"We did, and let that be enough for now. I have come to you because we need answers to critical questions. We discussed our findings with Prince William, General Abuahad, King Amder, King Glorfindel and Queen Eilol. General Abuahad had suggested a plan of attack, but, as you know, the difficulty is in the details.

"He suggested a simultaneous attack from all four sides. The Dwarves of the Mountains would attack from the south. Sir Domnall, King Fingolfin and Yurchist Linda would attack from the west. Duke Armjurst, King Aeradir and Clan Tazhela will attack from the east. King Richard and Prince William would lead their forces plus those of King Melwasúl and the Elves of the Brown Hills. Both King Glorfindel and Queen Eilol are leading their forces.

"General Abuahad suggested that Dwarves could tunnel into the rock beneath the walls. By doing so, they could build a tunnel beneath the walls and into the outer courtyard. If so, Duke Armjurst's entire army could pass under the walls, into the outer courtyard, isolating forces on the outer wall before attacking the inner wall. Further, if this attack was successful, we could repeat it to pass beneath the inner wall to attack the keep.

"I discussed this with my mother and father, King Amder, King Richard, Prince William, and General Abuahad. None of them knew if it was possible. They advised me that only Dwarves could answer that question. I could have asked my Jharl or my Thanes, but, since you are the ones who would perform the tunneling, I ask for your counsel in this matter.

"My Jharl, I am a Jharl of Clan Ghamarazh and a Thanelish of Clan Ez-Tansk. However, I am a Dwarf in name only. I do not have the abilities of a Dwarf, nor do I understand your gifts. Therefore, I must ask: can you tunnel through the rock underlying Shalal'm Caer, creating a tunnel under the outer wall for large numbers of Humans to pass through and capture the outer courtyard?"

The Jharl looked at me as though I was from another planet. I was, but what did that have to do with it? Anyway, he replied, "Rock is not rock. There are many types of rock, and every not every compaction of rock is a rock. Can you describe the formation?"

"Yes, and no. When we visited, I studied the entire structure. I can remember every facet of my exploration, and transmit my memories to others, if that would be of help."

The Jharl and his Thanes talked quietly among themselves. Then, Tazmatahela said, "Let me introduce Thane Pethelzha. Thane Pethelzha is a Master of Stone. He and his familial are those who construct and maintain our dwarrow. If there is one among us who can answer your question, it is he."

I nodded to the Thane. "I am honored to meet you, My Thane. Can you help me to answer my question?"

"Difficult it will be. Show me the structure."

"I can do that, My Thane, but to do so, we must join minds. You must let me enter your mind. Once there, I will show you my journey through Shalal'm Caer in as much detail as I can. Is this agreeable to you?"

"Loathe am I, My Jharl. Necessary is this?"

"Only if you want to observe the foundations of the fortress."

"Agreed, then. Prepared am I. Proceed."

I looked about, saying, "My Elves and I journeyed into Shalal'm Caer. We will commune with each other. Then, I will reach out to you, Thane Pethelzha. You will feel me, not the rest of my tribe. I also ask if others of Clan Tazhela desire to view the foundation of Beckworth's fortress."

"I shall," Jharl Tazmatahela declared, but he was the only one.

I sat quietly, joining with my Tribe. Once we were in harmony, I reached out to Jharl Tazmatahela. I encountered a solid barrier. "My Jharl, you must lower your barriers."

"Never have I lowered them in all my life. Difficult it is."

"Understood, but you must if you are to voyage with us."

He lowered his barriers just slightly, but enough for me to enter his mind. *'Do you feel my presence, Jharl Tazmatahela?'*

'Yes,' he replied.

I reached out to Thane Pethelzha. Again, he was resistant, but malleable. I wormed my way into his mind, asking, *'Do you feel my presence, Thane Pethelzha?'*

'Yes,' he answered.

'Then let us proceed.'

For the next hour, we revisited our exploration of Shalal'm Caer. Quite often either the Jharl or the Thane would ask us to stop and study a particular formation or feature. A few times, they asked us to touch or manipulate a particular stretch of rock. We couldn't because we hadn't done that when we explored the fortress. However, we could view them more closely, once even delving into the crystalline structure of the formation. They were very thorough.

When they were done, we relaxed and withdrew from their minds. "Well?" I asked.

Thane Pethelzha sat back, ruminating. After a while, he muttered, "Possible." He muttered to himself for some time, before uttering, "Tools." And still later, "Time." Then, after an extremely long interval, "Not possible." He then sat back as though he'd just announced the first law of thermodynamics.

We sat there waiting, but Thane Pethelzha had shot his wad. He just sat there nibbling on first meal. I looked to Jharl Tazmatahela, an eyebrow raised. When nothing happened, I asked, "Well?"

"Ah!" the Thane responded. "Although it could be done, we don't have the proper tools, so it can't be done until we get the proper tools, but we can't get them soon enough to attack, so it can't be done."

I looked at the Jharl, hoping he would explain what his Thane had said. He just nodded, knowledgeably, and reached for another slice of porg.

"I'm sorry, but I don't understand what's going on. We showed you the rocks, and you said you could do it, but you couldn't, but you could, but you couldn't. So which is it?"

"It is true," Thane Pethelzha, "Although mine the formation we could, we have not the tools, because to war we marched and not to mine, and, therefore, we cannot. Simple, My Jharl, it is."

I nodded, "Understand, I do. But, if I could supply tools, could you do it?"

"Oh, yes. These formations are granite, which is very hard and very strong. But, Dwarves we are, so we can travel through it as though it were air. But, Dwarves we are. Tunnels are different. You have with Dwarves walked through rock. But, through... not tunnel. Walk through air you do, but not build tunnel. Tunnel needs tools – pick, shovel, bracing, fire. Not Human tools; Dwarf tools. No Dwarf tools, no tunnel."

"So, if I could provide the tools you need, could you build the tunnel from the base under the outer wall that Duke Armjurst's army could use to get into the courtyard?

"Said that, I did!" the Thane answered, indignantly.

"Great! Now, what about the walls of Shalal'm Caer themselves? How strong are they?"

Thane Pethelzha laughed, "Oh, yes, strong… magical strong, but power is not knowledge." He laughed again.

"My Thane, I do not understand. Please tell me."

"Jharl Gilraën, magic makes the walls strong… too strong. They are so strong, they brittle. Hit them, bounce off. You say 'Too strong.' Not so. Hit harder… much harder. Rock splinter and crack and large chunk break bounce out… careful you be, or it hit you dead."

"So, if we were to use a catapult to throw a rock at the wall, it would bounce off. But, if we could hit it hard enough with a big enough rock, then the wall would spall pieces?"

He smiled broadly. "Spall, yes, but big rock," he replied spreading his arms wide.

My first thought was a trebuchet. I'd lectured about medieval warfare. PBS had a great program on catapults and trebuchets, and I'd watched 'pumpkin chunkin' on TV. Huge trebuchets could hurl massive rocks long distances with great precision. So, all I needed was lots of dwarf tools and trebuchets, neither of which I had, nor did I have the foggiest notion of how to make them.

First things first. "My Jharl, My Thane, I would like to bring other Dwarves into our discussion, if that's all right with you?" I removed my mirror from my quiver. I turned it southward, saying, "Jharl Morthanzhemian, speak with me!"

The clouds in the mirror swirled for several minutes until a face appeared. The face of Squire Althomozemian appeared. "Queen Jharl Gulámae, welcome. Indisposed is Jharl Morthanzhemian at this time. I serve you how?"

"Please wait for a moment, My Steward. I wish for Thane Defghamask to join us in this discussion. I will call for him now.

"Thane Defghamask, speak with me!"

Steward Tildorhamask's face appeared next to that of the Squire. "Jharl Gulámae, how may I serve you?"

"I wish to converse with Thane Defghamask or someone else in authority."

"The Thane is at the northern barriers. We are under assault, My Jharl."

"Has Jharl Worzhemacht reinforced you?"

"Indeed. Without Clan Worfellsten overcome we would have been. But we are hard pressed."

"I am also conversing with Squire Althomozemian of Ozhemia, so let me ask him about this situation. So, tell us Squire Althomozemian, is your clan reinforcing my Clan Ghamarazh?"

"Answer your question, not can I, Jharl Gulámae. Jharl Morthanzhemian is leading my clansmen in the north, but I have no knowledge of where our army is at this time."

"As you have heard, My Squire, *my* Clan desperately needs assistance. If we are not reinforced, all may be lost. It is necessary that I speak with your Jharl... now, My Squire, now!"

Squire Althomozemian blanched visibly. "I shall encourage him to communicate with you. If you will allow me a few moments to rouse him, My Jharl?"

"Please do, but hurry."

"So, My Thane, is Ez-Tansk beside you?" I hoped not, since I wanted them for the attack on the western wall.

"Indeed, both Clans are heavily involved. Beckworth tried to pass our left, but Azkhalish blunted his attack and turned it back on him."

"Well done, Ez-Tansk! Where are they now?"

"Closer, much closer. I am hoping I do not have to commit them, since they are my only reserves."

"What of Rhonzhafell, Vantazhak or Camazhule?"

"They are no help. Rhonzhafell is busy planting bulbs, Vantazhak is busy praying to the gods, and Camazhule is contemplating the meaning of Cadrazhulea's prophecy. We had hoped for some help from Dzarbish and Dzardan, but they are not communicating with us. Garmanch is too far away to be of help to anyone. We are fortunate in that the Orcs of both the Eastern and Western Meadows are allied with us. Although they are not within our dwarrow, they have protected the high passes into their lands and the interior of the mountains. Were Beckworth's forces able to penetrate the mountains, they could attack us from both sides, and it is doubtful we could protect ourselves from both sides."

Suddenly a face appeared in the mirror. "Jharl Gilraën, I am here," Jharl Morthanzhemian announced.

"My Jharl, I apologize to you for interrupting, but I have been talking with Thane Defghamask. He is under attack, and in desperate need of reinforcement. I ask if you can assist?"

"We were racing through the circumferential passage, but a large enemy force attacked us. We have driven them back, but discovered the passage you had described to us, Jharl Gulámae. We are sealing the passage from them, but shall reopen it when we need it. Regardless, we are rushing to your aid, Thane Defghamask, but holding back a force to defend the passage if they reopen it."

"So, My Thane, Jharl Morthanzhemian is rushing to your aid. Can you hold out?"

"We have lost the outer wall, but are holding the inner wall."

"I have one other question for you, which will affect the entire outcome of this war. I have investigated the rock formation underlying Beckworth's fortress. I have shown Jharl Tazmatahela and Thane Pethelzha the details, hoping Clan Tazhela could create a tunnel under the eastern walls of Shalal'm Caer to provide a passageway for Duke Armjurst's army to enter. They told me that they could if they had the proper tools. Obviously, they prepared for war, not to tunnel through hard rock. Do you know the tools of which they speak and, if so, can you supply them?"

"Of course. They are utterly common."

"Do you have enough for five hundred Dwarves?"

"Of course."

"If I were to have five hundred Dwarves on the eastern slopes of Beckworth's fortress, could you deliver the tools to them?"

"NO!" Thane Defghamask was adamant. "We are fighting for our survival and you want us to deliver tools thirty miles away? If they want them, let them come and get them."

"OK, I'll think of something. Get them ready and in one place. Get them as close as you can. We'll retrieve them when we can, but nothing happens until we do. So, are you satisfied, Thane Defghamask with the support you are getting from Ez-Tansk, Ozhemia and Worfellsten?"

"Yes, My Jharl, their help has been invaluable. Without them, we might have fallen."

"Let us remember this day. The four Clans of the Mountains united to defeat the enemy. If all the Clans were to stand together, who could defeat them?"

I terminated my conversation with them, wondering how I'd get a pile of Dwarf tools from Ozhemia to Shalal'm Caer. In the meantime, "Jharl Azkhalish!"

Duzhel's face appeared almost instantly. "Thanelish Gulámae, how may I serve you?"

"I need to speak with Jharl Azkhalish, Duzhel."

"Of course, Thane Gulámae. He will be with you in a moment."

Shortly, the Jharl appeared. "My Thanelish, how have your served your Jharl today?"

"My Jharl, I have ensured that Lord Beckworth's surprise attack has been thwarted. Clan Ozhemia is reinforcing Clan Ghamarazh. With their support, plus that of Clans Ez-Tansk and Worfellsten, they will defend their inner walls and recover their outer walls.

"Within days, we will go on the offense. Clan Ez-Tansk shall be honored by leading the attack on the western side of Shalal'm Caer.

Clan Ez-Tansk will mine a tunnel under the outer walls to lead the Orcs of Chrystal Crags and the Elves of the Blue Lake within Beckworth's fortress.

"As you lead them from the west, Clan Tazhela will lead Duke Armjurst's army beneath the east wall. At the same time, the three Clans of the Mountains plus the Orcs, Trolls and Octopods will attack from the south. I expect the Dwarves will attack from beneath the surface while the others take the wall. The fourth attack will be the largest, consisting of King Richard's entire army, plus the Elves of the Brown Hills and the Green Mountains and me.

"I have already discussed the massif with Jharl Tazmatahela and Thane Pethelzha. I have just made arrangements with Jharl Morthanzhemian to obtain the tools they will need. All I have to do is get the tools to them, and they will tunnel under the walls."

Azkhalish laughed. "And, you call this diplomacy, My Thane? Well done! You have united the Dwarves of the Mountains as never before. You have brought together a great coalition of Dwarves, Humans, Elves, Orcs and others as no one else could have done. You have brought great honor to Ez-Tansk and myself, your Jharl."

"Thank you, My Jharl. The honor of Clan Ez-Tansk is just one of my many responsibilities. I am grateful for your high praise. And, speaking of those other responsibilities, I must speak with others of this coalition. I shall ask Princess Cassandra to communicate with you, King Fingolfin, and Yurchist Linda regarding your dispositions and the timings of the attacks. Is there anything else, My Jharl?"

"No, My Thane, proceed, and may the stars smile upon you." He terminated the contact.

'*Whew*!' I sighed to myself. '*That went well. Next? Cassandra first, then Richard.*'

"Princess Cassandra, speak to me!"

A few moments later, her face appeared. "Gilraën?"

"Cassie, good to see you again. I haven't had the opportunity to congratulate you on the liberation of Coephalli. Well done!"

"Thank you. They weren't expecting us, and we swept through the city almost before they knew we were there. They had dispersed beyond the city harassing the countryside. So much of our job was cleaning up the mess they'd made."

"Where are you now?"

"We're just east pf Dungrampus, about one hundred miles from Soubister. I guess that's about two hundred miles from Shalal'm Caer. The war will be over by the time we get there."

"Yes, but your responsibilities won't be. You're in command of the Western Front. Blue Lake, Chrystal Crags and Ex-Tansk are under your command, as are Sir Domnall's Companies. I'll be attacking from all sides: Dwarves and Orcs from the south; Armjurst from the east; you from the west. Richard, William and I will attack from the north.

"Tactically, you and Armjurst will mirror each other. The Dwarves will build a tunnel under the walls. Your troops will enter the outer courtyard through the tunnels while your Elves surmount the walls.

"I'll coordinate the attacks. I want Beckworth concentrating on us in the north. That way the other three attacks have a better chance of success. So, I won't give the signal to break out of the tunnels until we've forced him to release his reserves on us. Sound right to you?"

"If you say so. However, I'd like to have someone who's right there in charge… perhaps Domnall as my second-in-command?"

"Good thought. Talk with the others. Emphasize that it is important that a Human be giving the orders. Otherwise, the Adjudicars will have cause to accuse either Dwarves or Elves of violating their contracts."

"Ah, yes, I'd forgotten that point. I'll let Domnall know, and then contact Fingolfin, Linda and Azkhalish, using your name."

"Excellent. Let me know if you have any problems. Terminate!"

'OK, last leg.' "King Richard, speak with me!"

A face appeared almost instantly. "Queen Gilraën, greetings. How may I assist you?"

"I need to speak with King Richard, Viscount Geoffrey, King Glorfindel and Queen Eilol. Please tell them my tribe and I will meet with them at King Richard's pavilion tomorrow after first meal. Is that doable?"

"Doable? Are you asking if it is possible to meet these nobles in King Richard's pavilion after first meal tomorrow?"

"Yes, Master Talbot, that's what I'm asking."

"I see no reason why not. I shall inform them and return your message."

"Thank you, Master Talbot, see you tomorrow. Terminate!"

I informed my tribe that we were leaving for Barstough, but before I did, I had to talk with King Séregon. Racing to his camp, I greeted him, "My King!"

"Queen Gilraën?" he asked.

"I have a problem I'm hoping you can help me solve. Clan Tazhela has informed me they believe they can tunnel under the eastern wall of Shalal'm Caer. However, they do not have the proper implements to do the job. I have communicated with Clan Ozhemia. They have the tools and have stockpiled them. However, neither Clan can transport them quickly enough. I am asking you if you and your Tribe can race to the lands of Clan Ozhemia, collect the implements they have accumulated, and then return with them for delivery to Clan Tazhela?"

He hesitated. "I wish you had informed of this earlier, Queen Gilraën. It would have been easier to arrange our route of march more to the west rather than through Bursk."

"I know it would have, My King, but then you would have exposed yourselves to attack. By taking the route through Bursk, your tribe and Duke Armjurst's army could support each other. However, I do apologize to you for this diversion. I only recently learned of the topography and geology of Shalal'm Caer and obtained the advice of Clan Tazhela this day. Regardless, will you undertake this endeavor?"

"Ah, I see. Duke Armjurst has informed me of your plan, and I concur. However, if Tazhela cannot tunnel, the plan must fail. Where is this cache?"

"Jharl Morthanzhemian is assembling it as we speak. Please use your mirror to contact him. Squire Althomozemian is a steward of the mirror with whom I have spoken."

"We will return with the implements on the second day.'

As I left Séregon's encampment I considered what I had to do next. This had been a busy day already. I focused on Justice, calling his name. I found him and tickled his defenses.

'Gilraën? Are you screwing with me again'

I giggled. *'Yup! Hey, were off to Barstough. That's where I want all of you. Have you heard from Artestius or any of his people?'*

'Barstough? We're half-way there already. Artestius and six of his friends are northwest of Barstough in the heavy woodlands. They say there's good pickings there. We were thinking of heading off to join them.'

'I'll meet you northwest of the town. Tell Artestius and his people to meet us. We need a sit-down with all those noble types.'

'Got it. We'll go on ahead and find Artestius' crowd. I'll wait for your tickle. Bye!' His mind sealed itself.

"Elves of the Maidstone Forest, are we ready to travel?" All twenty-seven were on their feet. "To Barstough!"

We shot off at a five-fold pace. On the way, we passed Prince William's Palace Guards. We slowed to the two-fold pace they were maintaining. "My Prince!"

William glanced toward me, a look of surprise on his face. "Gilraën? What are you doing here?"

"We are off to confer with your brother about the final battle plan. We will meet tomorrow after first meal. When will you arrive in Barstough?"

"We have made great progress. I expect we will arrive after this day, but after Mummia goes to rest. We have been speed marching.

We walk for one thousand paces and then run for one thousand paces. We eat as we walk, so we can travel great distances in half the time it would take any other army. But, this is a severe test for us all."

"Has Green Mountains overtaken you?"

"Oh, yes! We were trotting along when a gigantic wind overtook us. King Amder slowed long enough to pass the time of day, and then they were gone. I expect they are with Richard right now."

"Is there anything we can do to help you and your troops?"

"Carry us on your backs?" he jested.

"Are you declaring an emergency, My Prince?" I returned the jest.

"No, go ahead. However, do not awaken us tomorrow. We will need to recuperate."

"Agreed! To Barstough then!" We sped ahead, arriving in the town an hour later.

A sentinel stopped us at the five-corners in the center of the town. "Queen Gilraën! Greetings from King Richard. He is at his pavilion north of the town two miles, then east for a mile."

Ten minutes later, we walked into a huge meadow. Rank upon rank of tents stood before us. It took a moment for me to sort things out. Each of the Battalions of the army had gathered in a square of squares. A large space stood to the south, evidently for Prince William's Guards and the last two Companies of Baron Richmond's Battalion. In the central area between the squares stood a large, colorful pavilion bedecked in flags.

As we walked toward the camp, a large body of men blocked our path, halberds pointed at us. One man, a Captain by his tokens of rank, stood out, his palm raised. "Stop! Identify yourselves, Elves unknown."

My tribe spread out behind me. They were alert and ready, but none reached for a weapon. I stepped forward. "I am Queen Gilraën Gulámae of the Elves of the Green Mountains-Maidstone Forest, Jharl Regent of Clan Ghamarazh, and Thanelish of Clan Ez-Tansk. I am here to meet with King Richard of Umbeqjaralii. Please send my greetings to the King and tell him I am here."

At a signal from the Captain, his Company raised their halberds to the salute. "Queen Gilraën, I was told to expect you at this hour. I was ordered to lead you into the King's pavilion when you arrived. Please, come with me."

We stepped forward to follow the Captain. As we did so, the Company stood aside, making a passageway between them. When we approached, they raised their voices in a shout of greetings, as one troop of warriors might salute another. My Elves broke into song, conveying friendly greetings.

As we approached the pavilion, a tall Human stood forth. He had fair features, blondish hair, and light eyes. He was dressed in burnished steel armor with a long sword at his left hip and a long knife at his right. The tall, broad-shouldered and handsome man greeted me with a melodious baritone voice. "Welcome, Queen Gilraën. It is my pleasure to greet you once again."

"Greetings, King Richard, I am pleased to greet you once again. I presume you have received my message?"

"Yes, I have. What news have you?"

"I believe I have developed a basic battle plan. I need to speak with you and the Brown Elves to consider the final phases. I also come with other news. Your brother approaches with his Guard. General Abuahad follows closely, and Baron Richmond is just days behind. I believe that your army will be reunited in three to four days."

"That is excellent news, My Queen. Please, come into my pavilion."

"By your leave, My King, we have come a long way in just a few days. Perhaps we could establish our camp and find a meal? I'm sure I will be refreshed by tomorrow."

"Yes, of course. I have set aside a space for you. Captain, would you lead Queen Gilraën and her tribe to the place I had established for them?"

Moments later, we were in a small wood, near a brook that flowed northeastward toward the distant Phaed River. We quickly set our camp and left to find a field kitchen, leaving a ward to protect our gear. We found one on the edge of the King's encampment. By luck, we had also found Viscount Geoffrey's Battalion. They greeted us warmly and quickly found a place for us to sit and eat. However, we didn't stay long. It had been an exhausting couple of days, and we all needed a good night's sleep.

* * * * *

Chapter 3 – Catapults, Trebuchets and Siege Towers

Mummia was well up by the time I opened my eyes. My manic state had subsided. I felt satisfied with my efforts and their results. Things were on a path that should lead to victory. The last pieces were falling into place.

"Gilraën," a gentle voice called to me.

I rolled over to see Harold smiling at me. I leapt up and seized him in a great hug. "Harold! What a great surprise."

"Surprised? Why should you be surprised? We were Richard's vanguard, if you remember."

"Yes! You were. How are you all? Have you talked with the rest of the Tribe?"

"Oh, yes, we've been here for a little while. We're here to invite you to breakfast. Get your gear on, and we'll guide you to King Richard's kitchens."

I didn't have to be asked twice. Just moments later, all forty of us descended on the kitchens just behind Richard's pavilion. We had just sat when Richard and William joined us. What a wonderful time we had. It was a reunion as though we'd been parted for months or years rather than days and weeks. All pretenses of rank or privilege simply disappeared as our extended family swapped stories, laughed, oohed or cringed; each happy that we were alive and together once again.

Finally, Richard brought us back to the matters at hand. "I think they arranged things for our meeting. Shall we?" He rose, followed by the rest of us.

He led us around the pavilion and to a large grouping of tables. Turning to me, he said, "I do not have room for all of your tribe, but they may gather with my councilors and Captains to hear our discussions and to offer their advice."

Immediately, several Captains stood forward to usher my Tribe and Cavalry to seats near the central area. As they did, I noted that they had set up a table. A high chair stood towards the middle of the far side, with others surrounding it. One chair nearest me was unoccupied, and it was to this one that King Richard escorted me.

As I approached, King Glorfindel and Queen Eilol rose to greet me. "Welcome, Daughter," King Glorfindel said as Eilol kissed me on the cheeks. I sat between them as Richard passed around the table to sit opposite me. Viscount Sir Geoffrey sat to the King's right and his four Battalion Commanders on his left. Prince William sat with Baron Richmond, Sir Xander Deplos and General Abuahad to his left, while King Amder Melwasúl and Jharl Tazmatahela sat to his right.

Many mirrors stood at either end of the table. I saw the faces of Duke Armjurst and his father-in-law King Aeradir Séregon to my right. To my left was a second group with Princess Cassandra, King Fingolfin Sáralondë of Blue Lake, Yurchist Linda and Sir Domnall. A third group aligned with me showed the faces of Jharls Azkhalish of Ez-Tansk, Morthanzhemian of Ozhemia, Worzhemacht of Worfellsten, and Thane Defghamask of Ghamarazh

Obviously, King Richard had convened a council of war.

Before us on the table lay a huge map of the area around Shalal'm Caer, extending from Easbister to Soubister and into the Dwarf Mountains. As when William and I had mapped out this campaign, there were numbers of colored blocks each festooned with colored flags spread over the map.

A cup of wine appeared at my elbow, and Eilol offered me a baked cake.

Richard asked, "I hope this arrangement will be helpful in our discussions of the impending attack on George's fortress."

I stared at the board for several minutes. "Yes," I said, "this is mostly correct. I would only make one change." I removed a blue flag from the black block sitting within Shalal'm Caer. "We destroyed two battalions at Tamvill."

"Is that wise?" King Richard asked.

"I believe so," I answered. "When I explored Shalal'm Caer, I estimated the garrison to be about four thousand. When I consider the logistics I have seen, I estimate that number is close to the maximum that can be supported. There are two possibilities.

"First, Beckworth had that number, and sent one-quarter of his force into the east to turn our flank.

"The second is he did that, but replaced one thousand with recruits from Earth or some other planet.

"I know one Adjudicar was with Beckworth's forces in the east. So, that leaves only one Adjudicar who could transfer Humans to this world. I doubt he has the strength to transfer that many that distance in such a short time. So, I think my estimate is justified."

Abuahad cleared his throat. "Three thousand is more than enough to defend Shalal'm Caer. Even five hundred would be a sizable force that could hold such a defense against ten times that number for a year. There is little difference between three thousand and four thousand as far as we are concerned."

His was a sobering assessment. We sat staring at the one black block. Then, Richard reminded us, "We have the largest army ever assembled in this land. We have eleven thousands of Humans, Elves, Dwarves, Orcs and others. We have a variety of skills, abilities and powers such as never been assembled before in this land. If we cannot defeat this enemy, then we have lost nothing, for it is only a matter of time before the Usurper and his Adjudicars overcomes each of us, reducing us to slavery or worse. So, we will not lose heart. We will consider the words of Cadrazhulea the seer and follow Queen Gulámae to victory."

Heartened, I began to explain my battle plan. I started by moving the blocks representing Armjurst and White Cliffs to the east of the fortress. "Duke Armjurst, this is your attack." I told them of my discussions with Thane Pethelzha and his findings. "King Amder has volunteered to retrieve the tools Tazhela will need to tunnel through the bedrock beneath the fortress." They were both encouraged and relieved when they saw the strength of an attack by Dwarves, Elves and Humans, each using their unique abilities to contribute to their success.

I then moved the blocks representing Yurchist Linda, King Fingolfin, Sir Domnall and Jharl Azkhalish to the western side of the fortress. "Cassandra, this is your attack. As Tazhela is tunneling from the east, Ez-Tansk will burrow from the west. As Armjurst invests the eastern fastnesses, Linda will invade the west. As Green Mountain scales the eastern walls, Blue Lake will surmount the western. These attacks are symmetrical and overwhelming."

For the first time, Cassandra added her thoughts. "Great attack plan. I just wish I could be there to take part."

"Ah, that brings up an important point. As you know, I have named a Human to command each wing of this attack while I am nominally in command of Dwarfish forces. However, Cassandra is not in a position to command this attack directly. Therefore, with everyone's approval, I would name Sir Domnall of Dungrampus as her deputy, in tactical command of the western army."

Sir Geoffrey asked, "Should that not be my command?"

"Probably," I answered, "However, you and your Battalion have practiced with Prince William's army and marched with King Richard's. I believe that it would be better for you to remain with the army of the north in the main attack. That would give King Richard greater operational control, in that he could assign you to his army, Prince William's or an independent command, based on the most current situation. This is especially important, because his is the main attack, while all others are secondary, yet critical to the successful outcome."

I explained that, as these attacks are underway, the Clans of the Dwarf Mountains along with the Orcs of the Meadows and, hopefully, the Octopods would attack from beneath the surface, perhaps using the tunnel already created from the fortress into the mountains. Although removing Ez-Tansk from the direct attack, they would still be on the flank, supporting their kinsfolk.

"As with Princess Cassandra, I am removed from my Clans and my army. I retain my authority as commander of the armies of the Dwarf Mountains, and my titles of Jharl Regent and Thanelish of Diplomacy. Yet, my distance obviates against my tactical control of the battle. Therefore, I, too, need a deputy commander. I suggest that

Thane Defghamask be that person. He is the Thane of the General Staff and has directed the efforts against Beckworth since the initiation of hostilities. And, as my Thane, he has my confidence. But, this is an alliance. I ask Jharl Azkhalish, Jharl Worzhemacht and Jharl Morthanzhemian, and also you, Jharl Galmerstain, if my choice of deputy is agreeable to you, and if you will follow him into battle?"

When they all agreed, I got to our part. "We will attack the northern wall. I want you, King Richard, to attack the western half, including the gatehouse. William will attack the eastern half. I will disguise my presence and that of my forces, as I will explain later.

"I would have you, King Glorfindel and Queen Eilol with King Richard's forces, while I would like King Amder to be with Prince William.

"My basic battle plan would be as follows. William will attack the long northeastern wall, along with Green Mountains, Clan Tazhela, the Krelli and my forces. His objective will be to batter the walls down to provide access to the outer courtyard. Beckworth will have to divide his forces, and, hopefully, divert his reserves to face this massive attack. Regardless, his focus will be to the north.

"However, by focusing on the east, he will divert troops from the north, west and south. Armjurst's forces will attack the corner between the northern and eastern wall. Once again, Beckworth will have to divert forces and extend his reserves.

"Then, Cassandra's forces will attack from the western wall and northwestern corner of the fortress, while the Dwarves and Orcs will attack from the mountains to the south.

"We will have done everything in our power to draw his attention to the north and east. The large attack from the south and west will be so large and devastating that he will be unable to defend the walls against us.

"So we will have five simultaneous attacks, none of which he can ignore. He will run back and forth, expending his forces, committing his reserves, and no matter what he does, it will be too little, too late.

"As he is busy trying to defend the walls, Ez-Tansk will mine a shaft under the northwestern wall and Vantazhak will do the same under the northeastern corner. These should open the way for a direct assault into the courtyard between the first and second walls.

"However, we have a few problems if we are to attack the northern face. We cannot succeed if we can't breech the north wall. We need catapults to batter the wall, and siege towers to surmount the walls and gates. I don't know how to build these engines or how long it will take."

Richard leaned forward, smiling like the proverbial Cheshire cat. "Surprise! I know all about catapults and siege towers."

The King explained, "I have been preparing for this attack for many years. Our father, King Patrick, used to build catapults for fun. He used to throw loaves of bread over the wall, and all us kids would race around trying to catch them.

"We built all sorts of them. We started out with wound ropes, but they weren't strong enough. After a while, we graduated to steel springs. They were much better. We began playing with levers and augmented them with springs. It was fun, and we could really fling heavy stuff long distances. I tried to launch Cassie over the wall, but she screamed. When Dad saw what I was doing, he nearly skinned me alive. Damn, we had fun."

"Speak for yourself!" Cassandra retorted.

"You and Al almost killed me!" William added.

Armjurst was laughing so hard he could hardly breathe. "Gark!" he gasped. "Those were fun times. I'd forgotten about them. So, you went on building them? Great! But, I still don't know why you gave Shalal'm Caer to that whining brat. What got into you?"

"Obviously, it was a mistake letting Georgie have the biggest fortress in the kingdom. He made me feel guilty, so I did it despite what you, Cassie and Billie said. I gave in. I should have kept it and sent William to Jhal'm Thaer and Georgie to Shesol Vys. But, I really liked it up north in the old city. It's peaceful, quiet and in the center of everything. And, when Cassie wanted Blue Vail, everything seemed to be perfect. At first, everything was fine. Then Georgie turned nasty.

"That was when I began considering how to attack it. The walls are thick and heavily reinforced. The dungeons are huge and can store a year's food. A few hundred can defend the place, but it can easily house thousands, and from what Queen Gilraën has told us perhaps up to four thousand.

"I couldn't build a catapult big enough. So, I hired a master mechanic and his family. And then, we built a trebuchet. The first one wasn't very good, so we built more until we finally got it right. Now, I have two, both of which can hurl a 500-pound rock almost a mile.

"We also have ten of my old catapults. They can hurl a hundred pounds – or a loaf of bread - over a hundred-foot wall, if we can get them close enough.

"Then, we built six ballistae that can fire six, ten-foot arrows up to a hundred feet high. With them, I can clear almost any wall.

"I even have three siege towers. We can modify them to surmount almost any wall. We can build them from twenty feet to a hundred feet tall.

"All of them are in my siege train. It's large and slow. It'll dribble in beginning three or our days from now and continuing for a week or more. Then, it'll take a week to reassemble them. After that, we can begin the assault."

"How many men in the siege train?"

"It's only about four hundred, but they're all mechanics and engineers. They're a very special group. They have a portable sawmill, a small foundry and forge. They can repair or make most things. Whenever I need something, they build it – bridges, field fortifications, barracks, whatever. They remind me of Dad… always inventing things."

"So," I asked, "you actually know how to operate these things?"

"Oh, yes, we all do. We got good at catapulting all sorts of things."

"Fruits!" Albert mentioned.

"Bread!" Cassandra yelled.

"Cassandra!" William laughed.

Richard continued, "So, with that in mind, we need to prepare things in the order they will be required. I think the longest, hardest part will be preparing the ground along the main wall for the siege towers. Not only must the ground be prepared, but we must be able to roll the siege towers adjacent to the walls. That's a big problem."

"Oh," I interjected, "Artestius and a few of his friends are coming to our aid." I looked around at the blank stares. "Oh, yes, he's a Troll. We met him at Higgleston. Anyway, Justice says he's coming."

"Justice?" someone asked.

"Yes, Justice. He's a Krell. He'll be here with five of his friends. They're part of my forces, along with my Tribe and my Cavalry."

Richard nodded, saying, "Excellent. Trolls could be a huge help getting the siege towers into position.

"OK," I answered, "We'll need to protect the men clearing and leveling the ground, and building a ramp to get the towers near the walls. So, we'll need ballistae in place to clear the walls and to attack their catapults, along with gabions and fascines to protect the workers. I guess that puts them first.

"William's assault requires the trebuchets. That makes them second. While they're battering the walls, I can assemble the siege towers and get them into place.

"Of course, that means I will have to protect the siege engines while we landscape the grounds. That means I must have my troops in place. And, I'll need a strike force to counter any sorties Beckworth might throw at us."

King Fingolfin said, "I doubt that anyone could sortie successfully against either Brown Hills or us. We are rather quick, you know."

We all sat around, staring at the board. Nobody spoke. Everyone contemplated the colored blocks and their implications.

Queen Eilol said it for all of us. "All on one throw of the die!"

"Yes," I muttered, "We win or lose it all within the next two weeks. Until then, we have a lot to do. We need to get our troops into position. We need to establish supplies and routes. We need to establish communications. We need to ensure that Beckworth, his Adjudicars and his troops are tightly bottled up in Shalal'm Caer with no routes of escape. Dwarves must ensure they do not disappear under the ground. Elves must make sure they do not escape using magic… especially *transfer*. Humans need to make sure they do not sortie over land."

Quickly, the images in the mirrors faded. We stood, and slowly each of us went our way. Glorfindel and Eilol came to stand beside me, William and Richard. "Come with us, children. We need to be together, if for only a short while. Come, children."

I signaled to my Elves and my Ghillies to accompany me. William took me by the hand, as we followed Richard to the Brown Hills' encampment. The Elves of the Brown Hills and Fire Elves greeted us warmly. Moments later, they, my Tribe, and my Ghillies were off, laughing and enjoying each other's company. We, however, sat quietly. We knew that many of us were seeing our last days in this universe. And, we would be the ones sending them to their deaths… or, maybe, to our own.

"So, young William, you seem to have fallen for one of our daughters, again," Eilol chirped.

I've never seen such a bright shade of red before. William gasped. Richard laughed out loud. I almost fell through the earth beneath my feet.

"Now, now, Eilol, you've embarrassed the children," Glorfindel admonished her. "See what you've done? Perhaps we should change the subject?"

"Well," she persevered, "It's out in the open now, so why?"

"Because you've embarrassed them, my dear, and that is sufficient."

"I'm sure you're right, my dear," she replied. She clapped her hands, and a young Elf lad and lass appeared. "Wine and cakes, please," she asked.

Just moments later, a few Elves returned with small tables, a platter with white cakes, and a second with a carafe and several glasses. The wine was superb. I was never a connoisseur or anything like that, so I couldn't tell a good wine from a bad one. Personally, I liked California table wines, but that's me. This wine was superb. I'd had the cakes before. They were a combination between shortbread and yellow cake, but crisp and delicious. I wondered why Elves weren't fat with all this delicious food.

"Tell me," Glorfindel asked, "You talked about a trebuchet, comparing it to a catapult. What is the difference?"

Richard nodded and leaned forward to explain, "A catapult is a single-action machine. You load it up and release it. Typically, you load it by twisting a rope, or pulling against a spring, like a bow.

"A trebuchet is a two-step action machine. You have a weight – a big weight – which you raise. When you release the weight, it falls. This swings an arm, just like a catapult. However, the arm is attached to a sling. The arm pulls the sling, which holds the projectile, thereby combining the long arm of the catapult with the long length of the sling. It has to be big to hurl large rocks or iron balls. It has to have a long arm and a long sling to deliver the projectile at a distance. To throw an object a long distance means you have to create a lot of speed, which is power. So, when a trebuchet throws a large rock a great distance, it delivers a huge blow, which will smash almost anything it strikes. And, since it is precise, a trebuchet can hurl a projectile at almost the same place time after time. Eventually, whatever it is will be pulverized, and that includes rock walls."

Eilol asked, "Then why wouldn't you use it against a gate and just walk in?"

"Ah, because the gate is protected by the wall and the gatehouses. You see, the wall is the protection. Once it's breached, the protection is gone. The gate house is a double gate – the outer and the inner separated by a protected space. The gates are protected by towers, from which troops can fire arrows or pour fire down on them. The gates are protected by a drawbridge and a portcullis. Then, there's the gate itself. Once you're beyond the gate you are in a tunnel. The enemy can fire arrows, shoot spears, pour fire or whatever. Then, you've got another portcullis and a second gate. No, we design gatehouses to be killing grounds. Gates are the weakest part of the walls, so they are most heavily protected.

"That's why it's easier to tunnel under walls or use siege towers to go over them. Battering them is difficult and takes a long time. However, Gilraën's idea is a good one. She's using the trebuchets and the siege towers to cover the other attacks coming from the other three sides. Yet, because of the sheer numbers of troops and the massive siege engines, he can't dismiss our attacks. It's an excellent bit of subterfuge, and a game within a game. It should work, if everyone does their part, and the timing is right."

I had recovered from my embarrassment. "We will need to sing," I said to my Elvin parents. "We will need to overcome the magical resistance we will, no doubt, encounter. By singing, we can affect the structure of the walls themselves, increase the power or accuracy of our weapons and drive our enemies from their positions, while protecting our allies and ourselves. What do you suggest?"

"Tell us more about the walls, my child." Eilol suggested.

I opened my mind, showing them my exploration of the fortress, and also my more detailed study as directed by Thane Pethelzha. When I was done, I asked, "Well?"

"Although we have great powers, when it comes to rock, the Dwarves are the masters. However, we have powers they do not have. You may not have seen them, but we saw faults and inconsistencies that I believe we can attack. We can vibrate the cracks. We can find the tones that cause movement. We amplify the tones, making them loud enough to cause major changes and deformations deep within the structure of the rock itself. We can make it crumble from within. Were we to combine our song with your trebuchet, we could destroy the wall much more quickly.

"However, I'm sure Beckworth or one of his advisors has warned him of this. So, they have created magical defenses, and they will use their Sorcerers to blunt our attack."

"Ah!" I exclaimed, "That's what Pethelzha said! He talked about magic, saying power is not knowledge. He said that Beckworth had changed it, but he had embrittled the crystalline structure making it more susceptible to damage. The Thane declared it would spall if the impact were large enough."

"Then, wouldn't he also have placed wards to protect them?"

"I should think so, but I think we can overcome them both directly and indirectly. We can imbue Richard's projectiles with magical power. Then, we can guide and protect them during flight and ensure they hit the target with magical, explosive power. Altogether, I think our magic will be greater than theirs. And, as long as my tribe and I remain in hiding, Beckworth will not know who is doing it or how to counter it. His only choice will be to use his Adjudicars, and we're prepared to fight them."

Eilol gasped, "Really! My daughter, were it that easy, Glorfindel and I would have destroyed them long ago."

"No," I replied, "It's not that easy. I've met them twice. The first time, Caierne captured me. If it hadn't been for Miss Puss, I'd be a prisoner in Beckworth's dungeons. We also met one at Tamvill. I and seven of my Tribe fought him and two of his Sorcerers. It was a mighty struggle, but we were gaining the mastery. But they *transferred* before we could overcome them.

"I believe I am stronger than any Adjudicar I've met so far, but they are extremely powerful and not that easily overcome. Each of my tribe is among the most powerful of Elves. Together, I believe one of my cohorts could overcome an Adjudicar. Together, we are vastly more powerful than even several of them. Mother, when you created us, you did not understand how strong we would be. I doubt that even the Seeress understands what she has done.

"Which brings me back to the songs you will sing to help the attack. Obviously, they need to be songs of power, but what power? What do we want?"

Richard replied, "Protect our troops from enemy missiles and magic."

William added, "Make sure our missiles hit their targets."

Glorfindel added, "Make sure we can climb the walls. They're hard and glassy, with no imperfections we can use to climb them."

Eilol suggested, "Oh, that's easy. All we need is a limb long enough to reach the top of the wall. It's easy enough to climb one. So, we sing long limbs and cut them off. Easy enough."

"Protect the siege engines from magical attack?" William suggested.

"Good," I answered, "They're too important. And, since we'll be guiding the trebuchet's missiles, we must think about the catapults and ballistae. Oh, and since Beckworth has both on his towers, we must make sure be sure he can't hit anything with them. So, we'll use both offensive and defensive magic, and strong enough to overcome Beckworth's Sorcerers and Adjudicars."

Glorfindel asked, "So, when do we march?"

Richard answered, "As long as we have him enclosed within Shalal'm Caer, we don't have to hurry. We're all waiting on my siege train."

"Well, we can do something about that," Glorfindel replied. "If I were to deploy a hundred Elves, we could have your train here by tomorrow morning."

"You can?" Richard exclaimed. "That'd be great. It'll still take us a few days to assemble them and to get them into place."

I asked, "Could the Krelli and the Trolls help? They're big and strong. Krelli are smarter than Trolls, but Trolls aren't stupid, either."

Richard thought for a moment. "That could save two days. So, the only things holding us up are the rocks in the field in front of the castle and the moat. We'll need a lot of people clearing rocks and smoothing the surface. It doesn't have to be too smooth, because we have large wheels, but even small rocks could stop us cold. Then, the moat is wide – wider than the siege towers can reach. So, we have to fill them in enough that we can get the towers within ten to fifteen feet of the walls."

Eilol leaned forward, asking, "How are these towers protected?"

Richard explained, "We cover the sides with wood to protect our troops from spears and arrows. The structure itself is heavy enough to withstand impacts, plus the sloping sides make it difficult to hit effectively. Finally, we cover the wood with heavy cloth soaked in water. Even if they use fire arrows, they will be extinguished on impact. They could attack them with catapults, but they are not easy targets. Instead, they can use a sortie against them or simply observe where the tower is going, and place large numbers of troops, mobile ballistae or catapults at the point of the attack. That's why we have several of them to spread the defenses and hope at least one assault is successful. If one is, we will try to hold the wall, pour more troops in, and expand our invasion."

"I see," she nodded, "But if we were to add wards to it, would the extra protection help?"

"Oh, yes, assuming that the enemy doesn't know what they are and counteract them or turn them against us."

* * *

The following morning, I issued the orders to advance. Glorfindel was about to send one hundred of his Elves northward to speed the siege train, when I showed up with Justice and his friends in tow. Glorfindel staggered backward, reaching for his sword.

"My Father, let me introduce my long-time friend and boon companion, Justice. We knew each other from Earth and renewed our friendship when he almost killed me."

"Killed you?"

"Oh, yes. He tripped me up and had me at his mercy. But then, we got to talking and laughing and had such a good time, he couldn't kill me. We've been friends ever since. He loves my little 'quests,' don't you, my friend?"

"Oh, yes, but she doesn't have many of them. But, maybe this one will be more to my liking."

"However, my friend, before we can play, we need to get this siege train to the castle. And, for that, we need your help and that of your friends. Will you give them a hand?"

Justice laughed and clapped his hands together.

"Hilarious!" I laughed.

King Glorfindel looked askance at us. "What is this humor, my daughter?"

"Daughter?" Justice asked. "Since when are you their *daughter*?"

"Oh, the King and Queen adopted me. I am now their daughter."

"Oh? Well, if you say so. Anyway, hadn't we better be heading north if we're going to retrieve this wagon train?"

The King stated, "We will travel rapidly. Will that be suitable for you, Justice?"

"Oh, yes, Your Kingness. I've only met one Elf that can outrun me. I call her Road Runner, and she says..." He looked to me.

"Beep! Beep!"

We both laughed uproariously. The King looked at us as though we had both lost our minds.

"And inside joke," I tried to explain. But he didn't understand the idiom.

"All right," I said, "You'd better be off. Take care of yourselves, and I'll see you when you get back."

About a hundred Elves and five Krelli raced northward and were gone in seconds. King Glorfindel and I returned to his pavilion, where Queen Eilol was talking with King Fingolfin. "We've been talking about the assault. I know the Humans are skilled at their form of warfare, but we were asking ourselves why we shouldn't just hurdle the walls and sweep the defenders aside."

I replied, "I think you forgot how you got into this situation in the first place. You let the Adjudicars defraud you. They played you for fools. They understood your prejudices – your superiority attitude toward Humans and Dwarves. They played you like a violin. Before you could even figure it out, they had you sign away your lives. They had your promise not to intervene in the war between Beckworth and his step-brothers and sister. Then, they had you, all wrapped up in a big bag with a pink ribbon.

"Now, you can't attack him. You have a contract with magical implications. If you break it, not only will it have magical consequences, but they'll come after you, the same as they did with Queen Dominica. So, you must act under Human commanders, and this is the way they make war. Don't worry, you'll get lots of wall climbing, and will be critical for the success of this war. You'll know it; I'll know it, but the Humans won't, and that's the saving grace. As long as they think they're in command, they'll believe it, and the Adjudicars will have to believe them.

"The only other person they can blame is me. They've tried to kill me twice, and failed. Third time's the charm, as we say.

"Besides, what makes you think you can climb over those walls and defeat the thousands of troops defending the fortress? They've got big time magic, too, you know."

The three of them just stared at me a few seconds. Then, the Queen said, "You are right, of course. Dominica warned us, but we were too proud to listen to her. And, we suffered the consequences."

"So," I concluded, "shall we do it my way?"

At that instant, I voice emanated from my quiver. "Jharl Gilraën, I would speak with you."

It took me a few seconds to dig it out. As with any purse, whatever you're looking for had sunk to the bottom. Is that one of Murphy's Laws?

I turned with the mirror until I found a hazy cloud. "Who calls for Queen Gilraën?"

"It is I, Jharl Morthanzhemian. Heartening news, My Jharl, I have. At the head of his army, Jharl Galmerstain of Clan Zhaenstain has just entered our tunnels. He is come to support us, Jharl Gilraën. Again united are all Mountains Dwarves against the common foe."

"What great joy you bring to me, My Jharl. I was worried that using Ez-Tansk to support Cassandra's attack would jeopardize our defense. I had ensured that it wouldn't by staging the attack on the western corner. Now, I am assured that my Clan and our allies will prevail. Have you informed the other Jharls and Thane Defghamask?"

"No, to you I left this task most enjoyable."

"Thank you, My Jharl. If you would remain, I will contact Thane Defghamask, Jharl Azkhalish, and Jharl Worzhemacht."

I used the mirror to contact each of the other three Clan leaders. "Jharl Morthanzhemian has just told me wonderful news. I will let him tell you. Jharl Morthanzhemian, please tell them what you told me."

"At the head of his army, Jharl Galmerstain has just entered our tunnels."

All three beamed and chatted excitedly.

I continued, "I think we should contact Jharl Galmerstain and express our happiness."

I contacted him, joining him in our communication. "I understand from Jharl Morthanzhemian that you are leading your Clan to defend your neighbors of the Dwarf Mountains."

"No. Clan Zhaenstain is exercising. We have not exercised in many centuries. Clan Worphelia have moved their herds and flocks to eastern pastures, north and west of Armjurstton. Good is the grazing this time of year. We need not defend Zhaenstain border, so we exercise. Jharl Morthanzhemian agreed to let us pass. I request exercise with Jharl Marazhul, but Thane Defghamask rules. Now, ask Thane Defghamask to exercise."

"Ah, yes. I see the need for Clan Zhaenstain to exercise. All Clans should exercise, to prepare for times of need. Perhaps Clan Ozhemia will exercise with you? And, perhaps both your Clans could exercise with Clan Ghamarazh?

"Jharl Morthanzhemian? Thane Defghamask? Would you agree to exercise with Clan Zhaenstain? Is it convenient at this time?"

Jharl Morthanzhemian replied, "Odd, it is. At this time, Clan Ozhemia is exercising. Welcome you are, My Jharl, to join with us. Honored we would be to exercise with you."

"Great joy, My Jharls," Thane Defghamask replied, "Coincidence it is. Clan Ghamarazh exercises at this time. As Clan of War and Vengeance, Clan Ghamarazh exercises to maintain battle skills. Perhaps Clans Ozhemia and Zhaenstain would exercise with us to improve battle skills, in case of need in the future."

"Ah, the hand of kinship extended, My Thane? Accept I do. Honored we will be to exercise with you and Clan Ozhemia."

"I agree," I added. "As Jharl Regent of Clan Ghamarazh, I approve Thane Defghamask's plan to exercise. As Thane of Diplomacy of Clan Ez-Tansk, I seek your approval to inform my Jharl of this exercise. Perhaps Clan Ez-Tansk would seek to exercise. I do not speak for my Jharl, but I could place the proposition before him."

"Yes, My Jharl Regent," Jharl Galmerstain replied. "With Jharl Azkhalish I have not spoken in many years. Good it would be to speak with him again. I ask, Thane Gilraën, that you speak with your Jharl about this exercise."

"I shall do as you request, My Jharl. However, I must inform you that he is presently exercising with your neighbors in Clan Worfellsten. Would you be averse to joining an exercise with Jharl Worzhemacht?"

"Nay!" Galmerstain answered, "An old and trusted friend is Jharl Worzhemacht is. Eager am I to renew our kinship."

"My Jharls and Thanes," I addressed them all. "I am sure that such an exercise will only renew the bonds of kinship with all five Clans of the Mountains. I look forward to joining you as soon as I am able. I have other responsibilities to attend at this time, so I will leave you to communicate with each other and to finalize your plans for this exercise."

I terminated, laughing. What a farce! I wasn't sure of the game Jharl Galmerstain was playing, but by going along with the gag, I had reunited the five Clans of the Dwarf Mountains. But why the subterfuge? Jharlmor Azzele? Maybe. Regardless, my anvil was restored. Now, I had to get my hammers in place.

I returned to my encampment. My Elves and my Charioteers were lazing around, surrounded by an entire herd of zhaks. One of them saw me and whinnied loudly. Suddenly, I was in the midst of a stampede of half-sized horses. Each nosed me. Several stamped and whinnied greetings to which I replied in kind. Slowly, we wended our way back to where the rest of my troop was lazing about.

"Hey, Gilraën!" Harold yelled, "How's that for a welcome? They're thrilled to see you."

"And I am glad to see them, too. I'm also happy to see you all working hard."

They all laughed. I guess they've figured out my sense of humor.

"So, what's next?" Nienna asked.

"Well, it looks like all four armies are moving into their final attack positions. Clan Zhaenstain is reinforcing the Dwarves, and Brown Hills is expediting the arrival of King Richard's siege train. The only unit not in position is Cassandra's Battalion. Even if she takes the old road from Soubister to Shalal'm Caer, it'll take her five days or so to get here. Even so, now that Zhaenstain is arriving, Ez-Tansk can contribute to the western front. So, things are as good as they can get.

"And, that's the problem. It's like those old movies where the hero says, "It's quiet; too quiet!""

They chuckled.

"I may be an old worry-wort, but I'd prefer to be cautious. I want to send one Cohort to each front, just to keep an eye on things until the army arrives. Then, I want you Charioteers to come with me towards the front gate. I really want to see what's going on. So, which of you want to watch which side?"

None were eager to go to the more isolated western side, but, reluctantly, Galdor finally volunteered. Nienna took the eastern side, leaving Caranthir's with the Charioteers and me. We enjoyed a leisurely mid-day meal, then loaded up five day's supplies and departed to take up our watches.

Although it was only twenty-five miles or so from our camp to the frontier between Barstough and Beckworthshire, the trip took some five hours. By the time we got there, it was late afternoon, and by the time we'd set up camp, it was nightfall. We had sufficient numbers that we could set night watches of two Elves and three Archers. Although the Archers were Humans, they had benefited from their association with my Elves. Their senses were keener, with better hearing and night vision than most. And my Elves had learned from the Humans how to compensate for their sensory limitations through greater alertness and deliberate caution. Altogether, I felt comfortable with their abilities to sense intruders.

I wasn't surprised to be awakened in the night. Nessa touched my mind. *'Something's out there.'*

We formed a circle in a circle defense. The zhaks were in the middle. They understood the need to be quiet. The Ghillies arranged their chariots around the herd, placing themselves within the flimsy barricade like the old wagon trains when under attack. We arranged ourselves outside the circle, bows ready, spears at hand, and swords at our sides. I could sense something, but couldn't be sure of what.

A zephyr carried a smell I recognized – Goblin! I relayed that thought to my Elves, and hand signaled Harold. I cleared my mind, allowing my prescience to expand, seeking the slightest hint of a presence. I sensed two… maybe three that felt like Justice, but I sensed no magical being. A Master Sorcerer or an Adjudicar could disguise their presence, so my lack of detection didn't mean much.

Then I felt numbers. A large body of Orc-like creatures was advancing upon us. I couldn't tell how many, but there was a bunch of them. They appeared to be in an east-west line advancing northward. Again, I alerted my Tribe and my Charioteers.

The storm burst suddenly. Dozens of Goblins ran at us at full speed. They were utterly silent, but the dim light of Chrybda reflected from their long curved blades.

Quickly our circle collapsed. Elros and Idril were on my right; Lenwë and Alassë on my left. I knew that Caranthir was holding the rest in reserve, attempting to guard our flanks and rear.

I loosed my first arrow, and then my second, and my third, and my fourth. My first returned, and I loosed it, to retrieve my second and loosed it. I heard my flankers firing their arrows and realized the enormous firepower the five of us were generating.

However, our enemies had multiplied and were now attacking both flanks. Caranthir, Findecáno and Celebriän were to my right, while Uruviel and Nessa were on my left. I instructed Elros to join them, hoping his firepower would be sufficient.

It wasn't. We had to fall back, as the hordes extended their flanks.

We were barely holding our own, when I felt the Krelli attack from our rear. For just a moment, I thought we would be overwhelmed. But then, I heard Harold yell, "Fire!" I heard the twang of their bows as they loosed their first dozen-arrow volley. We retreated inside the barrier of chariots, and still we volleyed arrow after arrow.

A hand wielding a dark scimitar slashed at me. I blocked it with my slim shield and brought my spear upwards. I felt the sharp steel leaf slice through metal rings and dig deeply into flesh. I struck out with my bow, knocking a body aside, and stabbed violently at another.

I felt an Elf wounded. She cried out in pain… Celebriän Arcamenel. Uruviel rushed to her aid. Suddenly we had lost two defenders.

A monster bore down upon me. A sword as long as I was tall swiped at me. I caught it a glancing blow on my shield, deflecting it, but it spun me around as though an adult were disciplining a child. Vaerorderol appeared in my hand. The massive sword arced towards me. I caught it with my blade, turning it into the ground. Flexing my left wrist, I commanded, "Dashemba, Kill!" The monster fell backwards, grasping at his throat. Gallons of hot bloods geysered, covering me in its gore, as the monster fell, twitched and lay still.

They were gone! I lurched around seeking our enemies, but none were there.

"Gilraën! Help!"

It was Harold. He was covered in blood. I reached for him, but he pulled me aside. Faelnirv lay broken and bleeding. I looked around. Uruviel was busy attending to Celebriän. "Uruviel, I'm busy over here. Can you handle the rest?"

"I think so. Go ahead."

I studied Faelnirv. Her shield arm was broken – almost shattered. Her torso was sliced open and her intestines were trailing on the ground. She was within moments of death.

I concentrated on her, staunching the blood and delivering a shot of life-saving energy. With care and deliberation, I restored her intestines to her mesentery. Her liver was badly damaged. I worked on it for some time, healing much of it. I knew that if it wasn't too badly damaged, the liver could heal itself. I adjusted it in her torso, reattaching it with cartilage. I folded the intestines, pinning them in position with additional cartilage. Then, I began the tedious process of sealing and healing the muscles and tissues of her abdomen. When I judged her life to be out of danger, I turned my attention to her shield arm. It was a mess! Her humerus was broken in three places and her ulna in two. She'd taken a tremendous blow to her arm to break it in so many places.

Grasping her arm, I pushed the pieces back into place, trying hard to fit them exactly. Then, I worked from the inside out, nurturing the marrow, rebuilding bone, replacing calcium and phosphorous. By the time I was finished, I was exhausted.

I looked up to see all the Archers standing around me. The heads of three zhaks poked through the wall of humanity. "I think she'll be all right," I announced. They all broke into smiles of relief. The three zhaks whinnied and stamped. Each of them broke through the ring of Charioteers to nose me and then to Faelnirv.

I turned to find out who else had been injured, seeking Uruviel. She found me instead. "Three injured. Worst was Celebriän, but Findecáno and Caranthir also injured. Caranthir stabbed in back –

liver damage, but better. I will monitor him. Findecáno concussed – sealed brain bleed; dissolved blood clot. I will monitor him. Celebriän stabbed and with a broken arm and leg – nicked heart, but I got it in time. Broken tibia and humerus – both repaired. She will need intensive support for a day or two."

"Zhaks?" I asked.

Harold answered, "None injured, but they are frightened. We're working to calm them, but we may need help."

Everyone had heard our reports. All of us were concerned, but relieved nobody had been killed.

"How many did we kill?"

Elros Ancalímon answered, "More than thirty goblins and one Krell. We saw a second Krell badly injured and was carried off by a third one. We guess that we injured another fifty goblins before they withdrew."

"Recap. Elves? Charioteers?"

Slowly we discovered what had happened. Evidently, we were attacked by a hundred goblins and three Krelli. The goblins had attacked from three sides, penning us into a small space. Despite our barrage of arrows, the goblins had closed with us. Then the Krells had attacked from the rear. The Charioteers had fired their arrows, protecting themselves and their zhaks. They had defended themselves with dirks and shields. Celebriän and Faelnirv had fought one of the Krelli, coming off the worse.

"However, we punctured him like a pin cushion," Nasif boasted. "Another Krell hauled him off before we could kill him."

"In fact, My Queen," Elros explained, "the only dead Krell was the one you killed. By the way, how did you do that? According to everyone else, the remaining Krelli were filled with arrows and still escaped."

I smiled wryly. "I have my ways. Now, has anyone contacted the other cohorts?"

"No… at least I don't think so."

I concentrated on Galdor and Nienna. '*We were attacked by goblins and Krells. Several casualties; no deaths. One Krell dead; two to three wounded. Many goblins dead. Be cautious.*'

I went to visit the zhaks. They were nervous and frightened. I sat with Faelnirv's zhaks, comforting them, assuring them that Faelnirv was injured, but recovering. They were dubious. "Uruviel? Where is Faelnirv?"

"In my area."

"Is if OK for the zhaks to visit her?"

She gave me a caustic look. "Zhaks? She's recovering. She's got a long way to go, and you do remember infections?"

"Yes, but they need to see her, and assure themselves she's alive and recovering."

"Ok, I'll lift the tent flap so they can see her. But, they have to keep their distance."

"How's everyone else?"

"You did a great job with Celebriän, but she's got a long way to go. Caranthir's wound is healing, and his liver is repairing itself. Findecáno is conscious and cracking jokes. He'll probably be ready to return tomorrow."

I returned a few minutes later with Faelnirv's zhaks. They wanted to get closer, but I held them back. They whinnied and stamped, but Faelnirv just lay there. I tried to explain her injuries, but my command of the Human-zhak pidgin was limited, and I'm not sure I got the message across. The zhaks knelt down, but remained watchful.

I returned to the troop. They'd been rehashing events, trying to get the story straight. By the time they'd figured out the blow-by-blow, they concluded that if it had been Caranthir's Cohort or my Charioteers alone, they'd have died. It was the combined effect of Elves and Humans that won the battle. We all owed each other our lives. I didn't bother to tell my Charioteers that my Tribe could have *transferred* any time we'd wanted, and we would have escaped.

* * *

We had slept restlessly. Although I was relatively sure that Beckworth wouldn't try that again, I couldn't be sure. First thing, I checked with Galdor and Nienna. They hadn't been disturbed.

Elves were arriving at their siege positions. Dwarves and Humans were marching overland. They'd be in position in two days. They had attacked the twenty-one of us, but they would never attack a few thousand Elves, Dwarves and Humans.

As the Elves arrived to take up the guard, my cohorts returned. All of them were worried that their tribal kin had been attacked or injured. And they were worried that their Charioteer friends and the zhaks had been attacked and injured. None of us could figure out how they knew we were here or why they'd chosen to attack us and not one of the other cohorts. The only conclusion I could derive was that Beckworth was after me. If so, how did he know I was here? Well, it didn't really matter at this point. I knew where he was.

* * *

I made a pain in the ass of myself. I had nothing to do, so I kept trying to contact people. I quickly wore out my welcome, and for very little. The best news was that Cassandra and her bodyguards were racing toward us. She had left Sheldrick's Battalion east of Soubister. She'd headed across country, discovering the old road that had once joined Soubister to Easbister via Shalal'm Caer. It was overgrown, pitted and uneven, but it was useable for people on foot. Still, it was a good ninety miles. Even with the extraordinary stamina of the Royal family, it'd take two days, and then, she'd be exhausted and incapable of doing anything worthwhile for at least another day.

Justice and friends returned the following day. They had unhitched the draft animals and had hauled the wagons by hand. I guess if you're eighteen feet tall and muscular, such loads are trivial. More came via Elf-power. They just seemed to float along on the own. There were far more than I had figured.

By afternoon, they had lots of lumber laid out along with bits and pieces of iron. Even though I knew what all this was supposed to be, I couldn't picture it in my mind's eye. However, King Richard's mechanics did, and that was all that counted. The Krelli were of great assistance, moving heavy beams into place and such.

Then Artestius showed up with five of his friends. They arrived without prior notice, which called a mass of problems. Men and Elves leapt to their feet, arrows were aimed, and swords brandished. Artestius complained loudly, "Hey! Gilraën told us to come!" When they didn't listen, he yelled, "Gilraën! Help!"

I heard him and came running. It was a good thing I did. The Trolls had backed onto each other and were swinging clubs that were eight feet tall.

"Stop!" I yelled. "Hey, Artestius, don't hurt them."

"Huh!" he answered.

Sometimes, Trolls aren't that bright.

"Leave them alone. They're here to help." As our troops began to disperse, I told Artestius, "Come on with me. We're assembling equipment. Justice and his friends are helping, but you guys will really speed this up."

The mechanics didn't care whether they were Krell or Troll. They were big and strong, and that's all that mattered. Every time I checked on them, the build was progressing at a great pace.

William found me hanging around, watching. "Gilraën, come with me."

"Why?"

"Because you're disturbing the mechanics. You're making them nervous. They've got everything under control, so come with me. Richard wants to know about the ambush."

Despite my best judgment, I followed William to Richard's pavilion. That wonderful man knew the way to my heart.

"Thrak, Gilraën?"

I sat gently sipping the most wonderful of hot beverages. "Ooh, Richard, this is wonderful!"

"I'm glad you appreciate the things I do for you." He beamed. "Now, what can you tell me about that little spat you had?"

"We were just hanging around, when a whole bunch of Goblins attacked us."

"But, Gilraën, you were prepared for it. How did you know?"

"I had a feeling. I do not understand what triggered it. It had been going on all day. That's why I sent a Cohort to each front. Something was fishy, and I couldn't figure it out."

"You sent a Cohort to each side? Why?"

"Again, it was just a feeling. I stuck around with Caranthir Ancalimë's Cohort and my Cavalry. We had camped for the night and the zhaks were herded together where we could protect them.

"Suddenly, I had this overwhelming feeling that we would be attacked. Then, I smelled a Goblin. So, I told the Charioteers to surround the zhaks, and we created a larger circle around them.

"They were on us without warning. They sort of just appeared. We fired arrows as fast as we could, but there were too many of them, so we retreated until we were backed up on the chariots."

"Backed up on the chariots?"

"Yes, the Charioteers had created a barrier using the chariots. They and the zhaks were inside, and we were outside. But then, the Krelli attacked. At least two attacked from the rear, and at least one from the front. My Charioteers fought valiantly. They injured both Krelli so badly, they fled. I fought the other one and killed him. With the Krelli driven off, the rest of the attackers fled."

"That's interesting," the King evaluated. "A dozen archers drove off two Krells. That's significant. And you killed one. That's even more interesting. How did they drive oft two Krell?"

William interjected, "They are extraordinary archers. We recruited them specifically. Then, they've worked with Gilraën and her tribe extensively. They are superb."

Richard looked askance at his brother. "Really?"

I answered, "Yes, they instructed my Elves several times. They even beat them in an open competition."

"Well, that answers that," Richard concluded. "A dozen well-trained archers can drive off an attack by even two Krells. That brings us to my second question. How did you kill a Krell?"

I lifted my right sleeve, exposing the sheath. Then I slid it down.

William nodded in understanding.

Richard asked, "A knife?"

William responded, "They were Dominica's."

"Oh!" Richard responded. "One of her secret weapons?"

"Sort of, but not really," William answered. "Soul Blades!"

"What?" Richard exclaimed, "Those things exist?"

"Oh, yes," William answered. "I had her bow, her arrows, her blades and other of her possessions. I gave them to Gilraën. When she took them in her hand, they came alive as if they were in Dominica's hands. She has used them every since, and to great effect, I might add."

"I guess so," Richard agreed. He asked me, "Is this how you've killed the other Krelli?"

"Yes," I answered, "But, my arrows and those of my Elves are equally deadly. It's just that at close range, I didn't have the time or space for an arrow. He was on me, and I was on the defensive."

Richard shook his head, "I'm glad you're on our side. Does anyone else know about these weapons?"

"I think King Glorfindel and Queen Eilol know. And, maybe the Seeress, too. And, William, and my staff, and my Tribe, and probably my Archers, too. A lot of people know."

"What would happen if someone tried to take them from you and use them against you or us?"

I smiled, "Can't happen."

William explained, "These were Dominica's, so they responded to her. Gilraën is her image. I think that's deliberate. She may even be genetically related, since the Adjudicars had her body and could have used it to create an 'alter ego' to her. Therefore, her bow, blades, quiver and everything else that was Dominica's is now hers. No other person can use them, unless the weapons permit it themselves. And, to answer your next question, yes, they can make those kinds of decisions."

Richard persisted, "But, how did they know you were there?"

"I've been asking myself that question all night. I can't figure it out, unless somehow they can monitor my whereabouts."

"Well," Richard advised, "until you figure it out, be very careful. Keep a Cohort with you. No going off by yourself."

I glanced around. It was getting dark. "I guess I'll head back to our camp."

"Remember what I said, Gilraën." Richard advised. "Go nowhere alone. William, why don't you accompany here to make sure she gets there in one piece?"

"Do I have to?" he whined.

"No, I could do it," Richard jested.

"No, that's all right. I'll do it."

The brothers laughed, as William and I headed toward my camp, accompanied by a dozen of William's Guard. "So," he asked, "I heard you had casualties. Who and how bad?"

"Faelnirv the Archer and Celebriän Arcamenel the Elf were badly hurt. A few others were wounded, but it was those two that were the worst. They're recovering now, and should be fit by tomorrow."

"You were lucky, Gilraën. They could have killed you." William replied.

'Should I tell him we weren't really in trouble? We Elves could have escaped, but the Charioteers and their zhaks would have died. No, best let that be my secret.'

"Yes, but we weren't, and let's leave it at that."

We didn't speak of it any more that night. We ate with my Tribe and my Charioteers. We talked about the past weeks. The Charioteers were interested in the battle of Tamvill. We discussed how blind we were without a cavalry force scouting the lands ahead of us. They, in turn, discussed the trip south to Barstough. It was uneventful. Brown Hills had swept through undeterred. Evidently, that had been enough to frighten any would be attackers. Regardless, an army of thousands was enough to frighten off any attempts to waylay them. The Cavalry had explored all the way to the castle and had reported their findings to the King, but that was it. So, the Battle of Barstough was the most excitement they'd had in a weeks. When William and his Guard left, we bedded down, exhausted.

* * *

Richard's army moved south the next morning to take up positions immediately north of Shalal'm Caer. My first sight of the great fortress was awe-inspiring. I'd seen it from above and through the distorted view from the Void. It was different with just plain eyesight.

A broad open field extended in a long slope for more than a mile. At the summit great, gray walls erupted from the land. The road ran straight to a huge gatehouse with four massive towers and a great maw marking the entry. The drawbridge over the dry moat was raised, flags fluttered from the towers, and tiny figures rushed about on the battlements. Beckworth knew we were coming and was prepared for battle.

As agreed, Richard's forces moved to the right of the road, while William took the left. Clan Tazhela was at William's left flank, preparing to burrow through the cliffs under the northeastern corner to open the route for Duke Armjurst's forces to emerge into the courtyard between the two walls. Baron Richmond's Battalion stood to their right ready either to move in defense of the Dwarves or to follow Prince William into the courtyard between the walls. Sir Xander's Battalions were arrayed to their right with King Melwasúl's directly behind them facing the wall. When the time came, my Elves and I would lead the attack, along with Justice and his Krelli.

Artestius and his Trolls were pushing the siege towers up the long slope, protected by Viscount Geoffrey and Sir Xander. King Richard's Battalions and the Elves of the Brown Hills and Fire Elves advanced upon the gates.

Sir Domnall led King Fingolfin's Elves and Yurchist Linda's Orcs toward the western wall. Jharl Ez-Tansk advanced on their right, prepared to dig a tunnel under the western wall.

We were in a state of siege. Both the besieging army and those besieged were under extreme duress. Those on the inside were limited by the food and supplies they had in storage. Even the mightiest fortress had fallen low to the scourge of starvation.

Yet, the besieger was equally distressed. The besieging army was like a scourge of locusts. They would strip the locale of anything resembling food. As time passes, the army has to reach out further and further, devastating the lives and property of everyone in an ever-increasing radius.

The only advantage we had was the foresight of King Richard and his supply trains arriving from throughout the kingdom. Mighty wains, drawn by semi-domesticated ilanwaroch, ilanroch, and ilkarromb arrived from the vast farmlands of the Realm. A long stream of Orcs, each pulling a large, two-wheeled cart, arrived in Barstough, deposited their goods, and departed hurriedly. Yet, the problem was not the crops, herds or flocks. Regardless of their numbers, there just weren't enough carts, wagons, drays or wains to transport the vast quantities needed to supply ten thousand mouths.

'*Surely*,' I thought, '*we are better off than Beckworth, but our troops can desert, while theirs are trapped.*'

I had to keep them busy. If they were busy, they wouldn't be thinking about petty deprivations. Instead, they'd be busy preparing, attacking, retreating and reviewing their strategies and tactics. I'd use debriefings to encourage participation in all aspects of the assault on the fortress. Getting their feedback would make them feel as though they had an important role to play, and that I and the other bigwigs were interested in their thoughts and experience.

It was a matter of keeping everyone busy. It didn't matter whether they were Elves, Dwarves or Humans, boredom was the enemy. Activity was my friend and that of the alliance. So we needed to attack.

The Elves of the White Cliffs staged the first attack in Armjurst's sector. To carry it off, I had everyone else feint against the walls in their sector. The Elves used long poles laid against the walls. They quickly scaled the walls, seizing their summits.

Beckworth's troops reacted quickly. Within moments of the attack, the walls were well manned. Arrows whistled through the air, and boiling water poured through the gargoyles onto the heads of the Elves. Fortunately, Aeradir's Elves were prepared with both sturdy shields and powerful wards. None were killed, but many were injured. However, none of the injuries were beyond the skills of their healers.

The most important lesson we learned was the speed of Beckworth's response. His watchmen spotted the attack as it was forming. His men and goblins were on the walls within minutes. Had the attack been a serious effort, it would have been quickly and soundly defeated.

The second feint was more elaborate. Richard's army equipped themselves with ladders that were tall enough for his Humans to surmount the battlements. But, his was the feint.

Cassandra's army attacked the western wall. The Elves of the Blue Lake also used long poles to achieve the summit of the walls. Yurchist Linda's host followed closely. Using climbing ladders, they supported the Elves and achieved momentary success. Although they broke through the shell of the defense, they could not cross the outer courtyard and mount the taller inner walls. They retreated in good order with minimal casualties. Although the Orcs did suffer several deaths, the wards placed on Linda's troops by their Sorcerers protected the rest.

Again, it was a successful foray. We learned a lot. The most important evidence was the speed of the response. Beckworth's forces were ready to repel the attack from the beginning. His reinforcements arrived quickly. And, even though they were temporarily overwhelmed, they regrouped, counterattacked, and stymied the assault in the killing zone between the walls.

At the same time, we observed that Beckworth defended the northern wall with alacrity. As Richard's masses raced towards the wall, Beckworth's forces manned the battlement in force. None of the ladders remained in position long enough for the Humans to achieve the battlements. I wondered if the success of Cassandra's forces was at least partially enabled by the huge numbers of troops used to defend the walls against Richard's army. If so, we had seen the timing of his second surge of reinforcements.

During all this frenetic activity, Richard's mechanics were busily assembling their machines of war. Meanwhile, other troops were removing rocks and smoothing the plain before the north wall. Still others, including Krells and Trolls, were filling in the long slope to the walls, preparing to roll the siege towers into place.

I was surprised to discover that nobody on this continent had heard of using the gabion and fascine. Once I explained what they were and how to use them, Richard's engineers leaped into action, and within days, the long lawn ascending the slope to the walls was smoothed, long slopes created, and the gully before the walls filled with rubble and debris.

This extraordinary effort was impossible to hide. There could be no doubt that we were planning to assault the long wall between the gate and the western end. Yet, there was nothing that Beckworth could do to prevent it, unless he sallied in force and somehow destroyed our work. Still, it bothered me that he didn't even try. I expected some kind of effort. It was uncharacteristic of Beckworth to just sit back and wait. He was up to something, but I couldn't figure it out.

Like everybody else, my tribe and I needed to keep busy and hone our skills. We spent the next few hours trying to damage each other. We attacked using whatever magical arts in our possession trying to overwhelm each other. We did one-vs-one exercises. We did Cohort vs Cohort exercises. We did two cohorts vs one Cohort. We even tried everyone against me. It was exhausting to say the least.

We renewed our skills and rediscovered our strengths. We decided that our tactic would be to stick together as cohorts. The group of eight warrior-mages with one warrior-healer was extremely powerful. I couldn't defeat any single Cohort, although they couldn't defeat me, either. When all twenty-seven of them attacked me, they forced me into a full defense mode. They couldn't defeat me, but I was a tiny defensive ball barely capable of survival. I was so proud of them!

If I was correct in my assessment of the magical abilities of an Adjudicar, I could defeat one of them. If so, each of my cohorts could also defeat one of them. I knew there were two of them, which could mean three. We could defeat up to four of them.

Richard announced that that they completed both trebuchets. They also completed two of the three siege towers. Three catapults and two ballistae were ready to move into position. The Trolls moved the trebuchets with almost ridiculous ease. Justice and his Krelli half carried and half rolled huge rocks alongside the monstrous slingshots. We Elves levitated hundreds more and transported them to holding positions.

The Trolls rapidly cranked the trebuchet's gears, raising huge wooden boxes of rocks fifteen feet into the air. These were the counter-weights that would act upon the short arm of the lever. Once the boxes were raised to their highest, they folded the long arm back, and attached a long rope attached to the sling, which was drawn into position and locked in place with a hook. They stretched the sling forward and rolled a huge rock into it.

When all was ready, the mechanic in charge yanked a rope, which released the hook restraining the sling. Released, gravity accelerated the heavy box toward the ground. As the short end of the lever moved downward, the long arm whipped upward. At its peak, the arm struck a retaining block that stopped its forward motion. However, the sling had followed the arm, pulling the rock with it. When the arm stopped, the sling continued forward until it reached its apogee. At that a point, the rock hurled upward, rising hundreds of feet into the air. Then, it fell back to earth, colliding with the wall....

Except it didn't! The rock slammed into an invisible barrier, shattering into hundreds of pieces flying in all directions. Shards fell over a wide area. Fortunately, none of our troops were beneath the deadly rain.

"Ah!" I murmured. "So that's it, is it?"

I turned to my Elves. "It appears they are using magic to protect the walls. Let us seek this out and neutralize it. Concentrate with me. We will reinforce the rock and counter the magic."

Slowly, they reloaded the trebuchet. The entire operation took something over fifteen minutes, even with the help of Trolls and Krelli. When the machine was ready, I said, "Protect the rock." We annealed its surface, making it as strong and malleable as iron.

"When they fire, we will monitor their magic. We will have little time to act. Each Cohort shall act independently, seeking the spells in use. You will then counteract those spells to the best of your abilities. When you have done so, communicate your findings to the others. We will gradually find and neutralize all of them."

Again, the gigantic rock flew upward. Again, the rock hit an invisible wall and shattered, this time with a huge explosion.

Caranthir announced, "We have something." He transmitted the sensations of his Cohort. It seemed to be a spell that would project a barrier to passage.

"I shall work with you during the next shot. However, I'm sure that they will attempt to block us or will change the wards they are using. So, the rest of you should continue to monitor the magic and counter what you can."

A third shot flew into the skies. I felt what Caranthir had discovered. We neutralized it just seconds before the rock would have encountered it. The rock flew on… striking the wall. The noise was huge, causing everyone to clasp their ears in pain. A huge chunk of the upper segment of the wall spalled off, flying out from the wall and crashing to its foot.

All of us jumped up and down, cheering like children. I sent one Cohort to the other trebuchet so they could ensure that the rocks accomplished their goals. Trolls, Krelli, Humans and Elves worked side by side to load the sling, prepare the rock, load it into the sling, and raise the box to its full elevation. Suddenly, a rock flew from the machine to the right. The rock seemed to waver and fell short of the wall.

The machine to the left fired. This time the rock flew straight and true, striking the wall like a bomb. The other machine fired, but its rock veered far to the left, landing harmlessly. Slowly, but inevitably, the number of rocks hitting the outer wall, exploding and spalling huge chunks of rock from its face increased. At first, it was just one out of three that hit. Then it was half, and then three out of four. After six hours of bombardment, 9 out of 10 were smashing into the wall. The wall itself began to look like the cratered surface of Llombda.

As night fell, the bombardment ceased. The crews of the machines were spent. Even mighty Trolls and Krells were tired from the ceaseless exertions. But their work wasn't ended. The huge piles of rocks they had assembled for the day's work had fallen to a mound of just a few. New rocks had to be rolled or carried into place. Still others had to be carted in from as far away as the Phaed River.

The Dwarves of Tazhela had observed the bombardment. They analyzed our strikes and the rate at which the walls were being destroyed. They suggested that at this rate, the bombardment would topple the walls in three days.

I met with Richard and William, contacting Cassandra and Armjurst by mirror. I asked King Richard, "Will the siege engines and towers be in position in two days?'

The King turned to his engineers. They talked quietly among themselves until one of them replied, "The siege towers are ready to roll into position. All but one of the catapults will be ready, and all the ballistae. If we have the Trolls to help us, we can get them into position during the night so we will be ready to attack the walls first thing in the morning."

The King turned to me. "So, there is your answer. We will be ready in two days. When you give the orders, I will instruct my engineers to roll our siege machines into place during that night. I will have my entire army ready to attack the following morning."

I asked, "Prince William, will you be prepared to assault the battered walls in three day's time?"

William spoke immediately. "Yes, indeed! My men are eager to attack anything. They are alive with pent up energy. They have marched and fought and marched even more. They've been cooped up in camps and played at attacking the fortress. If anything, they are too ready."

Duke Armjurst explained, "The forces I lead include the Elves of the White Cliffs and the Dwarves of Tazhela. Elves see the universe in terms of millennia. A day here or there is meaningless to them. The Dwarves move at the pace of a planet. Although their world-view is not as long as that of the Elves, they live in the centuries. Only Humans live in the moment. Only Humans get excited about tomorrow's prospects. If I were to tell my army that we attack in one hour, one day or one year, few, other than the Humans, would change their preparedness. The Humans are eager for any activity. Just tell them what they are to do, and when they are to do it, and they will be in their proper place at the proper time ready to perform the proper actions."

William laughed so hard he almost fell out of his chair. "Gak, Albert! You are the biggest gas bag I've ever known! You haven't changed since we were kids. Ask you a simple question, it'd take you'd talk for half an hour but never answer the question. At least this time, you answered the question."

We all chuckled, as much at William's hysteria as Albert's loquacity. When we had recovered, I asked Cassandra, "And you?"

"Oh, yes. Terse enough? I just wish Sheldrick's Battalion were here. I have talked with Jharl Azkhalish. He and Domnall are old friends, it seems. So, the timing should be good."

Again, we all laughed. "Ok," I replied, "We're not ready to bring everyone into our plans. However, I think you've got to alert our various Kings, Queens, Jharls and Generals as to our plans. They have to know the plan, their part in it, and their ultimate goal. They will need to position their forces appropriately, and to be prepared to brief their unit commanders on their roles in the final assault.

"Inform your Elvin allies of Beckworth's use of magic to defend the walls. I expect he'll use everything he can to deflect a bombardment or interfere with either the positioning of the siege towers or the assault of the troops through the towers or over the walls. Perhaps Elves should lead the assault, with Humans supporting and reinforcing them."

That night, I sat with my tribe, the Krelli, Trolls and Cavalry. It was a bit boisterous, with everyone telling stories of their exploits during their treks from Shesol Vys to Barstough. I managed to slip in their assignments between funny anecdotes or frightening tales. The Trolls knew they were pushing siege towers into place. The Krelli understood they'd get the catapults and ballistae into place, but then prepare to follow us through the gap in the walls. In the meantime, the Charioteers would patrol the area around the siege works to prevent sorties against our preparations.

* * *

Early the next morning, Artestius' Trolls rolled the catapults and ballistae into place. The munitions for the catapults were firebombs. The engineers had soaked tinder in oil. They had packed ceramic pots with the kindling to destroy anything flammable on or beyond the outer walls. They also prepared the long ballistae arrows with oil-soaked windings. Not only would they kill anyone they hit, but if they missed targets on the walls, they would carry fire far beyond.

However, they all had to be calibrated to hurl their weapons where they would do the most harm. So, the first few shots were used to establish the range to and over the walls. Just as with the trebuchets, the first shots smashed into an invisible wall and shattered. I conferred with the Sorcerers from King Richard's court and told them what we had done to penetrate the magical defenses. Over the next few hours, the contest between 'ours' and 'theirs' raged hot and heavy. For the most part, 'ours' won. Then, the enemy would change their wards, and our missiles would go shooting off in some odd direction or simply stop and fall to the ground. It took some time for

Richard's Sorcerers to find the solution before the bombardment could resume.

However, by late afternoon, they had made considerable progress. At least eight out of ten firebombs either crashed into the battlements or onto the courtyard beyond. Similarly, ballistae bolts, directed by Richard's Sorcerers, were clearing the walls, destroying Beckworth's ballistae or killing their crews. In general, Richard's crews were making the defense very difficult, which could only improve our chances of surmounting the walls.

The trebuchets continued their inexorable task. My Tribe was busily directing massive rocks onto the walls, shattering them with enormous concussions that rang out beyond the battlefield. Occasionally, huge chunks of the wall would collapse, rumbling and tumbling down the slope from the wall towards the surrounding open fields, endangering the life and limb of anyone in the immediate area. Thane Pethelzha remained convinced that by the next day, the walls would be so reduced that troops could clamber over the debris and readily enter the outer courtyard.

In the meantime, Dwarves dug like obsessed badgers. Equipped with the proper tools obtained from Clan Ozhemia by the Elves of the White Cliffs, Clan Tazhela bored into the granite cliffs as easily as a child could poke a finger into white bread. Meanwhile, Ghamarazh and Ozhemia directed their efforts toward preparing the passage from their dwarrows into Shalal'm Caer. More than two thousand Dwarves were assembled, ready to burst into the fortress and beyond into the keep.

Clan Ez-Tansk dug from the western side beneath the walls, preparing to meet their kin beneath the walls. Hundreds of Orcs prepared to enter their tunnels to emerge within the outer courtyard. Elves along the other three sides busily prepared poles long enough to reach the summit of the walls. Such was the strength and agility of the Elves that they needed little other than these slim branches to clamber to the top of the walls faster than a frightened squirrel could climb a tree.

Thousands of men prepared scaling ladders. Yet, ladders were tricky things. First, they were very long. Once raised, the ladders sagged against the walls through much of their length. This made it difficult for men to achieve the necessary toeholds to climb. Therefore, the most agile among them were chosen to lead the assault.

Further, raising such long ladders into position was difficult. Other men stood beneath them armed with long y-shaped sticks to support the upper length of the ladders as they were raised. We expected the enemy upon the walls would try to topple them. They too would have long poles to contest the raising of the ladders, toppling them as quickly as we raised them.

In the meantime, other defenders would fire at us with bows or crossbows. Still others would dump boiling water or oil upon our heads. And when they could the defenders would set fire to the oil to cause horrendous and painful burns to all who were attempting to climb the walls.

It was my job to coordinate the multiple attacks. That night, I used the *waking sleep* to contact all the leaders. I reminded them of the order of events and how critical it was to stick to the schedule. I needed Beckworth to be overwhelmed not just by the size of our attack but its complexity. And it was that very complexity that could be our undoing. This was especially important for the Dwarves, who would be underground and out of sight until the very last moments.

Everyone was grim faced both with worry and fear. None wanted to be the ones to act prematurely or reticently, since either could lead to defeat. Equally, regardless of the success of the overall plan, Humans, Dwarves, Elves, Trolls, Krelli, Orcs and even Octopods would die. For my part, I worried about everyone and everything, but most of all my Cavalry. I was less concerned about my Tribe. We were warrior-mages, fully capable of using weapons or magic to harm or defend, as we needed. My Cavalry, however, were just mortals, both Human and zhak. They had nothing but their skill and speed to protect them. I just hoped they'd do nothing heroic.

As dusk overtook the field of battle, the last standing part of the wall fell to the interminable bombardment. All that was left was a pile of rubble, perhaps ten feet high. The inner courtyard was aflame.

Arrows and bolts still flew from the northern half of the wall, but harmlessly.

I fell into a troubled sleep, wondering, "What has Beckworth up his sleeve?"

* * * * *

Chapter 4 – Battle of Shalal'm Caer

It was still dark when my eyes snapped open. Unlike most mornings, I was suddenly and completely awake. I dressed quickly with my spear behind my back, my sword at my side, my quiver over my shoulder, and my bow in my hand. I wore my coronet and helmet to which I had affixed a plume so I could be identified quickly in the swarm of attackers.

When I emerged from my tent, my tribe was awaiting me. Each of us was armed similarly. Next to them were Justice and his allies. Each was wearing a mail over-shirt, greaves, braces and a close-fitting helmet. All of them hefted long shields on their arms. Two wielded huge maces; Justice and two others brandished swords with blades at least six feet in length and as broad as my hand.

We trotted off towards the battered section of the wall, where we joined with Prince William's army. I greeted him, King Amder, Richmond, Deplos and Justice "Hail! I see we are ready for battle."

They nodded, but said nothing.

"Then, let us get this day started."

I concentrated on King Richard, Princess Cassandra, and Duke Armjurst. "Let it begin!"

I felt them respond. That was sufficient. We had talked this day to exhaustion. It was now time to put our plans into effect.

At my signal, Dwarves began a frenzy of digging. Near at hand, Tazhela undermined the northeastern corner. Armjurst would follow closely behind. Upon exiting into the outer courtyard, he would turn left, toward the southern wall, to prevent Beckworth's troops from attacking the Dwarves as they undermined the inner wall. White Cliffs would scale the outer wall, attempting to secure the battlements.

It was our job - Prince William's, mine, and King Melwasúl's - to attack from east to west within the outer court, defending the Dwarves from attack from that quarter. Richard's attack against the walls was to protect us from troops on the battlements and to secure the western end of the outer courtyard.

"Justice, you and your Krelli are with me. My King, if you and your tribe would fall in behind me, we will begin. Prince William, we will walk forward until we can clearly see the gap in the wall. Then, we will advance at a run."

So saying, I set off at a quick walk. My Elves and the Krelli marched at my side. King Amder walked behind me leading five hundred of his kinfolk. Behind us, eleven hundred Humans strode stalwartly into battle.

The bright cusp of Mummia edged above the horizon, spewing rays of light that skimmed across the grassy field. The gap in the wall looked like a six-year-old's mouth.

"Let's go!" I shouted.

We sprinted forward, reaching the pile of rubble in just seconds. We Elves bounded from rock to rock, reaching the top in just a few bounds. The Krelli just leapt.

Justice struck something… hard! He rebounded like a tennis ball off a cement wall. I couldn't stop, either. I hit something that shouldn't be there. I found myself bouncing from rock to rock, ending up next to Justice.

"Crap! Gilraën, what was that?"

"Dunno, Justice. Let's find out."

By this time, the Elves were standing in a line, reaching out as though touching something, except nothing was there. I sat up slowly. My head was spinning. I stood, but the world was spinning around. Crap! Where was a healer when I needed one?

Justice had risen to one knee. "Damn! I don't feel all that well."

Uruviel Sîrfalas appeared at my side. "Are you OK?"

"No," I whispered. "My head is spinning."

"I'm not a bit surprised." She took my head in her hands and considered what he had discovered. "Yup, concussion." She mumbled a few words.

My head cleared. "Help Justice."

"Done. He's OK now."

We rose and clambered back up the rubble pile. "What's going on?" I asked nobody in particular.

King Melwasúl replied, "A magical barrier. It is a facsimile of the original wall of stone."

"But can we destroy it?" I asked.

"Patience, my young Queen. Let us analyze it. When we have evaluated it, then, perhaps, we can infer a solution."

My tiny little brain convulsed as I remembered saying the same things to my strategic analysis students. Basically, these were the three steps required to think critically. "Yes, I understand that, but while we are performing these mental gymnastics, the Dwarves of Tazhela are being slaughtered."

"Yes, young queen," he humored me, "but irrational and inconsiderate actions will only exacerbate the problem. We must take appropriate actions that will lead to a successful conclusion. Now, let us analyze this magic and then evaluate it."

"Yes, my King," I replied, like a little kid reluctantly complying with a parent's wishes.

"Gilraën," he requested, "Combine the strength of your Tribe with ours, and I will lead our examination."

I complied quickly, adding the magical energies of our twenty-eight to those of the five hundred thirty-two Green Mountain Elves. Inundated by their sheer numbers, I struggled to find Glorfindel's mind. A metaphorical hand reached out to me.

"A bit intimidating," he suggested. "Now, let us interrogate this magical edifice to see what we can learn."

I followed him along with hundreds of others, like a great herd follows the cow boss.

"Ah!" he exclaimed, directing our attention to what appeared to me to be a smooth surface. "Look deeply. See the structure? It is regular, almost crystalline. We shall cleave it! Come, let us create the wedge."

His mind conceived of an enormous chisel, which we had to place cross-wise to the upper surface of the magical wall. And that was the problem. The 'top' was far above the ramparts of the existing wall.

"*Try to rise!*" I commanded, and the chisel zoomed upward. My Elves and I rose with it, maintaining our magical connection with Melwasúl. We were several hundred feet above the fortress by the time we found it. Acting under King Amder's directions, we positioned the chisel, carefully orienting it to align with the crystalline structures of the magical wall.

"Now," he directed, "Lift the wedge. Ready? Strike!"

The world around us exploded. We were tossed like pebbles in a hurricane. Before we could even react, we found ourselves tumbling, falling, and plummeting to the ground. Frightened, confused and disoriented, I was helpless. For a moment, I knew I was going to die. My only thought was, '*Shit!*'

I was floating! Somehow, I'd avoided the ground. Looking around, I saw many of my Tribe sprawled awkwardly, lying on the ground.

"What the…" I asked the air around me.

"Queen Gulámae!" Melwasúl had appeared at my side. "What did you do? If I hadn't arrested your fall, you might have been killed!"

I struggled to my feet. "Attack! Maidstone Forest, Attack! Justice, Attack! Over the walls!"

We raced over the pile of debris the trebuchet's had created. We descended into the space between the walls, sealing the outer courtyard. Then they were on us. Goblins fell, pierced by our magical arrows, only to be replaced by still more of their kind.

Justice was beside me in two bounds, as were his companions. They cleared the way before us. My Tribe sprinted ahead, their bows at the ready, arrows nocked. More soldiers appeared… Humans and lots of them. They charged us, hurling spears and firing arrows.

We raised our shields, and our wards with them, as we loosed volley after volley of our magical arrows. Melwasúl and his Elves become as silver creatures of light, too bright to be looked upon.

"Ease off!" Justice shouted, pushing me aside. "You're having all the fun. Our turn!" With that, he and his friends raced forward, shields before them, weapons held high.

What should have been an overwhelming force frightening the enemy was met with derision. As Justice closed upon the defenders, six Krelli stepped out of the crowd and rushed to meet them. The clash was titanic. Enormous beings possessed of unimaginable strength and unworldly speed clashed. They were a blur. The sound of weapon on shield was cacophonous. Their battle spread from wall to wall, making it impossible to pass them even if we wanted to do so.

Suddenly, a massive body fell and was quiet. Another and another fell, as the giants fought each other. Several of my Elves rushed forward to drag the bodies from the fray. We didn't recognize the first one or the second. Both were alive, but badly injured. The third was the Krell we knew as Integrity. He was dead.

"Melwasúl, attack the other soldiers. We must clear the outer courtyard before they can reinforce. Prince William is coming behind us!"

"Come on!" I yelled to my tribe. "Spears and shields!

We were Elves in full battle fury. We accelerated in space-time, readying ourselves for battle at speeds unknown to mortals. A monster appeared before me for the inkling of a second. It swung a mace at me, which I ducked. For a moment, I was wrestling Vigash. I stepped aside and drove my spear into the back of his knee. As he fell, I stabbed him in his neck.

I moved beyond the struggle, seeing a pair of Krelli battling so closely they were biting each other, spitting out huge hunks of flesh. I recognized one of them as Justice. The other one was even bigger. They appeared to be evenly matched, but then the other one landed a telling blow with his mace. Justice fell forward as the other one swung his shield. He struck Justice in the side of his head, opening a massive wound.

The other one moved in for the kill. He raised his mace, but I stabbed him in the back alongside his spine. He arched his back, his mace arm reaching back at an awkward angle. Taking a page out of Vigash's playbook, I stabbed the Krell in his Achilles tendon, just above the ankle. The Krell spun, collapsing toward me, his shield about to behead me. I leaped aside, but the shield brushed my shoulder, crushing me to the ground. I rolled, gathering my feet under me. I spun, leapt and bounded to my feet.

The Krell had fallen to his knee facing away from me. I leapt onto his back, climbing upward to plunge my spear into the base of his skull. He twitched once... twice and fell on his face.

I leapt to the ground, looking around for my next opponent, but I was alone amidst a pile of bodies. Most of my Tribe was with me, spattered in blood and offal. Our healers were busy. Several Elves, including four of mine, were lying to the side, along with two Krelli. A mass of men was moving beyond us, pursuing the fleeing enemy. Evidently, our battle with the Krelli was so unnerving that they fled rather than await the outcome.

Green Mountain Elves were in hot pursuit. William's men followed, closely protecting the Dwarves who were busily undermining the corner of the interior wall. The battle was proceeding as planned. Now, what about the dead and injured?

I rushed to the healers. "Who? And how bad?"

Uruviel pointed to an Elf, "Fëanáro, crushed ribs, broken arm. He'll recover, but he needed food." She pointed again. "I don't know either of them. They must be Green Mountain Elves. That one had an arrow through the lung; that one's arm was severed. They'll be out of it for a while." He pointed to a Krell. "Dead. Head was crushed, and I couldn't save him."

"Who is he?"

"Your friend, Justice."

My breath wouldn't come. I gasped and sat down. *'Reu? Gone?'* My mind went blank, and I sat there staring at nothing. My friend... my oldest and dearest, pain in the ass friend was dead.

"Hey, Gilraën!" Caranthir grabbed me and lifted me to my feet. "Fight now; grieve later. You knew this could happen. It has. Now we have to fight Beckworth, so get your ass in gear, *Queen Gilraën*."

His words penetrated my grief. He was right. Now I had a personal reason to hunt down Beckworth and his Adjudicars.

I stood and went to the next healer, Lenwë Sáralondë. "Lenwë Tasardur injured his hand. He's fine now. These three are Mountain Elves.

I then went to Lessien Melwasúl, who was treating four more of Amder's Elves. "This one won't make it. Her brain is crushed, and I can't reconstruct it. The other three will survive, but this one has lost an arm."

"Maidstone Forest!" I shouted. "It's time for us to go! To me! Maidstone Forest, to me!" Quickly, all twenty-seven of them gathered around me. "Everybody OK?" They nodded. "Let's go. We have a job to do."

We bucked the tide of humanity rushing into the fray. We clambered over the rubble and into the field beyond.

My mirror came alive. "Queen Gilraën!"

I almost ignored it, but then remembered I was in command of this madness. "Who calls for Queen Gilraën?"

"King Richard. We have a problem!"

King Richard reported that the enemy had blocked the walls with magic. The siege towers couldn't approach them.

I reached for King Glorfindel's mind. '*Sing*,' I said. '*Disrupt the magic on the walls.*'

A chorus of power beset the walls. A shimmering haze of power fought power, slowly driving it back. Within moments, the Elves song of power had disrupted the spell placed on the wall.

When the siege towers were in place, the Elves burst into song once again as they raced up the tower and over the wall. Every spell placed in their path shattered as they raced along the walls, clearing them of all opposition.

One Battalion of Richard's army sped up the towers and over the walls, entering the outer courtyard. They battled their way to the massive gatehouses to open the outer gates for the rest of the army. However, the turrets were well defended, and denied all access to the gate mechanism, without which the enormous gates, portcullis, and draw gate could not be opened. Equally, the murder hole between the turrets could not be cleared.

The consequence to the assault was critical. Four of the King's Battalions were to have entered through the main gate along with all the Trolls. And we needed the Trolls for the assault on the inner gates. Even the battering ram needed to destroy the inner gate was to have passed through the main gate. So, it was necessary to open that gate.

Stymied, Richard redirected a second Battalion to the siege towers. In the meantime, he sought King Glorfindel's help. The Brown Elves were heavily engaged between the walls, and Queen Eilol's Fire Elves had mounted the outer walls to clear them of defenders. King Glorfindel and six of his strongest spell-casters raced to the gatehouse to consult with the Richard's generals. Together with six of Richard's sorcerers, they attacked a heavy, iron-reinforced door into the turret. Yet, in spite of all their efforts, the doors held, disrupting the entire assault.

I gathered my Tribe. "We have an important mission. The main gates are being held, and they cannot open them. The entire assault is endangered. We will transfer into the gatehouse, kill the defenders, and open the gates for the army. Let us orient ourselves. We can see the gatehouse, so we know where we are going. We must reconnoiter before we enter. Then, I will assign each Cohort a mission. Ready? Into the Void! *Balor ailai si Byr!*"

We stepped from the baryonic world into the infinity of the Void. We navigated quickly to the gatehouse and explored the baryonic world from our god's eye view. The gatehouses were massive. Both were large, square keeps with round turrets at the four corners. The gates stood firmly between them. The outer gates consisted of a drawbridge over a dry moat, a portcullis which guarded a pair of massive wooden gates heavily reinforced with iron bars. The gates were closed and locked with iron rods through the doors and into the stone above and below the doors. A massive reinforced timber crossed behind the door on heavy hasps.

A similar set of gates stood at the inner side of the gatehouses, providing double protection. Between the doors was a long killing zone. The walls were pockmarked with arrow slots, and the ceilings with openings the defenders could use to pour hot water or burning oil upon the attackers. Of all the features of this massive fortification, this gatehouse was the strongest.

We studied the mechanism used to raise and lower the triple gates. Because of the size of the gates, the mechanism was a gigantic series of iron gears. Similar gears existed in the two towers at each side of the entranceway. Both sets of gears had to be operated simultaneously to raise or lower them. It was a large and complex mechanism, designed to be difficult to operate. Both gatehouses had to be captured for an attacker to open their entries. Further, to achieve access to the outer courtyard, an attacker would have to seize both pairs of gatehouses.

"It looks to me like we have to capture five strong points at the same time: the four turrets and the killing zone. Let's break up into groups of five. Four will enter one of the turret's gate rooms, kill everyone there, and prepare to raise the gates. The fifth group will enter the rooms over and to the sides of the killing zone. Two Elves will enter the side rooms. I will enter the upper chamber. The three healers will be with me. This will be up close and personal. I don't think we'll have room to wield our spears, so it will be swords and shields. So pack the bows and spears.

"This will be hand-to-hand and bloody. Remember your training with Masters Perseus, Vigash, Drammon, Molotok and Chin. They taught us well. They prepared us for this battle."

We rearranged our numbers into four groups of five, and one group with me, and seven of my elves, including the healers.

"Ready to *transfer*?" They nodded. "Let's go!"

I stepped into a huge open room. Large numbers of men were busy tending fires beneath huge cauldrons. Several others stood with crossbows, looking from arrow loops over the inner court or outer wall. All were busy firing bolts, reloaded and firing again.

Immediately, I directed Nolofinwë and Eámanus against the bowmen at the outer loops and Lenwë and Celebriän against those firing into the courtyard. I sent each of the healers against those tending the cauldrons. I leapt at the few standing around and looking important.

We caught the guardians of the towers by surprise. Long before they could react, they were dead.

"Into the turrets!" I yelled. The four warrior-mages raced to the stairs and into the gate turrets. I ran to the western inner turret into a scene from an abattoir. Blood covered the floor, making it so slippery I almost fell. The walls were spattered with blood. Bodies lay in disarray. My Elves were grim faced. This was their first experience with killing up close and personal.

"Is everyone OK?" I asked. When they nodded, I contacted the other groups. Again, the speed and ferocity of our attacks had overwhelmed the defenders.

"Let's raise the gates."

It took a few moments to figure out how the mechanism worked. They used the same gear system for each of the gates. So, a set of ropes and pulleys had to be changed to operate each set. And it had to be done in order. The outer drawbridge had to be lowered first. Then each of the portcullises could be raised. We tried to open the gates, but failed until we examined them more closely. We had to remove the door bolts at the top and bottom of each door. Then we removed the crossbar. Only then were we able to swing the doors open.

A huge cheer erupted from the mass of warriors pounding on the front gate. Half a dozen Trolls raced in, nearly trampling us. Fortunately, we were able to back into the doorways leading to the upper chambers.

We transferred from the towers back to our encampment. A few of my Tribe were still horrified at the carnage they had wreaked upon the enemy. I alerted the healers, who worked to relieve the mental suffering of their kinfolk.

While our healers were busy with their charges, I contacted the other commanders. Sir Domnall reported that the Ez-Tansk had completed their tunnel under the outer wall and into the inner courtyard. Linda's Orcs had entered the courtyard and were now supporting the Blue Elves who were scaling the inner wall.

The Orcs of the Meadows had mounted their own attack against the southern wall and had scaled it entering the outer courtyard. Far more interestingly, the Octopods had also attacked. Mort and his family had easily scaled both the outer and inner walls. They were busy sowing destruction, wrapping bodies in silk and setting them aside to be carried back to their nests in the mountains.

Armjurst reported great success. Clan Tazhela had built a wonderful tunnel beneath the outer walls. The Elves of the White Cliffs had scaled the walls, singing songs of power and victory. They had met Armjurst's forces in the inner courtyard and driven the enemy back. The Elves then scaled the inner wall, driving the enemy from them.

With the northeastern corner defended from both sides and the upper walls, the Dwarves could go to work undermining the inner wall. Such a task was easy for them. Within an hour, they had created a tunnel over twenty feet wide beneath the walls. Minutes later, Duke Armjurst's army was flowing into the inner courtyard, supported by the Elves of the White Cliffs and Clan Tazhela.

It was easy to hear the heavy pounding of the huge battering ram on the inner gate. Well protected beneath a heavy timber roof, the Trolls swung the massive, iron-tipped log against the oak and iron door. I knew it would take a while, but I also knew that they would be successful in battering it to kindling. The enemy would pile rocks and debris behind it, but the strength of the Trolls and the magical power of the Elves would be too much for the defenders. They would clear a path for Richard's entire army. In the meantime, every one of Beckworth's men and goblins were fully engaged fighting ten thousand attackers.

Yet, I was worried. Massive numbers of Elves, singing songs of power in unison were far more than a few handfuls of Sorcerers could defeat. Elves and Orcs scaled walls in numbers so great they cleared the battlements, permitting Dwarves to undermine the walls, letting vast numbers of Humans follow them.

Yet, the Adjudicars had not entered the fray. What were they doing? Why were they not using their powers to defend the fortress? They had tried to protect the gap we had created in the outer wall, but since then, they'd done nothing. What were they doing?

As long as they did nothing, our forces would prevail. We had captured the outer walls and courtyard. We had penetrated the inner wall to the east and west. As soon as the Trolls had destroyed the inner gate, Richard's vast army would capture the inner courtyard, isolating the keep. And, when the Dwarves mined beneath the keep, it would be over. With Dwarves coming from below, Elves surmounting the walls above, and Humans pouring through the gates, the keep would fall in short order.

Or was this a cat-and-mouse game? We were waiting for them to make their move, but were they waiting for us to make ours? If so, they could have done something when I broke their magical barrier. If so, they could have done something when we transferred into the gatehouse. Why didn't they when they had the chance?

'Wait! Roger Norton! He had immolated himself in an explosion of nuclear proportions. What if all this was an elaborate plot to assemble this continent's armed forces into a small locale? An explosion such as Norton had created would wipe them all out at the same time. The resources of the continent would remain intact. The dwarrows would be open to exploitation. The Elf Realms would wither and die. Only the farms, laborers and lesser folk would survive. They would be easy to capture or subdue for the benefit of their conquerors. Could this be their long plan?

'That is a frightening line of reasoning. But, if so, what could I do about it? Surely, I couldn't pull our forces out now... not on the verge of victory based on my fears. Jubilation T. Cornpone, who snatched defeat from the jaws of victory? No, I needed more than that. But, what?'

I pondered my options. Which were...? I had no idea.

"Gilraën?"

I looked up to see Caranthir with a look of concern on his face.

"Are you well?"

"No, not really. I just had a horrible thought." I raised my voice, "Gather 'round. We may have a problem."

I spent several minutes explaining Roger Norton's self-immolation. I expressed my concern that this was a perfect opportunity to use such a weapon. I just didn't know how to test my fears.

Nienna replied, "You know, we could enter the Void and attack the Adjudicars before they can act."

I nodded, "Yes, I considered that. My question is, are they playing with us? Are they waiting for us? Is it a trap?"

"It could be, but we are twenty-eight; they are two."

"Still, they could have a plan in a plan to trap us."

"Then we don't all go at the same time. We could leave a Cohort in the Void, watching. If needed, they could rescue us. Otherwise, we'd be in the Void ready to cut off their escape. Either way, our numbers are our advantage."

I looked to my tribe, seeking their thoughts.

Galdor replied, "Yes, it sounds good to me. We'd planned on transferring, anyway. So, we do it before they can build up the energy needed to blow themselves to bits."

Caranthir added. "The only question is which of us stays and which of us goes."

"I think I'll leave that one to you. The Cohort that stays behind is critical to his operation. They need to save the rest of us if necessary. Otherwise they need to prevent the Adjudicars from entering the Void, and if that fails, capturing them and returning to the baryonic world with them. You nine will be on your own, and the rest of us will put our lives in your hands. Not that it's a big job or that important or anything."

After a long pause, Caranthir spoke. "I think Nienna should stay in the Void. She isn't any stronger than any of us, nor is her Cohort.

But, she always seems to have control of any situation. She always seems to know what we should do before the rest of us. If I'm in trouble, I want her to rescue me."

When Galdor agreed, I said, "So be it. Nienna, we place our lives in your hands."

She turned a delightful shade of red. "I thank you for your confidence. We will do what we can to protect you all. Will the healers be with me?"

I responded, "No, we may not need them as healers, but we will need their powers as warrior-healers. Their insights might be the difference."

With that settled, I polled my commanders, knowing once I entered the Void I'd be too busy to do it until I had dealt with the Adjudicars. King Richard reported the inner gates were shattered and that his army had entered the inner courtyard in force. Princess Cassandra responded that they too had entered the inner courtyard, but had no contact with the Dwarves of the Mountains. Prince William said he'd joined with his brother, and Duke Armjurst replied that his entire force was on William's left. He also reported a strange army of Orcs attacking the south wall and several extremely hostile Octopods that had withdrawn once a huge, black one had signaled to them.

Everything was in place. Now it was up to me and my elite Tribe.

"Balor ailai si Byr!"

We stood in utter blackness. There was no up or down; no left or right. Our only hope was our own ability to maintain our orientation to the specific space-time from which we had come. I led one Cohort from our starting point to the place I thought was the Keep. I peered from the Void to the baryonic world to discover I was immediately above the Keep.

I signaled to Nienna's Cohort to remain. Sixteen warrior-mages stood in a circle, swords out and shields raised. The two healers and I stood in the middle of the circle, ready to leap into action.

As we descended into the belly of the Keep, we saw huge numbers of men and goblins preparing to defend themselves. Roughly one-quarter of the way 'down,' we came upon a wide, open space. A large throne under a canopy occupied one wall. A long table ran parallel to the wall. Rows of tables ran perpendicular to the throne.

A man sat upon the throne. He looked familiar. He was about the same size as William, but looked a bit like Albert. However, he was pudgy, not trim; flaccid, not alert. He was much like his half-siblings, but just a bit different, and not to his advantage.

As we reappeared into the baryonic world, all my Elves created the strongest wards they knew. We enclosed ourselves in an invisible protective shield that would be impervious to anything we knew. At the same moment, each of them stepped forward, shield before them, sword at the ready. Before an eye could blink, each of them had advanced to the wall, slaughtering everyone in the room, except the man on the throne.

I stepped forward towards the seated man. "I am High Queen Gilraën Gulámae of Jaralii, Queen of the Green Mountains-Maidstone Forest, Jharl Regent of Clan Ghamarazh, and Thane of Clan Ez-Tansk. I am the leader of the army presently capturing this fortress. Might I ask with whom I am speaking?"

The man's eyes, which had been dead, suddenly came to light. A smile crossed his face, and he chuckled. "Ah, it's Miss High and Mighty who deigns to enter my trap. Welcome, prisoner. Once you have entered this domain, you were trapped and may never leave it. And now, your war is over. Within moments, Caierne and Thandekre will immolate me. I will vaporize in an explosion the likes of which this world has never seen. Then, you and I and my earnest brothers, sister, and cousins will die with me.

"Fools! You took the bait. I am their bait, and you fell into their trap. So much for the machinations of Nessa Narmolanya, the one who calls herself Seeress. So much for the ageless Elves, the dour Dwarves, and the impatient Humans. You will all die, and I will have brought you down – all of you!"

"Seize him!" I commanded. Together we surrounded him with rings of power, lifting him from his throne.

I concentrated on Nienna Lossëhelin.

Her reply was muted and scratchy, as though she was talking through a closed door.

"Pull us out. Him, too! Now!"

Suddenly, the walls disappeared. We were standing in the Void. "Gather 'round! *Transfer* to our encampment. Now!"

We stepped out on the trampled green grass, the bright sunlight blinding us.

"Watch him closely," I commanded my healers. "If he changes in any way, *transfer* him into the Void."

I checked with my commanders. Everything was progressing as planned. The Dwarves had tunneled into the Keep and had opened the gate. Elves had entered and were battling magicians of such great power that they were stymied and unable to advance to the higher levels.

"Has he changed at all?"

"Yes," they replied. "He seems weaker, almost as though he was starving."

"He might be. Use your skills to determine his status and heal what you can. However, monitor him closely. If he appears to be expanding and absorbing energy, *Balor* him into the Void, and leave him."

"The rest of us will return to deal with Caierne and Thandekre, the two Adjudicars. This time, we will search for them."

We *transferred* into the Void. "Nienna, you did a fantastic job getting us out of there. You did so well, I want you to do it again. The rest of you, same formation. This time, we descend until we find them. Then, we overpower them."

We assembled in a circle, with the two healers and me in the middle. This time we inched our way 'down' one level at a time. However, we also stopped long enough to kill everyone as we went.

We were four levels above the ground when we felt a huge surge of magical energy. "They are one level down. Protect yourselves. Be prepared to attack. Go!"

The center of the room was empty. Several men stood near a wide stone stair, the only entry into the level. Other than that, the entire broad space was utterly empty.

Caranthir's squad was facing in that direction. Instantly they raced forward, attacking with all their strength and speed. I was about to follow them when Galdor's Cohort raced past me to support their kinfolk.

Almost as quickly, they slowed as though they were trapped in molasses. Two men had spun to face us. Each held a hand toward us, palm outward. Eight of the mightiest Elves on the planet raised their palms and pushed back. They took a step forward. The two men gritted their teeth and lines of stress appeared in their foreheads.

Galdor's Cohort stepped to the sides of their kin, doubling their numbers. Together, they stepped forward, closing almost into touching distance. I joined them, adding my power to theirs. I felt the Adjudicar's resolve crumble. They withdrew within themselves. Then, one said, '*Transfer.*'

I stepped up and created a massive barrier around them, much like the one the Adjudicars had created to replace the battered wall.

They fought it with all their strength. One created a needle, which he pressed against my barrier. At first, the thin, sharp needle penetrated. I severed it with a sharp cleaver.

They tried combining their power, but it was too little, too late. I separated them with a second impenetrable barrier. Then I selected one. It turned out to be my old nemesis, Caierne.

"We meet again, Adjudicar!"

He knew of me, but unable to respond as he wished. He was, after all, somewhat constrained.

"You have met your match, Adjudicar. Prolong your agony, Adjudicar. Tell me who you are."

"Release me, and I'll tell you all you wish to know."

"Hah!" I laughed. "And, why should I release my hold on you?"

"Because, if you don't I won't tell you anything."

"Oh, no?" I probed his mind, and none too gently. He defended his mind well, but his present circumstance worked against him. In his tiny world, he couldn't access much power either to defend or to attack. So, my probe was as a hammer striking an egg.

It took him a while to recover sufficiently to resume our interrogation. I asked him, "Enough or should I repeat, Adjudicar? It should be obvious by now that I can peel your mind back one layer at a time, or you could simply tell me. Who are you? Where did you come from? What are you doing here?"

He was silent, trying to be adamant. So I tapped him. It was just a little one, but enough to get his attention.

"I am Caierne. I am an Adjudicar."

"Ah, the old name, rank and serial number? Well, it will not work. Try again.' I tapped him again.

"We come from a distant planet, which is unpronounceable in this form." His mind spoke a hissing, slithering, sliding sound.

"OK, so where is it?"

"From here? I don't know. I came from the planet called Gesh, which is 'pretty' in their language. Before that was Tschazhakh which is Orb of Smoke and Ash. Before that was... some other planet."

I saw worlds arise in his memory. Each was similar in that it was warm with a nitrogen and oxygen atmosphere. There was an abundance of liquid water and bluish skies. That is, they were all Earthlike, similar to this world.

"We conquer planets. Once we used force. It was expensive, bloody and wasteful. However, then we discovered magic. We didn't know how to use it. So, we manipulated our DNA. It took centuries for us to imbue magic into our very being, but we succeeded."

I saw tall, slim bipedal beings. Their arms and legs were long. Their heads were small with flat faces. They had small mouths and four eyes. Their brains were not in their heads, but in their upper chests, protected by the bones of their torsos.

"Over the centuries we became ever more powerful until we warred with each other. We destroyed ourselves in a war that left us mutilated in body and spirit. We thought our era of conquest was at an end."

His memories of that war were filled with fear and terror. Beings were destroyed in the most horrific manners.

"However, strange machines landed upon our planet. We knew some advanced race was reaching out to find other planets to explore. And so we laid a trap. We left traces of life in the path of their machines. It was only a matter of time before more machines arrived and then animated beings."

Small, squat beings descended from boxy machines that landed in plumes of fire. Like all explorers, they were wearing protective suits. Only later did they appear as bipedal, symmetrical beings with two arms, two legs and a large head.

"But we had changed. We were no longer mighty conquerors striding across the heavens. Instead, we had become mere remnants of our former glory. We had regressed millions of years, appearing as blobs of protoplasm, but with senses to perceive the world and a mind to understand and to remember.

"And so it was that when those would-be conquerors of our world walked upon it, we waited patiently. Then, when they fell to rest, we aligned our bodies with theirs, using our magic to becoming as one with them. Once within their bodies, we could control their minds. In that way, we regained our mobility, while disguising ourselves from others. We were now magical beings possessed of the great technologies of our hosts."

He pictured himself entering a body through the torso and affixing his body around the spinal column and base of the brain.

"Since then, we have conquered half the galaxy… one planet at a time."

He pictured the planets of which he had spoken earlier, a feeling of joy and accomplishment filling his mind.

"Have you always used this underhanded method?"

"Underhanded? NO! Eminently sensible. We seek out the ambitious, and offer them their world. They seldom refuse. We undermine their society, conquering one tiny piece at a time. We foment wars, weakening entire societies. Over time, we win. It is inevitable."

"And, how many of you are on this world?"

"Thandekre and I are here. There are others on different landmasses."

He pictured himself and the other Adjudicar. He also flashed images of several others, of which a few were of extraordinary power. I reviewed them several times, trying to burn their faces into my mind.

"How many are you in all the worlds?"

"Billions upon Billions. As I said, we have conquered half a galaxy. The only limit is our ability to travel between planets. Perhaps when we have conquered the entire galaxy, then we will have to consider other forms of travel."

His mind created an image much like that of Hubble Space Telescope. Thousands little pixels of light spread across a vast black background.

"Yes, how do you do that... travel between planets?"

"You have already experienced it, Anthony!"

I was shocked! '*Anthony? How did he know*?' "And, how is it you know such things?"

He choked a laugh. "Who do you think developed the games? Who do you think tested you? Who do you think powered the transport? Who do you think decided which of you would go where and what your form and function would be?

"You are the exception, Gilraën Gulámae. You escaped, to the ultimate destruction of our plans. You should have been the most powerful warrior-mage in the service of Lord Beckworth. You would have led his armies. You would have destroyed King Richard. The Elves would have cowered in their Realms, and the Dwarves in the dwarrows. With the Humans defeated, you would have led the

Krells against the Elves. And with them gone, you would have led
the Krelli, Trolls and Goblins against the isolated Dwarf clans. Only
then would you attack the final two: the Breccian Mountains first
and the Dwarf Mountains second. We would control this entire land,
leading our way to the total occupation and control of this orb."

His mind flashed with feelings of lust and joy.

"But, that interfering old biddy, Nessa Narmolanya, intercepted
you. She added her power to ours, changing you into an Elf, imbuing
you with far greater powers than we had anticipated or could have
granted to you. So, instead of profiting from your strengths, we have
fallen to them."

His resentment filled his mind, clouding all his other emotions.

"Is there any way I can extricate you from your host?"

Again, I felt the sensation of a humorless laugh.

"No, you can do nothing. When this host dies, separation will be
most difficult. It is likely that his death will be mine."

I felt a glimmer of hope. "But, not necessarily so?"

"No, not necessarily."

"So, you could go on and on, destroying world after world
throughout time?"

"Unlikely."

"But possible?"

I felt his concurrence.

"So, where on this world are your comrades?"

"No! That I will not give you. It is yours to find them. However,
they know of you. They are expecting you. They are already
planning your demise. You may kill me, but your death is already in
hand. Good-bye, Elf! My only joy is that you will soon join me
beyond the Void."

With that, his mind went blank. His presence disappeared, and
only a husk of protoplasm remained. However, I was not convinced,
and so burned it to destruction.

I turned to the adamantine box containing the Adjudicar, Thandekre, but he was also gone. And so, I utterly immolated his remains.

I addressed my tribe. "It is done. They are dead. Relax your spell, but be vigilant."

I engaged my prescience with Nienna. "It is done. Remove us into the Void."

Moments later the twenty-eight of us stood together. We clasped hands and simultaneously transferred to our encampment.

Our first thought was food. We had employed a huge amount of energy and had to replenish our internal stores. Bread and wine with slices of bhar and chedz sufficed for the present.

With my mouth still full of my first bites of the sandwich, I began contacting my commanders. I picked up the mirror and sought King Richard.

"Queen Gilraën, what is so important that you should commune with me in the midst of battle?"

"We have killed the Adjudicars and captured Beckworth. The war is won. We need only win the battle."

"That is wonderful news, indeed. We have entered the inner courtyard in force and are investing the keep. What had been fierce resistance has suddenly ceased. Is that your doing?"

"Yes, it probably is. We just killed the Adjudicars, so they are no longer defending it. You should be able to clear the keep, before you descend into the cellars and catacombs to destroy the last of Beckworth's forces."

I then contacted Prince William, Princess Cassandra, and Duke Armjurst, in that order. Finally, I contacted Thane Defghamask, and Jharls Azkhalish, Morthanzhemian, Worzhemacht and Galmerstain. However, as with all the others, I cautioned them that the enemy's leaders had been killed or captured, but not their armies, which were still alive and well and were fighting for their lives. I made doubly sure to emphasize the need of the Dwarves to clear the cellars and catacombs of all enemy soldiers.

And so, the battle for Shalal'm Caer continued throughout the day. By nightfall, we cleared the outer and inner courtyards of the enemy. The keep was still heavily defended, as were the subterranean chambers. Men, Elves, Dwarves, Orcs, Krelli and Trolls were relieved to eat and relax, while troops that had not engaged the enemy took up the forward positions. Gradually, everyone in the armies was fed and watered. The many slept, while the few stood guard.

* * *

Dawn broke, but we did not renew our attack. Mummia was an hour above the horizon before I stood within the inner court before the keep. I raised my voice so that all could hear.

"I am High Queen Gulámae, leader of the army that has defeated you. I have captured Lord Beckworth. He is under my guard. I have killed the Adjudicars, Caierne and Thandekre. My armies have captured your walls, your catacombs, and the depths of this castle. You are all that that remains of Beckworth's army.

"Surrender now, with honor. We will treat you as prisoners of war, feed, water, and clothe you. Your hurts will be healed, and your dead properly buried.

"If you do not, I will resume my attacks upon you. You will die ignobly, and the porg will eat your bodies.

"Come out without your weapons and with your arms raised."

We waited. Many minutes passed. Then a man appeared. A few more followed him. Then a thin trickle followed, which rapidly became a raging river. Over three hundred men and two hundred goblins arrayed themselves before the gates of the keep in the inner courtyard.

The war was over. I could go home… or could I?

* * * * *

Chapter 5 – Victory and Death

A ragged cheer began nearest to the keep. Gradually, it spread, encompassing more and more until a mighty roar of ten thousand voices rent the air. Men leapt up and down, holding each other in their arms. Elves raised their voices in songs of victory. Dwarves chanted lustily. Orcs shrieked. Trolls bellowed. Krelli hollered. Octopods clicked. The entire army rejoiced, as they had never done before in the history of this world.

Slowly, prisoners of war were gathered and shuttled into holding areas. Dwarves and Orcs scoured the deep caves, caverns and recesses beneath the fortress to root out the last elements of Beckworth's army. Beneath the keep were enormous armories. Living spaces had been rehabbed, becoming vast kitchens and storage rooms filled with foodstuff and ingredients. Cold cellars preserved meats, grain and roots. The fortress could have withstood a siege for many months, if not years.

My Tribe and I secured the throne room with a few well-chosen commands. We created a raised dais with me sitting in the high throne and my Elves and Ghillies seated behind me at three long tables.

My Elves and Charioteers found many long tables and benches. We found lots of individual chairs, which appeared to be similar in all respects. We even found the great galleys, with huge stoves, ovens, pantries and all the other facilities needed to feed thousands of people.

It took us a while to furnish the throne room to our likings. We needed an arrangement to seat the notables from Richard's court, and each of the courts of all the clans, tribes, families and other group entities that had worked so hard to secure this victory.

We arranged chairs and tables along other sides of the room. On the southeast side, I had chairs for Thane Defghamask, my deputy commander, and chairs for Jharls Azkhalish, Morthanzhemian, Worzhemacht, and Galmerstain. To the northeast, we arranged chairs for Duke Armjurst, King Aeradir, and Jharl Tazmatahela. On the northwest side, I had chairs for King Richard, King Glorfindel, Queen Eilol and Prince William. On the southwest, I placed chairs for Princess Cassandra, Yurchist Linda and King Fingolfin. We arranged tables and chairs behind the head tables. Hopefully, we'd have enough room for everyone.

I had talked with the Krelli and the Trolls inviting them to the soiree. The Trolls weren't interested; neither were the Octopods. The Krelli laughed, Integrity saying, "We couldn't even fit through the doors."

In the meantime, we managed to locate the cooks and galley staff. We brought them back from their hiding places and returned them to their duties. I also asked knowledgeable cooks from the courts of King Richard, the Elves, Dwarves and Orcs to lend their expertise for their particular races.

Late that afternoon, the nobles from all the tribes, clans, families and groups gathered. My Tribe assisted each to their tables and ensured that their favorite libations were in plentiful supply. Officially, I sat at the head table surrounded by my Tribe and supporters. Of course, some of the groups objected to the seating arrangements. All wanted to be closer to the top of the room. All wanted preferences of some kind or another. However, I squelched their arguments.

There were some complaints about the seating arrangements and which groups were adjacent to each other. I had deliberately placed them in battle order around the room. So, the Orcs and Dwarves, Humans and Elves were sitting next to each other. Despite their reticence, the effects of potent beverages and the joy of victory overcame all prejudices and past grievances.

Then, the food arrived, and the room suddenly went silent. The cooks had done what they could to satisfy the individual tastes of each group. We ate and drank and talked for hours. It was a joyous occasion for one and all.

Then it was time for the speeches. I began, "I was brought to this world as a stranger with a specific commission. I was to free this kingdom from the usurper, Lord Beckworth. I am a Human male by birth, an Elf woman by design, and a Dwarf by acclamation.

"I came here as a stranger. On my first day, Dame Eleanor, Viscountess Grampus befriended me. This was a most propitious meeting. She brought my little household together: Rosie, my maid; Beryl, my chambermaid; Daisy, my assistant maid; Dorothea, my cook. It was Dame Eleanor who taught me to act and dress properly. It was she who introduced me to her Princess Cassandra of the Blue Vale. And it was Cassandra who introduced me to her brother, Prince William.

"It was Prince William who introduced me to Master Perseus, Master Vigash, Master Drammon, Master Chin and Master Molotok. It was they who taught me humility, while teaching me to be a warrior.

"It was Prince William who introduced me to Master Talbot, Master Norton, Master Falsworth, Master Thackery and Master Richmond, Baron of Phaedham. It was they who introduced me to magic – its uses and abuses. It was because of them that I learned to protect Prince William. It was because of them I learned to hunt sorcerers and avoid Krelli.

"Yet, it was a Krell named Justice who did catch me, but then became my friend. He introduced me to Theriozemphia, Ozhemia's Shelf, Clan Ozhemia, and the people called Dwarves. He also introduced me to King Mort, who got so drunk he rolled up into a ball, and tumbled out of Ozhemia's Shelf down the hill all the way to the cottage of Ethyl, Wise Woman of Goerskim. Justice was of no help. He fell asleep in her yard beneath a large tree. He gave his life to free this land in the battle to seize this fortress and to capture Lord Beckworth."

"In my second expedition to discover Beckworth's dispositions, I discovered the great farmlands between Barstough and Brook's Tavern. I also discovered that they had imported farm animals and crops from Earth. These discoveries piqued my curiosity. Who would want to bring ruminant mammals or domesticated fowl across interstellar space?

"It was on that journey where I met Sir Domnall of Dungrampus," I nodded to him.

"It was also on that journey that I traversed the mighty mountain realm of Yurchist Linda. Let me apologize to you for not formally introducing myself at that time. We have known each other for many years. I hope that we will renew our friendship soon."

We exchanged nods and smiles. She raised her glass to me, shouting, "You look a damn sight better than you used to, Gilraën."

I laughed and continued. "It was after I left your wonderful realm that I returned to the Dwarf Mountains. It was then that I was hunted by another deadly predator – a Gaunt!"

There was a gasp from around the room.

"Yes, a full-grown Gaunt hunting food for her two kits. I was lucky to have shot her with an arrow otherwise my story on this planet would have been short. However, instead of killing her, I healed her. We departed as friends.

"I continued my exploration of the Dwarf Mountains, where an Adjudicar named Caierne captured me. Fortunately, he left me in the hands of a lesser sorcerer. Although I could not escape, I could use my mind to seek out other prescient beings, begging for help.

"That was the second time I met the Gaunt, who I had named Miss Puss. She killed or drove off those who would have dragged me, bound and gagged to the fortress of Lord Beckworth, thus saving me a third time. She then convinced me to mount her back, whereupon, she brought me to her lair, where I met her kits, Tom and Miss Cindy. They thought of me as a toy, and thoroughly enjoyed chasing me, catching me, tossing me and then licking my skin off. Fortunately, they were playing, and Miss Puss protected me when their play was too rough.

"I went hunting and fed them the kill from my hand. They came to know and trust me. So it was when Tom was caught in a gigantic foot trap, I had to save his paw. It is impossible to see those magnificent creatures playing, running, tumbling, climbing, and racing to consign one to a life of a cripple, which might even kill it because it could not hunt. Thereafter, I was as one with my blue, feline family.

"However, all was not well. When drawing water from a nearby stream, I found it was poisoned. I traced the poison back to its source in a nearby mountain. I followed it into the mountain to discover a huge cavern filled with Dwarves. I traveled through its length until I arrived at a great castle and keep. There, I met Jharl Azkhalish and Jharlish Emendahlia."

I nodded the Jharl, who hoisted a large mug in a salute.

"My information was important to the Jharl and his entire clan. They were deeply concerned that they were poisoning the stream, and ultimately the River Coulee. And so, Clan Ez-Tansk befriended me. Then, I discovered a plot to kill Jharl Azkhalish, his thanes and squires. I found the culprit and put an end to the plot. In return, Jharl Azkhalish honored me by naming me Thane of Diplomacy of Clan Ez-Tansk, and I have worn that coronet with pride and dignity since that time. I hope, My Jharl, I have honored our Clan." I bowed to him.

He stood and raised his voice. "Indeed, Thanelish Gilraën Gulámae, you have represented the highest values of Clan Ez-Tansk. We are proud you have chosen to be one of us." When he sat, every member of the clan pounded their tables and yelled Dwarfish approval.

"It was during that time that I discovered that Lord Beckworth was using the intricate network of passageways and tunnels in the Dwarf Mountains to surreptitiously transfer large numbers of troops against Dungrampus. Together, the forces of Jharl Azkhalish and Sir Domnall defeated them, but this was just the first skirmish.

"I then discovered that Clan Ghamarazh was permitting Lord Beckworth's forces travel unimpeded throughout the Dwarf Mountains. When I arrived at their southern gates, they attempted to capture me. However, I escaped, ferreted out their Jharl, and, using my Elvin capability to delve into another's mind, discovered his treachery, which I revealed to the Truth-Seekers. After they deposed him, I took up the Regency of the Jharldom of Clan Ghamarazh, naming Squires Gildnaramansk and Ranthathamghazk as judges of

154

the election of the new Jharl. In the meantime, I named Than Defghamask as the commander-in-chief of the army of Clan Ghamarazh, and charged him with the defense of his dwarrow and all of Dwarfdom.

"It was at that time that I discovered that both the Elves and the Dwarves had committed themselves to neutrality in the war between Lord Beckworth and King Richard. Any deviation from neutrality could lead to their utter annihilation, as had happened to the Elves of the Great Forest. I reasoned that if the Elves and the Dwarves were under the command of Humans, then they could be ordered to attack Lord Beckworth without violating their previous agreements. They could do this because they were ordered to attack by a higher authority than even the Jharlmor or the Seeress.

"Additionally, I, as both a Thanelish of Clan Ez-Tansk and the Regent Jharl of Clan Ghamarazh could command the Dwarves, alleviating them of any responsibility. When King Richard agreed to come under my command, this became my war against the Adjudicars.

"And so we sit here this night, savoring the fruits of our victory. Yes, we have won a mighty victory. And, most fortunately, because of our careful planning and the skills of our warriors, the cost in deaths and injuries was low. Yet, there are the dead, the maimed, and the wounded. I ask every healer to attend to those in need. Regardless of whether the injured are Dwarf, Elf, Orc, Troll, Krelli, Octopod or some other species, they are worthy of our skills. Their families should not suffer because their loved ones fought the great evil.

"Yet, we have won only a battle. The war is still ahead of us. Duke Armjurst has informed me of the plight of Narwortland. I know nothing of Farrowspike, but I must assume the poison of the Adjudicars has afflicted them. We must free all of Jaralii from their scourge.

"Finally, we must do what we can to create a world in which all of us can live in peace and harmony. We must establish borders within which each group can live and prosper… especially for the Humans. We know that Humans are a plague upon this land. They are grasping and conniving and covet lands beyond their own. Elves can defend their Realms simply by their creation. Dwarves, Orcs and others can only defend their lands through force of arms. Yet, Humans will win by waging continuous war from generation to generation, only because of their numbers. It is critical that we establish clear and unambiguous boundaries, defining those realms that are exclusively Human, Elfin, Dwarfish, Orcish, or of some other species and those which are common to us all.

"Therefore, I propose a governing body in which each species is properly represented. The Dwarves long ago reached a similar conclusion. That which had been a familial outgrew its ability to control itself simply because it had become too large a group. And so, Squires, and Thanes, and Jharls and ultimately the Jharlmor came into existence to settle controversies between Clans. Thus, I propose a governing body to settle disputes between claimants, to establish uniform codes of conduct, to establish the rules of commerce, and to maintain the peace among all the people of this land.

"I thank you all for your participation in this great endeavor. I congratulate all of you in your victory. I appeal to you all to make this the turning point in our history, to establish a new, just and peaceful world."

I sat.

Slowly at first, but then with ever greater enthusiasm every one of the beings in the room stood and cheered. They cheered and shouted. They shouted and danced. They danced and sang. They sang and drank and danced with abandon.

It was a joy to watch. Squat, heavy-legged Dwarves stomping with light, lithe and prancing Elves. William, Cassandra, Richard and I joined the merriment. I do not know how many I danced with or how much I drank. I remember talking animatedly with Linda. I remember dancing with Azkhalish until Emendahlia stepped in to dance with her husband. I warmly remember dancing with William, kissing him and feeling the warmth of his embrace.

* * *

I also remember awakening with Mummia in my eyes and the mother of all hangovers in my brain. I groaned and rolled over, but something was in the way. I bumped it, and it growled, "It's too early. Go back to sleep!"

'What the hell?'

I sat up. I was in my tent, in my bed, under my wrap. So was he!

"OMG!"

However, I did have all my clothes on. So did he. One of us smelled. I sniffed. It was me. I sniffed again. Him, too. I wished I were home. Rosie would have a gravy boat filled with hot, soapy water. Daisy would have fresh clothes. Beryl would have a hot cup of thrak awaiting me in my nook, and Dorothea would have a hot breakfast ready to serve.

William rolled over, his mouth partly open. Argh! He had a horrible case of halitosis! It smelled like a pig's sty on a hot summer day. It was too much for me, even in my condition.

I abandoned my quarters, seeking a place I could cleanse myself. I returned to the keep, seeking Beckworth's living quarters. When I found it, I located a bath, gravy boat and all. Now, I need a staff, but where to find them. Obviously, I needed chambermaids of some kind, but where to find them?

Then an idea struck me – Princess Cassandra! She has a staff, and she bathes. She must know how to obtain a staff.

I rushed to the western walls and searched out Princess Cassandra's quarters. She was suffering greatly from the previous evening's celebration. She looked at me with a caustic eye.

"YOU!" She said it much too loudly and grimaced. She whispered, "I hurt. Loud noises hurt. Bright lights hurt. Even moving is painful." She stood, none too gracefully, and staggered to a chair. She motioned for me to sit in a second one. "What can I do for you, Gilraën?"

"Cassie, I need a bath! I need clean clothes. I need to feel human… or Elvin or whatever!"

She tried to laugh, but grimaced instead. "Oh, my poor head. My poor stomach. Why did you let me drink so much?"

"Me? Since when am I responsible for your actions?"

"Since you declared yourself to be High Queen."

"Ah, so your hangover is my fault?"

"Yes. You served the brew. You staged the party. You danced and celebrated into the night. None of us could leave until you did. It was a good thing William spirited you off, or we'd still be there."

I tried to laugh, but the pain in my head was too much. I groaned, holding my head in my hands. "As my loyal subject, it was your responsibility to protect me from all hazards. You failed in your duty to your queen. So there!"

Her smile morphed into a grimace. "Well, you are half right. Anyway, what can I do for you?"

"Cassie, I need a bath! I need to be clean for a change. I need a fresh change of clothes."

She laughed again. "So do I." She called to her maid. "We need two baths prepared. We need a fresh change of clothes. Can you arrange that?"

"Your Highness, we have located a tub and can find another. And, you have two chests of clothes. It will take a while to heat the water. We do have soap, but it is common and a bit harsh. So, use it sparingly and not on your hair."

One hour later, we sat side by side, luxuriating in a nice hot bath. Our legs hung out over the end, and our uppers were too exposed, but it didn't matter. It was hot and wet, and we were clean and smelled like soap rather than sweat, blood and grime.

Her maid returned with garments fit for a princess. I contemplated them for just a moment. Then, I said to Cassandra, "Cassie, they are beautiful, but we're on a battlefield, not a castle. I would wonder if there is something more suitable for a warrior-queen?"

"Such as?"

"I really need leggings, boots and other clothes that I can wear on the battlefield. Then, I need to clean my armor and my weapons. Then, I have to inspect the troops, Clans, Tribes and other groups. Only then, can I become a normal person again."

Cassandra looked to her maid. She scurried off to return minutes later with clothes more suitable for battle.

"Cassie, since I've got to do it, shall I start with your army? Then, we can have something to eat before I rush off to one of the other armies. At least, we can be clean and have a bite in comfort."

We spent a delightful morning. First, we visited Jharl Azkhalish and Jharlish Emendahlia, who were gracious, as always. "Mine Thane, you have outdone yourself! You have fulfilled my every expectation of you."

We chatted with Sir Domnall, who was pleased to rekindle our friendship.

I hadn't really known King Sáralondë, but Cassandra knew him well. They were neighbors on the ends of the same river, which, thanks to several locks the Elves and Humans had constructed, the river was navigable its full length.

I then went south, into the Mountains. Squire Gildnaramansk and Squire Ranthathamghazk met with me. "Jharl Regent Gulámae, Clan Ghamarazh has chosen its next Jharl. We the Judges of the Election confirm that all the Thanes and Squires have agreed that Thane Defghamask has acted as our Jharl in the gravest and most difficult of times. We agree that he shall lead us in time of peace, having proven himself before the entire Clan."

"That is wonderful news, My Squires. I agree with all of you that Thane Defghamask has earned the loyalty of Clan Ghamarazh. When will the formal installation be held?"

"In two weeks."

"Obviously, I will be there. Be sure to keep me informed, so that I may place the crown of Ghamarazh on Jharl Elect Defghamask's head."

They bowed, saying, "We will be honored by your presence."

My meeting with Jharl Morthanzhemian was equally joyous. I asked, "I assume that Master Theriozemphia will now reopen Ozhemia's Shelf?"

He laughed loudly, "But of course. I expect the good master Theriozemphia will once again provide potables and edibles for the delight and enjoyment of all."

Jharl Worzhemacht was his grouchy, irritable self. "Everyone will seek repairs or replacements for armor, swords, helmets, shields and every other thing damaged or destroyed in this horrific war."

I commiserated with him. "Yes, I am sure that will be the case. However, yours is the Clan of Weapons, and none are like to them. I'm sure your artisans will be pleased for the work, and your treasury for the gold paid for their services."

He smiled wryly, answering, "Yes, it may take years, but we shall persevere."

I had never met Jharl Galmerstain. Maintaining his subterfuge, I asked, "My Jharl, I hope your combined exercise with the other Clans of the Mountains was worthwhile. Did you accomplish your objectives?"

Without the slightest hint of a smile, he responded, "Many thanks, Thanelish Gulámae, for inquiry. Much learned we. Experience much did we. Renewed bonds of kinship with all Mountain Dwarves. Attend installing of Defghamask Jharl you will?"

"Indeed, it is my duty. I am the Jharl Regent of Ghamarazh. It is my duty to pass on the crown to the proper Jharl, now that he has been properly elected. I assume that you will attend and extend your formal greetings to the new Jharl?"

"Dzha, not attending be gravest insult."

I moved on to the east, meeting with Duke Armjurst. "Without you, we would have lost," I told him. "You were courageous sending your armies northward, leaving your shire unprotected."

He smiled ruefully. "No, they were well protected. Green Glens extended their protection to the east, and Worphelia drove their herds to their eastern pastures, which are within my Duchy. By doing so, they also protected the lands of White Cliffs and Zhaenstain."

"Yes, I noted that, but I preferred to maintain the fiction."

"Yes, that is a good idea. We have rid ourselves of only half the Adjudicars in this land. Almost half of the lands of Narwortland is the Realm of the Elves of Green Glens. The Adjudicars are still powerful, and we don't want another Tribe annihilated."

"Yes, that will be our next objective, if I am permitted to do so."

"Why would you not?"

"I am here under contract. I have fulfilled my portion of that contract. I must be paid, and then I return to my life."

"Payment?" He scowled.

"Oh, yes. I shall receive a tithe of the treasury of Lord Beckworth, plus the gold guaranteed me, plus any booty that I capture or seize."

His eyes widened, swallowing his cheeks. "You will be the richest person in all of Trahe!"

"Probably." I shrugged (What else could I do?) "But, I was the one who won this war and took the greatest chances to do so. And, now, I leave, so that I shall not become the dictator of this world. They will remember me as its savior not as the most recent despot."

As we talked, Armjurst led me to Jharl Tazmatahela's camp, where he departed for his own. Thane Pethelzha greeted me. "You are come! Good. Formation was predicted. Good tunnel."

"How long did it take you to complete it?"

"Just two days. Very hard rock it was. Very steep. This way, that way, hard climb, but Armjurst climb it, beat Beckworth. Why you not protect him? We tunnel; you not there. Many hurt, killed. You come too late almost."

"Magic!" I responded. "They built a magical wall, and it took us some time to destroy it. We did, though."

"It is well you did, else they would have driven us back with great losses."

"Fortunately, we penetrated the magic, and we were successful. And, a large part of the credit goes to Clan Tazhela, My Jharl."

I moved on to King Richard's camp. Richard and William were both there, as were their commanders and supporters. General Abuahad greeted me most warmly.

"Splendid campaign, Gilraën. Oh, I'm sorry, Queen Gulámae. I was remembering our days at the castle. Those were good days. I am hopeful we will see them, again."

Suddenly, a middle-aged woman burst in upon us. She rushed up to me and embraced me. "Mistress Superior! How wonderful to see you, again. Just a few weeks ago we sheltered in the lea of half a barn. Now, we stand victorious on the field of battle. What a wonderful day!"

"High Mistress Gertrude, what a pleasure to see you again. Did you travel with Talbot?"

"Yes, and Brahms. We all had our jobs to do in this war. We were protecting William's battalions from Beckworth's sorcerers. We were successful, and our Battalions penetrated the walls and successfully drove back the counter-attack. We suffered light losses and have been able to heal almost all the injured."

"How many of William's battalions were killed?"

Abuahad answered, "Forty-four with one hundred six casualties. Of them, ninety-four recovered, nine will recover and the rest... we will retire with honors, befitting their injuries and status."

"And, Richard's army?"

"I can't be sure, but I believe I heard about a hundred dead, mostly from the towers and the gatehouse."

"Injured?"

"I have not heard anything. You should talk with the King."

"Good idea. Where are they?"

Abuahad pointed, and I wandered off in that general direction. I found large numbers of injured men, being tended by an inadequate number of healers. I summoned my healers, and we set to work.

After just a few hours, we had tended to a couple of hundred who would recover, and some whose injuries could not be healed. Them we counseled as well as we could.

By that time, I was tired and ready to eat. I intended to return to Richard's pavilion and beg a meal. I found the large pavilion surrounded by several large tents. Wandering towards them, several spear-wielding soldiers confronted me. They stood in front of me, halberd's points directed at me.

"Halt!" their leader demanded.

I would not put up with their crap. I waved my hand, tossing them aside like tissue paper in the wind. More than a dozen others raced to intercept me. Again, I waved my hand, dropping them on the ground. Suddenly arrows and spears were flying at me! I raised a ward, deflecting them all, then called to my Tribe, "To me! Fully armed! To me!"

Moments later, twenty-seven Elves surrounded me. "Kill all who attempt to interfere. We need to find the King and Prince William. Forward!"

We raised our shields and brandished our spears, extending wards around us.

"Spread out. Galdor, with me, forward. Nienna to the right; Caranthir to the left. Find the King and Prince; kill anyone who interferes."

Talbot, Gertrude and Brahms appeared at my side. "Gilraën, what is happening?"

"I don't know, but these soldiers are attacking me, and I have not located either King Richard or Prince William. Help me find them and protect them from whatever is happening."

I rushed to the large pavilion, trailed by Galdor's Cohort, Talbot and his family. I burst in to see Richard and William slumped in their chairs. Men, who I immediately determined were Sorcerers, stood behind them each with a large knife at their throats. Behind them stood... Beckworth!

I felt a huge force seize me, holding me in place. Instantly, I reinforced my mental defenses and prepared to attack.

He laughed. "Took you long enough, *Elf*," he sneered. "You killed Caierne and Thandekre, but you failed miserably. They were my underlings - mere dabblers in the true arts.

"Let me introduce my Sorcerers, Till and Chamworthy. No doubt you see their knives. If you make any move against me, they will kill brother Richard and brother William. You are mine!"

I knew what I had to do. I loosed the Soul Blades on my inner arms, letting them slip into my hands. I flipped my arms at them, commanding, "Kill!" The two Sorcerers were dead before they could flinch. I then reinforced my mental helmet and launched my attack, striking into the depth of his magical core with a spike of power.

He hit me like a ton of bricks… or a ton of most anything else, for that matter. Not only did he blunt my attack, but he almost smashed through my defenses. Before I could retaliate, Beckworth began to taunt me.

"Come on, *Elf*! You're supposed to be so tough? Hah! Now, you're going to learn the depth of your defeat. I have disabled your friends." He motioned to Galdor's Cohort, Talbot, Gertrude and Brahms.

His arm swept toward William and Richard. "Soon, it will be they who explode, killing all the Humans, Elves, Dwarves and everyone else who stood against me. All of you will die, and we will seize this land and this world, as we have so many others.

"You put up a good fight, *Elf*. I thought you had me when you appeared in my throne room. I thought I had sealed it against all intrusions, but you surprised me. I had to think quickly and get rid of you before you could undermine my plans completely. Either Caierne or Thandekre could have done it, but you murdered them before they could take action. Now I shall do what they failed to do.

"Prepare to die, *Elf*!" His grip on my mind tightened, threatening to crush my magical helmet and all.

With a growing sense of desperation, I fought him, rebuilding my defenses. He was immensely powerful. Perhaps I had bitten off more than I could chew. I needed time to renew my energy and reinforce my helmet. I wanted him to brag, to waste time, to tell me more that I could use to find and destroy any other Adjudicars on this planet. Fortunately, he didn't fail me.

"Ah, you struggle, *Elf*. Hah! *Elf*, indeed. You should have been mine, you know? Somehow that witch interfered, redirecting your transport from Earth, and using my power to change you into what you have become. It's a shame. With you, this war would have been over, and I would be master of this continent, and, ultimately, this whole world.

"No doubt, I'd have to convince the others to accept me as their leader. Your killing of Caierne and Thandekre actually helped me. When I kill you, it will show them that I am the most powerful on this continent, not them." Images of two others flashed through his mind: one tall and broad, the other short and massive. "They will have to accept my leadership or fight me, and they won't want to do that… not after I was the one to kill you.

"Then, I shall reach for the Supreme Council."

In his mind, he was sitting at a large, round table confronting four other Adjudicars. He pictured their faces clearly. I would recognize them when I next saw them. I got the impression that they were on different continents on this planet. I also got the idea that there were several Adjudicars in Narwortland and in Farrowspike vying for leadership positions among the Adjudicars.

I felt him exert his strength trying to end our confrontation. I guessed that he had said his all. As he was busy bragging, I was renewing my mental helmet, strengthening it, and burnishing it to a mirror finish. Feeling him weakening, I shot a spike deep into the heart of his magical center.

Beckworth recoiled only for an instant. He blunted my attack, renewing his own with redoubled vigor. The intensity of his attack was formidable.

His spike stabbed into my mind! I reeled in pain. For a moment, it seemed he would penetrate my innermost mind.

I deflected it with a mental shield, brushing it aside. I struck at it with a hammer, bending it, breaking it and driving it out of my mind. As I healed my helmet, I sliced and stabbed at his defenses, but with little effect.

His mental mace delivered a crushing blow, but I withstood it and delivered my own. I sliced at his mind with a blade of my own, determined to penetrate his defenses.

He blocked it, and returned a similar point. I deflected it, returning a powerful axe blow.

He dented the blade and returned a crushing blow as with a mace.

I shielded my helmet from the blow, enwrapping his mind with a simulated Faraday cage, blocking all energy from any source escaping. Then, I reinforced it, tightening it around his mind.

He stabbed at it, punctured it and tore the cage that was containing his mind. I repaired the holes as fast as he could make them. He slashed at it with a blade, but failed to dent the tough weave I had created. Then, he blasted it with an explosion, tearing a great hole that I couldn't repair.

He burst through, stabbing, slicing and battering my mind. I deflected his attacks, striking a huge blow, knocking him back.

For the briefest of moments, my mind was free of him. "Arzhenius, kill!" The Soul Blade leapt forward, but stopped, suspended between us. Arzhenius hummed with pent-up energy as it attempted to carry out its deadly mission.

"Ah!" Beckworth remarked, "That is where it went. When I have killed you, it will obey me or be destroyed."

However, I could see the strain in his face and the fear in his voice. His counterattack was frenzied, as though he had to end our battle quickly.

"Dashemba, kill!"

"Elf, you think they can hurt me?" he screamed.

Both Soul Blades stood poised before him. The pair of Soul Blades seemed to synchronize their attacks, producing a high-pitch scream.

I smashed at his mental shield with a mace, and then sliced it with an axe. However, he renewed his shield, and countered striking me with repeated hammer blows, hoping to dent and weaken my helmet.

Before he could concuss me, I expanded my helmet, padding it like those worn by football players. The combination of the suspension and the extra padding reduced his blows to a persistent annoyance.

His attack repulsed, I muttered, "Gamesha, Thesparius, Zhenesta, kill!" The high-pitched shriek the five produced was intolerable. I recoiled in excruciating pain. Half-blinded, reeling from the unbearable cacophony, I punched his aura with all my might.

With the appearance of three more Soul Blades, Beckworth recoiled. Ignoring me, he devoted his entire attention to defending against them. He twisted, and I felt him reach within himself, preparing to *transfer*.

"No!" I shouted, "You shall not escape me!" Vaerorderol appeared in my hand.

I stabbed!

He gasped and screamed, not expecting an attack against his physical body. He swung blindly and frantically, but ineffectually.

Five Soul Blades penetrated his chest, each drinking their fill

He staggered backwards and fell heavily, his mind panicking. "What have you done, Elf?"

"Killed you, Adjudicar. Killed you."

He gasped, and his mind flickered… flickered… and went blank. All resistance collapsed.

Removing Vaerorderol from his chest, I wiped the blood and gore that covered the blade on his cloak before returning my sword to its scabbard. "Be gone, Adjudicar!" I commanded, immolating his body.

I looked up to see my tribe gathered around. They had seen me in action before, but this was extraordinary. Talbot, Gertrude and Brahms lay on the ground. The power of our battle had stunned them.

"Healers!" I called, "The King and Prince William are in need."

As Lenwë and Gertrude attended to the King and Lessien and Uruviel cared for the Prince, I turned to my tribe. "He was an Adjudicar, after all. He duped us when we entered his throne room. He revealed there are many other Adjudicars on this planet, including one in Farrowspike and another in Narwortland. He intended to explode both Richard and William destroying the entire army. He, of course, could escape into the Void and return when the destruction was ended."

William groaned. I spun around and raced to his side. Lessien and Uruviel were still murmuring spells of healing, but he was recovering.

I looked to Lenwë to learn how he was proceeding. He was scowling and concentrating on the King. I melded my mind with his, supplying my power, while he directed it. The King had been savagely attacked. They had damaged his brain, his heart, liver, kidneys and lungs.

I summoned Uruviel to assist us. Lenwë worked to heal and restore on Richard's brain, while Uruviel and Gertrude healed his organs. I felt Talbot and Brahms join their powers with Gertrude's.

Even with six of us working on him, it was touch and go. Uruviel, Talbot and Gertrude concentrated on the King's organs. We healed his lungs and kidneys quickly, but it was the heart that concerned Uruviel. The left atrium and ventricle were destroyed, and if we couldn't repair them, Richard would die.

Yet, even if Uruviel could repair the heart, it would be for naught if Richard's brain died or even if it was badly damaged. I switched my full attention to Lenwë's efforts. Then I felt Lessien join us. Evidently, William was out of danger. Slowly… very slowly we staunched the intercellular bleeding and removed the clots. We restored damaged cells and rejuvenated nerves as much as we dared.

Then Lenwë withdrew. His face was chalk white, and I thought he would faint. "I have done what I can do. The rest is up to him. I need food!" He rushed out.

I sat beside Richard, monitoring Uruviel's and Lessien's efforts to heal Richard's heart, lungs and liver. Between the two of them, they repaired all the organs. However, by the time they had done their work, they, too, were spent.

"How is he?" William croaked.

"We have done what we can do," I replied. "He was beaten savagely and has suffered great damage to his brain and internal organs. The rest is up to him.

I reached out to hold William's hand. "Now, how about you? How are you feeling? And what did he do to you, anyway?"

"Ah, we decided – Richard and I – to renew our acquaintance with our half-brother. We brought him back to Richard's pavilion, intending to…. Well, I don't know what we really intended, but he is our half-brother. So, anyway, we decided to talk with him.

"No sooner had he arrived than he cast a spell on everyone around us. Suddenly, our soldiers turned on us and attacked us. Well, neither Richard nor I were ready to die, so we fought them. We drew our swords and killed many of them, but then they overpowered us. A few of them beat us up really badly, especially Richard.

"Then, Beckworth summoned two Sorcerers who bound us in the chairs. I begged him to help Richard, but he just laughed at me, and said, 'Let's just wait for your pet Elf to arrive. Then, I'll deal with all three of you. I'll take care of your sister later.'"

"What did he mean by that last comment?"

"Oh, he's wanted Cassie since he figured out the difference between boys and girls. That she was his half-sister didn't mean a thing to him."

"Gilraën!" Uruviel called.

When I arrived, she said, "He will not recover. I've been monitoring his brain functions. He doesn't respond to stimuli to his extremities, his eyes are not responsive to light, and he does not react to noise."

I turned to William. "Brace yourself. I don't think we can save him. William, take command of your armies. Talbot, protect William. Round up any other Sorcerers you think you'll need."

I stepped from the camp to find the rest of my tribe. My Cavalry had arrived and taken up defensive positions in front of the pavilion. Maidstone Forest had surrounded it, setting up a defensive ward.

Harold raced to me, "Gilraën!" He seized my shoulder. "Are you all right?"

"Yes... no," I replied. "Why do you ask?"

"Haven't you looked at yourself? You're covered in blood and gore. What have you been doing?" He looked around at the bodies lying around. "What's been going on around here?"

"Beckworth was an Adjudicar. He attacked the King and Prince. I had to kill him." I motioned toward the bodies. "Fortunately, I arrived in time. William is well on the road to recovery. I don't think Richard is going to make it." I clapped him on the shoulder. "I'm pleased that you are here. With my Cavalry surrounding me, nothing can go wrong."

"Damned straight!" Yashi yelled.

"Don't forget us!" Galdor responded.

"No, I can't forget any of you. You are mine, just as I am yours."

Cassandra raced up, but was blocked by the wards.

"Let her in," I asked them.

She raced up to me. "What's going on? I heard they attacked my brothers."

I explained what had happened. She rushed into the pavilion seeking her brothers. I followed her, leaving them time to speak to William without outsiders overhearing them. By the time I entered, tears were streaming down her face. She was holding onto William as though she would drown if she let go of him. She sobbed into his shirt, as William held her, tears rolling down his cheeks.

William reached for me and pulled me into their hug. We wept. Our joy was utterly destroyed. Elation gave way to despair. The sweet taste of victory turned to ashes in our mouths.

William moaned, "He fought for this day for ten years. Yet, the moment he achieved it, he was destroyed by the very thing he had vanquished. How can this be? We had him, but he came back. What shall I do?"

It was probably inappropriate, but I said it anyway. "William, the King is dead. Long live the King. Rule your kingdom, My King, that's what you must do."

* * * * *

Chapter 6 – Council of Jaralii

The momentary joy of victory dissipated completely in the morning light. Bodies lay strewn across the field of battle. Corpses hung on battlements. Piles of gore lay scattered throughout the inner and outer courtyards. Isolated arms, legs and the occasional head were sprinkled grotesquely.

The stench was overwhelming. Bodies… torsos pierced; intestines punctured. Digested and half-digested remains reeked. Hordes of flies had descended upon them, adding their filth to the bloating and exploding guts of rotting corpses.

Men and Elves, Dwarves and Orcs, each with a cloth wrapped firmly around their face, worked among the dead. Yet, the task was overwhelming. Of King Richard's armies, more than two hundred lay dead. Over one hundred Elves, who should have lived for countless centuries, lay wide-eyed serving as meals for flies. Almost one hundred Dwarves lay amongst their allies, while many hundreds of men and goblins who had defended the castle so vigorously, lay decomposing alongside their enemies in life.

This was horror beyond my darkest, my most dreadful dreams. As I stared at the field of the dead, I was reminded of the stories of so many generals, who described their battlefields as being so thick with the dead they could walk its length stepping only on the corpses. It had been just words – little blots of ink on paper. Now, it was a scene of utter disgust that would haunt my mind for the rest of my immensely long life.

I had to do something, but what?

I spoke with William and Cassandra. Both were still in shock. For their entire lives, Richard had been their big brother. Regardless of whether they argued, fought, planned or played, he was always the elder, bigger, stronger, wiser, whose opinion always carried more weight than both of theirs together. Now, he was gone. Their rock, their leader, their king was no more. Never again would they hear his laugh, see his smile, feel his touch, or put up with his terrible jokes.

Instead, William was now the King. He was the final authority. His thoughts, his words, his plans would decide the fate of thousands upon thousands of his subjects. Surrounded by those who loved him, he was alone at the pinnacle of power.

I sat quietly with them, trying to hold my emotions in check, but the ghastly sight of the field of battle kept popping into my mind's eye. "William, we face two problems, both of which you need to manage. First, we have far more corpses than we can cope with. Second, we must consider a funeral for your brother. I think both are related.

"I suggest a unification council of all the powers gathered to defeat Beckworth and his Adjudicars. I will propose that Shalal'm Caer become the seat of that council. And I will suggest that Shalal'm Caer become the burial place for all the dead, including King Richard. This will be a lasting memorial to all who died here. All delegates to this council will be reminded of the day we fought together as a united army to defeat the common enemy and be inspired by it.

"Would that be acceptable to you?"

"Oh, Gilraën, why do you do these things to me? I've just lost my brother, who was my king. How do I replace him? How do I govern a kingdom?"

"You can not replace him, but you must rule, because that is your destiny. It is unfortunate that you weren't given the time to recover from your grief. But, that's the way it is. You are the king, and you must make decisions starting from the moment Richard drew his last breath. King William, do your duty! Decide, my love!"

"Gilraën, you're a pain in the ass! Do as you will and be done with it!"

Cassie and I exchanged glances. She said, "Billie, you've got to be there for this to be official. So, get dressed, dry your tears, and suck it up. Let's go, brother Billie, you're the king, and we have work to do."

I left the pavilion to find General Abuahad. "My General, gather all the armies at the field before Shalal'm Caer. Be sure they are in the same relative positions they were in during the initial attack. Emphasize that you are acting under the orders of High Queen Gulámae. If you have any problems contact me, and I will arrive to solve it. Use whatever means you decide is most appropriate, but make sure they are there."

There were many complaints, especially from the Dwarves. It was their custom to bury their dead in stone, and as near to their home Dwarrows as possible. Humans wanted to return to their homes. Elves had no set procedures. They had so few deaths that they had no real need of such things. And, they viewed the corpses as mere husks, which once had contained a living entity. Octopods usually ate their dead; Krelli buried them just to stop the corpse from stinking, as did Trolls. Orcs, it seemed, had an elaborate death ceremony in which the body was laid aside to rot. Later, the bones were gathered and buried by the family. So, regardless of which group was involved, my idea was rejected.

Finally, I asserted myself… and begged!

It worked! Who knew?

* * *

The following morning, I was nervous. Winning a battle was one thing. Now, it was time to win or lose the war. The peace treaty was the key to the entire future of Jaralii. Slowly, large groups of Humans, Elves, Dwarves and Orcs assembled around the huge rectangular field that bordered the north face of the fortress. It had been well trampled by thousands of feet. Huge ruts had been plowed into the dirt by the passage of trebuchets, siege towers, catapults, ballistae and other engines of war. There was no doubt in anyone's mind that this had been the scene of blood and carnage… several rotting corpses still lay upon the open field.

I walked to the middle of the field, careful to avoid stepping on bodies, pieces or entrails. I raised my voice, amplifying it so that everyone could hear me.

"I am Gilraën Gulámae, Queen of the Elves of the Green Mountains-Maidstone Forest. We are met on this great battlefield for two purposes. The first is to honor the dead. I speak first of King Richard of Umbeqjaralii. He was the principal enemy of Lord Beckworth and his Adjudicars. Without his insight and leadership, this war could never have been waged. It was only because of his planning, his attention to the details of logistics that we have food, clothing, arms and weapons. He was the great architect of this victory, and it is to him we dedicate our future.

"We each suffered personal loss. My friend and long-time companion, known to you as Justice the Krell, died in battle defending me from Beckworth's Krelli. Both Yurchist Linda and I knew him as a friend, and both of us will miss him keenly.

"I'm sure that I am not the only among us who lost a friend, a husband, a wife, or someone else important to you. We are gathered together on this field of victory to grieve together, for all of us are lessened by these deaths, no matter how honorable and glorious they will appear in our songs. I ask that we all keep these losses in our minds as we consider the consequences of our victory, and the new world we have created.

"So, how should we proceed? What will we do to prevent such a recurrence or some future episode? What will we do?

"With King William's permission, I suggest that this very site becomes the most sacred, the most holy, the most honored for each of us, from this time forevermore. For it will be here that we bury our dead.

"This site has become hallowed ground for all of us. These grounds are steeped in our blood, whether Octopod or Elf, Troll or Dwarf, Orc or Krelli or Human. This ground," I reached down and dug out a handful of dirt. I held it high above my head. "This very ground is sacred to all of us, for it is saturated with our blood. And whoever will come here forever in the future will understand these are hallowed grounds.

"The lands around and about this fortress meet the requirements for each of our races. We have great rock formations to the East, West and South of Shalal'm Caer, which satisfy the burial rites of my Dwarves. These grounds are open to the land, the sky and the air, as is appropriate to my Elves. We have space to accommodate the death rituals of the Orcs, and ideal locations for each family's loved ones. And, we have an ideal location for the remains of King Richard and the brave Humans who fell in battle. We can also accommodate the wishes of Krelli and Trolls. And, I make a special request of my friend and ally, King Mort, that we have a special place for a tribute to his Tribe. In this way, these grounds will be hallowed by all to become a remembrance of these evil times to all who come here.

"But this leads me to my second purpose. I ask, 'How shall we conduct ourselves in this new world?' Shall we simply return to our homes, making believe our task is completed, and we have nothing more to do? Ask yourselves, 'Is the job done? Or is there more to do?'

"What of Narwortland? What of Farrowspike? They, too, are beset by Adjudicars.

"And is this the only land upon this planet? Are there no other places?

"Understand this: Before Beckworth died, he gloated over the body of King Richard, claiming there were two more of them, once each in Narwortland and Farrowspike, and five other Adjudicars on other lands. Could there be more? Where did they come from? How many more will come to enslave this world, to kill our loved ones, to destroy all that we know and love?

"Each of us has different wants, needs and desires. Each of us lives in different places and has different lifestyles and different aspirations. Some desires of the Dwarves differ from some desires of the Elves, but some are the same. Similarly, Humans, Dwarves, Orcs, Elves, Trolls, Krelli and Octopods have similar wants, needs and desires, yet we also have different ones. It is a property of life that all of us are identical in some ways and different in others.

"And so, it is inevitable that we will coexist at some times, and we will clash at others. However, as we have shown in this Great War against the Adjudicars, if we work together we can accomplish great deeds. I ask, 'How shall we continue this great coalition so that such opportunities to work together and such occasions to deter conflict will always be available to all of us?'

"We must seek a more permanent coalition of all the beings of this world. This place is the most hallowed in all our lands. Here all persons are welcome. Here all points of view shall be heard, discussed and adjudicated. Here and now we must form a governing coalition of all the peoples of this world, if that is your will.

"Therefore, I ask the Kings, Queens, Jharls, Yurchists and leaders of every group to meet with King William and me in the courtyard of Shalal'm Caer, where we will establish the foundations of this coalition. Those who wish to be a part of this new coalition will attend. Those of you who do not may leave and return to your lives. Remember this, however: such a decision is not final. If you wish to become a part of this council in the future, you will always be welcome."

King William and I marched off the field, through the main gates and into the inner courtyard. Chairs, tables, and benches were arranged in a rectangle upon the green lawn. I sat at the south side. Prince William sat opposite me to the north with Sir Xander. Cassandra, Yurchist Linda, and Sir Geoffrey sat at the west side, while Duke Armjurst sat to the east with Baron Richmond.

Slowly Kings, Queens, Jarls and important persons filed in and found a place to sit. The leaders of the four Clans of the Mountains sat with me. Clan Zhaenstain and White Cliffs Elves sat with Duke Armjurst. Blue Lake Elves sat with Cassandra. Brown Hill Elves, Tazhela Dwarves, and Green Mountains Elves sat with King William. Retribution the Krell wandered in and looked around. I waved to him, and he lumbered over, taking a bench to himself. Artestius, still heavily bandaged, limped in and sat at another bench near Retribution. The last to arrive was Mort. His very presence was upsetting to us all.

When everyone was settled in, King William rose. "I am William, King of Umbeqjaralii. This is my fortress. My father, King Patrick, received this fortress from his father. This is the place where Wayland, the first of our race to arrive on this planet, settled. This is where he first built a defense. This is where we first established our kingdom.

"I am loath to surrender this mighty fortress to anyone for anything. I will do so for one and only one reason. If this is to become the seat of this Congress of Jaralii, then I will permit it to be used for this purpose. However, if this is not to become that seat of the coalition of the powers of this land, then I shall not. I shall take up residence here, as my brother, King Richard, should have done when our father was murdered.

"We who are gathered here can establish such a Congress. Shall we do so, or shall we return to our homes, our prior lives and our prior enmities?"

A great silence hung over the gathering. Some stared thoughtfully at the ground or at the sky, avoiding the eyes of others. Some looked deliberately at others, trying to judge their sentiments. Still others shook their heads and muttered, or nodded and muttered, but regardless they muttered.

I was one of those who looked around trying to determine who would speak first, and whether they would be positive or negative. I knew I couldn't speak. Actually, I had no say in the matter. My Tribe and I were 'hired guns,' brought to this world as mercenaries to destroy the common enemy. And, until I/we established an Elf Realm of our own, we would continue to be outsiders.

William, Cassandra, Albert, Geoffrey, Frederick and Xander sat quietly. William looked around, an expression of curiosity on his face. Cassandra was biting her lower lip. Albert was drumming his fingers on the armrest, his eyes darting back and forth across the room. Geoffrey was staring at the clouds, while Frederick seemed to have sunk into a trance.

Linda was fidgeting. She kept looking at the few Orcs from the Eastern and Western Great Meadows. They seemed to be ignoring her.

None of the Elves appeared to be paying the slightest attention to anyone else. Oddly, they were not even trying to communicate mentally. They just sat like statues… cold, hard and immutable.

The Dwarves grumbled and muttered into their beards. Occasionally, one would glance toward another Dwarf, but, mostly, they watched the ground or the clouds as though expecting something dramatic to appear.

Integrity lay out on his back and was soon snoring loudly. Artestius' head sunk to his chest, his eyes closed.

We sat for one hour. Then we sat for a second hour. Finally, I rose to my feet. "I am pleased all of you are considering these propositions so carefully. I, however, am tired from my exertions. I suggest that we repair to our encampments, where our kitchens are preparing a midday meal. I suggest we meet at the second hour of the following morning. Each of us can use that time to consider such a bold proposition with our advisors. If we are agreed?"

I looked around. Everyone seemed to agree. So, after we had awakened those who were 'resting their eyes', I led from the inner courtyards, through the outer courtyard and the great gatehouse. When I arrived at our encampment, Harold asked, "How'd it go?"

I shrugged, (Yes, I did!) but I didn't reply.

We sat in a big group, sitting on the ground, eating a light lunch of local wine, bread, chedz, fron and porg. We discussed the various options that the delegates might take. I was most interested in watching the goings on across and around the field. The greatest movement appeared to be among the Orcs. The Dwarves were also busy. The Elves appeared to have made up their minds, or didn't care a whit about the outcome of our council.

That afternoon, I made the rounds. Of course, Azkhalish welcomed me with a huge hug. "Welcome to our deliberations, my Thanelish." I looked around to see all the Thanes and Squires of the Clan seated in a semi-circle facing the Jharl. He directed me to a chair which seemed to have been reserved for me. When I sat, I saw that Jharlish Emendahlia sat beside her husband.

She was the first to speak. "Tell me, Thanelish Gilraën, why we should trust the Humans or the Elves or any of the races who have invaded our world?"

"If you will excuse my impertinence, My Jharlish, the question is not that they are invaders. The question is, what do we do now that they are here?

"I see great power throughout these lands. Dwarves have great power over land and rock and the very planet itself. The Elves had a different power. They control magic and reach beyond this planet to the stars and beyond. The Humans have a different power. They create, discover and change the world around them. Krelli have powers; Trolls have powers; Orc have powers, Octopods have powers. Even the zhaks who pull my Charioteer's carts have power.

"How shall we survive in this changing world? By controlling the change itself. If we are not the masters of change, we will become its slaves. The council containing all races will not stop change from occurring. Instead, it will permit those who partake in it to be alerted to the changes that are coming, direct them in meaningful ways, and prepare for their outcome."

Evidently, my answer was thought-provoking, for there was a prolonged silence, broken finally by the Jharlish. "Thane Gilraën, gratitude is mine. Wisdom is in your words, but at all times does it apply? Cannot enemies use this council for their own purposes and against the interests of others?"

"Such things happen," I replied. "However, in such a council, each race with a different perspective, such selfish motivations will be redirected by the many to a more universal outcome. It is hard to be so surreptitious or so devious amongst the many that none are awakened to the possible detrimental outcome. When such an undesirable outcome is discovered by any one of us, it will be quickly disseminated to all of us.

"The second problem is more likely: one in which a group of the like-minded pit their strength against all others. A cabal might disguise its intent and the potential outcomes to the many. Could the Dwarves combine as a single power to the detriment of the Elves? No, not by themselves. However, if the Dwarves and the Humans and the Orcs were to combine against the Elves, then it might be possible. Equally, it is possible for all the others to combine against the Dwarves. But, they could do that with or without the council?

Such a conspiracy is possible, but it has not occurred in the ten thousand five hundred forty-two years in the count of the Dwarves of Jaralii.

"By its very nature, the council exposes such a conspiracy. Once exposed, the conspiracy will be discussed in open session where the merits of the position can be examined. In such an open environment, such a cabal must survive on its merits. And, if it does, it will be because it is merited.

"Again, to return to my example, if all the peoples of this world turned against the Dwarves, there must be some reason for their disposition. We Dwarves must have earned the enmity of all the other peoples of this land for them to despise us so. What could we have done to have earned universal condemnation? And, if we were guilty, should we not take appropriate actions to modify our position to earn the trust and respect of our neighbors?

"Please, My Jharlish, do not take this as an example of the attitude of all other people against us, for they do not have this attitude, especially at this time. The entire world has seen the courage, the fortitude, and the strength of the Dwarves of the Dwarf Mountains and the Green Mountains. King Richard had always declared his friendship with Tazhela. Princess Cassandra has always declared her friendship with Garmanch. Duke Armjurst has always declared his friendship with Worphelia. Viscount Grampus has always declared his friendship with Ez-Tansk. It was Justice the Krell and Mort the Octopod who introduced me to Master Theriozemphia's Hearth of Ozhemia's Shelf, which I hope will reopen in the very near future. The Dwarves of the Mountains are honored and respected by all.

"But, what if the Humans or the Elves or the Orcs earned the enmity of the other people of this land? A council of all the races would be the place to air these differences and resolve them before coming to the extreme of war. Alternatively, how could all the races of this land conspire to overcome any one race? It is impossible to do without someone speaking out, initiating the discussion, and striving to find a resolution short of armed conflict. And, this would be especially true if these meetings were being held in a war memorial, filled with the remembrances of alliances against the enemy and the losses of so many lives among all the races of this land."

* * *

I found Clan Ghamarazh deep in discussion. When I appeared, silence reigned. I stood before the three Thanes. "My Thanes, is this how you greet your Jharl?"

Defghamask jumped up, followed reluctantly by the other two. I sat where Defghamask had been. "Please draw up another chair, My Thane." He sat next to me displacing another Thane, who rapidly found a chair. "Please sit, my Thanes and Squires. What are our thoughts on the Council of Jaralii?"

Silence reigned.

"My Thanes, My Squires, Your Jharl requires your thoughts and ideas. Thane Defghamask, why don't you begin?"

"My Jharl, we are the eldest race. All others are invaders to our world. Now, we are facing the consequences of their actions, not ours. First, it was Elves. Then it was Humans. Now it's Adjudicars. And, you ask us to yield to them? You ask us to embrace them? You ask us to sit with them as equals that they can rule over our lands… our Clans? No, I say."

I nodded. Saying nothing, I called on the next Thane and the next. And then each of the seven Squires. There was little variance in their opinions.

"I hear, My Thanes and Squires. If this is the desire of Clan Ghamarazh, then so we shall vote. However, I suggest to you that there is a different argument.

"The Elves, the Humans, the Krelli, the Trolls, the Octopods, and even the Gaunts are here. They exist. They populate the lands. We need only look at the composition of the armies that defeated the Adjudicars. Of the eleven thousand troops, five thousand were Humans, three thousand were Elves, one thousand were Orcs. Only three thousand are Dwarves.

"They are here, whether we wish them to be or not. The question we must resolve is, what do we do now?

"I suggest we control the infestation. I suggest we find ways to limit and restrict the Humans, providing places where they can live: places for Dwarves, places for Elves, and, yes, places for Krelli, Orcs, Trolls and Octopods. For if we do not, the infestation will only increase until we must retreat within our dwarrows as though we are under siege.

"Then, what will we do? Will it not be too late to do anything? Will we not look back to this very moment and say to ourselves, 'If only we had take action when we could.'

"Thane Defghamask, I have other duties to perform. I direct you to speak for Clan Ghamarazh in the meeting to begin n the morrow."

I rose. The Thanes and Squires rose with me. "I will greet you all at the meeting." I left to return to my Tribe.

Harold greeted me first, as always. "Hey, Gilraën, how's it going?"

I wasn't sure. I mumbled something, but went to my pavilion and lay back for a quick nap.

* * *

"This will be interesting," I said to William.

"How so?" he asked.

I had taken a roundabout route to the meeting ground before the keep. As I went, I'd watched who was talking with whom, what groups they were near, and which ones they were avoiding. I answered, "Who will sit with whom?"

"Yes?" William half-replied and half-answered.

"Let's see which are allies and which are adversaries."

We didn't have long to wait. Cassandra, Geoffrey, Richmond, Deplos and Sheldrick entered, looked around, saw us and came over.

Cassandra sat along the same side as William, but in the corner some distance to the left of him. Geoffrey sat behind her, along with Sheldrick. Richmond and Deplos sat behind William.

Glorfindel and Eilol entered, hand in hand. They glanced at me, waved and then turned to the right, finding chairs. King Fingolfin entered, glanced around, and, seeing Glorfindel and Eilol, smiled and went to sit with them.

Linda entered, and, after looking around, waved to Cassandra and went to sit beside her. Almost instantly, they fell into a conversation, giggling like schoolgirls.

Armjurst arrived with King Aeradir. They waved amicably at me, William and Cassandra before heading to the side beyond Cassandra.

The Dwarves of the Dwarf Mountains arrived. They looked around, then huddled. When they broke, they headed to the left side, looking more like a herd of sheep rather than five mighty Dwarf lords. However, as they approached, Jharl Galmerstain redirected them towards Armjurst and Aeradir, acting like a bridge between the two groups.

King Amder and Jharl Tazmatahela came in together, looking like Mutt and Jeff. They smiled at everyone, but turned to sit between William and Cassandra.

Retribution bent to pass beneath the coverings, followed by Artestius. Both tried to stand, but the cloths were only twelve feet above the ground. Ducking low, they scooted to sit on the ground opposite me.

A loud skittling and scraping brought the muted conversations to a halt. Suddenly, a clatter of legs joined by a black body suspended three feet off the ground, scuttled under the tarps. Jerking and jumping left and right, Mort leaped and skittered into the corner on the far side, pulsing up and down as though preparing to leap upon his prey.

Everyone having arrived, I stood to address them. "Welcome back. I hope we are all refreshed and have considered the proposition before us. I invite you all to speak your minds." I sat waiting. And, I waited. *'Someone! Say something!'*

Yurchist Linda rose and cleared her throat. "I am Linda, Yurchist of the Orcs of the Chrystal Crags. The Orcs of the Eastern and Western Meadows have returned to their homes in the Dwarf Mountains. However, they have asked me to speak on their behalves. I believe I also speak for the Orcs of the North.

"In the past, we Orcs were hunted, persecuted and barely tolerated by all of you. For the first time in the history of this world, we Orcs have been treated honorably and as allies. We have fought side-by-side with Elves, Humans and Dwarves.

"As you are all aware, we are also farmers and herders. We have worked long and diligently to raise the food you all eat. We are more productive than any other persons or groups on this continent. We feed Dwarves and Humans, as well as ourselves.

"However, this has been our first opportunity to meet any Elves. We fought alongside King Fingolfin Sáralondë and the Elves of the Blue Lake. We came to know them, as they came to know us. We found them to be honorable… and good fighters, too." She smiled towards King Fingolfin. "We hope that they found our meeting as amicable.

"Now, we sit as equals amongst the races of this world. We are no longer outcasts, sought out only because you are hungry. We look forward to the time when we can take our proper place as equals in the governance of all Jaralii. Therefore, we support the suggestion made by Queen Gulámae," she bowed to me, "and, for our part, we accept the most generous offer made by King William." She bowed to him and sat.

Jarl Azkhalish the Fifth cleared this throat and stood. "Some time ago, I met Gilraën Gulámae for the first time. I was so impressed by her that I raised her to the high rank of Thanelish of Diplomacy for Clan Ez-Tansk.

"She united the Clans Ez-Tansk, Ghamarazh, Ozhemia, Worfellsten and Zhaenstain at the last moment. Had she not done so, we would surely have been overrun and defeated even before the united armies could arrive to do battle.

"Since that time, she has united the five Clans of the Dwarf Mountains and of the Green Mountains, the Elves of the north, the

Orcs of Jaralii, the Humans of Umbeqjaralii and of the Duchy of Armjurst, and the Octopods, as well as large numbers of Krelli and Trolls.

"This is unquestionably the greatest feat of diplomacy we Dwarves have ever seen in the ten thousand years of our existence.

"I declare before you all that Thanelish Gilraën Gulámae of Clan Ez-Tansk has succeeded far beyond my hopes. She has been so successful that I can come to trust her judgment. If she believes this is a foundation for a High Council of all the races and beings of this land, then we, the Dwarves of the Dwarf Mountains will willingly and eagerly participate in the desire to achieve peace, prosperity and unity of all of us who share this land."

So saying, he sat.

"Not of Dwarf Mountains is Tazhela," Jharl Tazmatahela declared. "Friends, allies, trade with Green Mountains and King Richard," he paused. "Nay, King William." He bowed to the King. "Stand with King William and King Amder does Clan Tazhela."

King Fingolfin Sáralondë arose, the first Elf to do so. "Five millennia ago, we found a land of great beauty. It was a lovely blue lake in a shallow valley. A great river flowed from it into a deep inlet of the northern sea. That is where I created the Realm of the Blue Lake. Thereafter, we lived in isolation. We did acknowledge our Seeress, Nėssa Narmŏlanya, and through her renewed our acquaintance with our kinfolk throughout this land. Thus it was with us for millennia.

"Then, some two millennia ago, our kinfolk from the Brown Hills communicated with us, inviting us to a meeting with them. This would not have been unusual, except that they had asked one Dwarf clan to this meeting. And, they had invited a third group which was new to these lands. This was our first meeting with the Humans, who had already befriended our kin and the Dwarves of Garmanch.

"Since that propitious moment, our relationship has grown, and we all have prospered from it. We have extended our influence along the northwestern coast of this continent from Coulee River to the North River. We have developed trade in produce and products, concepts and ideals, history and future. We have prospered, because we have opened ourselves to our neighbors, regardless of the fact that they are different from us, have different goals, different ideals, different concepts.

"We, the Elves of the Blue Lake, favor a greater community of the races of this world. We believe this Congress might be the first step to such a greater communion amongst us all."

King Melwasúl stood. "I have spoken with my neighbors, Jharl Tazmatahela and King William. We have long been friends and partners in this land, along with the Orcs of Umbeqjaralii. We would gladly take our part in a Congress, since our kin of the Blue Lake are also of that disposition."

After he sat, Duke Armjurst rose. "I have met with my neighbors, allies and friends from the White Cliffs and Zhaenstain. We, like the People of the Blue Lake and of the Green Mountains, have been friends since shortly after we Humans first arrived in northern Narwortland in the Eastern Dwarf Mountains. Our port is a beehive of activity because we trade not only with each other, our neighbors in Narwortland, and Clan Worphelia, but also with other lands far across the sea.

"In those distant lands, we often meet with and have commerce with the Elves of the Gray Havens and the Elves of the Sea. This trade, both within and beyond these lands, has been beneficial to all of us in northern Narwortland and the southeastern Dwarf Mountains.

"We echo the recommendations of the Elves of the Blue Lake and of the Green Mountains."

King Glorfindel and Queen Eilol stood. Eilol spoke for them. "Our daughter, Dominica, was the first among all the Elves of Jaralii to recognize the Adjudicars as the enemy of every sentient being in all of Trahe. She, and those others amongst us who were not blinded by our own fears, established the Realm of the Great Forest. But, Lord Beckworth and his Adjudicars sent Krelli against them, murdering our daughter, and annihilating her entire Tribe."

King Fingolfin picked up the narrative. "We blamed William, we blamed Beckworth, we blamed the outside world, and hid within our Realm, choking on our anguish until it transformed into hatred.

"Then, we discovered a stranger so alike to our daughter as to be almost indistinguishable. Like our daughter, she rose up against Lord Beckworth and his Adjudicars. Somehow, she became a Dwarf and a diplomat of Clan Ez-Tansk. She became a Jharl of the great Clan Ghamarazh. She befriended Krelli, Trolls, Octopods and even Gaunts.

"I met Queen Gulámae when we united to bring her Tribe to this world. I was awestruck by the resemblance to our daughter, both in appearance and in her resolve. When I spoke of this to my Queen, she was determined to meet Gilraën Gulámae.

"We owe much to Princess Cassandra, our friend and neighbor. It was she who first awakened us to our unjustified condemnation of the Humans of Umbeqjaralii, and our own irresponsible actions. However, it was the direct appeal of my daughter's mate that convinced me to renew my relationship with the Human kingdom.

"It was then that we met Queen Gilraën Gulámae. We found her to be everything that our daughter had aspired to be. So, we adopted her. Queen Gilraën Gulámae is the daughter of King Fingolfin of the Brown Elves and Queen Eilol of the Fire Elves. She is victorious over Lord Beckworth, and destroyed the Adjudicars who had murdered our daughter, Dominica, and annihilated the Tribe of the Great Forest. Our daughter avenged our daughter.

"Our daughter calls us to council with the other free peoples of this land. This time, we will hear her and acquiesce to her wishes."

Retribution the Krell tried to unfold his eighteen-foot height, but failed miserably beneath the twelve-foot ceiling. He flopped back to rest on the wall. "Like Queen Gulámae, they brought us here from Earth. On arrival, we found ourselves in this form. We were told that we were the good guys, and you were the bad guys. So, we fought you.

"Then Justice hunted Gilraën and discovered he and she were old friends from Earth. Then, Justice learned those things that were true and those that were false. Many of us were persuaded to follow her, but others were not. We fought to defeat Beckworth, who lied to us and turned us to evil. We, that is I and those who follow me, will join with the free people of this world to defeat the Adjudicars both on this continent and on all the others of this world."

Artestius was a mass of bandages. He didn't even attempt to rise. "I tell you, we Trolls of the Mountains are hunted, just as they hunt Orcs. We fought, because Queen Gilraën asked. We will sit in this council, but you will never hunt us again. You will cede our land to us, and we will live in peace."

Finally, Mort scuttled to the middle of the group. He clicked and hissed but his words were intelligible. "I leave one to bury. Arachnids will be in council. Honor us as we honor you. Leave us in peace, and we will leave you. But, remember we must eat. Our food is alive. If your animals stray, we will eat them, but we will not hunt in your lands. And, you will not enter our lands. We will attend council."

I stood, "Then we are agreed. Our first order of business shall be to bury our dead. Each Tribe, Clan or group shall bury their dead nearest to where you assaulted this fortress. We shall place monuments at those locations so that there will be a permanent record of each of our rolls in this battle. And, I suggest that this memorial contain the names of the dead, so that the delegates to his council will be reminded of their sacrifice. We must never forget why we waged this war and how much it cost.

"When these tasks are accomplished, we have three separate obligations. The first is the coronation of King William. The second is the coronation of Jharl Defghamask. The third is the initial meeting of the Council of Jaralii, wherein the type of government, its powers, limitations and responsibilities will be established. I leave you now to bury our dead, and grieve with King William for the loss of his brother. However, I suggest that specified delegates of the Council meet in the old throne room tomorrow at the second hour."

* * *

I spent the rest of the day helping to clean up the horrors of the battle. Most times, we could identify the dead, but in others we had only body parts. The only way we knew who was dead was that they were missing from the roll calls. The burials and the tabulation took two days. In the final accounting, we found that King Richard's army had suffered fifty-three dead and eighty casualties. William's forces had lost twenty-two dead and forty-seven casualties. Geoffrey's Battalions had lost twenty-one dead and sixteen casualties, while Sir Domnall's Battalion had eight dead and fifteen casualties. The tolls were not extraordinary, but the assault on the walls had been costly. Fortunately, most of the casualties would recover and return to their duties.

As I visited with each of my allies, I found that the casualties had been much less than I had expected. I hoped that this was, at least in part, because I had killed so many of Beckworth's Sorcerers or that my battle plan had been effective. Or, maybe, it was that our numbers were so great that we overwhelmed them.

Still, there were over one thousand dead or injured defenders along with more than fifteen hundred prisoners of war. About half were Goblins and half were Humans. The Goblins were like the Orcs of this world but smaller, longer in the arms, and less intelligent than the Orcs. Further, they did not know their origins. Either they were Orcs seized by Beckworth's agents and changed magically or they came from another world. About half the Humans were from Earth, but had only a vague recollection of who they were and where they'd come from. Most of the rest were from Jaralii, but some may have come from one of the other continents on Trahe.

What to do with them? I did not know. I consulted with King William, Yurchist Linda, King Glorfindel and Queen Eilol, and Jharl Azkhalish. "What will we do with them?" I asked.

William asked, "Can we send them home?"

I answered, "I'm not sure. The Adjudicars brought them here, so they are the only ones who knew who they were and where they came from… especially the Humans. Unless they know where to send them, I don't know how we can help."

"And the Goblins?" I asked.

Linda answered, "They aren't Orcs."

"But, what are they? Where did they come from?"

Linda replied, "I can't answer that. They just aren't Orcs, and believe me, I know Orcs."

"Ok, you know Orcs, but this still doesn't answer our problem."

William spoke up, "You know, we have empty forest to the north and northwest of Jhal'm Thaer. We could put them there until we know what to do with them."

Linda said, "That won't help. They do not know how to survive on their own. They aren't all that intelligent and don't seem to have any skills other than war."

I asked, "Are we sure?"

Linda replied, "Yes, we're sure. Maybe we can put them to use on our farms."

"Are they genetically compatible?"

"No," she replied, "but of a similar genetic profile, I think."

Jharl Azkhalish said, "Eovirs are primarily tree dwellers. These are land dwellers, but they climb extremely well. Then again, Orcs climb well, too." He nodded towards Linda, who smiled wryly.

"Well," I said, "We just can't kill them. We've got to figure out something. How about we try to fit them in with some other Orcs? If they can teach them to farm, they could be helpful, if the Orcs will take them."

Linda volunteered, "I'll talk with the other Yurchists. I don't have any contact with the Orcs of Umbeqjaralii. Can you provide one of my lords with an introduction?"

William nodded. "Sure, but they're not exactly my bosom buddies. I know them, but not well. We have a 'leave well enough alone' relationship, but maybe some of my subjects do.

"Now, how about the Humans? Gilraën, you have more power than any Adjudicar. So why can't you help to send them back?"

"I hadn't even considered such an idea. Hmmm," I answered. "That's a definite maybe. My tribe and I have great powers, but we don't know how to send anyone anywhere. Your Master Farmount is far more experienced that I am. And maybe I can elicit the cooperation of the other Elves. As a group, we have more than enough power to send one or two back to Earth, but we are talking about more than seven hundred.

"And, to where do we send them? If they don't know, how can we know where to send them?"

"You're right, Gilraën," Eilol replied, "but some of them do know. So, why don't we start by sending them back?"

"Great idea. Let's talk with them. Separate those who know their past from those who don't. We can start working on getting them home."

Azkhalish advised me, "But first, my Thanelish, we have a task to perform. We are burying our dead. We who survive must honor them according to our ancient ways. Come, My Thanelish, accompany me." He turned and walked away.

"Sorry, folks, but I have been reminded of my duty."

* * *

Dwarf funerals are long, lugubrious, and utterly tedious. My command of Dwarfish was elementary, but even with my somewhat limited understanding of the language it bored me out of my tiny little mind. We stood a lot. We keened a lot. We tore our beards or beat our breasts. Needless to say, I wasn't into mistreating 'the girls'. Some five or six hours later, the seventeen dead dwarves were interred in hard rock, as required by ancient tradition.

Then it was time for the interment meal. They named each dead Dwarf, which included his entire family back to the first Dwarf of his line. Typically, that was some twenty or more generations. Every Dwarf who knew the deceased spoke of their remembrances. The Dwarf's Squire spoke of his family and the deceased place in the familial. And throughout the ceremony, there was plenty of drinking. Each time the dead Dwarf's name was mentioned, everyone raised their glasses to drink a salute. By the time every Dwarf had said his piece, the night was well spent, and so was I.

* * *

My head hurt. No, that's not right. Pain was too weak... too limited a word. A super nova was exploding, and I was in its midst. I dared not open my eyes. The slightest movement resulted in vertigo and my stomach's upheaval. Had I eaten anything, it would have been spread all over the ground within my pavilion. Instead, I heaved and heaved, without effect other than my continuing, endless misery.

Finally, Lenwë took pity on me. He calmed my stomach and eased my headache. He prescribed toast with fron and watered wine. Oddly, it tasted pretty good. And, after a while, I could stand and move about.

When William saw me he laughed so hard, he bent over and gasped for breath. "Oh, Gilraën, you look awful! Did you try to drink with the Dwarves, again? I would have thought you'd have learned by now. One Dwarf can drink an entire Elf Tribe under the table and still walk away. And, they'll be sober in the morning, which you aren't."

"Do tell, William. Do tell!"

He laughed again. When he finally recovered, he asked, "So what's on the agenda today?"

My foggy brain considered his question. "We have to bury King Richard. It's got to be a big funeral, and we'd better do it before everyone leaves."

William nodded. "Yes, you're right. Can you contact everyone? I'll get Cassie."

"Sure, but where, when, what'll we do? You know, all that little stuff?"

"That's why we need Cassandra."

It took a while, but when Cassandra showed up, she saw me, and, in spite of her grief, broke out laughing. "You look terrible! What did you do?'

William answered her, "Drank with Dwarves!"

"Oh, you didn't! Nobody can, but Dwarves. Haven't you learned?"

I tried to laugh with them, but my head wasn't in it. "We're trying to bury Richard before everyone leaves. We need to know what to do."

"That's standard protocol stuff. We'll have to do it a little differently, but we can do most of it. Just talk with everyone and make sure they don't leave. I can handle all the details. You just get everyone set. The only things I have to know are where and when."

* * *

Two lines of soldiers stood thirty feet apart facing each other. The lines stretched from the northern end of the battlefield to the great gates of the outer wall. Beyond them, stretching the full width of the lawn stood the vast armies of Elves and Dwarves and Orcs, along with a few Krelli and Trolls, and one Octopod.

Six drummers stepped onto the field. They struck their drums and stepped. They draped their drums in black. They struck their drums and stepped. Their armbands were black. They struck their drums and stepped. They were somber, looking straight ahead. They struck their drums and stepped. The youngest, a mere boy, wept openly. They struck their drums and stepped. The eldest, gray and grizzled, bit his lip. They struck their drums and stepped.

Twelve Chariots, each drawn by three zhaks draped in black, followed them. The chariots were draped in black, and the Charioteers wore black honors in their helmets and black ribbons on their arms.

King William and Princess Cassandra followed, stepping to the beat of the drums. I followed, bearing the King's sword, point downward. My twenty-seven Elves marched behind me in three groups of nine.

Immediately behind us marched Duke Armjurst, Viscount Grampus, Baron Richmond and Sir Xander Deplos, each supporting one corner of the King's bier. The crown of Umbeqjaralii rested on the casket.

Following them on the right side the Kings and Queens of Elves marched in stately solemnity. Beside them, to their left, the Jharls walked, with stern looks on their faces. To their left marched Yurchist Linda and the Yurchists of the Orcs of the Eastern and Western Meadows, matching their attitude to the other mourners.

As the casket passed them, the mourners bowed their heads in sorrow and remembrance. When the last of the mourners passed them, they fell in line progressing towards the bastion of Shalal'm Caer.

The progression seemed to take forever. The damned sword got heavy after a while. Even my extraordinary muscles were quivering by the time we had slow-marched the mile or so to the great gate. Fortunately, once we got there, I could rest the blade on the ground.

The mightiest lords of the lands stood before the bier poised above the grave, which had been dug in the middle of the road directly before the gate. The Dwarves of Ez-Tansk had provided a large chunk of undressed marble, which sat at the head of the grave.

William and Cassandra stood at the head of the bier, looking out over the throng. William cleared his throat and then cleared it again. "My Kings, My Queens, My Jharls, Jharlish and Thanes, My Yurchists, Noble Lords and Ladies, allies, friends and all who are gathered here in this place and time, I am honored to greet you. However, this is not a time of rejoicing in our victory. Instead, we are here to honor our brother, King Richard of Umbeqjaralii of the honorable House of Wayland the Founder, Ulrich the Great, and Patrick of Jhal'm Thaer.

"King Richard was more responsible for this victory than anyone else. King Richard developed the farming communities that fed this army. He did that by establishing a personal relationship with the

Orcs of Jhal'm Thaer, of the Green Mountains, and the Jaralii Hills. He honored them, and they respected him.

"King Richard took special interest in the breeding programs established by our long fathers, King Ambrosius, King Adelbert, King Canisius and our father, King Patrick. Richard increased the number and kind of each of the draft animals, their training programs and their teamsters. He developed the wagons, carts and wains. He established the system of posts that sped the produce and products of the farms and fields to his army, that we could achieve this hard-fought victory.

"It was Richard who developed the armies of the Kingdom of Umbeqjaralii. It was he who nurtured the nobility of the realm. He developed the armies that now stand victorious on this field of battle.

"It was he who developed, built, transported, erected and used the engines of war that his armies used to destroy these walls, to surmount these walls, and to break these gates. Without them, we could not have penetrated this fortress.

"And, it was King Richard that the Adjudicar Beckworth seized in his final atrocity against all the races of these lands. I was fortunate to survive his hatred. Our brother was not, in spite of the heroic efforts of Queen Gilraën and her healers.

"And so, it is only fitting and proper that his body be interred here, guarding this gate to the fortress of Wayland the Founder, long father of our race. For it is by King Richard's great efforts that we stand here, victorious."

William rested his hands upon the casket. "My brother, I leave you here at the scene of your final victory. We will remember you for as long as this fortress and this kingdom shall last. All those who come to his place will learn of your dedication, your foresight, your victory, and the lasting peace that you made possible.

"I will miss you, big brother. I will miss your infectious smile. I will miss your wit. I will miss your sage advice. I will miss your presence in my life. Guard well this place. Usher in a new era of peace and prosperity for all these lands."

I retrieved the Crown of Umbeqjaralii. Cassandra and William placed their hands on the coffin and then stepped back. The Dwarves lowered his body into a rectangular pit they had dug from the living rock. My Elves, accompanied by those of all other Tribes, singing a song of sorrow, remembrance and power, lifted a large marble slab and slid it over the grave. Our song changed slightly, sealing the grave.

I walked to the gigantic rock at the grave's head. Picturing what I wanted it to become, I sang a song of power and creation. Slowly, the rock peeled away. The base was rectangular, four feet high and two wide. I pictured panels on the front and half-panels on the side, with scroll work on the top and bottom. Above was a spire some six feet in height, extending to a pyramidal peak. I left the rest of the rock unfinished, signifying an unfinished life. I created the following inscription in the front of the base.

Here lies

King Richard of Umbeqjaralii

Victor over the Adjudicars

Founder of the Council of Jaralii

Taking the Crown of Umbeqjaralii in my hands, I stepped to the foot of the grave. Raising the Crown above my head, I shouted, "The King is dead!"

William and Cassandra then stepped to the foot of the grave, facing the gathered throng. I stood behind William and placed the Crown on his head. I shouted, "Long live the King!"

Cassandra took two steps forward, turned and bowed to her brother, shouting, "Long live the King!"

All the lords and all the soldiers of Umbeqjaralii took up the cry, "Long live the King!"

Kings and Queens; Jharls, Thanes and Squires; Yurchists, nobles and all those gathered, picked up the cry, "Long live the King!"

King William took Cassandra by the hand to walk slowly down the long road to the end of the battlefield. Thousands cheered him lustily. Both he and Cassandra waved to their supporters, greeting many by name. It was only when he returned to the Royal Pavilion that the throng of well-wishers dispersed to return to their encampments.

I had tried to carry out my duties as sword master, but failed miserably. William and Cassandra stepped out before I could get in front of them. The masses of soldiers closing around their new king was so great that I gave up trying to keep up with the Royal Siblings. After a short while, I gathered up my Charioteers and Elves, and we scooted away to return to our camp.

As I settled down, my Tribe surrounded me, Galdor came close and whispered, "We found it. They hid it." They then dispersed as though nothing had happened.

We then sat and watched delegations from each of the Powers arrive at King William's pavilion. I did not want to be involved in the royal protocols or be a part of the formation of the first days of the rule of King William. Besides, I had other things to do.

With great discretion, I assembled my entire family, both Ghillies and Elves. I placed a ward about us, including a wall of silence so we could not be overheard. "Galdor, you said you have found it."

"Indeed, My Queen, but it was not I. Idril Ancalimë discovered it."

Idril quietly explained, "I was searching the grounds beneath the great gate, beneath the crypt of King Richard. There is a small room, one level below the catacombs beneath the castle. It is well hidden both physically and magically. I stripped the magical wards until I could pass through and then opened the cache. It is far more than I had expected. See my mind."

She expanded her consciousness so we could perceive and experience her memories. She had found a passageway below the catacombs. She followed it to a room almost directly below King Richard's memorial. The magical wards were many and complexly interwoven. However, she penetrated them enough to see within the room.

It was rectangular, roughly twenty feet by twenty feet by ten feet. Within were pallets of metallic bars. Each bar was about one foot long by six inches wide by four inches tall. The base of each pallet was a six-by-four array of such blocks. A similar array was stacked cross-wise on the first. A third was stacked cross-wise on the second and a fourth on the third. There were six such pallets.

"Oh, Wow!" I exclaimed. I performed a quick calculation. "That's like two billion dollars. That's a king's ransom and then some."

"Yes," Caranthir replied, "that's millions apiece."

"And," Idril added, "that's not all. There are alcoves dug into the walls. I investigated a few. They are filled with raw and cut jewels. When they are all properly cut, they're probably worth two to three times the bricks."

"With wealth like that, William can rebuild this world. And, we will each be wealthy beyond our wildest dreams." I thought for just a second. *"Everyone will want their cut. We'll have to figure out a reasonable distribution. Fortunately, there's more than enough to go around."*

Actually, there was, but parceling it was a problem. There were some 576 two-hundred pound blocks of gold just hanging around. Then, there were piles of jewels, which we had to divide evenly between Tribes, Clans, groups and people. Argh! It would have been a PITA even with a spreadsheet, but by hand and not even a calculator?

Further, this was my big payoff. I had the jewels I had retrieved from the Chrystal Crags, and some gold from William, but it was a pittance. By contract, they had promised me oodles of gold and other valuable stuff. It'd be easy if I just took ten percent, but I doubt it'd be that easy.

Worse, I'd have to figure out all those jewels. I wasn't sure of what gem was which. Anyone could fool me with brightly colored glass. Wanna buy Manhattan? Diamonds are harder than everything else, but quartz is pretty strong, too. Perhaps Clan Tazhela could be of help, but if they knew, then everyone would. But, that was the objective, wasn't it?

Obviously, William would get the lion's share. It was his castle after all. I mean ownership is… some parts of the law or something. I'd get the 10% agent's fee. I guessed that William would get 25%, a truly staggering amount of gold – something on the order of 4 tons. He would divide his share among all his nobles and troops. Even then, he'd end up with 40 bricks of gold, worth something around 145 million of Gold in his currency. The rest I divided between everyone according to whatever I thought was right. Regardless, it was a hell of a lot more than they had started with. By my calculations that would leave about one hundred ten gold bricks for the new Council.

We spent the next few hours breaking all the spells, hexes and wards Beckworth and his buddies had placed on the room, only to find out they'd booby trapped the gold and jewels. A few hours later, we could touch and shift the bricks and crystals. After that, I had little choice.

"Jharl Tazhela, I ask for your expertise. I need you to evaluate precious stones. Beckworth has a hoard of hidden wealth, which I am dividing among the Tribes and Clans. I can easily divide the gold, but I have no knowledge of the value of jewels."

"OH?" he said, a sudden gleam in his eyes. "Gold? Jewels? How much? Where?"

"I will bring you there. It's guarded, and I must get you past the wards. Whenever you're ready?" Ok, it was a lie. But Dwarves and wealth? Talk about temptation!

He was eager. "I can travel now, but only for a few hours. I will evaluate the treasure and then determine which of my Clan will be most suited for the tasks."

'Oh, no! Even more Dwarves!'

"Sure," I said aloud. "My Tribe is already hard at work. Hold my arm, My Jharl."

I transferred directly to the treasury. Tazmatahela's mouth fell open. This display of wealth was far more than he had imagined. "My Queen, this is amazing… breath taking… even beyond the greed of a Dwarf."

"I have apportioned the gold among the Kingdoms, Tribes and Clans. That's ready to go. You'll get tons of gold, as will they."

He gasped, "Tons!"

"Yes, tons. Our problem is these." I led him to the alcoves. Four wooden boxes were arrayed tightly. I pulled one out, revealing a horde of blue stones. The next alcove had a similar number of boxes of red stones. Similar alcoves contained green, violet, milky white, purple, yellow and black stones.

Tazmatahela gaped and stared. He started to speak, and his mouth moved, but no sound came out. He pawed at the stones and then turned to me stuttering nonsense. Finally, he uttered, "Fantastic!" and sat on the floor as though pole-axed.

After a short while, he clambered to his feet. "My Queen, I am beyond words. My mind is beyond my imagination. This is a trove beyond all our legends of hidden wealth. I will help you value it. Then, I will leave it to you to divide as you see fit. It is beyond me. In my greed, I would keep it all, hoard it, and sit within its treasure throughout the rest of my days. It is too much for any Dwarf. Perhaps you, in your wisdom will be able to divide it appropriately."

It wasn't all that easy. Large chunks of gold can be sliced into smaller pieces rather easily. Gold is soft, malleable and ductile. Jewels are chunks of crystal, often aluminum oxides, or, in the case of diamonds, carbon. They aren't easily divisible. Then, how much is a carat of ruby worth relative to a carat of diamond? Depends. The good part was the mass was so huge and varied, that we made reasonable piles for each Tribe, Clan, Kingdom or other group. I received six or seven each of rubies, emeralds, diamonds, sapphires, and other really pretty rocks. My Elves and Charioteers made out like bandits… well, you know what I mean.

* * *

The time for going home was almost here. I had only one thing to do before I left. I visited Clan Ghamarazh. "Jharl Defghamask, the army is breaking up and going home. I assume our Clan is returning to our Dwarrow?"

"Yes, My Jharl, in the morning."

"Have you given any thought to when you will hold the coronation?"

"Yes, My Jharl. I ask that we commit to the ceremonials on the day following the full brightness of Llombda."

I made a quick calculation… nine days. "Have you formally invited all the Clans, Tribes, Kingdoms and other important personages?"

"We have. You are the last to whom I speak. All the others have agreed."

"Then, My Jharl, I, too, agree."

I left rather quickly to talk with King William and Princess Cassandra. "We have a problem, William, Cassandra. Clan Ghamarazh intends to crown its Jharl in nine days. You don't have time to go much of anywhere before you head to our dwarrow."

William smiled, replying, "Yes, we know. A Thane led a formal contingent to invite me. Obviously, we're going, so we're marching south. Squire Ranthathamghazk has provided us with directions to our assigned quarters. We, Cassandra and I, will be accompanied by our Sorcerers, our Nobles, and a Battalion of troops."

"I assume your going to the northern gate?"

"I guess so. It's about fifty miles south of Shalal'm Caer."

"Yes, that's it. It's too rough for zhaks, but I want my Archers there. I'll go ahead with my Tribe. So, my Archers will be your scouts and skirmishers. I'm sure Richard had a Palace Guard, like yours, and so does Cassandra. Abuahad, Grampus, and Richmond each have a company. And, whomever else you were thinking of going with you. You'll want your very best.

"Now, what gifts will you bring to the new Jharl of Clan Ghamarazh?"

"We have nothing. We came to fight a war, not to attend the coronation of a Jharl."

"Well, you'll have to think of something. He is the Jharl of the Clan of War and Vengeance!"

"And, what will you bring?"

"How about a fortune in gold and jewels?"

"What are you talking about?"

I laughed, "We discovered a treasure house of gold and jewels."

"What?"

"I think you heard me. You will receive about eight thousand pounds of gold plus a wain-load of jewels. I suggest you send it under guard. Oh, you, too, Cassie, but you'll only get five thousand pounds and a load of jewels. That's only two to three hundred million Golds in your currency."

"Are you joking me?" she asked.

"No," I said, quiet seriously. "So, I'm going to split it among the different groups. Obviously, you, as the King, get a large share, but not all of it. The largest part will go to the Clans, Tribes and miscellaneous groups, although none will get as much as you, William. And, they'll have to split it up among all their people. You, William, have to run your kingdom, and you, Cassandra, are a Princess with royal responsibilities."

"Oh, and the Tribes and Clans that didn't join us, get nothing. I will be more than generous even with those who gave us minimal help. But, those who refused to assist us in any way get nothing."

William frowned mightily. "Wait a moment. You discovered a treasure trove in my fortress, and you take command of it. You determine who will receive what? Isn't that my province? Shouldn't I be deciding these things? After all, it is mine."

"No, it isn't. It was the Adjudicar's treasure. They stored it here, and my Tribe and I discovered and retrieved it. We have liberated it, and I will apportion it among those who fought against the Adjudicars or who aided us in our fight against them. This apportionment will, of course, include every soldier of Umbeqjaralii's army and that of Duke Armjurst's army to the amount of ten Golds for each of them."

"Ten Golds!" William exclaimed, "That's a fortune to a common man. How generous. I just hope they all believe it is from me, else I have only traitors in my ranks."

"Oh, yes. I have just allocated the funds. It will be up to you to disperse the funds to your subjects. I will distribute it to the allies, since I am their leader, at least for now."

"Gilraën, I know better than to argue with you, even if you are wrong. You are just too strong-willed. However, I will insist that you tell me, so I'm prepared when I am asked."

"Me, too!" Cassandra piped up.

It took me a long while to explain it all. The major Clans and Tribes would receive twenty two-hundred pound bars of gold and a cartload to jewels. Others would get less. Every major person received a brick or more. And, even the least soldier would receive ten Golds – perhaps a year of salary all in one lump sum.

"I've even left enough for the Council that they'll be able to get their government started. Of course, until they do, I will leave it in your custody, William. No sense in leaving four hundred million Golds lying around."

"Four hundred million! Where will I store it all?"

I just laughed. We should all have problems like that.

* * *

That night, while everyone was asleep, I contacted each leader in a *waking sleep*. I informed them I had a treasure for them as a reward for their alliance. Each was eager to receive an unexpected reward. However, they had to come to me so that we could transfer it properly.

For the most part, things went easily. Caranthir's Cohort was in the treasury along with five of Tazmatahela's Dwarves, who apportioned the jewels. I contacted them. They selected the appropriate trove and transferred it to me. Nienna's Cohort ensured that it arrived in the designated area and guarded it against intrusion. I informed the recipient of the amount of gold and the quantity and type of jewels. Finally, Galdor's Cohort transferred it to the appropriate location. With the Elves, we assisted the King or Queen to transfer the treasure directly to their Realm. In all other cases, we helped them distribute the treasure among the carts and wagons they had designated to haul their booty away.

Each of the four Elf Tribes was surprised and flattered. None had expected two tons of gold plus a huge trove of jewels. They had fought for ideals and survival.

The Dwarves were also surprised, but the moment I disclosed the gold or jewels, their natural avarice surfaced. Other than Clan Tazhela, each began to haggle, espousing their particular position and disparaging that of other Clans. I admonished Jharl Azkhalish.

"My Jharl, what is this I see? You entered into this war solely for the survival of our Clan. We were attacked by force of arms, by stealth and by magic. We resisted and found we were strong. We allied with the Humans, the Elves and our kin of the other Clans against the common foe. Never did we enter this war for a monetary reward. However, as your Thane of Diplomacy, I have found a treasure for our Clan. I am proud to add this treasure to the honors we have received in defeating the Adjudicars. But, My Jharl, do not expect greater honors than we have already received. It would not be appropriate."

Jharl Azkhalish glowered at me, his brow knit, and eyes flashing. "My Thanelish! Speak to me thusly you dare?"

"My Jharl, I have spoken honestly and openly, as I have always. Would you expect less of me?"

He sighed, "Nay, correct you are. In fact, cart is too small. I sent for a larger one. Two tons of gold is large, even by Dwarfish standards. And, the jewels are magnificent. Many will bedeck the Crown of Ez-Tansk, and many more the coronets of my Thanes."

A wagon pulled up, drawn by four dwarves. They loaded it quickly. A two hundred pound block of gold was a mere trifle to them.

The other Dwarf Clans were equally argumentative, except Tazhela. Jharl Tazmatahela nodded knowingly. "Well done have you been, your Majesty. It is well that you have done this, for I would not have trusted me to do it. Your name shall live in our Clan's history."

The last of the Dwarves to arrive was Thane Defghamask. He was astounded at the extraordinary wealth laid out before him. Before he could say anything, I asked, "My Jharl Designate, we must make a choice. Of all the Clans, ours suffered the most. The dwarrow of Ghamarazh has been a battlefield. We must rebuild, and we must recompense our people for their losses. Our kin have suffered mightily and are in need of restitution.

"You might take this treasure with you when you leave for our dwarrow. Alternatively, I could bring it with me when you are coronated. I will relinquish this crown to you and the responsibilities that are entailed in it. Then, as the High Queen, I can transfer this entire treasure before your throne. Your entire Clan will see the reward of their courage in the face of an implacable enemy. Their vengeance will be laid out before them all, and you will be the one responsible for leading them to victory."

"My Jharl Regent, I appreciate your many kindnesses. Let us consider another approach. I will take this treasure to our dwarrow, but I will not speak of it until you have placed the crown upon my head. Then, I will ask you to present this treasure to me and to explain it. I will accept it for Ghamarazh and begin the healing process with my Thanes and Squires."

"Excellent idea, My Jharl Designate."

Yurchist Linda greeted me warmly. "Gilraën, why have you summoned me?" she said, rather stiffly.

I reached out and hugged her. "Oh, Linda, Rue is dead!"

She hugged me back, and we sobbed on each other's shoulders for a few minutes.

We recovered our senses, dried our eyes and blew our noses. "I do have something else for you." The pile of gold and jewels appeared in the designated spot. "These are for you and your Orcs for all your assistance. I know you didn't ally with us for a reward, so this is an unexpected surprise."

"But," she giggled, "aren't all surprises unexpected?"

"Oh, you!" I giggled.

"Anyhoo," she continued, "what is this?"

"About two tons of gold and a pile of jewels."

"Oooh! My tribe will be elated... not so much for the jewels... we have plenty of them, but the gold is great. We don't have much of it, and we really need it to make our jewelry."

"Jewelry?"

"Oh, yes," she nodded vigorously. "We a make the best jewelry on the continent." She saw the look of surprise on my face. "No, really, we do. You should see my crown. It's tall and lacy, with jewels all around the band and throughout the lattice. It's stunning. We trade them all over this world to the very rich and very famous. When it comes time for your crown, talk with me. We'll make something very special for you. Just remember, ours are the best."

"And I'll pay for the best? No 'friends' discount?"

"No. We don't have to discount."

"Oooh! Talk about a sales pitch!"

"Well, I have been doing it for twenty years, as you know. I was a high quality jeweler back home. Now, my entire Tribe has learned these arts."

"Agreed, but it'll be a while."

"OK, you know where to find us."

"Now, I need to talk with the Yurchists of the Eastern and Western Meadows. They didn't respond to me. I have half a ton of gold and jewels for each of them."

"Really? They aren't expecting anything."

"Yes, but they earned it, and it's theirs if they want it."

"I could bring it to them."

"No," I replied, "I want to meet them and to thank them for their help. I want to encourage their alliance."

"I'll try, but they're going home."

"They don't care about the gold? Or the jewels?"

"No, not really. They're farmers… perhaps the very best farmers, herders, and such. Gold doesn't feed cows, and jewels are only good in chickens' gullets."

"But, gold and jewels have buying power. Surely they need money."

"Yes, and no. They have long-standing relationships with the Dwarves in the same way that the Orcs of Umbeqjaralii have with King Richard's… now King William's court. They are proud, self-sufficient, and are best when left alone to tend their animals and their lands. They sell their produce, because it is excess and would otherwise go to waste, which they would never allow."

"But what if they have a reversal? What if something goes wrong?"

"If they are in difficulties, everyone else is worse off than they are."

"OK, talk with them. If you can, persuade them to take their rewards. Otherwise, can you take it in trust for them? You're the Yurchist, right?"

"Sure, I'll watch out for them. If they need it, I'll let them know it's from you in remembrance of their service to the people of these lands."

"Perfect. Thank you, Linda."

Retribution lumbered up. "Hey, Linda, how are you," he rumbled.

"Great! And you, Retribution?"

"Good, thanks. Hey, Gilraën, you wanted something before we left?"

"Yes, Retribution, I did. I have something for you, Vengeance, Retaliation and your families. I don't know if gold or jewels are important to you, but I have a thousand pounds of gold and a pile of jewels for you. It's your share of the treasure."

"Treasure? What treasure?"

"Beckworth and his Adjudicars stripped this world of tons of gold and mountains of jewels. I've divided it up between us." I *summoned* five bars of gold and a small pile of jewels. "These are yours. I just require that you ensure that Justice's and Integrity's families are equally compensated."

"That's damned nice of you, Gilraën. We expected nothing, so this is really great. And, yes, we'll make sure their families are cared for. But, what of the other Krelli?"

"That's up to you. Right now, you are the leader of the Krelli. I won't interfere unless a Krell does something stupid. I will let you handle it, if you can. If not, I will."

"Yes, I believe you will. I've seen you in action. You're the only Elf I know that could. Look, I don't guarantee anything. There are only three of us left and four of Beckworth's supporters. I doubt we could control them. However, maybe they've seen the light and will come over to us. We're setting up on the back side of Ozhemia, just north of Zhaenstain, between the Dwarf and Wendle Rivers. We should be fine.

"As far as the gold and jewels are concerned, we'll take it all and gladly. I don't know what we'll do with it, but it's better to have it than not to have it. Many thanks, Gilraën, and if you have a quest in the future, call on me."

He stuffed the jewels into his oversize pocket and scooped up the half-ton of gold as though they were his groceries. He turned and almost bumped into Artestius. They greeted each other and Retribution was on his way.

"Gilraën?" the Troll mumbled.

"Artestius, it has been a long time since we met in Tamvill. I thank you for your alliance, your help and your friendship. I have a surprise for you." I pointed to the pile that I had *summmoned*.

"What's all that?" he asked.

"It's your share of Beckworth's treasury."

"That's a lot. And, the jewels, too?"

"Yes, it's for you and all the Trolls who fought against Beckworth. I do want you to share it with the others and attempt to control those who didn't. You are the one I know, and the one I will ask to help. Will you do it?"

"I can't. I can't control the others, not even with all that. But, I will try."

"Where will you be?"

"There's a nice valley south of the Dwarf River. It's not all that far from the Krelli, but far enough. It's between Worfellsten and Zhaenstain, but well hidden from them, and far enough from the Orcs."

"Very good and thank you. Do you need any help with that?"

"No, I have four others. It is a small load for five of us. Be well, Gilraën."

"Travel safely, Artestius." I waved to him.

I was looking around when a mass of legs scuttled to me. "Mort! You scared the life out of me!"

He clicked and clattered, hissing. "I am here, Gilraën. Your desire is what?"

"I have this for you." I pointed to the pile.

"What is that?"

"It is Beckworth's treasure… at least your part of it."

"I have no need of such things."

"You have no need of gold or jewels?"

"I am an arachnid, Gilraën. Just leave us in peace; that is all I ask. Be well, Gilraën." He scuttled off as scarily as he had arrived.

My mirror announced, "Queen Gilraën!"

I had to find my quiver. Then I had to remember which pocket I'd used to hide it. When I finally found it, I asked, "Who calls for Queen Gilraën?

"Queen Órelindë Telemnar Anwarünya." Her face appeared.

"My Queen, I welcome you," I responded.

"Queen Gulámae, I congratulate you on your victory."

"I thank you, Queen Órelindë. We could not have done it without your support and assistance."

"I thank you for remembering our service to you. Such services are generally forgotten. But, is that the reason for your instruction to speak with you?"

"We discovered a vast treasure beneath Beckworth's fortress. I know that your support cost you in time and effort. Your ships could have been trading across the sea. But, they weren't. Instead, you sent them to us. I need to not only say thank you but also repay you. So, I have a portion of the treasure set aside for you. I will transfer it to you if you will inform me of the location."

"Queen Gilraën, I am astounded, but how much is this treasure of which you speak?"

"Five two-hundred pound bricks of gold and about a dozen well-considered gems."

"That is a sizable treasure, Queen Gilraën. It will more than repay us for supporting you. The question is, how do we repay you? You freed us from the tyrant, the murderer and usurper. We are the ones who should be paying you."

"Oh, I am well compensated, I assure you. I can *transfer* it to you when you show me where."

She did, and I did.

"I have received the treasure, Queen Gilraën. You are most generous. End!"

"Queen Tári Lossëhelin Nenhámra!" I commanded.

"Who calls for Queen Tári?"

"Queen Gilraën Gulámae."

"Wait!"

'*Hmm*' I considered. '*A bit brusque.*'

I waited. And I waited more. Then, I counted to five hundred. "Terminate!"

'*If she doesn't want it, I won't give it to her.*'

"Nessa Narmolanya!"

"Hello, Gilraën, I have been following your exploits. Very well done. You have succeeded beyond my wildest hope. You defeated Lord Beckworth. You discovered he was an Adjudicar. You killed him and two other Adjudicars. You assembled an army of half the Elves and Dwarves, almost all the Orcs, plus Krells, Trolls and Spiders. Soon, you will crown a Jharl of one of the largest and most prestigious of all Dwarf Clans. You have re-established the Kingdom of Umbeqjaralii and placed the north on a new economic footing. You are quite amazing!"

"Well, thank you, Seeress. I have another surprise for you. We found the Adjudicar's treasure. It was huge! I've apportioned it among King William, the Tribes, Clans and other groups. I just tried to talk with Queen Tári, but she's not answering my mirror. I believe that none of this could have happened without you. So, I have allotted a share of the treasure to you. I am prepared to transfer it to you. Just provide me with an image of where you want it, and I'll put it there."

"How much is it?"

"A ton of gold and a pile of gems."

"A ton!"

"And a pile. It was quite a hoard."

She pictured a location, which I relayed to Galdor. He and his Cohort fixed the treasure in their minds and then the position to which it should be transferred. A few seconds later, it was gone.

"Oh, my!" she exclaimed. "So that's what a ton of gold looks like. It's not all that impressive is it? OOH! Those jewels are just lovely! Thank you, Gilraën. I shall have to consider how to set them."

"Aha!" I laughed, "I have the perfect solution. Talk with Yurchist Linda of the Chrystal Crags. They are expert designers and jewelers."

"Fine, I shall seek them out. Now, did you make provisions for you and yours?"

"Oh, yes, I'm set for life and then some."

"Now, you must remember that you have fulfilled your contract. You have limited time before you must return to Earth."

"Really? I have to return?"

"Oh, yes, that's a condition of your contract."

"How long do I have before I have to go?"

"I can't be sure, but soon. So, do what you must, but prepare to leave."

"How?"

"You must leave from the place you arrived."

"From a filthy ditch?"

"No, from the platform in Shesol Vys. Master Farmount will return you to the place from which you came."

"Can I bring anything with me?"

"Oh, yes. Whatever you are touching with your skin will go with you. But, remember that when you arrive, it will be you, not Queen Gilraën Gulámae."

"If I hold a bag, will the stuff in the bag come with me?"

"Oh, yes."

"So, if I lay on a bunch of gold bricks, they'd come with me."

"Oh, yes, that's correct."

"So, when I return, I could be really rich."

"Perhaps, but how will you explain your sudden wealth?"

I thought for a few seconds. "Yah, that could be a problem."

"And, Earth is not what it was, nor are you."

"How long do I have?"

"Only a few weeks… not more than a month."

"Good, I have a crown to restore to its proper authorities in nine days. Then, I have to establish a Realm for my Tribe. Oh, that's a good question. Do they have to return, too?"

"No, they didn't insist on an iron-clad contract, like you did."

"I see, so it's my fault."

"Oh, yes."

"And, if I don't leave, what then?"

"Oh, you will die."

"Die?"

"Yes. You signed a magical contract. If you attempt to break it, the magic of the contract will draw power from you until you have none left."

"Will it be sudden or a little at a time?"

"More sudden than lingering."

"And, when I'm back on Earth, I'll be same old me?"

"Yes, warts and all."

"But, what if I don't want to go?"

"You have no choice, Gilraën. No choice at all."

"Can I come back if I want?"

"No, you won't have any magical powers."

"Damn!"

* * *

Before we went to sleep, we *transferred* my fifty-nine blocks to Shesol Vys, William's forty-eight blocks to his treasury in Jhal'm Thaer. We *transferred* twenty-five blocks intended for Cassandra to Shesol Vys and twenty more to Armjurst's fortress in Narwortland. We sent fifteen blocks for Geoffrey in Coephalli, and fifteen more to Richmond in Phaedham. We *transferred* seven each to Domnall, Deplos, Cumbrie and Sheldrick. Each *transfer* included the appropriate jewels. I personally handed each of my Tribe and each of my Ghillies a brick of gold and a pouch of jewels. Each was astounded. This was extraordinary wealth for a common person... something on the order of 7.5 million Golds in local currency or about 3.6 million dollars.

Despite feeling wonderful about distributing Beckworth's hoard, I was upset on a personal basis. I really didn't want to go. Yes, when I got home, I'd be fabulously wealthy, but how could I spend it? Can you imagine how to explain seventy million in gold and perhaps more in jewels to the tax people? It might work out if I put it into the Caymans or Brazil or someplace, but how to get it there? Smuggle it through security? Not likely.

Besides, I liked it here. I really did. I had my own apartments with four wonderful servants who treated me like a queen. I was a Queen, which was another good thing. And there were my Elves... my Tribe. I had a family, and I could have a Realm, if I wanted to make one.

Where? There were huge forests in Umbeqjaralii. Maybe west of Sheshol Vys? Maybe the triangle between the West Highway and the Southwest Highway? It was nice there. Perhaps I'd use Triston as my point of entry. Maybe even extend beyond Triston to Shesol Vys? And Jhal'm Thaer? A big chunk of land. Lot of forest, but resources? I didn't know. Then there was that whole virtually uninhabited area north and east of Jhal'm Thaer. Wasn't that where Dominica was?

And that brought up another thought: William. I really like him. I mean, I **really** like him. He's so nice, and handsome and nice. I really enjoy holding him and kissing him and him holding me and him kissing me. And I get so HOT! He really turns me on. And, he's part Elf, so he has the stamina. And stamina is important. I giggled.

'Hold on, Tony!

'No, I'm not just Tony.'

That's right. I'm Tony there, but I'm Gilraën here. And here is here and there is there. And never the twain shall meet. Damn! I could be really happy here – family, friends, Tribe, wealth... a future I'd never dreamed not even when I'd been fully absorbed in one of my virtual reality/role-playing games.

What could I do?

* * *

I awoke almost as tired as when I'd fallen asleep. Tree creatures were chattering noisily. Birds were chirping their little hearts out. People were talking quietly. The smell of food cooking made my stomach growl with hunger. And 'nature' was calling – loudly.

I struggled to arise and dress. The urge was overwhelming. I didn't dress or arm myself, except I did grab Zhenesta. I had gotten into the habit of having one of the Soul Blades with me at all times. It was just an elementary precaution, especially when in the field.

I found a convenient spot. We had dug latrines in out of the way spots with plenty of nearby mosses, which took the place of toilet paper. I was just done, when I felt a presence... hostile... anger... hate! I leapt up, and spun around just in time to be hurled to the ground, a huge weight on my chest.

"Gotcha, bitch!" the Krell growled.

I took no chances. *'Transfer!'* I commanded, directing my arrival to my camp.

I stood looking at the fire where three Archers and five Elves lolled. "Krell!" I yelled and pointed. "To Arms!"

Galdor's Cohort appeared around us, fully armed, shields at the ready, spears extended.

"Krell! Attacked me over there."

The Cohort formed into line-of-battle facing towards my latrine. Nienna's Cohort joined us as the Ghillies and Elves that had been relaxing leaped up and headed for their tents. Moments later, twelve Ghillies surrounded me, arrows nocked and bows at the ready. Nine more Elves appeared at my side.

Nienna asked, "Perhaps you should dress, My Queen?"

It was only then I realized I was standing there in light shift, shaking from cold and fear. As I moved to my tent, my troop moved with me maintaining their guard about me. Moving quickly but not hastily, I donned my full armor and weapons to take my place at the head of my small army.

"Advance!"

My Ghillies had taken advantage of the few moments it had taken me to dress. Twelve chariots raced ahead in a skirmish line. Galdor's Cohort went right; Nienna's left. I went between them with Caranthir's Cohort around me just behind the Charioteers. Ours was a basic encirclement formation. Hopefully, we'd spread our flankers far enough to trap him and then to drive him towards the center, where we could capture him.

A monster raced toward me. He struck at a chariot caving in the left armor, knocking three zhaks down, ripping the chariot apart and ejecting the Charioteer. I stood at the center of a line of eight Elves, each of us determined to kill this brute. I felt a sudden surge of anger. He had hurt one of my Cavalry! He had hurt three zhaks! My blood boiled!

I held up my right hand and yelled, "Wall!"

The Krell ran into an impenetrable barrier. He looked like Wily Coyote! Splat! But I had no sense of humor.

I leapt onto his chest, Paer Jhaes at his throat. Eight Elves followed my lead, pinning his arms and legs, with spears pointed at his eyes. "Gotcha, bitch!" I growled.

He was woozy. His eyes didn't focus. He blinked once... twice. Then he growled and heaved! But we were too quick for him. He had one spear through each leg, one through each hand, one through each shoulder, one in his jaw and one that ripped open his face. I stabbed straight down into his throat. Blood spurted as he struggled to free himself.

"Stop, or you will die, Krell."

"I'm dead, anyway."

"Not yet, unless you want to die, in which case, we'll let you. If not, we'll heal you."

He ripped his right hand free of the spear, losing a finger in the process, and struck me. I fell off to his left, and he rolled after me. I rolled again, spun to my feet and leveled Paer Jhaes at his groin. Already, seven Elves were swarming him, stabbing and leaping back to avoid his wild swings. Timing his movement, I stabbed into his chest, penetrating a lung. Another slashing spear hamstrung him, and he fell heavily onto one knee. I stepped up, stabbing up under his chin just far enough to penetrate and lift his head.

"Krell, you will die if you keep this up. Surrender now or die."

He fell back. "You win, bitch!"

"Uruviel, heal the mortal wounds and the bleeding."

She bent over him, touching his wounds and muttering.

"Lenwë, check on the Charioteer and the zhaks."

I could see the effect on him, as color returned to the Krell's face. I stopped Uruviel.

"Now, Krell, who are you?"

"I am Shadow."

"So, what did I do to you?"

"You killed Beckworth."

"Yes, I did, and Caierne and Thandekre, and a bunch of other Sorcerers that used to work for him. And, I killed at least two if not three Krelli, and now you. So, why did you attack me? Do you think you can undo this war?"

"They swore me to kill you or die in the attempt."

"Sworn to whom?"

"Do you think those three are the only Adjudicars?"

"Tell me."

"They know who you are, and where you are, and who your friends are. They are all under threat from the Adjudicars."

"Do they know I'm coming for them?"

He laughed himself into a coughing fit. "You? You are nothing. They know you are not long for this world, but they fear that you might return. That bitch Seeress is powerful, and they don't trust her. She just might pull it off. So, they contracted me to kill you."

I was surprised. So, I asked him, "How did they know?"

"How do you think you got here? You contracted with the Adjudicars. If it hadn't been for that Seeress bitch, you'd have been one of us."

"So, which Adjudicar put a price on my head?"

"Doesn't matter, does it? They did. I failed. Someone else will try again until you're off this planet or dead."

"So, what am I to do with you?"

"Don't matter. I failed. I'm dead."

"You seem awfully alive to me."

"No, the next one will kill me, too."

"Oh? Do you really think a Krell can defeat any of my Elves? Any one of them is more than a match for the likes of you, and together, they can overpower all the Adjudicars on this planet. They'd better get off this planet before my Elves find them."

"Don't tell me. They don't listen to me. They just tell me what to do, and I do it."

Lenwë interrupted. "Rodriguez suffered a broken leg, but he is healing. Two zhaks, the stallion and a mare, were injured. He had a broken jaw; she had a bruised rib. The shielding protected them. Evidently, there were strong wards applied to them."

"So, they will be all right?"

"I'm sure, they will be fine."

With that worry out of the way, my mind returned to the problem of Shadow. I walked away, wondering, *'What to do?'* I ended up in William's camp, explaining what had happened.

William was irate. "They're hunting you? And you captured a Krell that was trying to kill you?"

"Yes, but what do I do with him? What do I do about the Adjudicars? How do I protect everyone?"

"Turn him over to me. I'll take care of him."

"What will you do to him?"

"What you should have done, but didn't."

"You're going to kill him?"

"Yes, and I will attach his head atop a pike above my castle's gate as a warning to others: Hunt us, you will die."

"That's murder, William!"

"Queen Gulámae, an enemy attacked you. As King of Umbeqjaralii, I sentence him to death. Execution is to take place, immediately. That is not murder, My Queen. That is the King's justice."

I tried to say something, but William had set his jaw and spoken in *that* tone. He was serious and adamant. And, worse, he was not only right, but he was within his rights. And the symbol of the head on a pike was ancient and recognized by all for its meaning.

"I'd rather you didn't. It's messy, and it smells after a while. Oh, and it's very unsanitary. Besides, what will killing him accomplish?"

"Getting rid of a Krell. I think that's sufficient. Remember, Gilraën, Krells killed Dominica. Krells murdered her whole Tribe. If it hadn't been for you, I'd have attacked Justice with my entire army, just to kill him. I want none of them left alive."

"You will have to make exceptions, William. Retribution, Vengeance and Retaliation are on our side. They fought for us and against Beckworth's Krelli. They are under my protection."

"If you say so, Gilraën."

I didn't know what to say after that, so I didn't. Abuahad had called to William, and they walked off in the other direction. So, I kept on wandering and ended up in Brown Hills' camp.

"My child!" Queen Eilol greeted me. "You are disturbed. What's the matter?"

I told her the whole story. She was shocked. "A Krell here, in the midst of the largest army in this land's history? And, you defeated him... with magic?"

"Not really. I created a solid barrier, and he ran into it. After that, there were ten of us."

She laughed. "Well, you did stop him. So, what will you do with him?"

"William has told me to turn the Krell over to him. He's going to behead him and stick his head on a pike."

"Kill him! That's barbaric! Why is he doing it?"

"An example to others. It's an ancient warning to other miscreants. It says, 'This is the consequence of your actions.' It's very effective."

"Is there no better way of handling such things?"

"I don't know of any that are as effective or efficient."

"Barbaric!" she sputtered. Then, she looked intensely at me, "But are you all right? You seem disturbed by more than just this Krell. What is it, my daughter?"

"Oh, it's just that my contract is fulfilled. I have to return to Earth, and, once I'm there, I can't come back. I really don't want to go, but I have to 'cause my contract says I must."

"Contract? What's a contract?"

"Oh, it's an agreement between two parties. I say I'll do something for someone, and they say that in return they'll do something for me. So, I contracted to come here and fight to overcome Beckworth. In return, they will pay me and send me home when I've done it. So, I did it. Now, I have to return to Earth and will be paid as agreed."

"With whom did you make this contract?"

"Whoever it was that was bringing people from Earth. I'm sure the Adjudicars were heavily involved, but so were King Richard and the Seeress. So, I have to return to Shesol Vys, where I was supposed to arrive, and they'll send me back to Earth. Since there's no magic on Earth, I'll live out my days as a fat, old man playing computer games."

"Are you sure of this contract?"

"Yes, the Seeress explained it to me."

"Does William know? Does your Tribe or Charioteers know?"

"No, I've just found out, and I don't know how to tell them."

"How much time do you have before you have to leave?"

"I'm not sure, but it's less than a month. Nessa says I have time to attend the coronation of Jharl Defghamask, but not much longer."

"So, I'll lose a second daughter? This is too much." She hugged me tightly. "At least I will have you for a short time. It is better than I had hoped. Come, sit with me, and we'll have a cup of wine."

* * * * *

Chapter 7 – Herald

When I returned to my camp, it was well after dark. Harold rushed up to me. "Where ya been, Gilraën? What'll we do with the giant?"

"I'm turning him over to King William. He's going to execute him and put his head on a pike."

"Yuk!" he exclaimed. "Messy!"

I nodded in agreement. "Any food left?"

"Sure, we kept something warm for you. There are three pots on the side of the fire. Dig in."

As I sat and ate, all of my Tribe and all of my Charioteers wandered in to sit around and stare into the hypnotic flames. "I have received disturbing news from the Seeress. It will affect all of you. My time here on this planet is limited. I must leave in a few weeks."

They all gasped. Harold, as always, was the first to speak. "Why, Gilraën? Why would you leave us?"

"I have no choice, and that's why I'm telling you. We all signed contracts when we came here. The normal contract was open-ended. Once here, you stayed here until you died.

"Mine was different. Mine is a closed contract. Once I had fulfilled it, I negotiated that they would return me along with my personal wealth plus whatever booty I could find. So, when I go home, I will be fabulously wealthy, if I can find a way around the IRS."

"Oh, that's easy," Erin said. "Just send it to an account in the Caymans under your name and social security number."

"It doesn't work that way. I have to carry it. It has to be touching me."

"Ah, let me think on that," she replied.

"So," I continued, "after we coronate Defghamask, I'll go to Shesol Vys and *transfer* back to Earth. In the meantime, we have to establish a Realm for you Elves, and a permanent home for you Charioteers and your zhaks."

Nienna asked, "Why not have the Charioteers and zhaks stay with us?"

"OK, let's consider that suggestion. First, you're Elves, and they aren't. Regardless of what you do, some of your magic will rub off on them. The longer they stay with you, the more they will absorb. Remember that it was my suggestion that the Archers get to know the zhaks started this whole affair. I tried to calm the zhaks by contacting them mentally. That was all it took."

"Is that bad?" Harold asked.

"I don't know, and that's the problem. The more intelligent the zhaks become, the more independent they will be. At some point, they might refuse to engage in such dangerous things as war. They'd figure out they could be killed for no reward for them. And, what if you Archers become magical? How does that change the dynamic or your missions? How will you hand on your skills to the next group of trainees if you rely on magic rather than skills to perform your role as Archers or Charioteers?"

"Will the presence of Charioteers affect us?" Galdor asked.

"Yes, but I don't know how," I answered as honestly as I could. "However, I ask you to consider it carefully. There is an upside and a downside, so you must discover each of them, evaluate them, and draw the proper inferences.

"Now, where would you like to live for the next few millennia or so?"

Orophin answered, "We haven't seen much of this continent, so it'd be hard to suggest anything."

"We can be of some help," Harold volunteered. "We've explored a lot of the lands south of Shesol Vys and found nothing all that nice. We've also explored a lot of the forest north and west of Shesol Vys. And, I know that Gilraën wanders through those woodlands."

He looked at me, and I nodded.

Harold continued, "They're nice. It's not all forest, although there are stretches of deep woods. There are broad meadows, steep hills and cliffs, streams and ponds, with lots of animals and plants. Many of the plants produce fruits or roots that the locals enjoy. It's really nice.

"We don't know anything about the woods lying east of Jhal'm Thaer. That was the Realm of William's wife, Dominica. They say that those woods are still under the influence of the Elves, and there's magic in the ground. They tell me that it's haunted, and the animals and plants are all more sentient and alive than elsewhere.

"I haven't heard anything about the woods towards the Brown Hills. And the north woods are almost uninhabited. The only place they tell me not to go is the lands south of the Nish River. It's somebody's Realm... probably the Green Mountain Elves."

"How do you know these things?" I asked.

"Oh, we talk with everyone. We talk with the Palace Guards, the household, the other troops, and even the occasional Orc."

"You speak Orcish?" I asked.

"No, not really. They speak a jargon of the common tongue, and we picked it up. It's not all that easy to talk with them, because they're very serious, especially about their families and farms. But, if you just sit and talk with them, they know a lot."

I laughed. "So, you are a natural gossip vine."

"No, but we keep our eyes open and our ears flapping, if that's what you mean?"

"Well," I joked, "it sounds like our Cavalry has done its job, once again."

"And," Galdor added, "it sounds like another reason to keep Gilraën's troop together, whether Elf, Ghillie or zhak."

"Yes, that's another plus, but you have to seek the disconfirming evidence."

"Huh?" Harold asked. "What's a disconfirming evidence?"

"When people try to justify their point of view, they seek evidence to confirm their preconceptions. In the process, they dismiss any evidence to the contrary. To counteract that, you must deliberately and conscientiously seek evidence that you are wrong. For every piece of evidence in favor of your prejudice, you must have an opposite one against you. Only when you have assembled all the pros and the cons can you begin to evaluate the merits of the position. You develop premises based on the facts you've assembled, using both the pros and the cons to validate each premise. You build an argument based on those validated premises to derive your conclusion. Sometimes you confirm your original position, but most of the time you modify it to account for the evidence you had deliberately overlooked or discounted. Regardless, your new position is stronger and more valid than it had been."

"And I thought I'd asked a simple question," Harold joked. "So, when do we head north to explore possible sites?"

"How quickly do you travel now, Harold?" I asked. I hadn't seen them in action for several weeks. During that time, they'd had plenty of practice and had been with my Elvin father and mother. Anything could have happened.

"We can do thirty miles a day with ease, and we can push forty when we want to do it."

"So, three days to Shesol Vys?"

"About that. It could be less – the zhaks are eager to get home."

"Shall we leave tomorrow? Is anything keeping us here?" None of them said anything. "Good, we leave tomorrow morning. We will tell the herds that you will return in three days. I'm sure they will be relieved. I'll tell King William we're going and make arrangements for our return to Shesol Vys."

As everyone packed and prepared to leave, I walked to William's camp. I found him in his pavilion with Cassandra, Abuahad, Geoffrey, Domnall, Richmond, Deplos, Sheldrick, the ever-present Talbot and three lords I didn't know. They were sitting in a circle around a series of stools that were bunched together. They'd had laid a map of Jaralii between them, showing the northern half of the continent.

"Welcome, My Queen," William said, standing. "Come sit with us. We are considering the new Kingdom of Umbeqjaralii."

I looked more closely. They had drawn a few balloons across the map. One included the entire west coast. The second include Shesol Vys and the entire southeast. The third included everything north of Shesol Vys. "I'm considering how to administer the Kingdom. It's much too large for one person to do it all. So, I'm thinking of dividing it up into duchies, counties and districts.

"Cassandra will remove herself from Grand Haven to reside in Shesol Vys. She will administer the Principality of Shesol Vys including Beck's Tavern to Shalal'm Caer, Wendleford, Talishport and Tazhton. Count Richmond will retain the County of Phaed. Lord Deplos' District will be in East Umbeqjaralii extending from Easbister to Wendleford to Eastport. Lord Abuahad shall retire from his present position to become Baron of South Umbeqjaralii, from Soubister to Easbister and including Shalal'm Caer. He will also be responsible for the Council of Jaralii.

"Duke Geoffrey will administer West Umbeqjaralii extending from Coephalli to Westport to Great Haven. Lord Henry will retain Grand Haven, Lord Domnall in Dungrampus, and Lord Atherton in Westport.

"I will reign over Umbeqjaralii. Further, I will retain ascendancy in the north and east, including those of Lords Oberon to the north of Jhal'm Thaer, Tullifore in the west, and Lacroix in the south.

"Because of the vast treasure you discovered, there will be lots of money to drive the economy… too much in fact. I will have to raise taxes to maintain roads, rebuild villages, introduce schools, and rebuild trade. I will need an enlightened, talented and energetic administration at all levels. For the most part, it will be my subjects who will be responsible for the changes I envision. But, they will need help and guidance from their royals and nobles as well. What do you think?"

I studied it for a while. Obviously, Cassandra had a huge job ahead of her. Hers was a smaller piece of the geographic pie, but it also contained most of the population of the Kingdom. This would have to become the driving force of the economy. Geoffrey would be responsible for Cassandra's old principality, now a Duchy. It was long and narrow, with two and possibly three sea trading hubs. But it seemed to have poor connections to the east with around four hundred miles from Coephalli to Barstough. And the north was desolate. There were two large fishing villages on the coast, but beyond Jhal'm Thaer was only empty forests.

He pointed to the northern lands. "I don't know what to do up here. It's really unexplored. Other than the North and East Highway, there's no hint of civilization up there. The journey from Jhal'm Thaer to North Harbor is an expedition, as it is to Fisherman's Bay, Grand Haven, and Blue Lake. There are no towns, inns or hostels to provide shelter or food for travelers, and no good reason for our subjects to settle there."

I asked, "Has anyone explored the area?"

"Oh, yes, we've sent out various parties to scout the lands. That's how we laid out the routes for the roads. Father always emphasized to us the importance of our road system. He said it was the future of our kingdom, and if we ever let them deteriorate, the kingdom would fail utterly."

"So, what resources are there? Who lives there now? What animals and plants exist there? What is the topography or the geology of the region?"

William's brows knitted. "I don't know. There are some scrolls and a few engineering drawings for the roads. But, we don't know much beyond five miles or so along each side of the road."

I suggested, "Back in the early history of my country, we purchased a huge tract of land adjacent to ours. The people from whom we bought it didn't know a lot about it, and their maps weren't the best. So our President sent an expedition to explore it in some detail. They took several people with them and received some support from the natives. It wasn't complete, but it opened our eyes to the possibilities and potentials of the wilderness.

"Then, to help settle the region, we established military outposts along the major trails. Typically, the large ones were a week or so apart, while smaller ones were just a day or two between them. The fact that there were roads was critical, as your father declared.

However, the protection provided by military troops and the sources of supplies ensured that people began to travel from the heavily populated areas to these newly opened lands. It didn't take all that long before towns and cities developed."

William sat back, staring at the map. "Explore the regions. Establish military posts. Encourage farming and industry."

"And," I added, "do it while you have the resources. Tax, yes, but not so greatly as to discourage farming and industry. And, I love your idea about schools. Education is critical. Boys and girls must learn to read, write, and perform mathematical functions. The most capable among them must go on to learn advanced skills. Some will want to learn to be better farmers. Some will want to become millers, tanners, weavers or whatever skills can be taught. Others will want to learn more about mathematics, astronomy, chemistry, physics, geology, healing or other advanced skills. And many will want to teach what they have learned to children or adults so they can have more productive lives. These people will become the foundations of an ever advancing civilization, developing technology and knowledge."

He beamed. "Yes, this will be most exciting. Perhaps, if we are successful, we will be remembered as are Ulrich, Alexander and Ambrosius."

A short time later, the meeting ended. Everyone returned to their camps, leaving William and me alone. I sighed deeply. I had to break the news, but I had to do it gently. My heart was breaking, and I didn't know what to say that would lessen his pain at my departure. I tried to let him down as gently as I could.

"Oh, two things you must consider. First, before I depart, with your permission and support, I will establish an Elf Realm for my Tribe somewhere within your Kingdom.

"Also, I suggest you make special arrangements for the Charioteers and their zhaks. They are unique and invaluable."

William was surprised, but then considered and answered, "Yes, Dominica had established a Realm, which she maintained until the Krelli murdered her. It was to the northeast of Jhal'm Thaer in the Jaralii Hills and beyond between the North and East Highways. It was lovely, filled with birds and beast, flowers and plants, never too hot or cold, never too wet or dry… an ideal place. I am told that the area is still magical, but none live there for fear of the magic that saturates the area."

Somewhat relieved, I continued, "I'm not sure where we will settle, but it will be near Jhal'm Thaer. Right now, there is sentiment towards the southwest, but we have not explored the possibilities."

Suddenly, he stopped and glowered at me, a look if disbelief on his face. Looking intensely at me, his voice choked with emotion, he stammered, "You speak of departing?"

"William, I will leave this world within the full phase of Llombda." There! I had said it. I felt tears welling in my eyes.

"Leave? This world? What are you saying, Gilraën?"

"The Seeress has told me that my time on this planet is coming to an end. I contracted to wage war against Beckworth. I have done so. My contract is fulfilled. I have received my share of the treasury of Lord Beckworth and the Adjudicars, which is very much greater than would have been my due. Under contract, I will return to my world with my treasure."

"I do not understand, Gilraën. Why would you leave?" He leaned forward grasping my shoulders. He gasped, pleading, "There is much to do. We have to overcome the Adjudicars of Narwortland and Farrowspike. We may be forced to wage war against others of the Adjudicars on other lands. We have to rebuild the Kingdom, establish the Council, and build a new era of prosperity. Why would you leave?"

"Because I have no choice, William," I replied hotly, tears streaming down my cheeks. "My time has come to an end. I either leave or die."

He fell back, slumping in his chair, "But, what of us?"

"This is the price I pay for victory," I sobbed. "We have won. We have preserved your kingdom. We have created an alliance that will destroy the last of the Adjudicars on Jaralii. And, when you are done cleaning this land, you will go forth to free this planet from their scourge, and my Elves will help, remembering my name. And, of course, there are my Charioteers, and they'll be training more Charioteers and specially bred zhaks."

William hung his head. "So, all my hopes are dashed. Victory is bereft of all meaning, and all is as if it were lost." A tear dripped from his chin.

Suddenly, he stood, shouting, "Leave me! I need to be alone."

I stumbled back to my pavilion. I closed the flaps and flung myself on my bed, weeping as though my heart was broken. I had lost! My wonderfully considered, well-conceived and idiot-proof contract was destroying me. My best laid plans had gone aglee, and I was broken, utterly.

* * *

I don't know how long I lay there, sobbing my heart out. I do know that when I awoke I was stiff, and my eyes were crusted shut. It took me a minute to get my eyelashes unstuck. Then, my long red hair was matted and twisted around the side of my head. Even my clothes were wrapped around me, thoroughly wrinkled, and they smelled… no they stank! I stank… or is that stunk? I don't know, but I was offensive to sentient life forms.

Cassandra! She had a bath!

I stripped and put on a caftan-like robe. When I opened the flap, the morning light struck me and, for a moment, I was blind. "Argh!" I croaked, much to the horror and amusement of all my Elves and Ghillies.

Harold guffawed, "Damn, Gilraën, you look like shit!"

"Thank you, one and all. I'm going to find Princess Cassandra and, hopefully, take a bath." I lifted my chin and marched as regally as I could to her encampment.

"Gilraën!" she exclaimed, "Are you all right?"

"No, I need a bath!"

Wrinkling her noses, she blushed "Yes, you do! Thera!" she called to her maid. "We need baths. In the meantime, we need thrak!"

"Oh, bless you!" I rejoined.

"Ah," she joked, "Please stay down wind!" She couldn't help herself. She just laughed and laughed. "What will I do without you?"

That did it! I broke down in tears, sobbing like a child. She rushed to me and held me, rocking back and forth. "That's all right, let it out!"

I blubbered, "I've been letting it out all night, and it's still there."

"Oh, you poor baby." She held me, and I just cried. I couldn't help it. "Here, try this." She pushed a hot cup into my hands.

I slurped at it. "Thrak!" I enthused. "Crap! I gotta blow my nose!" One thing this world did not offer was facial tissue. I did the best I could, and wiped the rest on my sleeve.

Cassandra dragged me to the twin baths. We slipped into the almost too hot water and lathered up. There was no doubt how filthy I was. I began feeling better instantly. The hot bath and the hot thrak slowly worked their magic.

Like Venus, I arose from my bath, refreshed. I slipped into a caftan, kissed Cassandra on both cheeks, and returned to my camp. I ducked into my tent and dressed in clean clothes. After arming myself as usual, I stepped from my tent. It took only minutes to pack everything up and watch it disappear into my quiver. I gathered my entire family.

Harold commented, "You look much better, Gilraën."

I smiled. "Thank you, I feel better. Now, we're going back to Shesol Vys. Before we go, we need to *transfer* our gold and jewels to Shesol Vys. I suggest we place it in the castle's treasury. We can retrieve it when we return. Is that agreed?"

When they all did, we concentrated on the fifty-nine bars of gold and the sacks of jewels still in the vault of Shalal'm Caer. Moments later, all the treasure was *transferred* to William's vault.

"Now, we Elves will *transfer* to Shesol Vys. We will talk with the herds to tell them to expect your arrival in three days. Will that be OK with you?"

Harold looked around to the rest of the Charioteers. Then he turned back to me. "Yes, as we said, we can do it in three days."

"Good, I just wanted to make sure."

I addressed my Elves, "Now, once we arrive, we must look around to determine where to create our Realm. Since I don't know anything about the North, I suggest we start there. Also, that was where Dominica established the Realm of the Great Forest. I'm pretty sure we can do it in three to four days.

"I have to see King William before we leave. So, figure half an hour. We'll all leave together. When we're well out of camp, we Elves will *transfer* to Shesol Vys. Let's give ourselves some time to get settled in. No doubt there will be a thousands questions, which we will have to answer. And, we must talk with the zhaks. So, we probably won't be able to get away until tomorrow. Then, we'll do three days of scouting a new home. Sound right?" When they nodded, I continued, "Good, I'll be back in a few minutes."

I rushed over to William's camp and to his pavilion. As I headed to it, Talbot stepped in front of me, saying, "The King does not wish to be disturbed."

"Talbot, it's me. I want to talk with William."

"My Queen, King William has given me specific instructions. He is not to be disturbed."

"Well, I'm going to disturb him."

"I will prevent it, My Queen."

I glowered at him. "Talbot, I have personally defeated three Adjudicars, several Krells, and countless Sorcerers. Do you think you can deter me?"

"No, I do not. Regardless, I will perform my duties."

"I will inform the King that you did so, and that I overpowered you. He will understand. And, Talbot, thank you for caring for him.

He is important to me, and I will be comforted knowing you are protecting him even though I cannot. Fare well, Master Talbot, and my very best wishes to Gertrude and Brahms."

I stepped past him, pushed the flap aside, and entered. William was sitting at a small table reading from a stack of papers. Without looking up, he growled, "I said I didn't want to be disturbed regardless…," he looked up to see me. "Oh, it's you."

"Yes, it's me. Talbot attempted to stop me, but I insisted."

I rushed to him and grabbed his shoulders, lifting him bodily. I hugged the stuffing out of him for several seconds. Although he resisted, I wouldn't let him go. When he looked at me, I kissed him. "Oh, William, what am I to do? If I stay, I'll die; if I go, I'll wish I'd died."

He relented and kissed me back. "Gilraën, what are *we* to do?"

"I don't know." I broke up, crying on his shoulder. "I'm miserable. Despite all my magic, I'm helpless. My heart is broken, and there is no repairing it."

We stood hugging each other for several minutes. Finally, he asked, "So what are you doing now?"

"We're returning to Shesol Vys. We'll tell everyone that we're victorious. I think I should also tell them that Richard is dead, and that you were gloriously coronated before the entire alliance of Elves, Dwarves, Orcs and other notables. And, I'll inform everyone you will attend the coronation of Jharl Defghamask along with the other monarchs, nobles and notables of the North. I'll also tell the zhaks to expect their kin in three day's time. When you return, there will be great rejoicing throughout your realm, My King." I kissed him again.

"So, that will be the last time we see each other?"

"No, we will see each other again at the coronation of Jharl Defghamask."

"It is just as well that I will be busy. I have a Kingdom to organize, the Council to establish, and a coronation to attend before I return to Shesol Vys. I'll install Cassandra and then head north to

Jhal'm Thaer. So, for the next month or two, I'll be very busy. Hopefully, I'll be able to get over you. It took me a few years to recover from Dominica's death, but at least I'll have Glorfindel and Eilol this time. Perhaps between the three of us we'll find some solace."

"And, I will have no one," I replied. "Perhaps when I return to Earth, I will forget you, like a wonderful dream." I sighed, "I will see you in nine days at the coronation." I kissed him and left, nodding to Talbot on the way out.

I rejoined my family. The Charioteers led out, smartly. The zhaks understood they were going home and trotted briskly. As we passed by the encampments of our allies, they lifted their heads in pride of their accomplishments. Our allies saluted and cheered us as we passed by. Half an hour later, we were well beyond them, and still some twenty miles south of Barstough. I called a halt to address my Charioteers.

"We will be leaving you now. You have a long journey ahead of you. I know you are eager to get home, but do not be hasty. There are still remnants of Beckworth's army about. And, there are always lawless brigands who might attack you. So, be alert. Be watchful and mindful. I hope to see you all in three days. Be well, my Archers; be well my zhaks. I will tell your herds to expect you. Get going, you have a long journey."

They marched off in good order. We waved at each of them as they passed by. When they were finally out of sight, I turned to my Tribe. "Let's go!" We joined hands and reappeared at the edge of the woods just south of Shesol Vys.

"OK, they're not expecting us. Let's give them a show, shall we?"

We spruced ourselves up as much as possible. We extracted our spears from our quivers and slung our shields on our arms. We burnished our helmets and armor. Then the Cohorts formed three lines.

"*Transfer!*"

* * *

The castle of Shesol Vys appeared in the distance.

"Ready?" I asked.

When they nodded, I stepped off at about a two-fold pace. It wasn't all that fast for us, but it was fast enough to make a good show for the sentries and lookouts in the castle. And, we'd take enough time for them to turn out the guard, what little there was, and to alert the citizens of our presence.

Sure enough, we heard horns sounding and drums rumbling. We saw lots of scurrying from the village, and several men at arms appeared on the battlements. Numbers of people rushed from the village to man the outer walls. They seemed to be preparing for a defense of Shesol Vys!

We arrived before the wall gate. It was closed, and they had lowered the portcullis. Half a dozen archers lurked behind the castellations, and several helmeted men armed with long pikes stood above the gate. One shouted, "Hold or we will shoot!" A single arrow landed some five feet before us. "That was a warning. Who are you, and what is your mission?"

I removed my helmet and shook out my mane. I amplified my voice so that even those in the castle could hear me. "I am High Queen Gilraën Gulámae of the Elves of the Green Mountains-Maidstone Forest, Jharl Regent of Clan Ghamarazh, Thanelish of Diplomacy of Clan Ez-Tansk, daughter of King Glorfindel and Queen Eilol of the Elves of the Brown Hills, and ally of the Kingdom of Umbeqjaralii. I come bearing tidings of victory to all of Umbeqjaralii. I have returned to tell the people of Shesol Vys that your victorious army marches to return to their homes.

"Master Thomas! Grant us entry!"

A horn sounded from the castle, followed quickly by a second and a third. Smiles broke out on the faces of the men at the gate. They raised the portcullis and opened the twin gates. Approaching the gates, we saw that the stern faces above us were very young or very old, but all were frightened and relieved. When we entered, people flocked into the streets. We walked to the right and then the left, slowly mounting the slope to the castle. The people cheered mightily. I studied them, seeing that they appeared worn and haggard, as though they had withstood a long, hard winter.

A little girl broke from her mother's arms and ran to me. She lifted both arms in the universal child sign to lift her up and carry her. Of course, I did. She snuggled into me and curled her fingers in my hair. She looked up at me and smiled, and my heart broke. I wept openly as I returned her to her mother.

"Bless you, child," I said, and I meant it.

Master Thomas stood at the castle gate, awaiting our arrival. Twenty men lined the battlements behind him. He raised his hand and said, loudly. "Who are you who request entry into the Castle of Shesol Vys?"

I re-introduced myself, concluding, "It is good to see you again, Master Thomas. We have much to discuss. Has my household been notified of my return?"

He didn't answer. Instead, four women broke through the line of men, their arms opened to me in greeting. Suddenly, I was enwrapped in the arms of four sobbing women. Rosie blurbled, "Welcome home!" Beryl sobbed, "We've been so worried." Dorothea broke away, saying, "I'll make a cup of thrak. Daisy, come heat bath water for the Queen. Hurry, girl, is this any way to act?"

Master Thomas dismissed the palace guard. "My Queen, I report that the castle and village of Shesol Vys is prepared for the return of the King. I welcome your return."

Obviously, he wanted to say more, but this, apparently, was not the time or the place. "You have fulfilled your duties admirably, Master Thomas, and I shall report that to the King. My Elves will now return to their quarters, and I will retire to my apartments. I ask you to attend to me in my quarters in two hours. Is that convenient for you?"

"Of course, My Queen. I shall inform the staff to return to their duties."

As my Tribe marched off to their barracks, I returned to my apartment, accompanied by Rosie and Beryl. By the time we arrived,

Dorothea had a cup of thrak waiting me. I took it in my comfy nook and sipped it gently. "Oh! This is wonderful! Thank you, dear Dorothea."

She beamed and scowled at Rosie. In turn, Rosie took my arm and led me to my bedroom, where she helped me removed my armor. "My Queen, I'm sure you have things that need cleaning, but I can't find them."

I brought my quiver to the bed and opened it. I pulled out all my clothes, making a considerable pile.

Rosie sniffed at the unsanitary mess. "Daisy, would you see to these?"

Daisy came in, took a sniff, and delicately lifted them with her fingertips.

"Aw, come on, they're not that bad!" I declaimed.

"My Queen, far be it for us to contradict you, but I must," Rosie whispered, seemingly afraid of what I might do when contradicted.

"Well... Oh yeah!" I replied.

"My Queen?"

"That was my snappy comeback!" I replied, laughing, "That's a silly way of saying, 'You're right, but I really don't want to admit it.'"

"Oh!" She smiled. "I hope you're not angry with me."

"No, you're right. I've fought several battles, killed countless souls, marched and run. I've fought for my life and that of our King. I've earned that stench, and I'm proud of it."

She smiled. "Yes, My Queen," she replied, somewhat facetiously.

"Your bath is ready," Daisy announced.

"Ah, blessed child," I replied, heading toward the bath.

It was wonderful... my second bath of the day! Thrak, soap, hot water, my rooms, my household ... ah, this was the life. Then it dawned on me. '*Damn!*'

"Daisy," I told her, "When I'm dressed, I want you all to meet me in the parlor. I have an important announcement."

I dawdled, I admit. I really didn't want to do this. However, it was necessary.

When I was finally dressed in an aquamarine dress, my hair done, makeup on and bedecked in jewelry, I went to the parlor. I sat in the two-seat sofa in the bay window overlooking the northeastern battlements. "Everyone, come and sit with me."

They all wanted to stand, but I insisted they pull up chairs around me. "I have something important to tell you. As you know, I come from a distant world." I looked carefully at them. I thought they knew, but I wasn't sure.

Daisy looked at me oddly. "Yes, Daisy, I am not from this world. I was brought here to wage war against Lord Beckworth and the Adjudicars.

"I have done so. I have waged war against him. I killed him, personally. My Elves and I killed his Adjudicars. I tried to save King Richard, but he died."

They gasped in unison. Each clamored for more information. Tears ran down their cheeks.

Trying to reassure them, I said, "I saved Prince William, who is now your King."

It didn't help. They sobbed. We hugged and wept. Even after we had brought ourselves under control, I didn't release them. I had more bad news.

"I have fulfilled my contract," I said "Now, I have to return to my home world. I will leave this planet in the next few weeks.

"I have two duties to perform. I have to establish an Elf Realm for my Tribe. I have to coronate Jharl Defghamask of Clan Ghamarazh. Then, I must return to my native world."

They looked at me as though what I had said was impossible, and that my words were the worst joke in history. Finally, Dorothea asked, "And, when will you return?"

"I won't. Once I leave, I cannot return. I have spoken with the Elvin Seeress, most powerful and wisest among the Elves. She has told me that I must leave or will die. I asked if I could return, and she told me I could not. So, I must say goodbye to you all. It's not immediate, but soon... very soon."

What little control we had established, dissolved. Each of them clung to me, holding me tightly. We slowly slid to the floor, a pile of women, sobbing inconsolably.

There was a knock on the door. We tried to untangle. Another knock. "My Queen, it is I, Master Thomas, as you required.

"Ladies!" I pulled myself together. "We have a guest. Comport yourselves. Beryl, the door; Dorothea, thrak. Rosie, Daisy to your tasks. I will be here. Escort my guest to me."

I gathered my thoughts and swallowed my emotions. It was time to become Queen Gilraën, again.

Beryl didn't look well, but she seemed to have herself under control. Master Thomas approached, hat in hand, and knelt. "My Queen, you summoned me."

"No, Thomas, I did not. I asked you to come. There is much that I wish to tell you, so you will know and you will be able to tell the others. There will be rumors and gossip and loose talk. You will correct this with the truth. Later, I will address all the people of the castle and the village. But, I need your help. Do you understand?"

"Yes, My Queen."

Beryl arrived along with Dorothea. She drew a small table next to Thomas, and Dorothea placed a mug of hot thrak upon it. She placed a second one on the table next to me. "Dorothea, Beryl, have Rose and Daisy join us. You all need to hear this."

When they had gathered, I told them the story... not every bit, but the full story, nonetheless. The telling took about two hours filled with oohs, ahs, oh no's, and gasps of horror, wonder or disgust. Had I been a storyteller, they have flattered me at their response. When I was done, I asked Master Thomas to gather the populace in the courtyard just after supper. I would address them from the wall, where they could all see me and hear me.

"My Tribe and I will attend the mid-day meal. Then, we will attend dinner late in the day. We won't attend supper, so prepare the food accordingly. We will eat early tomorrow. We will need a four-day supply of food for twenty-eight Elves. I'm sure everything you do will be most acceptable.

"Finally, let me tell you that you have done a superb job in caring for the King's castle, his subjects, and his properties. I will so inform King William when he returns. I will add my own praise for a job well done."

"Thank you, My Queen, I have done only my duty. I shall attend to your requirements." He bowed and left.

My household just sat, half in shock. I was almost inured to battle, pain and death. They had been my close companions for weeks on end. My hands would forever be coated in blood, and my soul scarred with death. But these were gentle women, whose bloodiest and most ghastly experience was a cut finger. My tale had horrified them, and they could barely comprehend it.

"I have to go to the paddocks and talk with the zhaks. I'll be back after a while."

I walked down to the paddocks and entered quietly. Taking a barrel of fruit, I walked to the central area and stomped three times. Every ear jerked forward. Every eye turned to me. Every one of them raced out to join me. Noses nuzzled me from all sides. I fed every one I could reach. I spread out my arms, seeking room. When I had some space, I began to stomp, wiggle, whinny, and shake my head, slowly but succinctly telling the story. When I told them their stallions and mares would all be returning within four days, they trumpeted and stomped in joy. The little ones bounced up and down as though they were kangaroos. They all mixed around me, rubbing me and whinnying softly. Slowly, they gathered in herds and returned to their paddocks, eagerly bumping and stomping and neighing quietly to each other.

I just grinned, enjoying their happiness.

I left as quietly as I had entered. I wended my way to the barracks. When I entered, my Tribe was sacked out. They were physically and emotionally drained. I understood them completely. I wondered why

I wasn't in bed and sound asleep. Then again, I had a deadline, and they didn't.

I returned to my rooms. Beryl was ready for me with a mug of thrak. I sat on my balcony remembering the nights William and I sat here looking at the stars and the moons. We had kissed and cuddled and almost.... I missed him. But what could I do?

I thought about reading. Then, I realized I hadn't seen an actual book since my arrival. *'Why not? Well,'* I considered, *'they don't have paper, as such. They don't have a printing press. They don't have book binding... duh, they don't have books. Do they read? William, Cassandra and the nobles do. The guildhalls do. What about regular folk? Can they do math, even at a rudimentary level? They do money, so they must do some math. What are their schools like?'*

"Beryl?" I asked, "Can you read and write?"

"Yes, My Queen."

"How did you learn?"

"My mother taught me."

"Did you go to a school?"

"No. Why do you ask?"

"I was wondering how many people could read, write and do basic mathematics... you know, like count, add, subtract."

"Oh, that is a mother's task. All mothers teach their children while they are young."

"How? Do you have books or teaching materials?"

"When we marry, we receive a scroll from the Town Master. We also have a new clay and stylus."

"How long do mothers teach their children?"

"Until they can do all the things in the scroll."

"Do you have a copy of the scroll?"

"No, but you might get one from Master Thomas."

"Does anyone go beyond their mother's teachings?"

"Some do, but they are exceptional boys. There are schools that take children at a young age to teach them. Many apprentice to learn skills, like millers, or tanners or smiths. Some learn to weave, or sow, or clothe. Some learn to farm or flock or herd. Some learn arcane arts like warfare, mapping, stargazing, or healing. But they are few."

"So, almost everyone can read, write and do some basic mathematics."

"Yes, My Queen. Why do you ask about such things?"

"I was here all by myself, and I began thinking about the future. Much of the future depends on learning as much as one can and then applying that knowledge to things that are not understood. Gradually, they invent new things, and they discover new ways. They gradually supplant the older ways, and then new things replace them. Over time, a civilization recreates itself, becoming ever more technological.

"For instance, in my world, we have machines of all kinds. Most of us have automobiles that we drive at high speeds over long distances, and we consider that to be normal. If we really want to travel long distances, we have other machines that can fly us halfway around the world in a matter of a few hours. We even have machines that can carry us to distant worlds. We talk with other people anywhere in the world and see pictures of them and their surroundings as they talk to us. It's like magic, but they are really machines that are doing the work, not magical abilities, so anyone can make them work."

Beryl just stared at me, looking as though I was insane or telling a children's story.

"Really, Beryl, that's the world I come from."

"But, it cannot be, My Queen. Such things cannot be real."

I laughed, "But, they are, and one of these days, such things might happen here. If so, I don't know what this world might accomplish. The combination of magic and technology would be extraordinary."

"But," Beryl sputtered, "why do you make these machines? You must use magic to do these things. How are these things possible?"

"That's why I'm asking. I have rid this world of a cancer on the body politic, but what have I done to improve the fate of its citizens? I have little time left, and I want to do what I can to make things better. I'm thinking of asking William to start a school system to educate everyone beyond what their mothers teach them. There is a whole universe of things to learn, and someone has to teach them. We need teachers to teach teachers how to teach so they can teach children beyond what they learn at their mother's knee."

Beryl's brow knitted as she considered my wild imaginings. "Perhaps that would be good, but I am not sure. There are many things we learn, because others show us how to do them. At first we try, but later we can do them."

"Such as?" I asked.

She looked around, saying, "This! I did not learn this from my mother. I learned it from other chamber maids and parlor maids and maids of all kinds. Such a job as this is hard to do, and much needs to be done correctly, because it reflects on you and this house and us. These are not the things from scrolls, but from others showing how to do it and why."

"So, should there be a school to teach young men and young women these difficult tasks?"

"I would not know. How many households are there for a parlor maid to serve? Surely, there cannot be that many."

"I don't know, but last I spoke with King William, he was considering three great households, plus many large households to administer the kingdom."

"Perhaps, but perhaps not. I learned, as did others, from those already doing the job. That is how I learned, as did she who taught me."

"Perhaps a school where all the skills are taught and learned. There are many needed to maintain any estate, plus all those needed by the people who live, work and defend it."

Beryl smiled, saying, "Those are pleasant ideas, My Queen, but I have my duties." And, she was off towards the kitchen, no doubt thinking I was some flaky dilettante.

My musings had whiled away the time. I was dressed appropriately, so I headed down to the great Hall, where I met Master Thomas and my tribe. "It is mid-day, and time for us to enter the great hall. Let us do this formally, Master Thomas."

"It shall be done, My Queen. If you will follow me, I will call the hall to attention."

He led out, followed by my tribe, arranged by Cohort. He arrived at the gate, announcing loudly, "Attend to me! Rise all and welcome High Queen Gilraën Gulámae and the Elves of the Green Mountains-Maidstone Forest."

I heard the sounds of many voices and the scrape of wooden legs on stone floors. Many feet slapped the floor, and the hubbub that had filled the hall suddenly ceased.

Master Thomas stood aside, and Galdor Míriel led his Cohort into the hall. Nienna's Cohort followed Galdor's followed by Caranthir's Cohort. They arrived at the top of the hall and stood around three tables just below the head table. As I appeared at the door to the great hall, they broke into applause. As expected, it was taken up by the thirty or forty men-at-arms and others who had gathered for their mid-day meal.

I entered and stood just within the hall. I nodded to the men who were the closest to the door. As I walked toward the head table, I nodded to each of them, sending positive energy and healing to each person as I looked at them. I doubted they would ever forget the experience of looking into my eyes, sensing my power as they experience feelings of renewal and health.

The applause continued until I had arrived at the throne, standing alone at the center of the head table. Master Thomas held the throne for me. When I felt the chair at the back of my legs, I sat. With that, the applause ended, and everyone else sat.

That was the signal Master Thomas was awaiting. Half a dozen women emerged from the kitchens, each bearing a tray. Master

Thomas disappeared into the kitchen before emerging with a tray. He brought it to the head table and placed it before me. As expected, I took the sharp knife from the table and cut a large slice from the meat. I slid it onto my plate. I cut off a piece and analyzed it carefully. I tasted it carefully. It was good – I mean really good! After weeks on the road, even properly cooked road kill would taste good.

"It is good!" I pronounced. "Let us eat!"

Everyone let out a sigh of relief. For a moment, all I heard was the sounds of ladles on serving dishes and knifes scraping on metal plates. I looked up to see one and all digging in.

Yup, it was good.

When everyone appeared to be finished, I stood. Before they could rise, I said, "Please, stay seated for a moment." I smiled warmly at all of them. "First, let me tell you how proud I am to be in the same hall, eating the same food as all of you. My Tribe and I have fought in distant lands for many days and weeks. We have seen many acts of valor and courage. Today, I compliment you for your fortitude and your service to your King. Even when faced by an army, you swarmed to the defense of your castle and your town. I shall so inform His Majesty.

"Now, I will address you and the entire town. Please exit the gate and gather all the town's folk and the people of the castle and the fields. I have news of great import for you all."

It wasn't quite stampede, but the bunch of them raced out, calling to the town folk to come to the courtyard. It didn't take long. Many were already standing around. More were arriving. My tribe and I mounted the battlements overlooking the courtyard some thirty feet below us. When everyone seemed to have arrived, I began.

"Rejoice all you standing here today! Rejoice all of Shesol Vys! Rejoice all of Umbeqjaralii! Lord Beckworth is dead!"

The crowd cheered and hooted. They danced and yelled. Several bottles appeared, and men passed them around.

When they had calmed a bit, I continued. "However, victory over Beckworth is marred by great losses. Greatest among them is the death of King Richard the Conqueror! The King is dead!"

Cheers turned to sobs almost instantly. Joy turned to grief. Elation turned to desolation. Even more bottles were passed around.

"The King is dead! Long live the King! Rejoice! King William reigns!"

The roller coaster of emotions rolled again! Tears of joy, which had morphed to sorrow, became elation! Even more bottles were passed around.

"The coronation of King William was the greatest in the history of the Kingdom of Umbeqjaralii. King Amder of the Green Mountains, King Fingolfin of the Blue Lake, King Glorfindel of the Brown Hills and Queen Eilol of the Fire Elves, King Séregon of the White Cliffs and all their Tribes celebrated King William's crowning. Jharl Azkhalish of Ez-Tansk, Jharl Galmerstain of Zhaenstain, Jharl Morthanzhemian of Ozhemia, Jharl Tazmatahela of Tazhela, Jharl Worzhemacht of Worfellsten and Jharl Designate Defghamask of Ghamarazh and all their warriors assembled for the King's investiture. Yurchist Linda of the Orcs of the Chrystal Caves and the Orcs of the Eastern and Western Meadows all stood by the King's side. Other notables included Retribution the Krelli and two other Krelli, Artestius the Troll and five of his kin, and even King Mort the Arachnid attended King William's coronation. I personally placed the crown on his head and lauded him before all the Kings and Queens and Jharls and Yurchist and nobles and warriors of the all the armies of the North attended the coronation of your king, William of the House Ambrosius the Beloved, descendent of Ulrich the Great, and Wayland the Founder. Hail King William!"

By this time, the number of bottles being passed around had multiplied. The effects were becoming obvious.

"Hear me, good people and subjects of King William! Rejoice! The armies of the King will attend the investiture of Jharl Defghamask eight days from now. The army will return ten days after that. Then, the King will lead his victorious army to Shesol Vys, where he will take up his reign. Return now to your homes.

Celebrate with your friends and families. Rejoice! Return to your homes with your families and friends! Rejoice!"

Slowly men, women and children wended their way down the hill towards their homes – some more steadily than others. As we left the walls, sounds of cheering and rejoicing echoed and re-echoed throughout the town.

My Elves and I returned to their barracks, where we could discuss our expedition. I began by spreading a large map of Umbeqjaralii on the floor. "Here's what I'd like to do," I said. "I'd like to start by moving westward to Triston. Then, we can explore this area." I pointed to the region between the West Highway, the Great Western Road, and the Southwestern Highway. "I know little about this region, other than it's the region of the five rivers. They start in the uplands to the west of Jhal'm Thaer and flowed almost due west to the West Sea.

"I suggest we separate so we can cover more ground. But, we should maintain mental contact so we know what everyone is seeing and doing. That way, we'll all know whether to explore it more closely.

"Then, we'll go into the northwest forests, between the West and North Highways. The Brown Hills Elves are already there, but in the far northwest corner. The area between the Northwest Highway and the North Highway might be the more interesting.

"Then, we'll explore the area between the North Highway and the Green Mountains. Two major rivers arise in the Jaralii Hills – the North River flows north to North Harbor and the Phaed River flows southeast through Phaedham ending flowing into the East Sea at Phaedport. The Nish River flows from the western Green Mountains to the marshes just north of the Green Mountains on the shore. From what I know, the area south of the Nish River is under the protection of the Green Mountain Elves. So, we'll confine our search to the area between the Green and the North Rivers. One other thing we should remember: these were the Realm of the Great Forest Elves under Queen Dominica, King William's wife. So, we must to tread more carefully there so as not to arouse King William's anger or suspicion.

"We'll leave at first light, if that's OK with all of you?"

They nodded.

"So, what are we looking for?" Galdor asked.

"I'm not sure," I replied. "What do we need? What do we want? What would make this more or less desirable?"

Silmarwen replied, "We need food, water and shelter."

"And, we need interesting stuff, too," Idril added. "I mean, we will live for thousands of years. What do we do with all that time? We need to have something to do that's worthwhile, interesting, and something that can grow as we grow."

"So, what do we do as a Tribe? What does each of us do as individuals? What is our purpose individually and collectively?"

My questions were real stumpers. I hadn't considered either question, and now that I was heading back to my old life on Earth, it really didn't matter to me. But it'd be unfair to abandon my Tribe without a Realm or a purpose. So, I considered those questions as though I were staying here for the next few thousand years.

"Hell," Elros exclaimed, 'the only thing I've been doing since I arrived here is hunting bad guys, whether they're Adjudicars, Krelli, Trolls or whatever. In fact, that's the only thing they have trained us to do."

Everyone nodded. I had to agree. I'd been the only one to explore any part of this land. Yet, come to think of it, Elros was right. They had trained me to fight, and I still had nightmares remembering wrestling Master Vigash. Yes, we had led the way against Lord Beckworth and the Adjudicars, but was that all we were? Is that all we would be for the foreseeable future?

Come to think of it, maybe that was what we were. We had learned the arts of war and had successfully fought the Adjudicars. I understood them better than anyone else in Jaralii. I knew many of their strengths and weaknesses. I knew that we were the only ones capable of meeting them in the Void. Perhaps if we knew more about the Void, we could trace them back to their planet of origin. Anyway, we were the ones who could defeat them. And I'd promised Armjurst we'd help him overcome the Adjudicars in Narwortland. Then we'd have to liberate Farrowspike. And there were at least four other continents infested with Adjudicars. So, we could eliminate them from all of Trahe. That'd be a worthwhile goal.

"You know, we're the only ones who can defeat Adjudicars?"

They looked at me as though I were some kind of nut. However, I refrained from saying anything further, letting my words sink in.

Caranthir asked, "Are you saying that we should be hunting down Adjudicars?"

"Not quite," I answered, "but we must remember why we were brought here. I was brought specifically to defeat Lord Beckworth and his Adjudicars. The fact that he was also an Adjudicar was unknown at the time, and one hell of a surprise to me.

"It was me and the entire council of Elves, headed by the Seeress herself, who brought you here to fight the Adjudicars and to liberate these lands from them. Therefore, not only do you have this ability but also the desire to perceive wrongs and attempt to right them. You are all Don Quixote's, jousting at windmills. Whatever else you do, you will always be paladins."

"Oh, crap!" Lenwë Sáralondë retorted.

We all broke up, laughing. He was usually a nice guy who always said good things about everybody or saw the good side of every situation. Such an exclamation was uncharacteristic of him.

"So, what else do we do communally or individually?"

"I used to make jewelry," Enelya volunteered.

"Automotive engineer," Galdor added.

Celebriän Arcamenel announced, "I'm a metallurgist. I ran steel mills for 20 years."

"I was a commercial airline pilot," Daeron said.

"Biologist," Uruviel volunteered.

"Marine Colonel," Caranthir stated.

"Petrochemical engineer," Findecáno said.

"Bicycle messenger," Lenwë Tasardur stated.

"Retired postman," Nolofinwë said.

Eö stated, "Truck driver."

"Hmmph, New York cabbie," Orophin supplied.

"Sailor. First mate on a tanker," Camthalion stated

"I was," Idril announced, "a computer techie."

Elros raised a hand. "Programmer."

"Foundry manager," Eámanus Calmcacil said, smiling.

Lúthien added, "Third grade teacher."

Fëanáro nodded, "High school English."

"Junior High Social Studies," Nessa added.

"College, business admin," Idril stated.

"College admissions," Eámanë Tîwele said.

Nienna raised a finger, "Cop."

Elrond smirked, "Fire fighter."

Lessien spoke. "I was a medical intern in my last year."

"Premed," Lenwë Sáralondë added.

Alassë said, "I was a retired garbage collector, dying of emphysema."

Silmarwen whispered, "Housewife and mother of four. My kids are all grown up, and my husband is dead."

We all looked at Celebriän Aldaríon. "OK, I was a chemical engineer in heavy industry. And you, Gilraën?"

"Oh, I was an IT Project manager."

"Hmm," I mumbled, "So, we have four computer types, five in engineering and manufacturing, three in medicine, four in education, an artist, six in transportation, one with military experience, four in public service, and one with home and family management experience. What a wonderful diversity. Now what can we do with that?"

Silmarwen suggested, "We don't have any computers on this world, so how does that experience apply?"

I suggested, "Well, computer programs depend on 'and' gates and 'or' gates. There are physical equivalents to both, which could help us in every field. And, we have a short-cut language of sixteen combinations of two characters that can communicate everything. Together, we have the capability to develop complex systems to develop, maintain and control complex systems, from roads, to manufacturing, to military planning, construction and processes."

"But what could a bicycle messenger add?" Lenwë asked.

"Two ways that I can think of instantly." Daeron answered. "First, it's the simplest and most efficient mechanical mode of transportation. Second, it's relatively easy to manufacture – except for the tires. We'd have to work on that."

"Hey," Uruviel retorted, "That's one of the things biologists do. We look for plants and animals for compounds and products we can use. There just might be something equivalent to the rubber tree that we could use."

"Or," Findecáno interjected, "perhaps we could manufacture some. I don't know about the petrochemical resources of this world, but we could explore it to find oil resources that we could use."

"Wait a minute," Silmarwen interrupted, "We don't want to screw up this world like we did ours. No pollution!"

Celebriän Aldaríon replied, "We have to be concerned about throwing around loaded terms like pollution. All processes have inputs and outputs. We are prime examples of a process with inputs and outputs. We eat; then we urinate and defecate. As long as we neither overeat nor over-produce waste products, we are just another part of the ecosystem. It's when we consume too many resources or produce too much output for the ecosystem to absorb that we have a problem. So, we can't do anything if we want a zero footprint. In fact, we can't exist, if those are the rules. However, the ecosystem can absorb what we produce, then it's reasonable and proper to use that process."

Lenwë added, "Yes, but some outputs are extremely dangerous even at low levels."

"That's true," I added. "That's how I met Ez-Tansk. I found they were producing arsenic, befouling the Coulee River. When I brought it to their attention, they accepted my findings and have worked to remove the effluent."

Alassë summarized, "So, we have a variety of off-world skills that could change this entire world. Yet, we are warriors at heart, driven to overcome bad guys and create a better society. So, the two halves of our existence on this planet can be synergistic, if we work at making it so."

We sat looking back and forth at each other. She made great sense. I nodded, "Sounds right to me."

She continued, "So, as we're walking around looking things over, we should think about what we could do to create our society, improve the general condition of everyone on this planet, and determining ways of destroying the Adjudicars, both on this world and in the other worlds they have conquered."

I nodded vigorously, replying, "Yes, that's what we should consider, remembering that we have virtually unlimited time in which to do it. More importantly, unless I can find a way back, you are on your own. I have only a few weeks left on this planet. I have to return to Earth, whether I want to go or not. So, I'll help to get you off on the right track, but after that, it's up to you."

When nobody else spoke up, I stood to leave. "I'll leave this with you to study. Have an early night. I'll see you in the morning."

I returned to my quarters, where Beryl met me. "My Queen, thrak?"

"Oh, yes. I'll be out on the balcony."

I went to my room where I extracted my mirror from my quiver. I wandered out to the balcony, pulling up a small table next to my lounge. After Beryl had delivered my thrak, I concentrated on the mirror. "King William!"

"Who calls for King William?"

I recognized Talbot's voice. "Master Talbot, it's me, Gilraën. Is William available?"

"No, My Queen, he is not. He is with the Elvin monarchs of the north. Most of the Dwarves have departed to their dwarrows, but will return to Ghamarazh for the coronation of Jharl Defghamask. Only Jharl Tazmatahela and his guards have remained. Most of the Orcs have left, except Yurchist Linda and her guard. Most of the Elves have returned to their homes, except for the Kings and Queens with their retinues. King William has sat in conference with them for several days. They are working on the terms of the Council of the Jaralii. There is much to discuss, evidently."

"I'm sure there is. Thank you, Talbot. Don't interrupt them. Have a good night."

I finished my thrak, and, having nothing better to do, I went to bed. I was sure I'd just lay there staring at the ceiling, sure I wouldn't catch a wink. I was wrong.

* * *

I awoke to the trilling of birds, the chatter of 'squirrels' and the morning brightness. I was refreshed and relaxed after a deep sleep in my own bed. I stretched, luxuriating in the strength and feeling of my limbs. I staggered into the chamber, relieved myself, washed my body and returned to my room. A new tunic and breeches lay on my bed, along with long socks and undergarments. As I sat and started to dress, Rosie entered.

"Pleasant day, My Queen," she said, "I have your thrak. How will you dress today?"

"Bless you, dear Rosie! Thrak!" I sipped the delicious brew. "The usual armor and arms. I'll be gone for four days exploring the wilds of Umbeqjaralii."

"Really? What do you expect to find?"

"I need to create an Elf Realm for my Tribe. So, we're looking for a suitable locale. We've never explored these lands, so this is our opportunity to do so."

Her bright mood seemed to vanish almost instantly. "Oh," she mumbled and started for the door.

"Rosie? What's the problem?"

"Nothing, My Queen."

"Rosie, tell me." I persisted.

"What will happen to us when you're gone? We don't belong in your Elf world, and you won't be here any longer."

"Ah, yes." I was stumped. What happens to wonderful servants after their employers leave? "I'm not sure, Rosie. I will have to speak with Princess Cassandra and Duchess Eleanor. I'm not sure if you will be together, but there must be positions for you somewhere. I do know that William is considering several new nobles to help administer the Kingdom. If so, there will be several additional great houses. Surely, those who have served the High Queen will find important postings."

She sniffled, "Perhaps, but they won't be with you!" She broke down in sobs with tears streaming down her face.

I rushed to her and held her in my arms. "There, there now," I commiserated with her.

Daisy arrived and broke down in tears the moment she saw us. Quickly the three of us were weeping as though we'd just lost our best friends.

Finally, I stood back and held them at arm's length. "Now, dry your tears. We are not parted yet, and we all have our jobs to do. Let's get going with our morning routine, shall we?"

They dried their tears, and Rosie helped me dress. I inspected my quiver, pulling some things out and placing other things inside it. One of the new things I hid away was a big map of Umbeqjaralii. I wanted to mark the things we discovered on the map, sort of an inventory of the Kingdom.

I inspected my bow, arrows, sword, spear, dirk and all five of my Soul Blades. I thoroughly examined my armor and shield. When I was satisfied that they were in perfect condition, I stored them appropriately, placed the coronet of Thane of Ex-Tansk on my brow, tucked my helmet under my arm and headed for the door.

Dorothea, Beryl, Rosie and Daisy were all standing there. I couldn't leave until I had hugged each of them. I was deeply touched.

When I arrived at first meal, I slipped in quietly, seating myself with my Tribe. "Well, have you any further thoughts?"

They looked back and forth at each other before Caranthir spoke up. "Yes, we've rearranged our numbers. Rather than travel as our accustomed cohorts, we've divided ourselves more with our specialties. So, we'll have scientists or engineers, transport, manufacturing, medicine and education with each of our three groups."

"Great idea," I responded. "What routes shall we travel?"

Galdor answered first. "We will take the western quadrant between the Southwest Highway and the West Highway. We will travel to northward to the rivers and explore westward, following them until they emerge into the plains of the Great Western Highway. We will then *transfer* to Jhal'm Thaer."

Nienna then replied, "We will investigate the north. We will *transfer* to Jhal'm Thaer and then explore northward between the Northwest and North Highway. We will congregate at North Harbor and then *transfer* to Jhal'm Thaer."

Caranthir said, "We will *transfer* to Jhal'm Thaer and then explore the east between the North and East Highway. We will end at Fisherman's Bay and then *transfer* to Jhal'm Thaer."

"And where would you like me to be?"

They glanced nervously at each other, hesitating to speak.

"Well?" I asked.

Galdor sighed, and then said, "Jhal'm Thaer."

"You don't want me to explore?"

"No," he replied. "We will be here for thousands of years, or at least until the Elves decide we should move to our next world. You will not be here. This will be our home, but it will not be yours. You have led us, but it is now the time for us to make our own way."

I was saddened and elated at the same time. I was saddened, because I would no longer be a part of the Tribe I had helped bring to this world. They were my family. I had taught them, led them, and lived with them. Yet, I could no longer be one of them. Soon, they would be but a memory of a distant time and place. If I had done my job, they would now be ready to take up their position among the Elvin Tribes of Jaralii. And it was almost time for me to return to my former... and my future life.

"Very well, but keep in close touch with me. I want to know what you sense – each of you. I will help and guide you towards the Elf Realm we will create. There is too much at stake, so I will be intimately involved. I will not have you fall to the same forces that murdered Queen Dominica and annihilated the Elves of the Great Forest. Do you understand?"

When they nodded, I told them, "I will head up to Jhal'm Thaer and introduce myself. I'll let them know what's happening and get a room for the night. After that, I may explore a little on my own. I will see you all in Jhal'm Thaer in four days. Enjoy your peregrinations."

I walked with them to their barracks. Once there, they rearranged themselves. Galdor's troop *transferred* to Triston. Nienna's group, Caranthir's group and I *transferred* to Jhal'm Thaer.

The great fortress, castle and keep of Jhal'm Thaer was magnificent. Shalal'm Caer was massive; Shesol Vys was storybook; Jhal'm Thaer was the acme of royalty. The castle itself was perched on a high massif of black basalt more than five hundred feet above the plain. A great wall, perhaps thirty feet tall, surrounded the mount. Within it and extending to the base of the cliffs was a large and prosperous city.

A broad road led to the massive gate, guarded by four turrets. The road led beyond, winding back and forth through the town between stone walls, which served as the outer wall of homes and doubled as mini-fortresses restricting the passages to invaders.

The road ran to the right, where a gatehouse barred the way. The road then turned to pass through a second wall and turreted gate. From below, the wall appeared to be enormous, but much of that was an optical illusion caused by looking upward. In fact, the wall was over fifty feet tall and twenty feet thick. Once through the gates, the road turned left and right and left again, passing through a large gate each extreme turn.

The road became a ramp crossing the face of the cliff below the castle. The first climb ran from left to right at a sharp angle. Then, it passed through a gatehouse and angled upward to a second gated turn. Finally, it rose to a massive gate into the castle. The walls of the castle seemed to rise out of the cliff face itself. From beneath it was impossible to guess their true height. Turrets guarded every turn. High towers rose behind the walls. A turreted keep peered over all, battlements surmounting its walls.

"Wow!" I exclaimed. My Elves agreed with me. We transferred to the outer gate, appearing suddenly before the startled guards.

"Hail, guardians of Jhal'm Thaer! Summon the Master of the Castle. I have come with tidings of war, death and victory!"

An older man stepped forward, his hand raised, palm outward. "Hail Elf! I am Barstow, Master of the Gate. Who seeks Farrell, Master of the Castle of Jhal'm Thaer?"

"I am High Queen Gilraën Gulámae of the Elves of the Green Mountain-Maidstone Forest, Jharl Regent of Clan Ghamarazh, and Thanelish of Diplomacy of Clan Ez-Tansk."

"Ah, Queen Gilraën, welcome. We have been expecting a herald to return to us with news of the battle before the gates of Shalal'm Caer. I would escort you to the castle, but my duty is to guard this gate. However, I shall send a message to the castle. I have no doubt that Master Farrell will be eager to welcome you and to escort you to the keep of Jhal'm Thaer. While we await him, would you accompany me within the gates, where I will offer you refreshment?"

I considered his mind for a moment. He was honest and bore us no ill will. If anything, he was extremely happy to be greeting an Elf, especially one with news about the war. "I am honored to accompany you, Master Barstow. Tell me of your watch. With the army gone to war, have you been troubled?"

"No, Your Majesty. Though there be few of us, either too old or too young, we are sufficient to hold the walls. And, should anyone be so foolish as to assault us, they would face the women protecting their children. Only a fool would attempt such a thing."

I laughed with him. "So, is it the custom among you to teach your women the arts of war?"

"No, quite the opposite. It is the wombmen who teach their children these skills. That has been true since King Ambrosius. It was Queen Goodwina who began this tradition, since she was the Queen, an Elf, mother, and warrior."

We passed through the gate into a small courtyard. There were two tables off to the left and benches along the inner wall. Barstow directed us to them and brought a pitcher of water with many cups. "I'm sorry I have no food to offer you."

"That's all right, Master Barstow, we just came from first meal." He went back to his position on the walls, leaving us to sit in the shade of the wall.

Shortly, a man raced to us. "Queen Gilraën?" I nodded. "Master Farrell has sent me to escort you to the castle. He asks if this is a formal entrance of the Queen or an informal entrance of an emissary of our King?"

"At this time, let's keep this informal."

A broad smile lit his face. "That is well. It would take us most of the morning if this were formal, but it would rouse the good folk. Follow me!" He sped away at a surprisingly high speed. We loped along after him, looking around at the walls, homes and gates. As we climbed higher, we could look out over the countryside far into the distance. The view was magnificent!

Even at our pace, it took a while to arrive at the long, back-and-forth slope. Then, it was a long hike up, and up, and up to the main gate. A man dressed in armor stood at the gate, a sword standing upright with the point in the ground and the hilt in his hands. Six other warriors stood behind him, and more than a dozen archers lined the parapets above him, bolts strung within their crossbows.

He raised his hand, palm outward. "Hail, good Elves. Master Barstow's message tells me we are honored by a High Queen of Elves. With whom am I conversing?"

I explained.

"Welcome, Queen Gilraën. I am Farrell, Master of Jhal'm Thaer. Do you have news of our King?"

"I do, but it might be best if we speak in private before we address the village. I shall stay here for a few days. My Elves," I pointed to them, "will be leaving, but they will all return in four days. I require quarters and the passwords so I may leave and enter at my will."

"It shall be done, Your Majesty. Let us enter the courtyard and then proceed to the hall. I would then instruct my messenger to lead your Elves to the outer gate, if that is convenient?"

"Very well, Master Farrell. Lead on."

We followed him through the massive gatehouse, across the green courtyard, through the turreted main gate into the castle. It was a magnificent structure, right out of Disneyland or Harry Potter. The turrets were over one hundred feet tall with great spires and multiple balconies from which defenders could rain destruction upon their attackers. We were in a courtyard. A castellated wall fifty feet high surrounded us. High windows, balconies and arrow slots broke the walls, establishing unassailable defenses.

Farrell marched ahead to a high, broad reinforced double door. A man-at-arms stood to either side. We walked in, passed through a wide hallway, and through a pair of interior oak doors. We entered a huge, broad, high hall. Dozens of large tables were arrayed on the main floor. Perhaps one thousand could dine there in comfort. A balcony swept around three sides. A stage some three feet high stretched across the upper end of the hall. At the far end was a huge fireplace. The central firebox was tall and wide, but very shallow, perfect for radiating heat. To each side were deep fireplaces, with tripods and sconces over the flames and ovens on each side. Smaller doorways on either side led to rooms behind the brickwork.

"I'll see you in four days," I said to my Tribe, as Farrell led me through the door on the right, into a large kitchen. Several cooks and their assistants were hard at work. Farrell led me beyond and to the right into an alcove. A small window overlooked the city, plain and woodlands to the east.

He led me to a small table at the window and indicated a chair. When I sat, he asked, "May I sit, Your Majesty?" pointing to the chair opposite me.

"Of course, Master Farrell. This is your castle after all. I am just a guest here."

"Far more than a guest, Your Majesty," he replied, sitting to face me.

"I have much to tell you, Master Farrell. First, let me tell you that Lord Beckworth killed King Richard. William is now King of Umbeqjaralii. He was coronated before all the Kings, Queens, Jharls, Thanes, Yurchist and everyone else of importance in the northern alliance and their entire armies. It was the largest, grandest and most well-attended coronation in the Kingdom's history.

"I killed Lord Beckworth, who was himself an Adjudicar. I also killed both his Adjudicars.

"Our armies liberated Shalal'm Caer, killing or capturing over one thousand Humans, goblins, Krelli and others defending it.

"Our losses were minimal, thanks to the many Elves and our Sorcerers.

"I do want to address the people of this city and the guardians of this fortress of the King. I would gather people in the courtyard, and I would stand above the castle's gate to address them. Is that acceptable?"

"Of course, Your Majesty."

"I sense hesitancy, Master Farrell. What would you suggest?"

"We customarily use the balcony overlooking the courtyard in the east wall for such occasions. The sound travels best from there. Queen Goodwina created it especially for such occasions. They used it over the years to announce the death of Kings, the birth of children, the King's annual address, and all other important functions."

"Perfect! What other things should I know or do when addressing the King's subjects."

"The order of entrance is important. The seating is important. The people with whom you make eye contact is important. The order of exit is important. The people invited to the main hall before the convocation is critical. Those invited to the main hall after the convocation are more important. The…"

"Stop!" I exclaimed. "Master Farrell, it is obvious that I need your help. Please, help me. This is important – the death of the King, the coronation of the King, and all that."

"Certainly, Your Majesty. It would be impossible for you to know all our protocols. I am pleased to serve."

There was much to do. Jhal'm Thaer was a big city, especially when the surrounding lands were included… and they were. There were various lords, squires, and other large landowners. And, of course, there were Orcs to be considered. Then, there were the various guilds, artisans and shops. Each had a position in the crowd and guarded it jealously. It was all too much for me, but Farrell had it under complete control. However, with all the preparations, it would take until the following day before all the arrangements could be made and all the people gathered and situated properly.

That gave me the entire day to work out the speech. I ran it by Farrell, who suggested I make it longer and to address each contingent by name and in the proper order.

I balked.

"Master Farrell, I think I want to make something abundantly clear to everyone. I am the High Queen. This was MY army. King Richard and all of Umbeqjaralii were under my command. The Elves of Blue Lake, Green Mountains, Brown Hills, the Fire Elves and the

White Cliffs were under my command. The Dwarves of Ez-Tansk, Ghamarazh, Ozhemia, Worfellsten, Zhaenstain and Tazhela were under my command. The Orcs of Chrystal Crags, East Meadow and West Meadow were under my command. The Krelli, the Trolls and the Octopods were under my command. I am the Queen of the Elves of the Green Mountains-Maidstone Forest. I am the Jharl Regent of Ghamarazh. I am a Thanelish of Clan Ez-Tansk. I am the daughter of King Fingolfin and Queen Eilol. They are here to attend to me, not the other way around. I will do what I can to follow the established protocol, but I will not be a slave to it. I'm an Elf, after all."

"Of course, Your Majesty," he replied, somewhat condescendingly. "However, if I did not instruct you in the proper protocols, you would be held up to ridicule and King Rich… William would be angry with me. I'm not sure which would be worse – an angry Queen of Elves or an angry King of Umbeqjaralii."

I had to laugh. The poor man was caught on the horns of a dilemma. "Then let me thank you for your kindness and patience. I will speak to the King and inform him of your diligence."

He smiled half-heartedly. "Now, shall we go over this one more time?"

I didn't want to, but Farrell was probably right.

An hour later, he sat back. "I believe that you will insult no one, if you say what we have agreed. As for the content, it is your tale. It is well that you extol the virtues of King Richard and King William. However, you do place your role in the whole affair above that of the King. Is that wise?"

"I led the armies, Master Farrell. I led King Richard and Prince William and Princess Cassandra and Viscount Geoffrey and Baron Richmond, and four Elvin kings, one Elvin queen, five Dwarf Jharls, one Orc Yurchist, and Krelli and Trolls and Octopods and ten thousand warriors. I, personally, killed three Adjudicars, including Lord Beckworth. I tried to save King Richard's life and failed. However, I did save King William's life, and that's the only reason you even have a king. I'm giving King Richard full credit and then some."

"If you say so, My Queen." He nodded a bow.

I gave him 'that' look. You know the 'You doubt me? Really?'

He bowed his head, far more abjectly. "Is there anything else I may do, Your Majesty?"

"Yes, if I'm staying overnight, I need suitable quarters and staff."

"Of course; if you would follow me?"

We returned through the great hall to the entrance hallway. We turned left and left again around the outer wall of the hall. We went up to flights of stairs, turned right and turned right again. He stopped at a large double door and knocked.

The door opened inward, where a tall, youthful woman stood. Master Farrell bowed. He turned to me, intoning, "Your Highness, I introduce you to Dame Philidae Oberon of Jhal'm Thaer." He turned to the woman. "Milady, I introduce Her Majesty, Gilraën Gulámae of the Green Mountains-Maidstone Forest."

"Yes, yes, Master Farrell. Where have you been keeping her? Where is her baggage? What have you been doing with her?"

"She had none, Madame."

"Well, get on with your work, while I attend to Her Majesty's needs."

As he bowed away, the Dame took me by the arm and escorted me into the quarters prepared for me. We entered a large, squarish room. It was bright with sunlight flowing in through six 'French' doors, each of which led to a large balcony with a waist-high wall. She escorted me to the right and through a door to a boudoir with attached bath.

Dame Philidae hovered, asking, "Where are your clothes, Your Majesty? Surely you have more to wear than just your armor."

"I do, but it is well hidden." I flopped my quiver on the bed. For several minutes, I pulled clothes from the hidden pockets until I had a small pile of tunics, breeches, undergarments, socks and other articles of clothing.

"No gowns? How do you expect to meet the nobles of this land?"

"Dame Philidae, I am an Elf. I am not just a Queen, but a High Queen." I pointed to the clothes spread on the bed. "Those are the clothes of the High Queen of Jaralii. They are more than sufficient for me, so they are more than sufficient for the King of Umbeqjaralii and all the nobles of this court."

She gulped. "Of course, Your Majesty, as you say."

"Now, Dame Philidae, do you have any suggestions regarding how I might attire myself for a more formal occasion?"

Her entire demeanor changed. "Indeed, I do, Your Majesty. If I might, I would have my seamstress attend you?"

"Excellent suggestion, My Dame. What is the fashion of the court?"

Dame Philidae clapped her hands and three women bustled into the room, armed with several gowns, yards of cloth, scissors and thread. I just hung around as they poked and prodded and stretched and snipped and sewed. Then one approached me with a corset.

"No!" I held up my hand. She staggered backwards. "This shall not be."

"But,…" Dame Philidae sputtered.

I glowered at her. I raised my index finger and waggled it at her. "NO!"

She shrugged. (Yes, she did!) "If you feel that strongly, Your Majesty."

I said nothing. I thought my declaration to be sufficient.

"On which side do you wear your dirk?" she asked.

I was taken aback. "Pardon me?"

"On which side do you wear your dirk?"

I leaned to the bed and slipped Vaerorderol from the quiver. "This is Vaerorderol. I wear it on my left. This is Gamesha, a Soul Blade. I shall wear this in my bodice." I lifted my coronet. "Jharl Azkhalish presented this coronet to me as the Thanelish of Diplomacy of Clan Ez-Tansk. I wear it without other adornment."

None of them seemed the slightest surprised. Instead, two of the women began snipping threads, pinning seams and stitching nimbly. Some time later, they stood, and Dame Philidae said, "Let us slip this over your head, My Queen."

They did. Then the ladies gathered and pinned and stitched a bit more. Then, one slipped a golden belt around my waist, and snugged it tightly.

Dame Philidae said, "Would you slip the scabbard through this loop?"

I did, and they adjusted a few links in a triple chain that attached the scabbard to the belt. When their work was done, the sword hung straight down my leg. This initiated another round of gathering, pinning and stitching until they were satisfied.

"If you will, would you insert the blade into the pocket in your bodice?" she asked.

I reached for Gamesha and slipped its scabbard into the pocket inside the bodice. They then turned me to see myself in a full-length mirror.

The gown was blue teal with green and gold highlights. It was ankle length, with a tight bodice revealing my upper chest and throat. The sleeves were three-quarters length, tapered on the forearm. The sword extended slightly above my waist. The scabbard slipped through an oval tube held in place by three chains. The scabbard itself was cleverly hidden within the folds of the skirt. My hair was up in the front and sides, exposing the coronet. It had been gathered and fell behind my ears and down my back. They had stained my lips with a red berry, my cheeks with ochre, and my lids with a touch of ash. I must admit, I looked fantastic!

"Ladies, you have outdone yourselves. My compliments. I will see that you are suitably rewarded."

"Your Majesty," Dame Philidae announced, "We are expected in the Great Hall. If you are ready, I will lead you there."

As we approached the doors to the Great Hall, Master Farrell joined us. "Your Majesty," he said, "The nobles of the court will precede you. I will enter bearing the Great Sword. You will follow. I will lead you to the throne at the center of the head table. I will place the Great Sword on the table before the throne. Then, I will step back, and I will seat you. I'm sure you are familiar with the rest of the ceremonial."

I smiled, "If not, I'll fake it, Master Farrell." I stood aside as the noble women of the court approached me, curtsied and then entered the hall. When they had passed, Master Farrell waved a hand and then lifted a huge broadsword, blade upwards.

Horns blared and drums rolled. Master Farrell stepped forward at a slow but steady pace. As he passed the doorway, I heard the distinct sounds of chairs and benches being slid on a stone floor. I heard large numbers of feet scuffling on stone. I stepped forward to see a huge number of people. They had squeezed more tables onto the main floor. I guessed that the balcony had been similarly treated.

As we marched slowly up the center of the hall, the people began applauding. The blare of the trumpet and beat of the drums complimented the clapping. Many voices were raised, and soon the entire body, mostly women, were cheering me wildly.

I was deeply affected. I smiled as broadly as I could and waved to the people on either side. I nodded and waved to the widely smiling and cheering faces all around me. It was as though I were the conquering hero accepting the plaudits of my rabid fans. Then, it dawned on me: I was.

Master Farrell turned to the right. I followed. He sped up the four stairs to the dais. I maintained my pace, while Farrell led the way to the throne, stepped between it and the adjacent chairs and laid the broadsword above my place. Then, he stepped back, pulling the throne back to allow me to stand between it and the table. When I felt the seat press against my legs, I sat. As I did, the nobles and the folk both on the floor and in the balcony took their seats.

Dame Philidae, on my right, leaned in to me. "You are not expected to speak before they serve the meal. You will cut the meat and declare it fit for consumption. But, after they clear the food, you are expected to say a few words."

"I think I will welcome everyone, if that's acceptable."

She nodded, and I stood. When everyone else began to stand, I waved my hands, saying, "No, my good nobles and esteemed subjects of the King. Please sit. I simply rise to welcome you to this feast of victory. Tomorrow, I will address you all regarding the campaign against Lord Beckworth. Tonight, I will enjoy your hospitality. Please, let the meal be served."

As I sat, I nodded to Farrell, who waved to the sides of the fireplace behind us. A stream of women, laden with vast trays or serving dishes emerged from both sides of the fireplace, marching the length of the hall to deliver their burdens almost simultaneously to every table. As they did, other servers emerged in the balconies, where more than a hundred good folk were seated.

Several women passed in front of our table, placing a huge covered tray before me, with three tureens to surround it. When the lids were removed, I recognized a large porg. The tureens contained tavor, foss and tans. Another platter contained a brown brot with fron on the side. Finally, goblets were filled with a red vin. It was a feed fit for a king... or a High Queen, for that matter.

I lopped a generous portion off the beast and laid it on my plate. I cut a mouthful off and lifted it to my nose. As I did so, I used all my faculties to analyze it. Not only did it smell delicious, it was perfect! "It is good! Let us eat. Enjoy!"

The hubbub resumed as everyone dug in. However, within just a few minutes, the only sound was knives scraping on plates.

I leaned over to Dame Philidae. "Introduce me to our dining companions... between bites, of course."

She smiled, leaned forward, and indicated the woman to my left. "Queen Gulámae, meet Lady Jane Dalimore. Her husband is a Captain in King Richard's army. Lady Jane Dalimore, meet Queen Gilraën Gulámae." She stopped and took a bite of porg followed by a slice of foss.

She looked to her right. "Queen Gulámae, let me introduce my closest friend, Dame Delian Millicent. Dame Delian, please meet Queen Gilraën Gulámae. Her husband is the Senior Captain of First Battalion of King Richard's army.

"I'll introduce you to the rest of them after dinner. We'll all meet in your quarters after we eat. They're a great group. But, we haven't eaten like this in months. This is all for you, Queen Gulámae. Frankly, our clothes were getting too large for us. It'll be great to fit into them once again."

"You mean you've been on a strict diet?"

She laughed, "No, we've been on three-quarter rations for six months. Since the King marched south, we've been on short rations… not quite half rations, but close. The men have eaten more than we women, but they are looking thin… almost gaunt. We all look to the day when King Richard returns. So, I took advantage of this situation.

"We're eating full rations tonight, and I've invited more than one thousand people to this meal. Tomorrow morning we will have first meal and morning meal. I've invited hundreds of others. We will distribute all the leftovers to people who I couldn't squeeze in. I'm hoping that everyone in the city will be fed decently for the first time in weeks. It's only right that we should celebrate the victory we all worked so hard to achieve."

I laughed out loud. "Wonderful! I love it! You are a conniving woman. I'm proud of you, and I won't tell anyone what a wonderful woman you really are, unless you want me to do so. In which case, I'll announce it from the palace gates."

She smiled shyly, "No, I don't think you should announce anything. Perhaps we could talk about this after the meal?"

"Of course, My Dame. May I call you Philidae?"

"Philly."

"Gilraën. Sorry, but I haven't got a nickname. I mean Queenie just doesn't fit, somehow."

She laughed out loud. She pointed to the woman to my left, saying, "Janey." She looked to her right. "Deli." She looked carefully at me. "And, Gillie. We just can't have you going through life without a friend name."

"A friend name, eh? I must tell Cassie and Ely."

"Cassandra and Eleanor?" she asked.

"Yes, Princess and Duchess, respectively."

"Yes, them. We miss them. We all used to be together until Ely married and Cassie went off to Grand Haven."

"Yes, this is too much for the dinner table. We will have to get together over thrak and cookies."

"Cookies?"

"Small, sweet cakes?"

"Ah, sweet cakes."

"I assume that we have a cook in my temporary quarters?"

"No, but we will." She looked around, signaling Master Farrell. When he came to her, she whispered in his ear, and he left hurriedly. She winked at me.

After that, the meal went well. We conversed lightly, trying not to say anything of import. When the meal was almost at a close, I signaled to Farrell. He signaled to the staff, which began clearing the tables. That was my signal. I stood and cleared my throat.

Before anyone could leap to their feet, I said, "Please, remain seated. We have enjoyed a wonderful meal. My thanks to the kitchen staff and Master Farrell for this magnificent meal." I clapped my hands and nodded in his direction.

Everyone took my lead and applauded.

I stopped and waited for everyone to settle down. "You have welcomed me with the hospitality of the King. I accept this greeting in the King's name.

"Tomorrow, I will address the entire population of Jhal'm Thaer. I know you will be there to hear the full story of our victory. Tonight, we celebrate the beginning of the end of this war. Your King and your army will return in just a few weeks. At that time, you will begin the recovery.

"Recovery is a difficult time. Soldiers will return from the war to a time of peace. In all those months of training and war, others have taken up their roles. Yet, when they return from war, our men will expect to return to their former lives. Disruption will lead to disruption. The transition from war to peace will be traumatic, for these and many other reasons.

"Yet, recovery is possible. I have seen this, and I know it can be done. So, keep my warning in mind as peace overtakes you, for better or for worse.

"For now, let us enjoy the warm feelings of friendship and full stomachs. Let us return to our homes, our quarters, and our residences, and remember this night for all the rest of our lives. I bid you a pleasant and restful sleep."

I turned to Philly. "Let's go. I'll lead."

As the women at the head table rose, so did everyone else. I edged around the throne and led the way down the stairs and the length of the room. As we went, the room broke into applause, but this time it was real and in appreciation. When we exited the hall, Philly took the lead, showing us the way to my quarters on the second floor above the ground.

When we entered, I smelled the rich aroma of thrak. Philly shouted, "Karen!"

A small, middle-aged woman emerged from the left with a tray. A tall pitcher and several mugs were on it. She deposited them on a table before a settee surrounded by six chairs. I sat on the settee. Dame Oberon sat to my right, with Dame Millicent to her left, and Lady Dalimore to hers. Five other women sat in the other chairs. Philidae began his introductions.

"Queen Gilraën, the woman to your left is Dame Veronica Tullifore. Her husband commands the 2nd Battalion. The woman to her left is Lady Tonsoria de Lacroix. Her husband commands the Third Battalion. The woman next to her is Lady Xanthia Gimble. Her husband is Senior Captain of 3rd Battalion. We are the wives of the highest ranked officers in King Richard's army.

"Now, let me introduce Gillie. Gillie, this is Ronnie, Tonie and Thia."

"Please, enjoy your thrak."

They all sipped. "Now, tell me about yourselves."

We fell into 'girl talk' in just moments. However, there was an underlying tension. I knew that the only thing they really wanted to know was if their husbands, brothers, sons or perhaps even daughters were still alive. And that was the one thing I couldn't answer. I knew none of their men. I only knew a few of William's troops, mainly their commanders or officers. Regardless of their concerns for their loved ones, we all had a wonderful evening. They left early, promising to meet me for first meal.

I retired to my bed, where it was quiet and peaceful. I opened my mind to my Tribe so that we could commune. Each of the groups had split into sub-groups of three to explore their quadrants more efficiently. Galdor and his group were first. They had started in the west, near the Southwest Highway, and had headed west along the lines of the small rivers. Their thoughts continued to describe the beauty of the region. The small rivers arose on the uplands, flowing in streams and brooks through gentle valleys between rocky ridges. Birds and beasts lived in these isolated valleys leading seemingly separate existences from those on the other side of the crests. They had found few natural resources or abundant foods, but they had only explored the eastern uplands.

Nienna's group reported thick woodlands of immense trees. The undergrowth was thick, mostly bushes which might produce berries in their season. There were few birds or animals living in the thick vegetation, and they had discovered no resources.

Caranthir's group was enthusiastic. They extolled the size and majesty of the trees, which they described as tall and of great girth. The undergrowth was spongy while firm, described as 'walking on a cloud' whatever that means. They described the area they had explored as 'magical,' which it probably was since it had once been the Realm of the Great Forest. They reported large numbers of animals and birds, a wide variety of edible plants, berries and roots. In fact, the region showed all the earmarks of having been carefully grown and tended, but now allowed to be fallow. They noted rich iron ore near the Jaralii Hills, and indications of coal nearer the Green Mountains.

When all the information was assembled and considered, the choices seemed to be in either the west or the east, but not the north. However, there was much to be explored other the next two days, and we were a long way from making any final decisions.

That night, I fell asleep with a real sense of accomplishment.

* * * * *

Chapter 8 – Jaralii Wood

I awoke refreshed and ready to take on the day. Although it was early, I still had some time before first meal. I dressed quickly in just a tunic and breaches, arming myself with Vaerorderol and all five Soul Blades. Placing the coronet on my head, I sat before my mirror. "King William!" I commanded.

As I had expected, Master Talbot responded, "Who calls for King William?"

"Talbot, it's me, Gilraën."

"Ah, My Queen, the King has barely risen. I will inform him."

The mirror showed the interior of a tent and remained that view for several minutes. Finally, William's face appeared. "Gilraën, what are you doing up and about this early in the morning?"

"I thought I'd catch you before you started your day. I have some questions. I met with several women up here in Jhal'm Thaer."

"Jhal'm Thaer? What are you doing up there?"

"Oh, we're looking for a good place to establish an Elf Realm. We're looking to the west, north, and east of Jhal'm Thaer, but we haven't come to any decisions yet."

"Well, Dominica did that years ago, and decided on her Realm out east of the Jaralii Hills. I went there many times. It was very nice, especially if you like enormous trees, which she did. It was something about growing up in the mountains, but I never understood it. So, what did you want?"

"Oh, yes. I met with six women last night. They are the wives of the Commanders and Senior Captains of the Army of Jhal'm Thaer. I was wondering if they survived and their condition."

William turned aside. "Talbot, what do we know about the commanding officers of Richard's army? Were any of them killed or injured?" He turned back to me. "He'll find out in just a minute. So, what have you been doing?"

"Well, two days ago, I addressed the people of Shesol Vys and told them the story. They know that Richard is dead, and you are King. They know that you are detained because of the coronation of Jharl Defghamask, and you will be returning in about three weeks.

"Yesterday, we came north. Today, I'll deliver a much longer speech to the people of Jhal'm Thaer. Master Farrell has been very helpful in the areas of protocol. I did not understand how complicated local politics is up here."

William roared with laughter. "Yes, it used to drive Richard crazy. That's a big reason why Shesol Vys is so important to the Kingdom. It's much less formal. We can work and train in relative anonymity, peace and quiet. We have few nobles, no guilds, and fewer self-important persons. I used to get away with all sorts of stuff. Now, it'll be me imprisoned by protocol, and Cassie will have all the fun."

He turned away from the mirror. He talked with someone for a few minutes and then turned back to me. "Good news. Let me get this in order. First Battalion Commander Lord Falner Oberon, injured in left arm, expected to recover completely. Sir Desmond Dalimore was badly injured in the attack on the wall. He is healing and will recover. Second Battalion Commander Lord Egbert Tullifore alive and well. Sir Malcolm Millicent alive and well. Third Battalion Commander Lord Julius de Lacroix was injured, but will recover. Sir Guilford Gimble is alive and well."

"Oh, that's good news! So, what are you doing today?"

"I am meeting with the Royals or their representatives to formalize our agreements on this Congress of Jaralii. We've decided that we should not exclude anyone, which is important, I believe, if we are to bring a lasting peace to this land and protect ourselves from the Adjudicars on other continents. I think we will tear down the inner wall to create a green space between the outer wall and the keep. We'll retain the keep, but expand it to accommodate administrators from each realm. So far, the negotiations are proceeding smoothly."

"Sounds great. I'll talk with you later. I have to attend first meal."

"And, you are keeping me from my first meal." He beamed. "I miss you, Gilraën. By the way, talk with the Seeress. I hear there are Seers or Seeresses on each continent. If they all work together, they should be able to find a way to get you back here. At least that is my hope. Terminate."

"Mine, too," I said to my reflection.

I found my way to the Great Hall and slipped in unnoticed. I was sitting at the head table by the time anyone noticed.

Master Farrell rushed up to me, breathing hard. "Your Majesty, what are you doing? You should not have entered thusly. We were waiting for you!"

"I have spoken to you about this, Master Farrell. I am above your rules, systems and protocols. I am the High Queen. Whatever I chose to do is correct at that time, and others will have to adjust themselves to me, and that includes you. Now, escort whoever is waiting to their places. If it is my friends, the women who sat with me last night, just send them in. They are probably hungry and need to get on with their day. Now, be off with you!"

Several minutes later, a parade began at the double doors entering the Great Hall. Everyone stood, as did I. I smiled broadly at the people as they entered, nodding to many who I thought I'd recognized. Lastly, the six wives entered. I waved to them and smiled. They were reticent at first, but quickly overcame their embarrassment to wave back to me. As they arrived on the dais, I reached out to them, hugged them and helped them to their places. I moved to my throne, and we all sat in unison.

"Welcome, good women. I ran afoul of Master Farrell's protocols, again. I had to inform him that I was not subject to them, regardless of his desire to maintain control of me." I giggled. "But, I'm glad you are all here. I do have news, but I think I should wait until they serve the food. There are many hungry mouths to feed."

By this time, servers were hurrying through the hall and in the balconies. This time, the meat was thinly sliced and fried porg... perhaps the remains from last night's meal? Additionally, there were scrambled oyes, large loaves, tavor, graz, guk and fron. It was almost a standard all-American breakfast, except for the tankards of ale-like brew.

I tested the foods and found they were wholesome. After the ceremonial taste of the porg slices, I announced, "It's good!" Then we all dug in.

I gave everyone five minutes or so to get the edge off their appetites, before quietly addressing the women. "I have spoken with the King, asking about your husbands." As each of them looked expectantly at me, I continued, "They are all alive." They all breathed a sigh of relief. "Now," I continued, "Philly, Falner was injured in his left arm, but they expect him to recover completely. Janie, Desmond was badly injured in the attack on the wall. He is healing and is expected to recover. Tonie, Julius was injured, but they expect him to recover. I'm sorry I don't have any other information, but that should relieve your minds."

Suddenly, I was swamped by a swarm of arms and a sea of sobs as all six of them gathered me up in a group hug. Such a show of emotions was probably unheard of in these august halls, but we didn't care. After a short while, we resumed our places and finished our meal. After the meal, they were eager to tell their families and households the good news.

I signaled to Master Farrell, who hurried to me. "When you have the time, please show me how to arrive at the balcony from which I will address the throng. At what time of the day will they be ready for me to address them?"

"My Queen, although I could cease in my duties and lead you there immediately, I beg your indulgence. I have many duties to perform preparing second meal and mid-day meal. You are expected to address His Majesty's subjects the first hour after the mid-day meal. If I might call upon you mid-morning after second meal, I would have more time to show you what you need to know and also perform my duties to the house."

"Of course, Master Farrell. I understand you have many duties to perform. I will meet you at my quarters. I will need some assistance, since Dame Philidae has other duties as well."

"As you say, My Queen, Dame Philidae has made appropriate arrangements. Your staff awaits you."

When I returned, a woman awaited me. She was of average height, a stern face with bright blue eyes, and dark hair held in a bun at the back of her head. She was dressed in the manner of a working woman, with a neat, gray dress and a white apron. Curtsying deeply, she announced, "I am Carnela, your maid during your stay. We are short of staff in the castle, but I can fulfill most of your needs. If you have additional needs, I can summon others from their duties to attend to your needs."

I smiled, reached out to her and took her hand. "Rise, Carnela. When we are alone, you need not curtsy. I'm not a formal person, as good Master Farrell has discovered. Now," I said, leading the way to the bedroom, "I will address the populace after the mid-day meal. They expect a show, and I'm going to give them one." I giggled conspiratorially. "So, we're going to clean and shine my armor and weapons. I will address them in full battle gear, with full armor and armaments. I do expect to overawe them all."

"Yes, Your Majesty. How shall we proceed?"

"Well, first, we can order some thrak. We do have some, I assume?"

"Well, Your Majesty, not much. You and the officer's ladies consumed more than half of our supply."

"That was Karen who served it. Is she a cook?"

"Oh, yes. She's second cook."

"And you? What is your position when you're not attending to a Queen?"

"I am the senior maid of the noble's chambers."

"And, am I the only noble in the castle at this time, or do the women I was with also reside here?"

"Oh, no, they have their own lands or estates. However, when you arrived, Master Farrell alerted Dame Philidae, who made the other arrangements. We have not had an Elf in this castle since Queen Dominica."

We set about cleaning my clothes and my armor. There were a few things that she couldn't touch – like my Soul Blades. However, by the time Farrell called for me, my clothes were clean, my boots polished, my armor gleamed, my blades shone, my helmet and coronet were burnished, and my shield buffed. All I had to do was dress.

I left Carnela in charge and followed Farrell. It was an easy trip. We returned to the staircase and went up one flight. We walked toward the 'front' but there was a winding staircase in the corner. It led into one of the spired turrets. The balcony was on the first flight opening on the courtyard parallel to the wall. It was a perfect firing position enfilading any attack on the keep's gate.

I could see why this was such a useful speaking platform. The shape of the outer wall was slightly convex as was the outer wall of the keep. Sound from this balcony was channeled between the walls so anyone could clearly hear.

I returned to my quarters. Carnela was busy cleaning, dusting, and doing all those other things needed to maintain a presentable accommodation. I told her, "I'll be reviewing my speech, so if you hear me mumbling, it's just me mumbling."

I spent the next hour considering how to say everything that I needed to say. But, it was like one of those high school assignments: 'What did you do on your summer vacation?' in five hundred words. The mid-day meal came and went. I was too nervous to eat. I began to dress. It was old hat. I'd been doing this for weeks.

I stripped and pulled on my leather socks, breeches and tunic, slipping the padded shirt over my tunic. I worked from the ground up, attached mail to my greaves on my lower legs and cuisses on my thighs, and poleyns on my knees thereby protecting my ankles and knees. Then I attached mail to the bottom of my breastplate and backplate to cover my hips and backsides. After slipping on a protective collar of plate and mail around my neck, I donned my padded cap and mail coif. I attached the belt around my waist and slipped the scabbard of Vaerorderol through the loop on my left and my dirk on my right waist. After I slid my five Soul Blades into their usual places, I placed my coronet onto my brow and my helmet onto my head. Finally, I slid my left arm into Paeraelaes and seized Paer

Jhaes with my right. Studying my reflection in the tall mirror, I decided I was as ready as I could get.

I stepped out the door to find Farrell standing there about to knock. His jaw dropped when he saw me. "My Queen, are you going to address the subjects of the King dressed as a warrior?"

"Master Farrell, we have had this discussion. Have you learned nothing? I am THE High Queen. Whatever I do is right, proper, mete and moot. We will NOT have this discussion again, will we?" I moved close to him, staring him in the eyes, an angry look on my face.

"No, Your Majesty, we will not. May I lead you?"

"Please do."

He turned and led me by the same route to the balcony. I peeked over the edge. The courtyard was packed... literally wall to wall bodies! There had to be over a thousand people packed shoulder to shoulder. I turned to him, asking, "How many people are outside the walls?"

"Many! Far more than are here."

"Crap! Is there any way I can speak to everyone inside and outside at the same time?"

"Only if you stand on the wall between them."

"Great idea, Farrell. How do I get there?"

He looked at me as though I had a screw loose.

"Really, Farrell, how do I get to the wall?"

"Follow me," he replied.

We wandered down to the main floor. We walked the length of the ell, emerging through a postern door, across the narrow space to the stairs leading to the wall. We clambered up, and we made our way across to the gatehouse. I climbed into the inner turret, which was taller and allowed me to be seen from the courtyard and the outer court and into the city below..

"This will do. Thanks, Farrell."

I concentrated on increasing the volume of my voice. Trumpets blared, commanding everyone's attention. "Subjects of the King!" I shouted, trying to get their attention. "Because there are so many of you, I have chosen to stand in the gatehouse turret so I may address you all. Can you all hear me? If you can hear me, wave your hands." I peered to the edge of the crowds, seeing raised hands. *'Here goes!'* I thought.

I went through the litany of nobles, semi-nobles, almost nobles, not quite almost nobles and everyone else Farrell had told me to address. "I come with news of victory and defeat, death and life, destruction and renewal."

For the next hour, I enthralled them with tales of marches, battles, strategies, weapons, falling walls, desperate fights, delving Dwarves, singing Elves, trebuchets and towers. It was magnificent, if I do say so myself.

"But then, our victory was robbed of its sweetness. I had killed both of the Adjudicars, freeing our lands of their ilk. Unbeknownst to me, there was one more, hiding in plain sight.

"I walked to the King's pavilion to rejoice with King Richard, Prince William and Princess Cassandra. Men-at-arms lay dying. A magical wall isolating the pavilion from the rest of the army. I summoned my Tribe and my Charioteers. We destroyed the wall, fought the mass of soldiers preventing us from advancing and entered the King's pavilion. There, smiling, as though he had conquered us all, stood Lord Beckworth, revealed as the third and the Master Adjudicar.

"Two Sorcerers stood with him, one with a knife at King Richard's throat, the other with a blade at Prince William's. Both of them were unconscious, having been brutally attacked, most foully. Despite the threat, I killed the two Sorcerers and seized Beckworth's mind with mine. We wrestled mightily and for many minutes, until I overcame him and destroyed him as I had destroyed the Adjudicars Caierne and Thandekre.

"Then my Tribe's healers and I attempted to heal our King and our Prince. It was a mighty struggle. Other Elvin healers and our Sorcerers joined us, working to heal the damage done to them.

"We were only partially successful. Our King Richard of Umbeqjaralii died in spite of our best efforts."

I waited as the sounds of sobs, cries and shouts rebounded from wall to wall throughout the city. I waited minute after minute until the initial shock had worn off.

"However, we did save the life of King William, for he is now your King of Umbeqjaralii."

Tears of sorrow turned to tears of joy. Shouts of anguish and pain became cries of joy and rejoicing.

I led the chorus: "The King is dead! Long Live the King!"

When the hubbub lessened, I continued, "Behold, William, son of Patrick, was coronated before the Kings or Queens of Five Elvin Tribes, the Jharls of six different Dwarf Clans, the Yurchist of Orcs, and mighty Krelli, Trolls and even Octopods. All the lands of the north rejoiced in our happiness."

The throngs cheered mightily and yelled at the top of their lungs.

I waited for the commotion to die down. "King William is now engaged in the most delicate negotiations with the other Tribes, Clans and other groups to develop a new community of nations. We all hope that this community of nations will engender a renaissance of cooperation among nations and peoples. In this way, we shall rid ourselves of Adjudicars and all those who would enslave us to their own purposes."

I let that sink in. "Finally, the great Clan Ghamarazh is without a Jharl. The most noble Thane, Defghamask, has led his dwarrow against the enemy. Our King William will join with Jaralii's Kings and Queens, Jharls and Yurchists to celebrate Jharl Defghamask's coronation in the dwarrow of Clan Ghamarazh.

I raised my hand above my head and punched the sky, shouting, "Long live King William! Long live King William! Long live King William!"

When the entire city was shouting and pumping and jumping and rejoicing, I stepped down and returned to my quarters. My job was done. I'd broken the bad news, creating a hero. I'd introduced their new King, and made him an object of adulation. Not bad for a day's work.

I returned to my quarters and stripped out of my armor. Dressed casually, I relaxed on the balcony. "Carnela? Are you still here?"

I heard a noise coming from my left. I turned to see Carnela emerging from the kitchen.

"Thrak, My Queen?"

"Oh, you wonderful woman! Thank you!"

She poured a small mug of thrak from a heavy ceramic jug. "If you drink from a small mug, the rest will remain hot in the heavy pot. That way, you will not waste any."

"Oh, I didn't know that. It makes sense, though."

"I heard your speech. I was so sad that King Richard is dead, but I have hope now that William is our King. He was always nice to me and everyone else. And, Dominica was wonderful. And, you so remind me of her."

"So I've heard. King Glorfindel and Queen Eilol adopted me as their daughter I so resembled Dominica."

"Oh, that was nice of them. Everyone needs family. Is there anything else?"

"No. Thank you. I think I'll just sit here a while and commune with my Elves. They're spread all over Umbeqjaralii, exploring the Kingdom."

She smiled weakly, saying, "That's nice, isn't it." She nodded her head and returned to the galley.

I relaxed and 'tuned in' to my Tribe. They were all quite busy trotting along through wooded areas, leaping over rivulets, climbing trees, exploring ruins…! Exploring ruins?

I concentrated on Caranthir's thoughts. He was exploring a large, tall tree. He had climbed at least a hundred feet into a bulbous, hollow area. There was a balcony with a railing around it and a stairway spiraling around the trunk going upwards and downwards.

I concentrated next on Celebriän Arcamenel, who was exploring a pile of rocks. I established my link with her. *'What are you studying?'*

She seemed shocked to hear me, but then acknowledged my presence. *'This is a smelter. It's quite sophisticated, especially in its handling of the out gases. It's not big, but could produce a ton a day, which is more than enough for small-scale manufacturing. I'm looking around for other signs of metal working, such as forging and stamping. That will give me some idea of what they were doing.'*

'I'll let you get on with it then.'

I contacted Nienna. *'I'm amazed,'* she said, *'This is a large, trackless forest. The trees are mostly deciduous with moderate undergrowth everywhere. They could be berries. The trees bear some kind of fruit or nut. There are large numbers of charder, bhar, porg and other herbivores. There are packs of candimaers and some smaller carnivorous animals that we haven't quite identified. It could be some kind of cat.'*

'Cat?' I asked, suddenly concerned for my Tribe. *'How big?'*

'We think it's something around the size of a house cat or a bobcat, but not large.'

'Oh, good. Were it a gaunt, I'd advise you to be ultra-careful. Regardless, it'd be interesting to determine what this other carnivore is. Now, what about resources and stuff?'

'Nothing! That's what's so amazing. It's just forest and more forest. We find no evidence of iron or coal. There are no real rivers, just little streams and quiet lakes. It's mostly flat, with occasional marsh lands, but that's mostly because it's so flat. I guess if the woods were cleared, it might be good for farming, but I'm not sure of the soil or the climate. There's nothing exciting here, so far.'

'Fine, I'll just maintain a low-level contact.'

I tuned in to Galdor. *'Anything new or exciting?'*

'Yes, and no. This is a delightful land. The rivers are small, swift and bubbling. The uplands are varied and beautiful. There are lovely caves – some of them run for miles. We've found two caves that are

deep and undisturbed filled with crystals. They're probably quartz, but they are huge and stunning. We've tried our best not to disturb them.

'The trees are bountiful, but neither large nor small. The undergrowth is manageable. The animal life is plentiful. We've seen charder, bhar, porg, and spiner as well as candimaer. As for the soil itself, it appears a bit rocky to me. I don't think it'd be good farming lands, but maybe herding.'

'Any natural resources?'

'No, but we're just approaching the long slopes to the sea. We'll see.'

'OK, I'll just maintain contact.'

A voice cried out, *'Oh My God!'*

It had to be one of mine. I searched my Tribe, finding one standing and staring in shock. It was Uruviel. *'What is it?'* I asked.

She stared at a hillock. *'Horrible!'* she exclaimed. I couldn't see what she was seeing. *'I've found them.'*

'Them?' I asked.

'The dead Elves.'

I looked more closely, trying to discern what she was seeing. She moved closer and reached out to touch a stick or something sticking out of the mound. As she did, the stick suddenly resolved into an arm. Only then did I see what she was seeing. This was a death mound. The bodies of scores of Elves were piled one atop the other and left to rot. This was the fate of the Elves of the Great Forest.

'Clarify your position, Uruviel.' I demanded, as I headed to the bedroom to put on my armor, rearm myself, and transfer to her location.

I arrived about five minutes later. Uruviel was kneeling next to the pile of bodies, with tears streaming down her cheeks. "This is what the Krells did. This was what the Adjudicars did to them. I'm glad we killed them."

I reached out to her and held her hand. "Yes, we killed them. Now, we have to hunt down the rest of them and kill them, too."

Caranthir, Celebriän Arcamenel, and Lenwë Tasardur arrived shortly. Each approached the pile slowly, hardly daring even to speak. Enough time had passed that the dreadful odor of death had subsided. The sticks of bone were covered with dried, leathery patches of skin. Skulls were bereft of eyes or skin, making them unidentifiable. Were it not for the place we were in, we would not have known they were Elves.

I stood back and brought my entire Tribe into my consciousness. "*See with me!*" I commanded. I looked at the pile of corpses, reaching in to lift an arm or a foot. I focused on a skull, bashed and battered. A body lay on a sword. A smashed shield and a broken spear lay to the side. "*This is the remains of the Elves of the Great Forest. It is our duty to inter them and memorialize them. Come to me. I will raise the Elves of Jaralii.*"

I stood aside and focused my thoughts on Nessa Narmolanya. '*Seeress, attend to me!*'

'*Queen Gilraën?*' she replied, appearing in my mind.

'*See with my eyes,*' I intoned. Again, I went to the pile of corpses.

'*OH! NO!*' the Seeress anguished. '*What is this?*'

'*The final resting place of the Elves of the Great Forest. This is the work of the Krelli of the Adjudicars. My tribe and I are about to bury them and memorialize them. I will contact Father Glorfindel and Mother Eilol. I will also contact King Amder, King Fingolfin and King Aeradir. However, there are many among the Elvin Tribes I know not.*

'*We will seek an appropriate place to inter their remains. And, we will consider how we might best memorialize them. However, I think that all the Tribes should see this, to know why we fought, and to renew their resolve to continue our war against the Adjudicars until they are driven from this world.*'

The Seeress replied, '*Yes, they will all want to attend. You must contact those of your allies. I will contact the rest, and I will attend myself. This will be a turning point in Elvin history.*

'However, I do not want you or your Tribe to do anything. The others must see this with their own eyes. This vision must be burned into the Elvin consciousness for all time. Do nothing, Gilraën. This horror will be our inspiration.

'Do make the appropriate preparations for their interment and for a memorial. Tomorrow will be a day none of us will forget.

'When you are done communing with those tribes return to me.'

As we broke our mental contact, I began to see the legacy I might leave behind me. For good or for evil, I would unite the Elves of Jaralii in a crusade against the Adjudicars.

I roused myself from my reverie to look around me. All twenty-seven of my Elves stood nearby, staring in horror at the remains of the Great Forest Elves. "I have communed with the Seeress. We will commune with the Kings and Queens of the Elves. They will attend on us tomorrow.

"It is important that we do nothing to disturb this horror, so that others can see it and experience it. This is the price of appeasement and cowardice. They all need to see this, so that it will be burned into their minds for all time.

"However, we must do two things. First, we must determine an appropriate burial site for these Elves. Second, we must consider an appropriate memorial that all Elves for all time will see and understand its significance. Let us set a ward around this so that no other harm may befall them."

We joined our thoughts and ringed the mound with a barrier that extended above and below them, sealing them in an impenetrable shield.

"Now, let us look about to find the best spot to bury them. As we do so, let us also consider an appropriate memorial for them."

We fanned out to find a suitable site to bury their remains. In the process, we discovered other bodies, lying singly or in small groups, cut down, hacked and beaten. We found body parts, isolated heads, arms, and torsos. And we found weapons, broken and despoiled. It was the scene of battle, retreat and massacre.

Finally, we found a knoll overlooking the mound of bodies. The crest was bare, with a ring of birch surrounding it like a crown. Here, we would bury them.

As night fell, we returned to the area Caranthir had explored. The trees were the largest I'd seen since I visited the great rain forests of the American northwest. These magnificent trees were both taller and broader than even the mightiest of the sequoias. The Elves had created rooms and passages both within and between the monarchs of the woods. Their now abandoned city could easily house hundreds, and could readily expand to thousands upon thousands.

We dug into our supplies, making preparations to eat. But Uruviel Sîrfalas announced, "Wait a minute. I've been looking around. These Elves had enormous food gardens. There are groves of fruits and nuts. There are stands of bushes for fruits and berries. There are plots of tubers and mounds of fruit or vegetable vines and grasses. This is a garden spot that could feed hundreds all year 'round. If we wanted a break, we could take a few minutes and extract some potato-like tubers, tavor and foss to add to our provisions. Given a day or two I think I could analyze the entire crop. I even think they had flocks or herds, either for wool, milk and cheese, or meat."

We all agreed that some fresh veggies would be a great supplement to the dried foods we had in our packs.

While several went with Uruviel, others went in search of water, while still others used the fireplaces they'd discovered to begin the cooking fires we'd need. An hour later, we were sitting back having enjoyed a wonderful meal.

"You know," I began, "this is a very nice place. It has all the comforts of home. We have water. We have gardens that need tending. We have homes that are already prepared for us. We have natural resources of iron, coal and limestone. We don't have to start from scratch. We could build on what the Great Forest Elves started, honoring them and remembering their sacrifice. If I ever find a way to return, this is where I would make my home."

"Can you ever return?" Nolofinwë asked.

"To be honest, I don't think so. I've spoken with the Seeress, and she says it's all my fault. When I made my contract, I insisted on returning to Earth, and now I have to do so. I asked if there was any way I could come back, and she wasn't encouraging. I will say that if I can find a way, I will."

I looked around. "Did any of you find a better candidate for our homeland?" The others looked back and forth and shook their heads. "Then, let's spend as much time as we can in the next few days exploring this area. Agreed?"

When they all agreed, I said, "OK, now let's contact the Elvin Kings and Queens that we know. Let's start with my parents, King Glorfindel and Queen Eilol. Are we one?" We joined our minds. *'King Glorfindel, Queen Eilol, it is I, Gilraën.'*

'Gilraën? You sound grave. What is the matter?'

'We have found the remains of the Elves of the Great Forest. There is a pile of bodies rotting in the midst of the forest. Fix my location in your minds. Come tomorrow. The Seeress is gathering all the Tribes. We will bury them and raise a memorial to them.'

Glorfindel was grim; Eilol anguished. *'Of course, we will be there, along with all those of our Tribes who wish to attend.'*

'I must go, Mother, Father. There are many others we need to contact. The Seeress may also speak with you.'

I terminated our mental contact and went on to King Amder Melwasúl. *'My King, we have made a discovery of the highest importance. This day, we discovered the bodies of all the Elves of the Great Forest. They were piled into a mound, where their bodies were exposed to the elements until they rotted. Tomorrow, we will bury them and create a memorial to them. We ask you and your Tribe to attend. I expect the Seeress will also contact you.'*

'I don't understand, My Queen. You discovered the bodies of the Elves of the Great Forest?'

'Yes, My King, that is what I am telling you.'

'Tomorrow? We will be there.'

In a similar manner, we contacted King Fingolfin and King Aeradir. Both assured us that they would be in attendance. Finally, we returned to the Seeress.

'I have contacted the monarchs of the other Tribes, Gilraën. They will all be in attendance.'

'Even Hidden Lakes?'

'Yes, but only Queen Lessien. The others will lead large contingents.'

'There will be a traffic jam, if we're not careful. Off the top of my head, we can view the remains in the morning, and perform the interment at mid-day. In the afternoon, we can discuss a lasting memorial. Oh, and this very well could be where we will establish our Realm. I will discuss it with Father Glorfindel and Mother Eilol, but I think they will approve.'

'I would also approve. The location is ideal, as I once told Dominica. I hope your Tribe will enjoy their Realm throughout the coming millennia.'

'Seeress!' Caranthir interrupted, *'Our Queen, Gilraën, will be forced to leave us. None of us want that to happen. You brought her here initially. You, the monarchs of the great Tribes and Queen Gilraën brought us here and gave us our powers. Is there no way we can circumvent her contract so she might return to us? Surely, with our strength added to that of yours and the other Tribes, we can accomplish this.'*

'You speak of things I am considering. Perhaps it is possible. I am not sure of the terms of the contract or of the power that might be needed to circumvent it. However, I shall convene the Supreme Council of Seers to consider the possibilities. I can guarantee nothing, other than I will recommend it most strongly.'

Suddenly, she disappeared from our minds.

"Well, that's something. Thank you, Caranthir. I hope something comes from it, but I won't hold my breath and neither should you.

"So, where do we sleep? I haven't explored this area, so what do you suggest?"

Caranthir pointed to a really big tree. There's a huge apartment up there. It's several stories high and crosses between three trees. We might try there."

We chose to walk up the long, winding staircase. Despite our Elvin strength and endurance, I was breathing hard and my thighs ached when we finally got to the lower entrance. I glanced down. We had to be two hundred feet up.

We stepped into a large room. It appeared to be a reception room. Staircases disappeared to the right and the left. I chose the right one. It wound upward to the next floor. There were three rooms: a larger open room with a small galley to the left and a bedroom/bath behind and to the right. I went back out to the stairs and up another flight. There was a similar apartment within the tree and a doorway to the outside.

A long, covered bridge led to the next tree. This one was even bigger and fatter than the one we had climbed, except it didn't have a stairway. I could see a second bridge leading to a third tree. That one also had an external stairway.

"It looks like a castle, except it's a couple of hundred feet up. You have to use either this tree or that one to get to the middle one. And, look at that huge bulge," I commented.

The middle tree featured a huge balloon that ran from the height of the bridges upwards one hundred feet or more. A long way up, a web of bridges ran between the middle tree and several around the periphery. As I looked, the web extended out in every direction for as far as I could see. It was a city of immense proportions – far larger than the number of bodies we had discovered.

'*Why,*' I wondered.

"I'm going to investigate that." I pointed to the bulgy tree.

The covered bridge was well constructed. There was almost no sway or bounce as I expected when I first stepped on it. At the other end was a large wooden door. I reached for it to open it and felt a tingle. The door came alive and opened wide.

"Definitely Elvin," I commented.

I entered to find a hallway extending to my right and left, running along the inside of the trunk, but outside the balloon. I turned to the right and wound around to a pair of doors. Again, I reached for them and felt a tingle as they opened for me. I was standing at the bottom of the huge egg. Long tables were arrayed near large ovens built into the walls. Wide doors opened into long shafts that descended along the outside of the tree to the ground. Heavy ropes ran the full length to the broad dumbwaiters that brought food, wood or other supplies to the kitchens.

Immediately to my right and left were stairs that wound upward to the next floor. At the far end near the vertical wall were other stairs that also led to the next level. I turned to my left and bounded up the stairs to find a huge, egg-shaped open space. An enormous array of balconies climbed upward and around almost the entire circumference and height of the eggshell. Opposite was a magnificent stage extending one third of the way across the width of the egg. Flights of stairs led behind the balconies each level. Typically, each balcony contained a large table with eight to ten chairs. There were perhaps one or two hundred balconies overlooking the stage.

The stage area was bare. Evidently it could be used for productions or for assemblies or just about anything else. But how to get there? I tried to climb up and around the beehive of balconies without success. I descended to the kitchen level, but found no way around.

This time I went to the left. At the end of the hall was a large double door. As usual, it required a tingle in my palm to open it. The broad hallway wound to the right and a huge lift. I found a stairway and ascended to the rear of the stage area. Tables and chairs were piled up in one corner. All sorts of props were hanging from the rafters. It was a real stage set up for real productions. However, it was large enough to house almost any event needing a large audience and with plenty of room to show off.

I exited the way I came and was about the start down the wide hallway leading out. However, I noticed a large door to my right. I tingled it open to find a wide staircase winding around the eggshell to the right, which I climbed up and up beyond the auditorium. I guessed I had traveled the full circumference of the egg, but now maybe a hundred feet above its base, when I came to a golden double door. I laid my hand on it, but it didn't tingle.

Knowing nothing else to do, I said, "Open!" To my everlasting surprise, it did!

The room was white and round with a high ceiling. To my immediate right was a triple dais. On the top level as a huge throne of light wood that reminded me of birch. The wood was inlaid with varieties of darker wood. Large jewels encrusted in gold were inlaid within the dark wood.

Several smaller thrones were arrayed on the second step. Many ornate chairs were aligned on the lower step. The central part of the room was bare. However, there were many chairs and small tables around the edges. I guessed that this was the formal throne room, but I wondered how everyone was supposed to get there.

I walked the length of the room to a double door, which opened with the usual tingle. They opened outwards into a large anteroom. Double doors led from the anteroom to a broad bridge that branched halfway to three different trees. Each of them had broad stairs winding down to the ground over three hundred feet below me. However, there were no doors leading off the anteroom. So, I returned to the throne room, looking for other entrances.

On the opposite side of the dais from which I had entered was a hidden door. To all appearances, it was just another panel, but I could feel a difference between it and the wall to either side. I touched it, but there was no tingle.

'Hey, it worked last time,' I said to myself. "Open!" I commanded.

Click! It swung inward. Another broad stairway wound away to the right. It stopped at a landing with another set of double doors on my right. I lay my hand on it, and commanded, "Open!"

Click! They swung inward, exposing a beautiful room. I stepped as though to enter, but found resistance. I could see what was inside, but not pass. "Open!" I commanded, but the passage remained closed. I lay both hands on the invisible barrier and said quietly, "Open for your Queen." The barrier quavered, and I stepped through.

The room was laid out for multiple small groups. There were five tables: three for three, one for four and one for five. A wide door broke the interior wall. I opened it with the familiar tingle. A hallway led off to the left, and a door faced me. I opened it to find a lovely anteroom with a tall window to my right overlooking the forest. Two small settees and several chairs took up the center of the room. A smaller doorway stood diagonally across the room. I opened it to find a magnificent bedroom, with a large four-posted bed, a full-length double window, and a deep closet.

I turned and exited the anteroom and turned right down the hallway. The first door was a privy with an attached bath. The second was a kitchen with a large window. The one on the end led to another set of stairs. At the landing were four rooms. Each had a bed, closet, vanity, and a small table with three chairs. Exploring, I found women's clothing, makeup, combs and brushes.

'Have you each found suitable quarters?' I asked. When they all answered they had found a place that seemed to have been created for them personally, I told them, *'I have found the Queen's apartments. I will stay here for the night. I will meet you at the base of the first sentinel tree for first meal.'*

I returned to the bedroom and explored, knowing I was peering into the life of an Elf woman who was almost my twin. Her closet was neatly divided with gowns, heeled shoes, and more formal clothing on the right, and more athletic clothing including breeches, tunics, jackets, and boots on the left. To the rear was an empty rack for armor and weapons.

I removed my armor and dressed it upon the rack. The five Soul Blades seemed to snuggle into a familiar place when I placed them in their slots. Divested of my armor, I removed my outer clothing, wondering how to get them cleaned. It would have been nice to have a staff, but….

I turned to the right to see a slim, tall door. Opening it, I found a full set of clothes similar in all regards to the ones I was wearing. I removed them, finding them clean and fresh smelling. I hung them in the available slot on the left of the closet and replace the ones I had removed with my own… even my undergarments.

I then noticed a lovely gray and silver peignoir set. I lifted it from its hangers and slipped it on, finding it fit me perfectly. I returned to the bedroom and slipped beneath the light and fluffy blanket. My head hit the pillow, and....

* * *

It was morning. A bird of some kind was whistling loudly. I rose and looked out the window to see the bird sitting on the sill of my window. Curious, I opened it. The bird cocked its head to me and hopped through the window and onto my hand.

"Good morning, bird," I said.

It cocked its head, peering closely at me. It trilled lightly and then hopped out of my hand, onto the sill and flew away. '*What a delightful way to start the day,*' I thought to myself.

I gathered the clothes I had liberated from the small closet and went around to the privy and then the bath. I found no spigots, but there was a 'nose' hanging into the tub. Not knowing any better, I said, "Warm bath!"

Almost instantly, water began flowing from the nose. I tested it with my hand and found it was the perfect temperature. I looked around for a cloth and towel, seeing a closet at the end of the tub. Opening it, I found a washcloth, two heavy towels and a mat. I lay the mat down on the floor, took the washcloth, and stepped into the tub. I wondered about soap, but stopped wondering about it as I wiped myself with the cloth. My skin tingled as I wiped myself, and the dirt just seemed to slough off. I rinsed the cloth in the bath water, which then swirled and drained, replaced with more delightfully warm water from the nose-like spigot.

Although I could have lain there an hour, just soaking up this delightful experience, I knew there was a lot to do today. Reluctantly, I rose from my bath, ala Venus, and dried myself. I replaced the linens in the closet and dressed quickly. Returning to the bedroom and the closet, I retrieved my armor and weapons. Swiftly dressing, I went to the vanity, where I did my hair and makeup, and adjusted my coronet.

'Food?' I thought and looked around for a quicker way from my apartment to the ground. Finding none, I descended through the throne room, around the egg, over the bridge, and down the stairs to the ground. Even at 'Elf speed' it took some time.

I looked around to find my Tribe, each dressed in full battle array. "Have any of you thought of food?" I asked.

Silmarwen laughed, "It's just like being at home again. The children arrive first thing in the morning asking, 'Mom, what's to eat?' Well, children, I have thought of it. And, thanks to the Elves of the Great Forest, there is food aplenty. It requires application of sight and hands, and a touch of magic to replenish the stores. And, I found a communal kitchen and assembly hall. But, I do need volunteers to help cook and prepare."

Lenwë Tasardur said, "Sure, lead on, *Mom*!"

Alassë Tur-anion agreed. "Lead on, Mom, and I will follow. Yeah, food!"

I asked, "Where's this assembly hall?"

Silmarwen waved, "Follow me." She led us to another huge tree with a winding stairway around the outer bark. We raced up a hundred feet or so to a wide belly in the tree. An expansive veranda ran around the tree. A series of windowed double doors were arrayed around the tree providing access to an interior hall containing arrays of tables and chairs pushed back against the walls. At the rear of the hall was a partition separating the main area from a large and well-appointed galley.

"Wow! This is great!" Fëanáro exclaimed. "Let's get some chairs and tables outside." Quickly, we rearranged tables and chairs throughout the interior room and the wide balcony. It didn't take us long to determine that two hundred could occupy the main room with perhaps two-thirds as many on the veranda.

Eámanë asked, "Has anyone else noticed that this place is built for hundreds of people?"

"Yes, I had," I responded. "How many of you saw the opera house over there?"

A few had, but not all. I continued, "You've got to see it. It looks like La Scala or one of those European opera houses with box seats piled up and around a huge stage. It must be able to seat a thousand. The throne room is above it, and might hold a few hundred at a time. This place is far larger than the numbers of the dead. I wonder what happened to them?"

Caranthir posed answers, "Escaped? Captured? MIA? Or, was this place built with the idea of expansion?"

"How many of these places were occupied, do you think?" I asked. "For instance, I found Dominica's apartments. I found clothes in her closet. I also found quarters for four staff. They still had clothes and personal stuff in them. However, there is no sign of the servants."

At that point, Silmarwen rounded the partition, shouting, "Come and get it!"

We stood and followed her into the kitchen. She, Lenwë and Alassë had the food laid out like a cafeteria. We lined up, picked up plates and flatware, and then loaded our plates from chafing dishes and wound our way back to the main room. We walked out onto the balcony and took seats overlooking the forest. When our cooks arrived, we stood and applauded them. They proudly took their places, accepting the plaudits of their cohorts and friends.

As we ate, we considered the sequence of the day's events. None of us was sure what we'd do. The Seeress had made some suggestions, but we weren't sure of how to carry them out.

Lenwë Sáralondë pointed at the ground. "Oh, look!"

A pack of candimaers had killed a porg. They had dragged it into the open area beneath us and were busily devouring it. They reminded me of a pack of wolves. The largest male was eating his fill. When another pack member approached, he bared his teeth and growled. When he withdrew, several males tore at the carcass. When they were done, the females and pups clambered over the carcass. By the time the eight adults and two pups were sated, there was little but bones left. Somewhat lazily, the alpha male grabbed a thigh bone and gnawed at it. The smallest pup approached and sat beside him, watching the leader splintering the bone. The little one seemed undisturbed when the alpha growled at him. Instead, the little one reared up and grabbed the male by the ear. However, his grip wasn't that strong, and he fell off rolling over on this back. As he righted himself, the male picked him up by the scruff of the neck and deposited him several feet away. As he returned to his bone, a large female raced in, grabbed the pup by the nape of the neck and carried him off. As we watched, other adults grabbed various bones, disassembling the corpse like a team of butchers. Just as suddenly as they had arrived, the pack departed, leaving an unsightly pile of half-chewed bones behind them.

Lenwë remarked, "Messy eaters! We must teach them to clear up after themselves." She evoked a chuckle from all of us.

I waved my hand, sending the remnants into a hole in the ground, which I then capped with the dirt I had removed.

"Are we ready?" I asked. When they nodded, I asked, "Where? It looks like the clearing right below us is the best place to greet them. When they arrive, we can lead them to the mound of the dead, and then into the wood nearer to the burial hill."

When everyone agreed, I said, "Let's contact the Seeress first. We'll let her decide on the protocol of the order of the tribes. I do want Brown Hills and Fire Elves first. They were Dominica's parents, and they are my adopted parents and will be your foster parents to you when I'm gone. I'm thinking that Green Mountains and Blue Lake should come second and third. Then, White Cliffs, since they were our allies. I guess Gray Elves and Sea Elves should be next, because of their behind-the-scenes assistance. But who next, we can leave to the Seeress."

We joined our minds, and I commanded, "Nessa Narmolanya!"

"I am here, children!" We looked up and there she was, standing amidst us on the balcony. "I agree with your order of precedence. Shall we descend so we can welcome your guests?"

We raced down the long stairs to the ground. We stood in a broad arc. I asked the Seeress, "Would you do the honors?"

She smiled.

Almost instantly, over one hundred Elves appeared. King Fingolfin and Queen Eilol stepped forward and hugged me. Fingolfin held me. "Oh, my child, we are so distraught. You found the remains of the Tribe of the Great Forest? It must have been a ghastly sight."

"Father, mother, we have not disturbed it. It is as we found it." I turned to Galdor. "Would one of you escort the parents of Queen Dominica to the death mound and then to the burial mount?"

In quick order, King Amder Melwasúl appeared with one hundred of the Green Mountains. King Fingolfin Sáralondë and many of his Tribe followed them. King Aeradir Lúinwë Séregon was next, then Queen Órelindë Telemnar Anwarünya and then by Queen Tári Lossëhelin Nenhámra.

'Who is next?' I wondered.

Queen Amarië Ancalimë and about one hundred of the Elves of the Clouds appeared before me. "Queen Gulámae," she stated, standing imperiously before me. She turned to the Seeress, "Nessa Narmolanya."

I was affronted. Regardless of our lineages, I had just led the coalition that had defeated the Adjudicars, killing three of them, one by my own hand. I was thinking of something cold and biting to say, but I heard the Seeress in my mind say, *'Don't.'*

Instead, I smiled. I turned to Galdor, reiterating, "Would one of you lead Queen Amarië to the death mound and then to the burial mount?"

Imperiously, Queen Amarië spun on her heel to follow Eö Sîrfalas to the death mound, followed by the others of her tribe.

I turned to the Seeress, demanding, "What's up with her?"

"My dear, you have supplanted all others in power and glory, and, if I might remind you, in wealth. She's jealous. Don't let her get under your skin, or you will make an enemy of a rival."

She was right. I nodded ruefully, but asked, "Will Hidden Lakes be coming?"

"Let us see, shall we?" She winked at me.

King Arafinwë Glorfindel Lossëhelin and one hundred of his Tribe arrived. "Hail, Queen Gulámae. I am displeased to greet you on such a somber occasion. Perhaps after this day, our Tribes will not be estranged."

I felt genuine artifice in his all too glib greeting, but I didn't want to leap to a false conclusion. "Greetings, King Arafinwë. Nothing would please me more." I turned to Nienna, "Would one of you escort King Arafinwë to the death mound and then to the burial mount?"

Queen Lessien Calmcacil and a dozen of her tribe appeared. Well, it could have been anyone, as far as I was concerned. They were all about the same height, dressed in blue teal robes that fell to the ground with heavy veils disguising their features.

She stepped forward to whisper, "Hail, Queen Gulámae, Conqueror of the Adjudicars. We have been told of the tragedy you have discovered and have come to offer our condolences to the family of Queen Dominica."

I was pleased to hear her plaudits, but cautious. "We are appalled and outraged that such a thing has occurred. It was a most disturbing discovery, and we needed all of Elfdom to mourn with us." I turned to Caranthir, "Would one of you escort Queen Lessien to the death mound and then to the burial mount?"

We were about to leave for the burial mound, when the Seeress asked us to wait. When we were reassembled, she addressed us. "This is a momentous occasion. Never in all our long history has a Tribe been annihilated. In fact, until this time, were any Tribe attacked, all of Elfdom would have risen up against the enemy. So, this is a monument to their shame and to your victory. Be not overly proud, but humble. You have shamed us by your example, and we are mortified. If you were to rub salt into this wound, you will make enemies of them all. However, if you are humble, expressing thanks to those who fought alongside you, acknowledging those who supported you, and be gracious to those who did nothing, they will live in shame, for their part in this is well known to all. We will use this to our advantage at a later time. Come now, my children, we have a duty to perform."

We joined our distant kinfolk at the base of the burial mound we had chosen. I asked King Glorfindel and Queen Eilol to join the Seeress and me at its summit. The Seeress told the story of the founding of the Elves of the Great Forest, acknowledging both Glorfindel and Eilol. She also mentioned prominent Elves who had left their Tribes to follow Queen Dominica. They had come from every tribe, except that of Hidden Lakes. As she named them, I saw Elves from their familial tribe weep unashamedly for their lost loved ones. As Glorfindel and Eilol mourned their daughter, I, their newly adopted daughter, held them in a three-way hug.

When she had concluded her elegy, she said, "Their bodies were desecrated by the elements and the wild creatures. It is now our duty and our right to bury them in the Realm of their creation. This place - the crest of this hill surrounded by a crown of white trees – shall be their burial site. Let us now join our minds to do our duty to our kin."

I felt us all join in a single gestalt of such immense power that even I felt awed. The Seeress led our minds to the death mound. There she disentangled each body and with infinite grace and humility transferred it into a discrete grave on periphery of the hilltop. As we interred each body, a small block of stone sprang out of the ground to mark its place. When the last body was buried and marked, she led us in creating a spire of white granite at the peak of the hill. Then, we sealed the entire cap of the hill so that this place would stand the rigors of time and the elements as a permanent memorial to Queen Dominica and the Elves of the Great Forest.

As I descended the hill, Glorfindel, Eilol, their Tribe and mine joined me. We led the way back to the clearing, where the Tribes mingled. I found Silmarwen, and asked, "Mom, you know more about this than I do. I think we should feed these people, but I don't know how. What should I do?"

"Oh, well played!" she jested. "My children never learned to manipulate me that way. If they had, I might not have been such a bitch. Anyway, you'd be worse than useless. Go on and meet our guests. I got this. Actually, the way this is set up, it's easy. Oh, I'll ask Silmarwen and Alassë to help. I'll let you know."

"Thanks, Mom!" I giggled.

She slugged me in the arm. "Get out of here!"

I returned to the throng, finding Glorfindel and Eilol almost immediately. They greeted me enthusiastically. "We never came here," he said. "I was so upset with her that I refused to admit she had left us to found her own Tribe. When she was killed, I blamed William. Even when I first saw you, when Nessa brought you here, I was angry and refused to have anything to do with you. I am so ashamed. At least I had a second chance. I hope I acted more commendably with you than I did with Dominica."

Eilol caressed his face with her hand, "Yes, you did, dearest." She grasped me in a familial hug. "We are united with our adopted daughter, and will be forever."

I couldn't let it go. "No, it won't be forever. I have only a few weeks left on this planet before I must return to my previous life. You know that, mother."

She burst into tears. "No! I won't have it! You must stay. I lost you once, and I will not lose you again."

I appealed to Glorfindel with my eyes. He pulled her away and walked away with her sobbing on his shoulder.

Silmarwen's thoughts appeared in my mind. *'We are ready. Cafeteria style.'*

I raised my voice. "Good Elves! Silmarwen Felagund, Lenwë Tasardur and Alassë Tur-anion have prepared a meal for us. Please understand, we arrived here only yesterday. Neither Silmarwen, Lenwë nor Alassë were assigned this task, nor do they do it as a normal part of their duties to our Tribe. Instead, they have volunteered their skills, time and effort to feed you in our time of mourning. Ascend the stairs with me. Follow in line and take the foods you wish. Then, either join us on the balcony, sit in the main area, or descend to the ground to eat your meal. Please, follow me."

I led the way up the winding stairs to the kitchen and back to the balcony. When Glorfindel and Eilol emerged, I waved them to join me. I then waved Amder, Fingolfin and Aeradir to my table. Queen

Tári emerged, saw us, and asked if she could join us. When we agreed, she waved to Queen Órelindë who also joined us.

"This is quite delicious, Gilraën." King Aeradir commented. "What is it?"

"You know, I'm not sure. Evidently, Dominica's Tribe found or created several new roots that are quite palatable. The Elves of the Great Forest Elves were excellent gardeners. We found large plots, groves, bushes, trees, and many tended areas that still remember them. They sprung to life as we entered, and they are providing quantities of food sufficient for the number of people who are here.

"In fact, we are astounded by the proliferation of constructions we have found. This Realm is habitable by many hundreds if not thousands. We have barely begun to explore it, but have already found this facility and an auditorium that could seat more than a thousand for organized activities and entertainments. It is truly an astounding place."

"Nay, Gilraën, it was Dominica's idea to create an Elvin city planned in such a way as to allow growth without destroying the lands, the air, the streams or the other lives within her Realm. I visited here only once, although many of my Tribe visited often. It was always a place of delight and joy, filled with song, story, entertainments and wonderment. Not since we Elves were young and vital has any Realm been so. It was as though I were reborn a child when I came here. And, that is the story I have heard from all who came within her sphere."

"Well, that settles one of our great concerns. Although we were distraught at our findings of death, we are concerned that somehow we had missed hundreds of others. We imagined them captured, tortured or enslaved in distant lands. Just how many were they?"

"Only a few hundred, more is the pity. Had they numbered in the thousands, they might have defeated their assailants, even though they were Krelli."

I thought for a moment about Justice. "Yes, it would have taken many hundreds to defeat the force of Krelli Beckworth sent against them. Even then, it would have been a close thing. The protection of a Realm was their only true defense, and without it… without their Queen, they were doomed."

Amder replied, "But now, the Queen has returned. Surely, you and your tribe will re-establish this realm."

"No, I will not. I will help my Tribe to establish their Realm, but I shall not be here to sustain it."

Queen Órelindë scoffed, "Surely you play with us as a gaunt would a langstem."

"No, I don't. I will help my Elves build a Realm, but thereafter it's up to them to maintain it. I will attend the coronation of Jharl Designate Defghamask, since I am the Jharl Regent. Then, I will return to my home world to take up the rest of my life."

Queen Tári sputtered, "You achieved victory only to abandon your Tribe? You defeated a few Adjudicars, leaving us to the vengeance of those who still inhabiting our lands? Had I known that, I would never have assisted Armjurst in this insane attack on the Adjudicars."

I looked down at the table and shook my head. She'd learned nothing. She was still the coward who would abandon her kin, sacrificing all others in the vain hope of avoiding the same fate.

As I was formulating my reply, the Seeress appeared at my side. "Shame be upon you, Tári Nenhámra! Your blood runs thin in your veins. Have you learned nothing in all the eons of your existence? Those with whom you sit formed the greatest alliance in the history of this land. Together, Elf and Dwarf and Human and Orc and all their allies united to bring down one of the most fearsome enemies we have ever encountered. But, you prefer to cower like the langstem hiding deep in its lair? When will you learn you are an Elf? When will you remember that we are mighty beyond the shadow of our enemies?"

She raised her voice so that all could hear. "Yes, High Queen Gilraën Gulámae will leave us. She chose this destiny. She chose to achieve victory or face death. She chose that if she were victorious, she would leave us having taught us the lessons of strength in unity, while ensuring that she would not become the victim of mindless adulation.

"She is not a goddess, and she does not pretend to be one. She is not omnipotent, even though she led us to victory – in spite of some who are here at this memorial of another brave and intrepid Elvin Queen who stood against the tyrants. Instead, she had the wisdom to choose victory or death – something none of you did although you could have led us to the same end had you chosen courage instead of cowardice.

"Now, because of her commitment, she must return to her home world, whether she wishes to do so or not. She has no choice, which is not true for any of you.

"I suggest that before she leaves us forever, we provide her with the choice to return, if she should change her mind. I will speak to all of you at a later time."

She disappeared.

I turned to Glorfindel and Eilol, laughing. "She has a way with words, doesn't she?"

He guffawed, and Eilol giggled. Tári puffed up and sputtered, "Who is she to talk like that?"

"Oh, come on, Tári!" Eilol joshed her. "She's the Seeress. She's been doing this forever, and she's always right. That's why she's the Seeress. So, what are you going to do about it? What are you going to do for our daughter?"

"Daughter? Nothing. She is gone beyond the Void."

"No, Tári, this," she grabbed me and held me closely, "is also our daughter. Glorfindel and I adopted her as our daughter. She is alive and well. She saved us from three Adjudicars. She united the North. She allied Elf with Dwarf with Orc with Human. She fought them hand to hand and won. Reconsider yourself, Tári. We did, and discovered just how wrong we can be – despite our many eons of life, learning and wisdom."

Queen Amarië Calmcacil strode up to our table. "You may have hoodwinked these simple-minded fools, disguising yourself as their daughter to worm your way into their affection, but you have not deceived me. I know your kind, and curse you for your duplicity. Take your ill-gotten gold and jewels. Be gone from this world. Good riddance, I say."

She turned Glorfindel and Eilol. "And, when the Adjudicars appear before your gates, do not plead to me for succor. I will give you none, for you are the cause of all our troubles. Had your spawn not angered them, the Adjudicars would have left us alone, taking only the lands of the Humans. Instead, she brought them down on herself and now all of us! Cursed be you for all of your reigns."

The Elves of the Clouds disappeared.

A tall form dressed in blue teal robes and a heavy veil over her face sidled to my side. "She speaks with anger and fear. The free people of Jaralii are most grateful to you. We of the Hidden Lakes support you in our hearts and minds, but do not ask us to support you in deeds, for we shall not. It is our affliction, not our desire. I will seek the Seeress for advice. Blessings be on the Elves of the Green Mountains-Maidstone Forest. May you find your Realm and prosper."

The Elves of the Hidden Lakes disappeared.

"What was all that about?" I asked Glorfindel and Eilol.

They shrugged. (Yes, they did.) However, Fingolfin replied, "Once they were the fairest of all our kind. Then, we came to this world. For some reason, they withdrew into the Hidden Lakes and have had no intercourse with any of our kind. We have asked for explanations, but they have never been forthcoming. Yet, they do not appear to be unfriendly. They just wish to be alone. And so, we have acquiesced to their desires."

King Amder Melwasúl took the place of Queen Amarië. "Wow, you three have really stirred up a hornet's nest. Even the Seeress got into the action. What caused all that?"

King Glorfindel replied, "Egos! It appears that our daughter did not solve all of Amarië's problems. Gilraën only killed three of the Adjudicars, leaving the rest for others to battle. As usual, Amarië blames everyone else for her shortcomings."

Amder laughed boisterously, causing Tári to scowl at him. "She's been that way since she was born! She's always whining and complaining, but never doing anything to help herself or her Tribe. It just goes to show you that power does not equate to intelligence."

All the elder Elves laughed. Eilol giggled, "If that were the case, I'd be High Seeress."

Glorfindel, ever gallant, leaned over and kissed her. "Of course, dear, I've always said so."

She kissed him back. "Unless you disagreed."

"Me?" he replied. "When did I ever disagree with you? Or, when have I ever dared disagree with you?"

"Beyond count, dearest. Beyond count!"

We all had a good laugh.

"Seriously, though," Melwasúl persisted, "What are we going to do about you, Gilraën?"

"Me?" I replied. "I don't think there is anything you can do. I must return, take up my previous life and finish the contract I have already committed myself to completing."

"And, what is this contract that is so important?"

"Ah, it's one of those technological things that is a part of my world, but not of this world."

"Oh? Tell us about this technological thing."

"My company has just installed a new computer network and linked it to the cloud, where they can interface with the rest of the client's world-wide business. I will install their new business system, modifying it as needed, and complete their on-site training. Then, I'll hang around solving spot problems until they sign off on the final installation. It should take a month to six weeks, and then it's on to the next contract... whatever that is."

"So, you when you complete that contract, you are done?"

"Yes, that's about it, I guess."

"Hmm, interesting."

"Interesting?"

"Perhaps, but I will have to consider it before going any further."

I shrugged. (Yes, I am ashamed to say I did.) "Ok. Sure!"

"I will say this," he continued, "should your tribe renew the Realm of the Great Forest, I will welcome them as I had the Realm of Queen Dominica. I am sure that after your stout defense of Tamvill alongside Clan Tazhela that Jharl Tazmatahela will welcome you with open arms. Now that William is King, we could establish an economic and social coalition that will be the envy of every power on this continent.

"Consider also, with the relationship between your Tribe, Gilraën, and that of your new parents, this coalition could easily extend across the north to include Brown Hills, Blue Lake and even Clan Garmanch. And, with your long-standing friendship with Yurchist Linda, we could encompass the Orcs of the Chrystal Crags. It could become a major coup… all a result of your successful prosecution of the war against Beckworth. So, even though you are forced to leave this world, your legacy will live long after you, just as the memorial we created today will be an enduring commemoration of those whose deaths ignited the war against the Adjudicars."

"I am pleased. In my old life – my future life – I played my games. I was often a heroine, because I could use the male ego to my advantage. I was very successful, which is why I was selected to come here. In fact, I was so good that Adjudicar Beckworth intended me to lead his forces against you. Had he been successful in procuring my services, it is unlikely that you would be here. Can you imagine a Warrior-Mage with my magical powers? I can't, but I would have been invincible.

"Regardless, in my games, everything was imaginary. It was only real within the non-reality of the computer game. This life – you, my Tribe, the Adjudicars – is all too real. I leave a world better off than when I arrived. I did something positive with my life. When I die, I will have a smile on my face."

* * *

After everyone left, we cleaned up our new home. With magic, such things are easy. All of us were tired. Entertaining several hundred Elves from nine different Tribes was exhausting. We all slept in. It was half to mid-day when we gathered in the cafeteria. Each of us had figured out the magic involved, so we each made a meal to our liking. I've always been partial to bacon and eggs with toast.

We decided to fully investigate this city and its surroundings. The more we looked, the better we liked it. We found the structural fortification that had not been completed. We found the sources of iron ore, pig iron and some high carbon steel. We found an armory with several superb swords, two exquisite shields, a helmet and a pair of vambraces. Each had been specifically created with Elvin skills and magic. Eámanus and Celebriän Arcamenel were especially impressed, remarking on the metallurgy, the production methods, and magical properties at great length.

Nessa Melwasúl returned from her explorations with several lengths of string. "You gotta see this," she said, showing them to Uruviel and me.

"What are they?" I asked.

"That's exactly it. I don't know. But, look at them. This," she handed me a thin, slippery and strong thread, "is one of them. This is a different one." She handed me a long white thread, thicker and coarser. Then, she handed me a thick, hairy thread.

"What are they?" I reiterated.

"They are filaments growing from a grove of trees over there. They are growing from different trees just over there," she said, pointing.

We went over to the grove, where we found trees with long threads hanging from them in great profusion. At the edge of the grove was a stand of those gigantic trees. In the first, there was a large room, fully open to the world, with several old-fashioned spinning wheels along one side. In the next was a bunch of vats with colored goop in the bottom. In the third was half a dozen looms.

We glanced at each other with one of those 'Aha!' looks. They were making cloth. They made thread from the filaments. The thin stuff was like silk; the medium was like cotton; the heavy like wool. They dyed the thread and then wove it.

Celebriän Aldaríon rushed up to us. "I've got a big one for you!" He was really excited. "Come here and see at what we found." We rushed off to find Galdor, Elrond, Findecáno, Celebriän Arcamenel and Eámanus Calmcacil standing over a pit next to a tall, massive, U-shaped, brick structure. "You know what this is?"

"No," I answered.

Findecáno answered, "We think this is a destructive distillation apparatus."

Their answer was entirely uninformative. "Huh?"

"Yes," Elrond replied, "We're thinking coal, but it could be wood, too."

"So what?" I asked.

Eámanus replied, "This answers many questions. They are coking coal. They capture the off gases and liquids. They get coal gas, which is flammable and could be used to heat a forge, for instance. They also get aniline dyes, which they could use to dye cloth, leather and other stuff. They'd also get ammonia, which they could use as fertilizer or as a generic base. This is where big companies like BASF began – aniline dyes from destructive distillation of coal. This is first generation industry."

Light dawned on marble head! "So, they have developed an integrated manufacturing using coal for coke and dye, iron and steel, and cloth dyed to order?"

"That's what we think," Findecáno replied.

"Can you reconstruct the industry?"

"Given time, sure," he replied.

"So, we have trees producing thread, a coal distillation process, a foundry and forge, a weaving and dying operation. What else?"

Uruviel arrived with a bottle of gook. "This is interesting."

"Oh," I replied.

"If this is what I think it is, it is the answer to everything."

"Everything? Do you know what Eámanë, Elrond and Findecáno discovered?"

"No, why?"

"Well, they think what they discovered is the answer."

Findecáno explained. Uruviel nodded in understanding. "Then this makes sense," he replied, shaking the bottle. "If I'm right, this is rubber!"

The five of us just stood there trying to get a grip on our discoveries. This was mind-boggling. Dominica and her Tribe were developing a nascent industrial society with 'all natural' raw materials and minimal effect on the local environment.

I spent much of the day exploring our new home. I found Eö, Eámanë Tîwele, Lúthien Séregon and Idril Anwamanë exploring rows of vegetation. "Whacha doin'" I asked.

Eö answered, "We are looking at this stuff. Obviously all this," he waved his arms in a great circle, "is food. We're trying to figure out what's what. Like this stuff over here is root vegetables, that stuff is vines, and that stuff is grasses. So far, we've found tavor and foss here, tans here, jhig and maidzh over there. But there's other stuff, too. We're trying to figure it out.

"There's something like potatoes and maybe parsnip with the roots. There's fruit with the vines. Some could be peppers and some could be cucumbers or tomatoes or something. Then, there's wheat-like stuff with the maidzh.

"Now, over there are groves. There are four different kinds of fruits. Some look like crab apples. Some are like quinces. Then there are apple-like and pear-like fruits.

"And, way over there are nut trees. There are at least two types, maybe three. One is sorta like cashews, and one is like walnuts. We're trying to figure out how to tend them. If we're going to live here for any length of time, they'll be our major source of sustenance.

"Oh, there's a small pen and abattoir over in that direction. There's only room for a couple of animals, so it's not like they have huge herds of cattle or anything. Maybe it's just one or two at a time or for special occasions.

"Now, we have found nothing for oyes or guk. You mentioned that you'd seen chickens and cows in your journeys in the piedmont of the Dwarf Mountains. Maybe we could go down there and get some. I don't know where we'd keep them or what we'd feed them."

I replied, "Good thought. When we get together tonight, let's talk about it."

I met Camthalion, Orophin, Daeron and Lenwë Tasardur talking seriously. As I approached, they looked up and waved me over.

Lenwë said, "You know we need better roads and stuff around here. This Elf city is great… it really is. But, it's isolated. If we're going to go anywhere, we either find our way using game trails or *transfer*. But, we're talking about some kind of commerce with Tazhela, Green Mountains and Jhal'm Thaer, at the very least. We need better roads, or at least wider trails."

Camthalion added, "And, we need to use the rivers. The closest is the Green River. And, there's the North River. We need to use them if we're going to send or receive goods, services, people, raw materials, and other stuff. That could mean locks, barges and other stuff associated with river work. Oh, and if so, Fisherman's Bay could become a center of shipbuilding, coastal traffic and even overseas shipping."

"Wow!" I exclaimed. "You guys are thinking big. I like it, but it's a big project."

By that time, it was mid-day, and I was peckish. I wandered up to the cafeteria and began puttering. Suddenly, Silmarwen was at my side. "Can I help you?" she asked.

"No, I'm just looking for a nibble."

"Ah, yes, you're all like my children raiding the refrigerator so that when I do make a meal, everything I had planned to serve has been eaten, and there's nothing for me to make for the meal. So, I'm taking over. Well, Alassë Tur-anion and me. He's a great cook. And, as long as there are only twenty-eight of us, we can more than take care of everything. I do need to call the grocery store, though."

I suggested, "You'd better talk to our gardeners: Eö Sîrfalas, Eámanë Tîwele, Lúthien Séregon and Idril Anwamanë. They're working to figure out what's there. So, talk with them to figure out what to serve. Meanwhile, oh mighty Mom, what's for lunch?"

She clucked, "Go out there and sit down. I'll get you something."

I did, and she did. She had prepared a delicious vegetable soup with maidzh bread and a cup of vin.

Enelya Ringëril joined me. She held a one-inch square emerald and placed it on the table. "What do you think of that?"

I laughed, thinking of Scotty in Star Trek, "It's green!"

"Seriously, pick it up."

I did, and it tingled in my hand. I studied it more carefully, but couldn't find anything unusual. "What about it?" I asked.

"Reach into it with magic," she replied.

I extended a tendril of my mind into the crystal. It was curiously excited. I couldn't understand what I was seeing. "Yes?" I asked.

"I was working on this, using my mind to manipulate it. As I did, I found that it was storing some of my energy. So, I concentrated on depositing energy in it. Then, I concentrated on the energy I had stored and could restore myself. I've tried it several times, and I think I've found something. These ordered crystals can store magical energy and release it on demand."

She pulled a ruby as big as a chicken egg from a purse at her waist. "I want you to try with this one. Use whatever energy sources you can find and try to deposit them in the crystal. If I'm right, we could each have a crystal like this for our own use. Each of us could charge it like a battery during our quiet times. Then, when we needed the energy, we could retrieve it to restore ourselves. Just think how this would help us transfer or enter the Void."

"OK, I'll try it."

"If it works," she continued excitedly, "I could adorn the pommels of our swords or dirks with a crystal of choice. It'd look like decoration, but be personal, retrievable energy right at hand, literally."

"Yes," I replied, "I had tried this already. It works. Go with it!"

She grinned and skipped away.

Caranthir joined me. "I've been watching everyone scurrying around. I went from group to group, to find something to do. I know nothing about farming or metals or medicine or jewelry or any of the things others are finding so interesting. I'm a military man. I know training, logistics, weapons and tactics, and strategy and all that other stuff. It's been my whole life. I don't know what to do if I'm not engaged in martial arts of some kind. What can I do around here?"

"How about security? You and Nienna are both in that general profession. Why not talk with her?"

"Good idea. Let me find her," he said wandering off.

For the next week, everyone was very busy with their new responsibilities. Idril Ancalimë became our administrator, trying to coordinate everyone's activities. Fëanáro Coamenel became interested in Nessa Melwasúl's cloth and dye operations, and Elros Ancalímon began programming the looms. Nolofinwë Culnámo, always interesting in quality footwear, assisted Uruviel in developing our rubber industry.

We spent much of the following week orienting ourselves, figuring out what our predecessors had done, and determining the limits of our Realm-to-be. Eö Sîrfalas and his team had all the gardens, groves and fields blooming and fruiting. The two Celebriäns were coking, smelting, forging and finishing up a pile. Nessa and her team spun and dyed and wove to their heart's content. The rubber industry of Uruviel and Nolofinwë was rebounding. Our medical team was working on the universal cure for every ailment. Enelya had adorned every pommel with a new jewel. Caranthir and Nienna had secured us. Camthalion's team was riding high with new transportation schemes. And Silmarwen and Alassë were feeding us better than we could have imagined.

My time on Trahe was rapidly coming to an end. I had only two responsibilities before I left. It was time to fulfill the first. I sent Elves to the limits we had chosen for our Realm. It was a sizable hunk of territory. We took the eastern half of the Jaralii Hills, leaving the mines the Humans had dug and enough rich iron ore to last them for a century or two. We had plenty of iron, too. We extended our line across the end of the Green Mountains, abutting the territory claimed by Clan Tazhela, but including extensive anthracite deposits. We extended along the piedmont to the Green River to the point it met the East Highway. We then extended a line to the North River and back. It was a triangle roughly two hundred fifty miles by two hundred miles – more than enough room for even the largest Tribe.

We agreed to establish a Realm in a Realm. We'd establish an outer Realm that would not be a deterrent to passage, demarking our extent. Within that outer barrier, we would establish a magical realm that would deflect hostile intent, but otherwise permit passage. Within that we would establish an inner core – a true Elf Realm within which we could live without interference. Our Inner Realm would enclose our mines, our wood, our homes and our interests. The Realm would exclude all entrance of those on two legs, except those we specifically permitted.

When everyone was in position, we joined our minds and entered the Void. From there, we directed our energy to create void-space around our Realm. The outer barrier was physically weak, but contained a magical element that detected sentience and intent. The second barrier detected sentience, evoking confusion, slowly forcing whoever it was beyond our Realm. The inner barrier was as powerful as we could make it. No sentient creature could pass without us performing specific magical spells that would permit limited rights of passage.

Getting it right took all day. It was difficult and required considerable effort. The problem wasn't the power required. Any of us could have created a smaller Realm, but each of us was more powerful than any Elf King or Queen. However, we had chosen a huge area – much larger than any other Realm. Second, we had a triple Realm, again unlike any other Realm. Finally, we had specified restrictions, which added to our defenses.

* * *

My final duty was the coronation of Jharl Defghamask. We arrived at first light outside the northern gates. They weren't as impressive as the southern gates, but they were more accessible to the royals, nobles and notables still in Shalal'm Caer working out the details of the Congress of Jaralii.

Tagamask, the Leader of the Guard, met us at the gate. "Greedens, Jharlish Gilrun. Gome. Tagamask goes."

I understood his pidgin and led my Tribe the long trek through the dwarrow to the ceremonial center to the north of the castle and citadel of Ghamarazh.

Squires Gildnaramansk and Ranthathamghazk greeted me more formally. "Hail, Jharl Regent Gulámae. We, your Judges of the Election, greet you. We see you have brought your Tribe. Although they are welcome, they may not accompany you from this point forward. Instead, Leader Tagamask will lead them to a position of honor that they may observe the coronation." They bowed to my Elves.

I suffered my Tribe to be led away under the guidance of the Leader of the Guard. I followed the Squires up and into the castle. We climbed to the fourth level, where three Dwarf maids clucked at me as they removed my armor and clothing. Then they dressed me in the traditional garb of a Jharl. They started with yellow sandals that covered my toes in a steel cap. Then, I stepped into brilliant red, heavy pantaloons that flopped as I moved. They slipped a bright yellow tunic over my head. It was of the same heavy material and texture and long – coming down below my hips. Both the collar and the cuffs were the same brilliant red as the pantaloons. They then slipped a short-sleeved tunic of heavy silver mail over my head, gathered it at my waist and attached my sword to the belt. They combed my hair straight down my back. Finally, they gathered my hair and made it into two long braids.

When I was properly prepared, we went down two flights of stairs emerging in a small room. Squires Gildnaramansk and Ranthathamghazk joined me. Gildnaramansk instructed me very carefully as to my duties. When I was clear on what they expected, we stepped out of the room and began the ceremony.

Drums rolled and horns blared. Gildnaramansk and Ranthathamghazk stepped out of the small room at half-step pace. We stepped off on the beat of the drums. Of course, these were Dwarf steps, which were already half my stride. I tried to match their steps, and ended up shuffling. When we finally arrived at the throne, the two Squires took me by the arms and guided me to be seated.

That was the signal for Defghamask to begin his long walk. I was tempted to look around, but, remembering my duty, I remained calm and placidly looked forward over the throng before me. I tried to use my peripheral vision as much as I could to see what was happening. It wasn't clear, but I did it anyway. Gradually, Thane Defghamask came about ten feet from me, and turned to face me.

The two Judges of the Election stood forward, faced inward to each other and then to me. They bowed and then stood erect.

It was my turn. "Judges of the Election of the Jharl of Clan Defghamask, have the Dwarves of Clan Defghamask elected a Jharl?"

Squire Gildnaramansk said in a loud and clear voice, "Yeah, the Dwarves of Ghamarazh have elected a new Jharl."

Squire Ranthathamghazk said in a loud and clear voice, "Yeah, the Dwarves of Ghamarazh have elected a new Jharl."

"Bring the Jharl Designate forth."

The two Squires turned to face Defghamask and went to his side. Taking him by the arms, they led the Thane before me.

I spoke so that the furthest Dwarf could hear me. "Do you Thane Defghamask seek the high office of Jharl of Clan Ghamarazh?"

"I do!"

"Do you seek this office for to obtain personal wealth or privilege?"

"Nay, I do not."

"Will you lead Clan Defghamask according to its ancient laws and customs?"

"I will."

I spread my arms looking up, then right, then left. "Do you, Clan Defghamask take this Dwarf, Thane Defghamask, as your Jharl?"

The entire congregation of Dwarves rose in unison and shouted, cheered and celebrated as one. It took several minutes for them to become quiet.

I nodded to Defghamask, who stepped forward and dropped to both knees.

It was my turn. What I was supposed to say was formulaic, but this was an exceptional circumstance. "When the Truth Seekers of Clan Ghamarazh revealed the treachery of Jharl Marazhul the Twelfth, I took the Crown as Jharl Regent. Many claimants vied to become the next Jharl. Squire Gildnaramansk and Squire Ranthathamghazk eschewed the position and attempted to depart. I knew that these two Squires placed their duty to the Clan above their personal ambitions. Therefore, I selected them as Judges of the Election.

"I ask you, Squire Gildnaramansk, is Thane Defghamask is worthy to become Jharl of Clan Ghamarazh?"

He glowered at me for just a moment, before he answered, "Aye, My Jharl Regent, he is."

I turned to his partner. "I ask you, Squire Ranthathamghazk, is Thane Defghamask is worthy to become Jharl of Clan Ghamarazh?"

He promptly answered, "Aye, My Jharl Regent, he is."

I lifted the crown from my head and held it high above my head. "It is my honor, my duty and my right to crown you, Jharl Defghamask of Clan Ghamarazh."

As I placed the crown on his head, he rose to a thunderous roar of approval. He turned to face his Clan and raised both arms out wide. As he did, I stepped aside. He took one step back, and then a second. I took him by the arm and guided him to the throne. I then stepped before him and bowed my head.

I turned to the throng, shouting, "Hail, Jharl Defghamask of Ghamarazh!"

The throng took up the chant as the Jharl stood and walked briskly out of the hall and beyond into the open area before the castle. He marched up a few stairs to a dais where he could readily be seen by the thousands gathered to rejoice in the inauguration of the Jharl. The entire mountain shook with the mighty roar of thousands of Dwarfish voices. Seemingly from nowhere a mug of Dwarfish brew was thrust into my hand and a smiling Dwarf face cheered lustily and clanked his mug on mine.

I knew better than to drink with a Dwarf. I really did. But one thing led to another. Then, my Tribe, the Judges of the Election, the Jharl, and even Steward Tildorhamask - all quite inebriated, surrounded me. We sang and danced and shouted and did all those things one does when celebrating a most joyous occasion.

It was late, or early – it's hard to tell when you're under a mountain – when we were escorted to our quarters. Three dwarf maids led me to an attached room, where they undressed me, returned my clothes and armor, and led me to a private bedroom. I fell on the bedding and remembered nothing for many hours.

* * *

I awoke with a terrible pain in my head. '*What a fool,*' I thought. '*Only a fool would drink with Dwarves!*' I tried to stand and failed miserably. I groaned and lay back on my futon.

A bleary-eyed Caranthir Ancalimë stuck his head around the door. "Decent?" he asked.

"And if I weren't it'd be too late, wouldn't it?"

319

"True, but you're not, and they're serving food."

"Gark! What a horrible thought!"

"William is there."

"OK, you got me. I'll try to move, but no loud noises, please."

"Agree. We're all walking around on tip-toes, trying not to make any noise."

I dressed in my standard togs, armor and weapons. Despite my fevered brain, I looked the part of an Elvin Queen. Unfortunately, Jharl Defghamask was in a wonderful, joyous and exuberant mood.

Suddenly, I was seized around my waist, lifted off the ground and twirled about. I squiggled around, not sure whether to fight. It was William! He was utterly exuberant, laughing wildly and spinning me around. "Gilraën! I'm so happy to see you! You were great!"

My heart almost burst with joy. He was so cute, so handsome, so... manly! I hugged the stuffing out of him. Our lips met and lingered. I engulfed him, wrapping my arms and legs around him as he carried me off.

"Harrumph! My King?"

We detached, and William put me back on my feet. He asked, "What is it, Talbot?"

"My King, My Queen, Jharl Defghamask has called a meeting of all the heads of state in his throne room."

"Now?" William whined.

"Yes, My King."

"Lead on," he sighed.

We followed Talbot into the formal throne room on the third floor. In comparison with the ceremonial room on the floor below, this was much smaller and far more intimate. Jharl Defghamask sat in golden High Throne sat the far end of the hall on the third step of a dais. Four Thanes sat in smaller thrones on the second step; nine Stewards sat in chairs on the first tier. Rows of chairs lined the two walls, with a long open aisle down the middle.

Tildorhamask escorted us to into the hall. Every Elvin King or Queen and Yurchist Linda sat along the right side of the hall. Every Dwarfish Jharl sat on the left. Tildorhamask led us to the front of the hall, seating me at the first chair just off the dais, with William to my left. Opposite me was an empty chair. Jharls occupied all the other chairs on that side of the hall.

Tildorhamask left the hall only to return moments later, leading a Dwarf. This male was somewhat taller and slimmer than other Dwarves I had met. Further, unlike all other Dwarves I had met, this Dwarf was a blond, with flowing hair to his shoulder. Although dressed similarly to the other Jharls, this one wore a purple sash from his right shoulder under his left arm. He also wore an elaborate crown with six points and a high conical cap topped by a large diamond.

As he entered, all the Dwarves, including Jharl Defghamask stood and applauded. Not knowing any better, I did, too. Seeing me stand, William also did and joined in the applause. However, I notice that I was the only Elf standing. It really didn't matter to me. Obviously, this was an important Dwarf, and I was still a Thane of Clan Ez-Tansk. I glanced over at Jharl Azkhalish, who smiled and nodded at me, before returning his attention to the important Dwarf. Ultimately, Tildorhamask escorted the Dwarf to the chair opposite me. Only then did I recognize who he was. This was Jharlmor Azzele!

Then, I fully realized the honor they had given me. I was seated opposite the leader of all Dwarfdom. They accorded me the highest rank of all non-Dwarves - the leader of Elves, Humans, Orcs and other sentient beings. Quite an honor.

When we were all seated, and the room had come to order, the new Jharl stood. "I, Jharl Defghamask welcome you to the Dwarrow of Ghamarazh. I owe this moment to many people who are today gathered here. I express my gratitude first to High Queen Gulámae. She is responsible for discovering the treachery of Jharl Marazhul, which led to my appointment as war leader of Ghamarazh. She is also responsible for the alliance of Dwarves, Elves, Humans, Orcs and other sentient beings against the Adjudicar Beckworth and his allies. She relinquished the crown of Ghamarazh and coronated me as its elected Jharl. To her I owe this day.

"I express my gratitude to my neighbors: Jharl Azkhalish of Clan Ez-Tansk who first came to our aid; Jharl Worzhemacht of Clan Worfellsten without whom this dwarrow would have been overrun; Jharl Morthanzhemian of Clan Ozhemia who came to our aid; and Jharl Galmerstain of Clan Zhaenstain who came to our aid. I also express my gratitude to Jharl Tazmatahela, who marched from the Green Mountains to come to our aid.

"I express my gratitude to King Amder Melwasúl, who led his Tribe from the Green Mountains to come to our aid. I also express my gratitude to King Fingolfin Sáralondë, who led his Tribe from the Blue Lake to come to our aid. I express my gratitude to King Glorfindel Huor Ancalímon and Queen Eilol Thösaendas who led their tribes from the Brown Hills to come to our aid. I express my gratitude to King Aeradir Lúinwë Séregon who led his Tribe from the White Cliffs to come to our aid.

"I express my gratitude to Yurchist Linda, who led the Orcs of the Chrystal Crags to our aid. I also express my gratitude to her for her efforts to build our alliance with the Orcs of Eastern Meadow and the Western Meadow.

"Finally, I express both my condolences and my gratitude to King William of Umbeqjaralii. Without the efforts of King Richard, there would have been no opposition to the Adjudicars, nor would there have been an army to engage them, nor would we have been properly supplied. Without the efforts of this Human King, the Adjudicars would now reign over us all. His death is a great blow to all of us.

"I express my gratitude to Duke Armjurst, who led his armies to our aid.

"However, we now welcome King William to the throne of Umbeqjaralii. We express our gratitude to him for his strength in battle and leadership of the forces that came to our aid. We also express our gratitude to him for his sponsorship and patronage of the Council of Jaralii. It is our greatest hope for the future of our land.

"I shall also express my gratitude to those Krelli, Trolls and Octopods who allied with us to defeat the Adjudicars.

"However, I condemn those who did not support the alliance against the Adjudicars. I cannot speak to the cause of the Elves. I will leave that to your own councils. However, I can speak to those of my kin who did not come to our aid. I refer to the prophecy of Thane Cadrazhulea:

"A High One among High Ones shall come from Beyond.

She shall wear an old face of the Verdant Hills

She shall befriend the Mighty and the Weak.

She shall unite the High, the Deep, the Many, the Few

The Usurper shall fall before her; all will rejoice.

Unite and be Free."

"I ask, 'Where were you in our time of need?' You," he turned to face Jharlmor Azzele, "of all of us, you recognize the prophecy of a Thane of Seers. You abandoned us to our fate, while the High One among the High Ones came to our aid, uniting the free peoples to conquer the Usurper.

"Where were you, Dzardemazhael? Or you, Thaemagarmz ? Or you Rhonzhastem? Or you, Bethmathalia? Or you, Manzhakthalia? Are we now so isolated, so remote, or so secluded that we are estranged even from our kin since the beginnings of our race? These are questions that we, the Twelve Clans, must discuss.

"However, this is not the time for this debate. Instead, it is a time of joy and celebration. I welcome you all to my court, and I express my desire to extend the friendship of Clan Ghamarazh to all who are gathered here today.

"Finally, I announce the complete and absolute support of Clan Ghamarazh for the Council of Jaralii. I pledge that Clan Ghamarazh will cooperate with all the members of that Council to extend justice, prosperity and peace throughout the lands.

"Come, now and enjoy the hospitality of Clan Ghamarazh."

He stepped down, and, followed closely by his Thanes and Squires, led us outside the castle and into the open expanse beyond. Evidently, the entire nation of Ghamarazh had gathered with every kind of food and drink that was possible to imagine. The normally staid and dour Dwarves were exuberant and excited beyond all measure. This was especially true for a people who had suffered so greatly as had Clan Ghamarazh.

I wept for joy!

I found my hand in his. William was at my side, laughing and singing and dancing. And so was I. We drank and caroused. I danced with Dwarves and Elves and Humans. I kissed William and hugged him close to me. We collapsed in his quarters, holding each other, kissing and caressing. And then he was inside of me. My legs were wrapped around him and my body was on fire with love and lust and joy. And we held each other and fell asleep in each other's arms.

* * *

I awoke. I was on my side, with an arm wrapped around me. At first, I was apprehensive, until I remembered. The fog slowly lifted, and I rolled over.

William smiled at me. "It's about time. I've been lying here waiting for you to wake up. You've been quite comfortable."

I smiled. "Yes, I have. And you seem to be as well."

He smiled. "Yes, I am."

I rolled the other way, and slipped out of the bed, heading to the privy. A mirror on the wall revealed my disheveled state.

In spite of his entreaties, I refused to rejoin William. I dressed slowly, because I was sore where I'd never been before. My brain seemed foggy, and I couldn't help but smile. It didn't help that he came up behind me, hugged me close and nuzzled the nape of my neck. He was just so nice!

* * *

I woke. I was lying on the floor. William was shouting, "Gilraën!"

Uruviel appeared at my side. "My Queen! What is the matter?"

"I don't know. I just blacked out. When I came to, William was yelling, and you were here." I sort of checked myself, wondering what was wrong. For some reason, I felt weak. I just wasn't myself.

Nessa Narmolanya appeared at my side. "My child it has begun. You are dying. Unless you leave this world, you will die."

William was distraught. "Die? Why should she die?"

"It is her contract, young King William. She must return to her home world before she dies in this one. Say your farewells now. I will take her to the point of departure and send her on her way."

He leaned down to me and kissed me. "I am broken once again. I love you, Gilraën."

"And, I love you." My voice was weak and tremulous. "If I can find a way, I will return. Be well, My King."

* * *

We returned to my apartments. Nobody else was there, which was unusual since my staff was devoted to me. Nessa said, "With your remaining strength, gather your gold and jewels in the transport chamber of Master Farmount. I will provide you with my own strength to help you."

I considered my pile of gold and transferred it to the room where I had entered this world. I reached into my cabinet and removed a leather bag filled with jewels.

"Now," the Seeress instructed, "remove your armor and place it on the rack."

When I had, she said, "Place it under your seal, and in William's protection."

I did, placing armor, quiver, bow, sword, dirk, Soul Blades and all under a spell such that no one other than William could touch them.

"Now, remove your clothes and wrap a blanket around you. Remember that you will be much different when you arrive."

I nodded in agreement.

As we entered the Transport Room, Nessa held me closely. She released me and looked deeply into my eyes. "Child," Nessa said, placing a box in my hand, "This contains a charm created by me and the full Council of Seers with the support of the Congress of the Elves of Jaralii. You have a contract to fulfill, and so you must. You must take up your own life as it was and pursue it as you would have done.

"However, once you have done so, you might need to return to this world. If you must return, then open this box and break the talisman. You and all you touch will return to the Transport Room here in this place.

"You will now travel to your point of origin on Earth. That will also be your point of departure should you choose to return.

"Now, lie here." I lay on a cross of golden bricks. I tucked the bag of jewels under the blanket. I reached out until I was touching my hard-earned wages, Nessa's box firmly in my hand.

"Blessings on you, my child."

Master Fairmount entered. "Ah, leaving us? Do come back any time."

He mumbled a few words, and Nessa mouthed a command I didn't quite hear.

* * * * *

Chapter 9 – Home?

I was sitting at the window in my living room. It was evening. I looked through the bottom slats of the Venetian blinds. A car drove past.

I was home.

I stood, still draped in the blanket, but otherwise stark naked. I looked down across a hairy chest, a larger-than-I-wanted-it-to-be belly, the hint of a penis above hairy legs and long, white feet. Definitely not the '*me*' of the past few… what? Days? Weeks? Months?

I looked further to see I was standing on a golden dais. In one hand was a leather pouch; a small black box in the other. I opened the drawstring of the pouch and peered inside. Within was the most expensive collection of jewels this planet may have ever seen. In fact, I was one damned wealthy man… if I could figure a way around the IRS.

I stopped for a moment to calculate. Roughly 3,300 pounds of gold at $2000 per Troy ounce: $80,000,000. That was the smaller yet heavier part of my treasure. I had no way of computing the value of my jewels. I had one emerald that was roughly 4 inches square and three-quarters of an inch thick. There was no such thing on Earth. I had rubies the size of chicken eggs. I had a sapphire that was three times the size of the famous Stewart Sapphire on the rear of the Empire Crown. And, on it went. They were so large and so perfect they were beyond price.

I had to put all this somewhere while I tried to figure out what to do with it all. I did have a finished basement with a solid concrete floor. That was where the HVAC system and the water heater were. It took two hours to lug the gold ingots down the stairs and into the small room. I lined the floor with them and piled them up the rear wall. When I was done, I threw an old blanket over them, and closed the door.

By that time, I was sweating like a pig, and I was sore from stem to stern. I needed a hot bath, but I had the gas turned off... no hot water. I searched my bedroom for my cell phone, but when I found it, the battery was drained. I located my laptop. The battery was drained, but I had one in reserve, which still had some power. I contacted the gas company, the electric company, and the network for my TV, internet, landlines and modems. They'd be turned on by the following day at the latest.

In the meantime, I carried the bag of jewels upstairs into my study. I swung the picture aside revealing the safe, into which I deposited the jewels and the black box. Then, I returned to my bedroom, where I found my old jeans, a T-shirt and sandals. Putting them on, I became my old self, for better or for worse.

I trundled downstairs. There in the front hall immediately before the door were my suitcases, the bag of toilet paper, and my 38-caliber pistol with ammo – all just where I had left them. I reached into the rucksack and pulled out my recharger, wallet, house and car keys. Grabbing my phone and laptop, I stepped out, locked the door and wandered down to the local coffee shop, where I plugged in the recharger and my computer. A few moments later, I discovered it was Thursday. In four days, I had to report to work.

It took a while to recharge my computer's battery. I ordered a light meal while I surfed the net. Much of the news was troubling. International tensions were mounting, and threats were becoming more commonplace. I didn't like it, but I had no superpowers to intervene.

After a while, I shifted to battery power while my phone recharged. It took a while, but I finally caught up on all the doings of countries, politicians, sports teams, races, weather, scientific progress and other events of all kinds.

When my phone was fully charged, I switched the power back to my computer. I opened the new software they expected me to install. I had to become an expert in it before next Wednesday, when I would be in Vancouver, installing it, training everyone in its use, setting up the company's books and other files and developing the human systems needed to maintain and use the system and to provide the information the higher ups would need. It was really complicated, because the company was involved in international banking and investing. So, theirs was a constant updating of exchange rates, stock prices, labor and shipping, and those thousands of other things, all of which added up to profit or loss.

I quit at about 10:00 PM and went home. It was dark, and I no longer had Elf vision. Fortunately, it was my house, so I didn't stub my toe too badly. I found my bed successfully and fell into it.

Scenes of Jaralii filled my dreams. I felt the warm caress of William's hand and heard his wonderful, soft voice crooning my name. I laughed with Cassandra, Eleanor, Rose, Beryl, Daisy and Dorothea. I played with Ms. Puss… with Tom and Ms. Cindy.

I awoke, struggling. I was completely wrapped in my blanket and barely able to move. The sun was shining brightly into the room, a broad warm patch across my bed. With some effort, I unwound myself and fell from the bed onto the floor.

I got dressed and stumbled downstairs to make a pot of coffee. I had water, but no gas or electricity. Bah! I walked to the coffee shop to grab coffee and breakfast. While there, I called AAA to recharge my car's battery and inflate the tires. No doubt I'd need to bring it to the dealer to get it ready for the road. I intended to get to Vancouver. It'd be a leisurely drive followed by a ferry ride across the Sound. It'd be my reorientation to the real world.

The Triple-A guy arrived and got my car running. The dealer had a spot open for me, and I was out three hours later. I drove to Rueben's house and very carefully tried the door with no success. I looked through the window to see a layer of dust on everything. I found the same story at Greg's and Linda's – nobody home, but plenty of dust. I guess that's the answer. I'd been hoping I'd be wrong.

By the time I was heading home, it was rush hour. Of course, that's a complete misnomer. Nobody was rushing anywhere. Long lines of bumper-to-bumper traffic edged along super highways. And it stank! I'd gotten used to clean air. The smog hurt my eyes; the smell of exhausts made me ill.

By the time I got home, I was crabby. Fortunately, both the gas and the electricity were on. However, I didn't have any food. So, I was off again. The Piggly Wiggly was just a few blocks away. I decided to forego a big shopping day and just get the essentials: moo, OJ, bread, eggs, bacon, butter, coffee, TP, a six-pack, a frozen pizza, and cereal for the morning.

When I got home, I nuked the pizza, popped a cold frosty, and plunked myself in front of the tube. *'I must show the cooks how to cook a pizza. William will love it!'*

'William? What am I thinking? He's there, and I'm here, and we'll never see each other again... unless. No, that's wrong. I won't be going back there.

'But, why not? He is cute.

'Cute? Where did that come from? I'm a guy, and so is he. I know it can happen, but not for me. I'd be a damned poor "bottom."

'Is that why I left so abruptly? I was attracted to him, I must admit. But, if it's to be a boy-girl thing, I want to be the boy.

Or do I?'

The news interrupted my musings. The announcer was talking about the Middle East. Iraq was threatening Israel – again! North Korea was threatening the USA – again. China was siding with the Koreans, and, for some inexplicable reason, Russia was supporting them in the UN. The UN was in an uproar, but nothing would come of it. The US was holding naval maneuvers in the Atlantic with Britain and Canada, while also holding maneuvers with Japan and South Korea. The two-ocean navy strikes again.

However, this sounded like more than just saber rattling. There was a tone to the reports that was more ominous than the ones when I'd left. Still, nobody in their right mind wanted a shooting war between the Big Powers. That was the kind of thing that had led to World War I. Surely, we'd learned not to do that again.

The pizza was good. I'd gotten a thick rising crust, which, along with a couple of beers, was a really delicious meal.

I Conquered

I awoke still sitting in my recliner. The TV was blaring something I didn't recognize. I hit the 'off' button, switched off the light, and then climbed the stairs to my bedroom. I stripped and was asleep in minutes.

I was in William's arms, looking from my balcony over the fields and forests watching Chrybda chase Llombda skyward. The night was cool, but not cold. His arm and warm body next to mine felt good.

He turned his face to mine, looking down into my eyes. His eyes were bright blue. His nose was long and straight. A smile turned the corners of his mouth, and his eyes sparkled.

His face came closer to mine. I stretched my neck towards him and kissed him on the mouth. He tasted good. He smelled good. His arms felt good around me, crushing me to his chest.

I was aroused. I wanted him. I wanted him deep inside me. I felt his manhood thrusting...

"What the hell?" I woke, aroused and ready, but confused. I was ready for sex, but not the sex that I had dreamed. "What the hell?" I repeated.

I got up and stumbled into the bathroom. I flicked on the light and grabbed at the aluminum cup at the side of the sink. My fingers were shaking, and I knocked it into the sink. It clattered and clanged, making far more noise than something that small and thin should have done.

I cornered the damned thing and filled it halfway with water. Drinking it down, I stared at myself in the mirror. There I was... me. I was just a normal fifty-ish guy. My hair was gray, as was my beard. I was not hirsute, but I did have a few hairs on my chest and around my nipples. My belly was flopping and fat bulged over my hips. My hands were broad with long, powerful fingers.

This was the 'me' I knew and understood. 'She' was new and exotic. I was middle-aged; she was young. I would age, perhaps not all that comfortably. She would live forever, barring the unforeseeable circumstance. I was ordinary. She was extraordinary.

But, overriding everything, I was a man. She was definitely all woman.

But the dream had been all too real. Had I been there, William and I would have…. But I wasn't. I was here, getting ready to cross over to Canada, install a new system, train the people to operate it and help them get it up and operating. It was something I'd done a dozen times before. It'd take me three weeks – four at the outside. Then, I'd be home, getting ready for my next project. It was a good life, but not forever.

I got back to bed, but I couldn't fall asleep. My mind was busy with recollections of the past few months. I worried about my staff. What were they doing now that I wasn't there? I worried about my Charioteers and their zhaks. I worried about my Tribe. I worried about William. Had he arrived home safely? How was the Congress progressing? Would they support Narwortland and Farrowspike?

* * *

A goose was honking right outside my window. It was worse than the alarm radio's buzz. I stumbled out of bed, open the blinds and looked out. There was a bunch of geese – not quite a gaggle. For some reason, they had decided it was time for the goose chorus as they honked back and forth at each other. Then, as though on command, they flapped once… twice and were flying off honking madly at each other.

Well, it was day. I glanced at the clock radio – 8:03 AM. Probably time for me to get some breakfast. I threw on a robe and eased my way downstairs and into the kitchen. I started the coffee, pulled the box of OJ out of the frig, and found a clean glass. I poured half a glass, put the box back and sat at the table. I grabbed the remote and turned on the small TV that sat opposite me on the table.

Again, the news was all negative. The President had called up the Reserves, which was an ominous sign. NATO was on a higher alert status. China was making threats. I switched the channel to find Scooby Doo cartoons.

Digging out a frying pan, I dropped a rasher of bacon into it. As the bacon sputtered, I pulled out the eggs and butter. I popped two slices of bread into the toaster. When the bacon was cooked, I tore off a sheet of paper towel and transferred the bacon onto it. When the toast popped, I buttered it. Then, I cracked two eggs into the hot bacon grease, where they popped and sputtered, the edges burning lacy and brown. I pulled down a plate from the cabinet, and a knife and fork from the drawer. After I extracted a spatula from the hook over the stove, I used it to splash bacon grease over the top of the eggs. Gradually, the top of the yolks turned cloudy. I scooped them onto the plate, depositing the bacon and toast onto it.

I dipped a piece of the toast into the warm yolk, drawing the yellow liquid into the nooks and crannies. I bit off a chunk of bacon savoring the combination of yolk, toast and bacon. Delicious!

Scooby Doo ended, and some Japanese cartoon began. I'd never gotten into them, so I turned the channel looking for something interesting. I settled on Murder, She Wrote. Angela Lansbury's program had been on the air for half a century. Even though she was long dead, her heirs were still raking in the residuals.

By the time the program had ended, I was done. I washed my dishes, dried them and put them away. Then, I dug out my computer and began to work with the program I was to install and train. It was mostly the same program I'd worked with for a decade. However, this 'latest and greatest' version had some interesting tweaks. By the time I'd figured them all out and had studied the installation instructions, it was afternoon. My back hurt, my hand hurt, and my eyes ached.

Sore and tired, I climbed upstairs and laid out some decent clothes. Then I drew a nice hot bath. This was a big tub in which I could lay out in comfort. I added hot water twice, before I stood under the shower to wash my hair.

I thought of my gravy boat and laughed. *'When I get back, I'm going to have a real tub made so I can lie down in it,'* I commented to myself.

"Whoa!" I said, thinking, *'What's this "when I get back?" I'm not going back.'*

After I'd dried my thinning, graying hair under the blower, I dug out my electric beaver and sheared the graying bristles from my face. When I returned to the bedroom to get dressed, I glanced around looking for my armor, and laughed to myself. Instead, I had laid out a pair of tan, gabardine slacks, a light yellow short-sleeved shirt, and tan loafers. After I'd combed my hair, I went down, got into my car, and headed to my favorite Friday night hangout.

Leo's Bar and Grille was a typical Western motif bar and restaurant. On the weekends they had a small country-western band, with dancing. Typically, there were more young women than men. Why, I never knew, but I'd taken advantage of the ratio more than once.

When I entered, Bill, the barkeep, yelled, "Hey, Tony, welcome back, man. Where you been?"

By the time I was seated at the bar, he had a draft poured. "Out of town. The usual," I answered.

"Hell, man, it's been a couple of months. You know, I don't see Reuben or Greg, either. What's up with you guys?"

"I don't know about them, but I had a big problem to solve. I was out of the country on a confidential project. It was a tough one, but I'm back for the weekend. Then, I'm off to Vancouver for a month. You know, no rest for the wicked? So, who's on stage tonight?"

He mentioned some group I'd never heard of. What's new, right? "Usual crowd?"

"Yeah, I guess. Plenty of chicks. They come to ogle the band." He waved as he rushed to the other end of the bar to assist a thirsty patron.

I took my beer to the small table on the other side of the room, nearer the stage, but not too close.

A waitress (Debbie?) appeared with a menu. "Another beer?"

"Sure."

She was off before I could order. Instead, I studied the menu I'd memorized. The steak sandwich with fries and salad with bleu cheese dressing looked good to me. While waiting for it to appear, I looked around at the rapidly filling hall. There were gaggles of girls flocking to the tables closer to the stage. Guys appeared, hanging around the bar, drinking beers, and gabbing with their friends.

I felt a little out of place. When it was the bunch of us, we had numbers. Yes, we were all older than the kids here, but there were half a dozen of us, so we were never alone. Now, it was just me and lots of youngsters. And there was no chance the old group would ever reassemble. I'd seen Reu fall, or was it Justice who had died? I'd avenged him, but that wouldn't bring him back. Linda was now Yurchist. Although I had a good idea of Greg's whereabouts, I'd lost track of Tammie's or anybody else's, for that matter.

The steak sandwich was good. It'd been a long time since I'd had real food. Yes, the food on Trahe was good, but it wasn't the food I'd eaten all my life. Then, the music began to play, and, suddenly, I was home.

A bunch of the patrons began to line dance – the Texas Two-Step. That one I could do. I got into line and began stepping left and right, spinning around, and stepping again. It'd been a while since I'd been here. The girl to my left was cute. I smiled at her, but she ignored me. The gal the other side of me was also cute, so I smiled at her. She sorta laughed, seemingly scorning my approach. I shrugged, thinking, '*Plenty of fish in the sea. If not tonight, some other night.*'

A few hours later, another young lady smiled back at me. By the time we got back to my place, we were thoroughly enjoying each other's company. We enjoyed each other all night long. However, I made sure she enjoyed it far more than I did. For me, it wasn't all that great, but that was my fault, not hers.

Saturday, I made a full installation of the software and thoroughly tested it. I ran simulations of various scenarios that I knew would arise. And I created test series including different problems for the client to solve.

Sunday, I rested, watching the Sea Hawks lose to the 49ers. It was a good game, but it didn't turn out the way I wanted. The late game was the Falcons and the Jets – a thoroughly forgettable affair that didn't keep me awake.

Monday, I showed up at the office bright and early. The boss was happy to see me. "Good vacation?"

"Yup, just great!" I enthused.

"Ready for Vancouver?"

"Yup. I'll catch the ferry this afternoon. I'll be there first thing tomorrow."

I gathered my stuff and headed out. The drive was uneventful, as was the passage across Puget Sound. I passed through Canadian immigration and drove to my motel room. The next morning, I began my routine. I'd done this so many times, I could have done it in my sleep.

* * *

The weeks passed quickly, and I was home.

I was happy to return to the grind of day-to-day office work. It was good to just putter with no pressure to perform anything out of the ordinary. I called my old clients, just checking to make sure all was well with them and that our competitors hadn't stolen my accounts.

However, with my more relaxed state of mind, my dreams had become more troubling. I dreamed of William holding me, kissing me, getting me so hot that I wanted him inside me… again.

On another night, I dreamed I was sitting in my nook surrounded by my three children. I was pregnant and explaining to them that they were about to have another brother or sister.

I dreamed of my Elves, exploring their new world. They found a deep cave in a limestone cliff. Inside were huge crystals of quartz lying about in profusion. In another dream, they discovered water emeralds, rubies, sapphires and amethysts growing in profusion. In a third, they found deposits of gold, silver, copper and zinc ores.

In another series of dreams, I saw my Charioteers helping their zhaks foal. Suddenly, a dozen or more little zhaks trembled and quaked with their first steps. I awoke laughing as one tiny, little thing tried to get those overly long legs under it, but fell repeatedly on its nose. Then, when it finally stood, albeit shakily, we cheered and laughed. That's when I awoke.

These recurring dreams were exhausting. I was tired at work and fell asleep at my desk more than once. I took to napping during my lunch hours, nibbling at breaks in the morning and afternoon. It actually turned out well. My productivity returned to normal, and I lost a few pounds.

I was becoming more fearful as the international situation grew ever more perilous. Korea was demanding reparations from the Japanese for World War II. They were also demanding reparations from South Korea and the US for damages incurred in the Korean War. They were threatening Japan with nuclear war.

America stood four-square with Japan. Over the years, we had helped Japan build up a missile defense system, primarily aboard their expanding fleet of destroyers. And we had pushed a third carrier battle group into the Pacific. There was no telling how many SSBNs were lurking out there, each loaded with hundreds of nuclear warheads. There was even a news report of B-2s landing in Guam. This was not good!

That night, I had the most vivid dream ever. Nessa Narmolanya came to me.

'*Queen Gilraën, the time has come for you to return. This is your destiny, and you must act. The peace you had hoped to establish has not materialized. The lands of Narwortland and Farrowspike have fallen under the spell of evil Sorcerers or worse. The Elves have withdrawn into their Realms, the Dwarves into their dwarrows, and the Orcs into their dens. Your family and your friends are in danger. You must return before your world is destroyed. Prepare to depart at a moment's notice. Your life and the fate of an entire world are in your hands.*

"*I shall return, but only to deliver a final warning. Be prepared to depart to Trahe, or die on Earth.*'

I awoke in a panic. I was sweating bullets and frightened half to death. Could my dream have been *Waking Sleep*? Could the Seeress have that much power to transmit her thoughts across interstellar distances? If anyone could, it'd be her.

I tried to get back to sleep, but couldn't. Nessa's warning was all too vivid and all too real. If she was warning me, I'd better respond accordingly.

It was early AM, but I made a pot of coffee and began making a list of the things I'd want to bring with me. First and foremost was my wealth in gold and jewels. Wealth is power, and I'd need it in Jaralii. My weapons and armor were still in Umbeqjaralii, as were all the clothes I'd need. I considered my pistol, but rejected it.

What would be important on a world such as Trahe? Jaralii had plenty of things, but was still a low-level of technology. They relied on magic to solve problems, so had never developed a technology much beyond medieval Earth. So, what knowledge would I want to bring with me?

I ran a quick Google search to discover Man's most important technological discoveries. There was fire and the development of smelting processes. Paper was a critical invention. A critical development was the first standardized screw, perhaps the 'secret' of future mass production. Also of importance was the steam engine/pump. Firearms were important, but I wasn't eager to introduce them to Jaralii unless I had to do it. The internal and external combustion engines were also a big technological development that I wasn't anxious to introduce. There was a discussion of the basic sciences: physics, chemistry, geology, astronomy, metallurgy. The development of processes to produce acids and bases were critical for all industrial applications. Finally, it was critical to turn science theory into engineering practice.

Obviously, I couldn't suddenly learn how to do all this, but I had books. However, books were large and heavy. I could use my Kindle, but that would require batteries and electricity. I could upload and read Kindle books and other stuff to my cell phone, but the battery would fail after a time, making it useless... unless I could find a power source. I had a solar panel and converter. It wasn't all that powerful, but it could charge the phone's batteries in a couple of hours. I checked both my chargers and the solar panel and converter. It all worked, and would for a while… I hoped.

I spent three days downloading masses of data to 20T SIM cards or 10T thumb drives. I used both my phone and my computer to double the rate of data acquisition. With the very high-speed modems I used for my gaming systems, I loaded three hundred SIM cards and another five hundred thumb drives. Finally, I grabbed all the software I used as well as a bunch of programs I didn't know anything about, but figured I might need. Ideally, I had all the essentials I'd ever need to build a technologically advanced civilization from scratch.

I then called in, saying I'd work from home today. The boss agreed, and I started my preparations to leave. I raced to the store, where I bought two more large solar panels, three converters and half a dozen batteries for each.

I was just congratulating myself, when I remembered Nessa's last words to me. "You will now travel to your point of origin on Earth. That will also be your point of departure should you chose to return."

Damn! I spent the next three hours toting hundred pound ingots upstairs and into the living room. Thirty-three trips up and down stairs were almost too much for me. I was gasping for air. My back, legs and arms ached. And I still had to gather my jewels and electronics.

After two more trips, I stumbled into the kitchen, grabbed a cup of coffee and a fried egg sandwich. Somewhat refreshed, I assembled the bars of gold on the floor. I could lie on them, touching each. Then, I placed the sack of jewels, my cell phone, solar panels, converters, rechargers and memory cards on top of them.

I needed some leather bags, so I had to go shopping, again. I found three: two were big shoulder bags, the other a largish backpack. When I got home, I put all my electronics into the backpack. I dumped the jewels into the shoulder bag. I also brought a mirror, comb, brush, some nice soap and a few other things. Then, I draped a big woolen blanket over it all, knowing I'd need it.

I returned the kitchen and turned on the tube. "Shit!" I exclaimed, watching the streamer along the bottom of the screen. Korea had issued an ultimatum. Japan had responded. China had issued a warning declaring they would attack anyone who attacked North Korea. In turn, the US declared it would defend Japan against all aggression. Russia declared its support of China. NATO declared they would consider an attack against the United States an attack on themselves. It was another house of cards, just as it had been before World War I. That one had cost some twenty million deaths and casualties. World War II had cost almost fifty million. The toll of this one would be in the billions.

"Shit!" I reiterated, as the picture switched to the UN. The people pictured were grim and looked worried. The speaker was calling on the world's leaders to stand down and to begin negotiations. However, North Korea was notable by its absence. Only one person was in China's position. The tight-lipped US ambassador sat in the midst of our delegation.

Suddenly, there was a break. An announcer came on the screen. "We're breaking into this program to hear from the President of the United States, speaking from the Oval Office."

"Shit!" I exclaimed. Then, I yelled, "Shit!" again, realizing that the box that I would need to transport myself to Trahe was upstairs on my dresser. I dashed upstairs and opened the box. Within was a glass sphere hanging on a golden necklace. I wrapped the chain around my wrist, the sphere at my fingertips.

Returning downstairs, I sat in the living room on my bars of gold, watching the tube. The situation was rapidly deteriorating. I checked my bags. Everything was there. I stripped, sat on the gold bars and draped the blanket over me.

The announcer broke in. "We have just received information that North Korea has attacked Tokyo. We have no word on casualties." He looked off camera. "The President is speaking from the Oval Office."

The screen switched. "…learned that Tokyo has been attacked. Pyongyang has claimed responsibilities for that attack. The United States has responded to this outrageous breech of international peace. We urge all citizens of the United States to remain in their homes until this emergency has passed."

I cried. I couldn't help it. Nobody can win a nuclear war. If we hit North Korea, will China strike us? If so, it's all over. The US can obliterate China, but China can hurt the US badly. And what of Japan? Caught in the crossfire, they would demolish the Land of the Rising Sun.

I lay back, placing my purses on my legs, torso and chest. I pulled the blanket over me, tucking my arms inside and along the line of bars. Taking the sphere in my right hand, I snapped it between my fingers, just as a blinding flash of white blazed through the window.

* * *

The room was smoky and stank. Master Fairmount stood to the side, mouth gaping. "My Queen? Queen Gilraën? Is that you?"

* * * * *

Thus the third and final prediction

of the Seer, Cadrazhulea of Camazhule, has been fulfilled:

The Usurper shall fall before her; all will rejoice.

Unite and be Free.

The End of Gilraën and the Prophecy

Coming Soon!

Gilraën and the Doom of the Adjudicars

<u>Special Offer</u>

Who's Who in Jaralii

Want a guide to the characters in the Gilraën and the Prophecy?

E-mail your request to my official site:

JaraliiChronicles@gmail.com

Jaralii Chronicles: Gilraën and the Prophecy

Book One: I Came (E-Book)

https://www.amazon.com/Gilraen-Prophecy-Came-Jaralii-Chronicles-ebook/dp/B083PQNNCT

ISBN: 978-1-7344680-0-7

ASIN: B083PQNNCT

Book One: I Came (Paperback)

https://www.amazon.com/Gilraen-Prophecy-Came-Jaralii-Chronicles-ebook/dp/B083PQNNCT

ISBN-10: 978-1-7344680-1-7

ISBN-13: 978-1734468014

ASIN: B083PQNNCT

Book Two: I Saw (E-Book)

https://www.amazon.com/Jaralii-Chronicles-Saw-Gilraen-Prophecy-ebook/dp/B0849NV8HC

ISBN: 978-1-7344680-2-1
ASIN: B0849NV8HC

Book Two: I Saw (Paperback)

https://www.amazon.com/Gilraen-Prophecy-Came-Jaralii-Chronicles-ebook/dp/B083PQNNCT

ISBN: 978-1-7344680-4-5
ASIN: 1734468041